THE MAJESTIC 311

Also by Keith C. Blackmore

Mountain Man
Mountain Man
Safari
Hellifax
Well Fed
Make Me King
Mindless
Skull Road
Mountain Man Prequel
Mountain Man 2nd Prequel: Them Early Days
The Hospital: A Mountain Man Story
Mountain Man Omnibus: Books 1–3

131 Days
131 Days
House of Pain
Spikes and Edges
About the Blood
To Thunderous Applause
131 Days Omnibus: Books 1–3

Breeds
Breeds
Breeds 2
Breeds 3
Breeds: The Complete Trilogy

Isosceles Moon
Isosceles Moon
Isosceles Moon 2

The Bear That Fell from the Stars
Bones and Needles
Cauldron Gristle
Flight of the Cookie Dough Mansion
The Majestic 311
The Missing Boatman
Private Property
The Troll Hunter
White Sands, Red Steel

THE MAJESTIC 311

KEITH C. BLACKMORE

Podium

ISBN: 978-1-0394-8356-9

Published in 2024 by Podium Publishing
www.podiumaudio.com

THE MAJESTIC 311

1

The Wait

A cloud stretched as tight as a hangman's rope cut across a full moon. Stars hung in brilliant tatters around that radiant face, and their combined celestial might illuminated the wintry countryside with a beauty that would make the day ache with envy. White-capped mountains had their faces shaded, but their craggy shoulders glowed under the night sky. Snowy slopes ended in thin collars of fir and spruce. Farther down the high country, patches of white shone through a thickening cloak of forest. Snow blanketed the wilderness towards the mountain base, whitening everything and burying most of the known passes.

Down in one gully, nestled between a series of frostbitten hills, eight men sat upon horses. They waited, faces set, their shoulders hunched like vultures. Some of them studied the midnight lustre of the sky, their thoughts deep and private, while others stared at the stretch of railway tracks before them, almost entirely obscured by snow. They wore clothing of the season, heavy coats of leather over double sets of wool pants and shirts, thick scarves and gloves. Their hats were prairie felt and, though similar, not the fancy Stetsons that were gaining popularity down south.

Not a breeze disturbed the riders. The mountain air was so crisp, so pure, that to breathe it in tasted like a sip of chilled holy water.

"This is horseshit," Eli Gallant grumbled, breaking the silence, loud enough for the others to hear.

A smirk stretched across Nathan Rhode's face, one concealed by a scarf pulled up so high, only his eyes peeked out.

For moments, no one said anything.

"You cow fuckers hear me?" Eli spoke again, a touch louder. "Horse. *Shit.*

All horseshit. I must be out of my goddamn mind to come up here. Waiting in this forsaken ass crack of the world, on a goddamn horse in the middle of goddamn winter. Horseshit. That's what I think, by Christ."

No one said anything for several seconds.

"Go on back if you want," Leland Baxter said with quiet indifference. "We can make do."

"Oh, I'm thinking about it," Eli said, rising in his saddle and making the leather creak. "Goddamn right I'm thinking about it. And right now, I'm thinking it's all horseshit, Leland Baxter. *All* horseshit. You put that in your fancy fuckin' pipe and make curls out of it."

Silence then, as Leland Baxter—the leader of the group—refrained from commenting, allowing those last few words to sink into the heads of the other men. That was Leland's way. If there was grumbling to be done, let the malcontents grumble. Let them moan. Give them time to bitch, and let them bitch until the bitchin's done.

But always, *always*, make the effort to hear them out.

Or, at the very least, *appear* to be hearing them out.

"Why do you say that?" Leland finally asked.

Nathan lowered his head. He cringed at the foulness of his breath trapped within the folds of his scarf. He hadn't known Baxter for long, having only met the man two weeks prior, but in that short time sharing the ex-miner's company, Nathan learned that the man was willing to listen to his men's complaints. He might not do anything about the complaining, mind you, but he would definitely listen, sure as God above.

"Why do I say that?" a confounded Eli Gallant finally blurted. "Why the fuck do I say that? Your eyes frozen in your head, Leland? I mean can you *not* see the shit on them tracks? Them rails are goddamn *covered* in ice, for Christ's sakes. *Covered.* I mean, look. Just *look* at them. Ain't too dark to see you can't see them things. Look!"

Nathan glanced to his left, where Leland Baxter sat astride his brown gelding. In the deep reckoning shadows rolling off the majestic Rockies, the outlaw leader didn't move. Didn't flinch. A profound silence surrounded the man from Fraser Valley, and he didn't disturb it. His gloved fingers wrapped about the saddle horn as if he were some judge presiding over a longhorn court. Like them all, Baxter had a thick scarf around his neck and shoulders, but he hadn't pulled the wool up over his mouth. His mustached face stared ahead, the profile as dignified as marble stone, while a right eye twinkled, not yet dried out by the winter air.

Leland had a scar up his right cheek, a deep cut made by a ring, earned in a fistfight with some drunken bastard from Saskatchewan, delivered when a killer of an uppercut missed his jaw by a hair.

But the ring left its mark.

Cut me like a hot knife through butter, Leland had declared, his mouth hidden by the monstrous dust collector that sprouted from his upper lip.

The outlaw leader looked toward the icy tracks, inspected them, and lifted his face to the night.

"Well?" Eli demanded.

"They are indeed glazed with ice," Leland agreed. "You are correct in that. However, there's nothing I can do about their frigid state."

That stark assessment stunned Eli Gallant into silence, but not for long. "Sweet Christ Almighty, Leland. It's fuckin' *cold* up here. Them tracks got a coat of ice on them thicker than your pecker, and I'm willing to bet the twenty dollars I got in my pocket that your *train*… ain't coming this way tonight. No sir. That big ol' chunk of pig iron ain't coming this way *ever.*"

Baxter exhaled, answering with steam, and searched the heavens for what, Nathan did not know.

"Why ain't the train coming this way, then?" asked Milton Floss, his words muffled by his own thick scarf, and his eyes peeking over that crust of bullet-stopping cotton. Milton was a cattle thief from Big Muddy Valley, looking to branch out into other fields. He figured robbing trains sounded promising.

"It ain't that the train *ain't* coming this way," said fellow rustler Mackenzie Cass. "It's the incline of the slope."

"The grade," 'Shorty' Charlie Williams supplied with a low, contrary rumble.

"The grade," Mackenzie said. "Exactly. Thank you kindly, Shorty. The ice will make it so that the grade is slippery. But they got fixtures these days. To apply to the front of a steam engine in heavy snow and ice. I heard tell of it a while back. Big plows they attach to the front. Scoops up the snow and slings it two hundred feet into the air. Designed by a dentist out of Toronto."

That was met with silence once again.

"Horseshit," Gallant finally scoffed.

"Ain't horseshit," Mackenzie countered in a calm, distracted tone probably inflicted by the cold and the beauty of the night sky. As far as Nathan could tell, in the short time they'd all been together, where Milton was something of a simpleminded soul, quick to laugh and to fight (but not in an evil way), Mackenzie was different entirely. Both were in their late twenties, but Mackenzie was no simpleton wrangling cattle herds. The man knew things, or at least *sounded* like he knew things, and wasn't afraid to share that knowledge when the opportunity presented itself.

"Ain't horseshit a'tall," Mackenzie repeated, while Milton glared a warning at the mouthy Gallant. "Fella's name is… hold on now… Elliott… J.W. Don't ask me what the J and W stand for. He invented the thing. From what I hear, his first design didn't take with the railway folks, so he partnered up with another man. Guy by the name of Orange Mull. Or wait… maybe that's Jull. Yeah, I think it's Jull. Anyway, together they got it right."

Leather creaked as Eli turned and leaned in his saddle, fixing his disbelieving wrath upon Mackenzie. "You tell me that a goddamn *dentist* made up a plow? For a *train*?"

"I'm just saying. S'up to you if'n you believe it or not."

"Horse… shit," Eli stated in a defiant voice. "A goddamn dentist rigging up a train to shovel snow. The hell he know about shoveling snow, huh? The hell he know about trains for that matter?"

"It doesn't shovel snow. It scoops it. Then slings it."

"Yeah, well, I've shoveled enough bullshit in my time to know it when I smell it."

"You're gettin' on my nerves, Gallant," Milton warned.

"Think for a minute, then," Eli Gallant challenged. "A dentist. From *Toronto*. Thinking up a plow… for a *train*? When he'd come up with that? While he was yankin' teeth outta folks' faces? Huh? Christ Almighty, what's next? Clergy inventing boxes that help you converse with the dead? Hm?"

"Already got them fancy buggies that go on without a team of horses," Mackenzie said.

"You're a goddamn fancy buggy yourself, Mackenzie."

Neither Milton nor Mackenzie appeared to like that. In Nathan's mind, Mackenzie was an educated man, but that didn't mean he allowed himself to be pushed around by foulmouthed bloodsabitches like Eli Gallant. Especially not in times of growing duress, as what they all were being currently subjected to.

"Don't you worry," Leland Baxter declared, quieting the whole works of them before fist fights broke out. "Not one bit. That train's coming this way. I know it."

That greatly interested Eli, and he traded looks with his own companion, an Albertan rancher-turned-gun runner by the name of Gilbert Butler.

"The tracks are covered in *ice*, Leland, goddamnit," Eli stressed with poisoned contempt. "You know what's gonna happen? I'll tell you what's gonna happen. On the other side of them mountains there, the train's gonna come on through the underpass. Cut straight on through 'til it pops out on this side. Then it's gonna hit all that…" Eli swept a gloved hand at the snow-covered tracks. "And *then* it's gonna start spinning wheels. Spin, spin, spin. After that, that train is gonna slip right back down that tunnel. Just like a slick piece of shit going back into an asshole."

Nathan grimaced at the image.

"You have a way with your similes," Leland Baxter said.

"My what now?" Eli asked.

"Similes."

"'Similes'?"

Leland sighed.

"Speak fucking English for a change, Leland," Eli barked. "I get goddamn mesmerized between the likes of you and Mackenzie over there. One talking about 'similes' and the other talking about goddamn dentists clearing snow from railways. Try and speak simple like, for the simpleminded among us. And for those who might not know what a goddamn 'simile' is."

"Or for those able to say it," Nathan muttered.

A moment's silence then as Eli shut up, absorbing the insult. Leather groaned again as he leaned forward to direct a murderous scowl at the last speaker, a look that made the night that much colder. "I wasn't talking to *you*, Nathan Shit-flinger *Rhodes*. So you just shut your shit mouth before I do. Understand?"

Nathan scowled back. He didn't rightly know Eli Gallant's reputation except for a few stories from the others, but Nathan was positive Eli didn't rightly know *his* reputation either. Or what he was capable of doing when he got his anger up.

Because Nathan Rhodes was capable of a lot.

"Oh someone's feelin' scrappy," Eli declared with steamy breath, his eyes narrowed. "Don't he look scrappy to you, Gilbert?"

"Looks scrappy and then some," Gilbert agreed.

"Goddamn right he does."

Nathan didn't look at Gilbert, who probably only went to the shitter when Eli Gallant okayed it. Instead, he continued giving the evil eye to Gallant.

"Stop it," Leland said, his level voice booming in that snowy mountain gulley. "Right now. That's an order."

That got Eli's attention. "Yeah? Or what?"

A resounding silence followed the question. Then, "Or I'll have Shorty deal with you both."

'Shorty' Charlie Williams rode the biggest horse of them all. A big black breed, some seventeen hands high, with a head broad enough to punch through a wall. The animal was more suited for heavy labor than long riding, but no other animal could support Shorty's size. The man towered over the collection of rogues and scoundrels Leland Baxter had gathered to his fell purpose, a full head in some cases, and Nathan wasn't a small man. On top of that midnight horse, Shorty was every bit as ominous as a black garbed hangman, just waiting for a word from his employer. Broad of shoulder and of face, quiet, with an unruly chin rug that might've been ripped off a grizzly's ball sack, Shorty wasn't one for conversation. In fact, Shorty didn't rightly speak unless spoken to, unless when supplying a thought needing to be aired. Nathan couldn't say if the man could fight or not, but the big man certainly exuded the willingness to partake in violent confrontations, if someone felt brave enough to challenge him.

Or if Leland Baxter gave the word.

And Leland Baxter seemed on the verge of doing just that.

Eli considered the threat, gauged Shorty as being more than willing, and, with a shadowy glare at Nathan, he settled back into his saddle. Nathan didn't look at Shorty, but he felt the man's heavy attention upon him. Snorting steam, Nathan straightened and gazed ahead, content to be done with the matter.

The situation had diffused itself.

Nathan considered the snow-white patchwork of fir and spruce that covered the mountains, illuminated by a moon so bright he could almost tell one tree from the other. Stars dusted the heavens, producing a glitter that could mesmerize a man. He looked for the constellations, remembering that his mother knew them all. She even tried teaching him the names of those constellations, but most never took to his memory. Not that his mother minded. She never minded much when it came to her only son, and Nathan loved her for that. She'd died in her house upon the Saskatchewan prairies, where a terrible winter had blown into her lungs and struck her with a powerful bout of pneumonia. Nathan's father died shortly after, of a broken heart. That left a thirteen-year-old boy alone and sick with misery, to deal with his two passed-on parents for the remainder of the winter months.

And, somewhere around that time, a part of Nathan died as well.

Winter. He considered the railroad tracks and saw that they were indeed icy, and wondered if the train might slip after all.

"Have no worries, Nathan," Leland Baxter said with a calmness that was pleasing to the ear. "The plan hasn't changed. Fact is, the plan's only gotten better."

"How's that now?"

"Well," Leland carried on. "What do you think will happen when the train starts to climb the slope?"

Nathan thought about it, glad to be distracted. "Slow down?"

"That's right. And if the train does indeed slip on the rails, what do you think the engineer will do? The same man charged with getting the train and all its passengers and cargo to its final destination?"

Nathan had to think about that one, too. "Apply the brakes?"

"Well done, Nathan." Leland said, clearly impressed. "You're a thinker, after all."

The compliment straightened the young man's back.

"Yes," Leland resumed. "The engineer will apply the brakes, and that's all the better for us. We were planning on stopping the train anyway, until our business was concluded. This snow only works in our favor. Understand now?"

Nathan nodded.

"Understand, Eli?"

"Yeah, I understand," Gallant grumped as if he'd just lost a fist fight and a few teeth besides.

"What was that?"

"Said I *understand*," Eli huffed. "Christ Almighty, Leland."

"Not so worried now, are you?" Leland asked.

"Guess not."

"Never doubted me at all, did you?"

That was pushing his luck, but with the likes of Shorty watching you, Eli Gallant decided to be smart. "Guess not."

That satisfied Leland. "Good."

"Just saying I think it's horseshit a dentist made up a plow for a train," Eli muttered. "That's all."

Nathan exhaled, the scarf capturing his polluted breath. He'd expect nothing less from a piece of shit like Eli Gallant. The man was a complainer, a tormenter, and an instigator, and Nathan again wondered why and how it was Leland who brought Gallant and his buddy Gilbert into the plan.

But then he remembered the guns.

Eli had brought them guns. A lot of guns. Got them all from Yankee gun runners down in Montana. Say what you will about the Americans, but they made the best guns, far superior to anything available north of the border.

Even the vaunted North West Passage Police Force were said to be upgrading with American firearms, as their current selection was of a poor and unreliable design.

Nathan was equipped with a Winchester Model 1873, which held fifteen rounds. He wore a pair of Colt Navy 1852 revolvers on his hips, and he was given enough ammunition for both rifle and revolvers to feel like he was going to war.

"Good thing you're up front," Nathan heard Milton say to Eli.

Silence then, but everyone knew Milton had picked a fight.

"Whattaya mean by that?" Eli demanded.

"I mean exactly what I mean. Good thing you're up front."

"You sayin' something there, peckerhead?"

"What he means," Mackenzie spoke up, "is that it's best you head to the front of the train and stay away from the passengers. You're liable to hurt someone."

"Oh no," Eli said, picking at that bone. "That ain't what he said. He didn't say that at all. Trouble is, I *know* what he said. Well let me tell *you* something, *Milton.*"

"Eli," Leland warned.

A poisoned-looking Gallant flustered, let off steam, and gradually simmered back down.

The eight riders became quiet again.

"What if the train stops on the other side of the mountain?" Milton asked, breaking that alpine stillness. "Do we go get it?"

"No, we do not," Leland answered. "We wait right here until it comes through. That part of the plan doesn't change. The train will push through any snow covering the tracks. Especially if it is indeed outfitted with a plow, the likes of which Mackenzie has described. To tell the truth, I would very much like to see such a device."

Eli sighed in unchecked disgust.

"Wouldn't want to go through all that snow," Nathan said quietly. "All the firepower I'm carrying. Feels like a ton."

"You can dump it, if you wish," Leland Baxter said. "After we rob the train. Once we deal with whatever security might be on board."

"Shame," Mackenzie said. "Too bad you couldn't find out if the military was gonna be on that thing. Or the Northwest police. And how many."

"Shame indeed," Leland agreed. "Which is why it's better to have more than enough ammunition. We can thank Eli and Gilbert for that."

That note of gratitude didn't placate Eli Gallant. "Have enough," he sneered. "I swear, Leland. You have a way of understating things. Damn right we have enough. We're ready to start a goddamn *war* here. I mean, don't get me wrong, Leland. Each and every one of you sonsabitches are paying me for what you're carrying after the fact. You hear me? And that's ammunition included. I don't care if you shoot one goddamned shell or one hundred. You're paying for every brass nugget you got on you. You're *all* paying. Hear me? I ain't taking none of it back. Too much trouble bringing it all up here in the first place."

"I'll pay what you're owed," Leland said. "Have no worries of that. We all will. Soon as we rob the train."

That brought on a series of assurances from the other men.

"Didn't hear you, Nathan," Eli pointed out.

Nathan didn't answer right away. "I said I'd pay you back not a week ago. And that's all I got to say on the matter."

Eli didn't say anything to that. Instead, he looked at Leland and said, "I have a question." The hard case actually raised a gloved hand.

The men waited for Leland Baxter to respond. He sighed heavily. "Go ahead."

"Why the hell am I up front?" Eli demanded. "You don't think I can handle a car full of Northwest police? Or soldiers for that matter?"

"On the contrary," Leland explained with the patience of Job. "I think you're more than capable of handling whatever security has been assigned to that train."

"So why am I going up front?"

"What I don't think you're capable of, Eli Gallant, is controlling the passengers between us and the payroll car. I think you'd be every bit as short of temper and disagreeable as you've been these past few days riding up here. Which is why I chose you to control the engineer."

Eli absorbed that. "All right, but what if the payroll car has more men than you figured on? What then?"

"Well, in that case, I'll send you on back. To help suppress the security detachment. Until Jimmy has time to persuade them otherwise. With the dynamite."

That quieted the men, each and every one of them.

The last man comprising the gang of train robbers was James "Jimmy" Norquay, a Metis buffalo hunter out of Tail Creek, a small Albertan town burned to the ground some twenty years ago and never rebuilt. Jimmy didn't say much, spoke only when spoken to, and generally stayed off to one side of Leland as if waiting to be called upon for some fell purpose. When he did speak, it was calm and measured, his words inflected with a slight English accent, hinting at a childhood spent in residential schools. Word was—and Nathan learned this from Milton—that Leland and Jimmy had actually *met* at one of those residential schools and became good friends, which sort of made sense. Nathan remembered his interview for this outfit. He remembered the little back room of that trader's post where he first met Leland Baxter, where half-filled spittoons gleamed in the shadows and the air stunk of spilled whiskey and sour piss. Shorty Charlie Williams stood shotgun outside that closed door, but when Nathan went inside, Jimmy was right there, standing all still and such, right behind Leland, who sat at the only table.

That was the first time Nathan had to apply to a gang, and the first time he met Leland Baxter and his two henchmen.

Nathan shifted in the saddle and rubbed his nose in his scarf. He had nothing against the Metis, but Jimmy honest-to-God disturbed him in some supernatural way, and it took everything he had not to reveal that unease. Knowing that Jimmy possessed one dozen sticks of dynamite underneath that cattle hide coat of his didn't truly alleviate that unease. Dynamite was… unpredictable. To Nathan anyway. He'd heard plenty of stories of the material exploding at very inconvenient times, resulting in missing body parts and untidy deaths. Leland assured him that it was fresh dynamite they carried, bought from the Grand Old Powder Company itself, and that he need not worry about the sticks going off until needed.

Nathan had believed Leland at the time.

He also suspected Jimmy's silence was a result of *having* all that dynamite strapped to his person. Like most of them, Jimmy had his scarf pulled up around his face, rendering his profile stoic and mysterious. The man was bearded underneath, however, with a good head of hair, and a look about him that spoke of a quiet intellect.

Nathan figured he wouldn't be much for talking either, if'n he had to carry those Godforsaken firecrackers tight to his ass.

"Listen," Eli said in a rare moment of reason. "All grumblin' aside. I think it's best me and Gilbert are back there. Just in case there is a carload of soldiers on board. Chances are, they'll cut loose on poor Mackenzie and Milton. And none of us needs to see or smell Milton shittin' his britches when the lead starts flyin' past his head. You need someone willin' to get harsh, and harsh pretty damn quick if you get my meanin'."

"Why don't you—" an annoyed Milton started to say.

"—You make a good point," Leland Baxter interrupted.

Milton and Mackenzie traded looks as if just hearing something profoundly unfair.

"You aren't gonna listen to that bastard, are you, Leland?" Milton asked.

"He raises a fair point."

Milton and Mackenzie traded looks again.

"You aren't gonna change the plan, are you, Leland?" Mackenzie asked.

"I don't wanna change the plan," added Milton.

"We've already planned to look after them passenger cars," Mackenzie heaped on.

"Herd them all into one, nice and quiet like," Milton heaped on further.

"All I said was he makes a good point," Leland said. "And he does. Controlling the passengers is all well and good, but perhaps it's best to have Eli and Gilbert go on ahead of you. Just in case."

"Well shit, he changed the plan," Milton muttered in disgust. "All because of you."

Nathan didn't know if Eli Gallant was happy or not, but he suspected the contrary bastard was.

"Give me a moment," Leland said. He thought it over.

Eli nodded eagerly at Gilbert, as if they were about to receive a ruling in their favor.

"All right," Leland announced. "I've decided. Eli and Gilbert will go forward with Jimmy. Gilbert will herd the passengers to the front of the train, well and away from the payroll car. Once that's done, Gilbert will return to Eli and Jimmy and hold at the last car they've cleared. I'll be along once the train's stopped, and with a little luck, we'll take the payroll without a drop of blood spilled."

"Why do we haveta move the passengers to the front, anyway?" Eli wanted to know.

"Hostages," Leland Baxter said. "If we approach from the rear, the Northwest police or soldiers or whoever is in the payroll car will be between us and them. All the reason why we're waiting here, on this grade, for the train to emerge, slowly as she climbs, traveling at such a speed to easily board her from the front. My hope is, if we gather up the passengers quietly, we can use them as leverage, to make the security force surrender themselves."

"And if they don't?"

Leland paused for effect. "Then we inform them of our dynamite. And our willingness to use it. And that whatever they're being paid to protect the payroll isn't worth their lives."

Milton shook his head, not pleased with his new role of babysitting.

"How many might be on that train, y'figure?" Mackenzie asked.

Leland thought about it. "About twenty passengers to each car. That seems comfortable. Roughly four cars. Say, eighty people, thereabouts."

"And no idea about soldiers or police?"

"The payroll train is a guarded secret. A large contingent riding the train would give away that something of importance is on board. My sources say no more than ten men, including an officer and junior officer. And ten men is plenty deterrent, if needed."

"What about this source of yours, Leland?" Eli asked. "You never did say what happened to him."

"That's right. I didn't."

That ended the conversation right there. As patient and authoritative as he might be, Leland Baxter wasn't one to fool around once he settled upon a course of action. And he'd never flinch about pulling a trigger. Nathan respected that. The man might've been a lawman in a past life.

The pack of eight waited, the winter night chilling them despite their extra layers. The stars continued to shine, unhindered by any significant cloud, their sparkle growing even more pronounced as the night wore on, if such a thing was possible.

"You sure that train is comin' tonight, Leland?" Eli wanted to know.

"I'm sure."

"Because it sure would be a goddamn shame if we humped all the way up here and got the night wrong."

"There's ice on them tracks," Mackenzie said. "So no train's come by here in a while."

"Well, shit, Mackenzie," Eli growled. "That snow might've blown down there earlier this day. We'd have no way of knowing. A good snow squall could blow through here and dump five feet of snow in five minutes. That's guaranteed."

Nathan had to admit, the man had a point there.

"The train's coming tonight," Leland assured them all. "We're just early is all."

"We're just freezin' our peckers to our saddles, is all," Eli muttered. "Jesus Christ Our Savior. I bet we missed her."

Leland didn't dignify that with an answer.

"That would be goddamned hilarious if'n we did," Eli continued. "Missin' the very train we came to rob. Holy shit, I'd laugh. Long and loud. All them careful laid plans gone to hell. And we're up here with only the grub and water we carried."

They did have a few pack mules back at the campsite with extra supplies, but Eli's thoughts placed a flicker of concern in Nathan's mind.

Leland, however, maintained his silence, staring as if his spine was somehow a length of iron.

"Heard some stories," Milton began, his words low and wicked, "where some folks who'd been trapped in the winter wilderness, hadta draw straws, to decide who got eaten first. So the others could survive."

"Goddamn figured something like that'd be on your mind, Milton," Eli remarked. "Who's gonna be the one to eat your pecker?"

"I didn't say that," Milton shot back.

"You were sure as hell gettin' around to it."

"Be quiet," Leland got in. "All of you. Right this instant."

Silence ruled again, but Nathan figured it wouldn't last long. Not with this group. They'd only been together a short time, and the peace was holding, but the trek up and into the mountains had stressed them to a point where some of the men were probably wondering if the reward was worth the effort.

That included Nathan.

"Well," Eli started up again, perhaps restless with the cold quiet, "I tell you all one thing. I ain't stayin' up here too much longer. Either that goddamn train shows up soon or me and Gilbert head on back to the campsite. See if'n we can't fire up a can of beans or something. Get some tea goin'. The rest of you shitty assholes can stay up here and—"

Leland's hand went up, and much to Nathan's surprise, Eli not only saw it, but he shut up.

But only for a second. "What?" he asked.

Then he heard it.

As did Nathan, and everyone else in the gang.

Distant, but unmistakable. Floating through the mountains like the voice of a lonesome ghost.

A train whistle.

2

The Interview

The town wasn't really a town. Wasn't even a village. It was one long strip of a frozen mud puddle filled with shattered ice and generously pickled with horseshit, which got Nathan wondering. There weren't many horses on the road. In fact, he didn't see any. There were exactly three small houses on the right side of the road and two others on the left. Smoke rose from chimneys, which reminded Nathan of crooked, hand-rolled cigarettes, the kind forgotten in breast pockets but discovered a few days later, still serviceable, but with a few strands sticking out here and there. A few bare elm trees nestled in between the houses, their limbs white with snow and no doubt beautiful in any other season. Probably beautiful under a sunny winter sky for that matter, but not today, not with heaven's dark, bloated guts hanging low and promising to drop a blizzard upon the scrawny settlement at any given moment. Nathan couldn't see any townsfolk, but he felt eyes on him, from the windows, where the sun rendered the darkened glass as fine as mirrors. There weren't any faces pressed up against the glass, but they watched him all the same, sauntering through atop a brown gelding.

Nathan steered the horse through Main Street, or what he considered Main Street, and spotted his destination. Wasn't hard at all, just like the telegram said. Small town south of the Canadian Pacific Railroad, a few houses, and one trading post at the very edge, the last thing you'd see on your way to the Rockies. The mountains loomed over the hills and treelines in the distance, their great craggy peaks hidden in that ominous January gloom brewing overhead.

Nathan didn't rightly care. He'd found the trading post. Saw that it was still standing, and that its chimney issued smoke. A big red barn leaned up against the shop, making the establishment the biggest structure around these parts.

He stopped at a deserted hitching post, where the previous night's snow still coated the wood, and slid off his horse's back. There was no splash when his boots hit the ground, only the contact of his heels sinking into half-frozen dirt. Nathan pulled down his scarf, revealing about three days' worth of stubble on a somewhat square face. He had thought about looking for a shave once in town, but upon seeing the state of the place, he decided that wasn't going to happen. He'd be fortunate just to have a warm wash.

Hell, he'd be lucky if he found a room for the night. As it was, with only three dollars left to his name, he had a strong suspicion he'd be sharing the barn with his horse. And whoever else was bunking down for the night.

He stepped up to the front door, eyed the faded sign that read "SWYER'S TRADING POST!" and took firm hold of the latch. He pulled the door open and a miasmic stink of tobacco smoke and juice, spilled whiskey, and God-only-knew-what-else stopped him in his tracks. Nathan stepped inside, wincing as if he'd just nailed his thumb with a hammer.

Sparse light somehow bled through windows in need of a scrubbing, illuminating the interior in a dreary gloom. A pot-bellied stove with a respectable stack of firewood spread heat into the place, and for that, Nathan was deeply grateful. Three square tables, rough and old, with chairs were arranged around the stove. A wide lane separated the drinking area from a log counter. A crooked wooden sign that read "TRADING POST" hung over one section and had a couple of sparsely stocked shelves behind it to back up that claim. Further down the log counter were two barrels, on their side at about waist-high, the knobby spigots well out of reach of any long-armed bastard thinking to stretch across the counter and serve himself. The sign "BAR" hung prominently over the barrels, laying to rest any mystery as to the contents. Nathan noticed that the BAR sign was much larger than the TRADING POST one, as if vying for the customer's attention. Brass spittoons, grazed by dusty sunlight and in need of a lavation, were positioned at either end of the counter. Nathan imagined even the flies avoided the receptacles.

There were two men in the room, watching him quietly, wondering his intentions.

Nathan tipped his hat at the one behind the bar, a tall gangly fellow in a black coat that looked suitable for the spring. Broad buttons were smartly fastened to the neck, where the ends of a dapper mustache drooped. The barman watched him carefully, no doubt wondering what had just come in from the approaching storm.

"Cold out there," Nathan said and smiled, flashing teeth he'd hadn't picked in a couple of days.

"Damn right it's cold out there," the barman said, unblinking. As if remembering his chores, he reached under the counter—all the while watching Nathan—and produced a washcloth. He got to scrubbing down the bar's surface.

"You got rooms for the night?" Nathan asked.

That stopped the scrubbing and earned him a glare. "Rooms? Can't you read?"

"Yeah. I can read."

"So why are you asking if I got rooms for the night? I don't got any rooms for the night. This ain't a hotel. You see the sign out there? In here?"

The barman punctuated each question with a chop of the hand.

"I saw them," Nathan replied.

"And you can read?"

"Said that I could."

"Then you're wasting my time," the barman scoffed and got back to some very energetic scrubbing.

"All right," Nathan said, taking a settling breath. "I'm looking for someone. Got a telegraph telling me to meet him here. Tall. Mustached. Though not quite like yours."

The barman stopped wiping down the counter a second time and glared. "Something wrong with my mustache?"

That backed Nathan up. "Nothing wrong with your mustache."

"You're goddamn right there's nothing wrong with my mustache. I take care of my mustache. Ladies love my mustache. Hell, I got men come in here and admire my mustache. They come in here all the time and say, that's a right-fine mustache you have there, Eddie. Right fine. See, I trim it and comb it out every day. I was just getting 'round to waxing it before you came in. You damn well wish you had a mustache like mine."

Nathan left all that alone. "As I was sayin', I'm looking for a man. Name's Robinson."

"Robinson?" the barman said and looked towards the other occupant of the room, standing near a back wall. He was big, broad of shoulder, and wearing a black beard that might've been inspiration for a children's story or two. He was dressed in an equally black duster opened to the waist, exposing a thick shirt underneath. The big man eyed Nathan something fierce, but all that was secondary, because, almost perfectly concealed behind a large leg, was a shotgun, pointed at the floorboards.

Nathan could draw, even draw fast, and he could certainly shoot, owning a pair of Colt Navy revolvers strapped to each thigh, but those prized guns were under his own coat. That shotgun would put him through the door and well into the road if the owner wished it.

So Nathan did the sensible thing. He lifted his hands and slowly tipped his hat.

"You Robinson?" he asked, just as a blast of wind rattled the windows.

Eyes that were either green or blue gazed back at him. "Nope."

"Oh. Sorry. Well then, anyone know—"

The big shotgunner stepped aside, revealing the door he was standing up against. Nathan had to admit, the distraction of the shotgun made him miss the door completely.

"Go on in," the shotgun man said, one-arming his weapon to his shoulder.

Nathan hesitated and decided that neither well-mustached Eddie or the shotgun man were going to do anything rash. So, with footfalls that echoed throughout the empty trading post, he proceeded to the door.

Which swung open, revealing a simple but serviceable poker room. The walls were dark and bare spruce timber. A couple of windows were placed about neck-high, on either side of a support beam. Smoke drifted from a cigarette held in one hand.

"Mr. Robinson?" Nathan asked upon placing a toe on the threshold.

"I am." The man smiled pleasantly, enjoying his smoke. "Mr. Rhodes?"

"That's me."

"Won't you come in?"

Nathan glanced at the shotgun man, who had lowered his head as if asleep. Just inside the door was yet another individual, bearded, with a full head of black hair, and studying the newcomer with a thoughtful expression.

Nathan nodded in his direction.

"Have a seat," Robinson instructed.

"Thank you," Nathan said and pulled out one of four chairs around the table. A bottle of Three Clover Whiskey stood at the center, along with four shot glasses. Nathan had been on the road for a week, and a whiskey bullet appealed to him very much. He sat down.

"The door, Jimmy, if you please?"

The bearded man did as he was told. Nathan scooted himself toward the table, trying hard not to look at the bottle, for politeness' sake.

"Keep your hands on the table," Robinson ordered softly and squinted as he took a draw off his cigarette.

Nathan did just that, very carefully.

"Have any trouble finding us?" Robinson asked.

Nathan smiled. "Not too hard, seeing as you're the only people around for miles."

Jimmy walked around the room until he stood at Robinson's back. Quietly, surely, he pulled out a revolver before crossing his hands before him. All the while, that thoughtful, schoolmaster's expression didn't falter.

"Don't mind Jimmy," Robinson said. "He's just here to make sure you don't try anything. I don't think you're going to try anything. Are you?"

Nathan smiled again, but it wasn't as broad this time. "No sir. Not me."

"Good," Robinson said in a grandfatherly way. "Now then, let's see… you were recommended to me by…"

Nathan waited until he realized he was expected to say something. "Bob Sanders. Ah, *Lone* Bob Sanders."

"Lone Bob had a bit of trouble, didn't he?" Robinson inquired with a frown and a smoke.

"Yes sir, he did. He did."

"What happened to him?"

Nathan gazed into Robinson's face, then remembered Jimmy with his gun at the ready. "His horse tossed him. Animal got contrary and bucked him off its back. Bob landed square on his feet, but in a gorge he was riding alongside before he got bucked. Broke both legs below the knee. Skinned out both hands something terrible. Probably would've died if not for a wagon-load of Christians going by, later in the day. Still well after the cold got to nibbling on some of Bob's parts."

"Excellent," Robinson said. "You are Nathan Rhodes."

"I am indeed," he replied, relieved he'd passed the initial questioning.

"Had to make sure, you understand," Robinson continued. "In case someone might've waylaid you. Attempted to … assume your identity. Chances are it wasn't going to happen. Not to you, but call me being careful. And a bit paranoid, I suppose."

Nathan swept his hands over the table's surface. "Think nothing of it."

"Keep your hands on the table, please."

Nathan immediately did so, his uncertainty returning.

"All right, then," Robinson started. "Where are you from?"

"Little place in Saskatchewan. Not quite a town. Gonna be one, though. If that Melville fella has his way."

"Charles Melville? Hays? Head of the Grand Trunk Railway?"

"S'pose so. Only know him as Melville."

"That's him. There's no other." Robinson took another draw off his smoke. "Can you shoot?"

"Yes sir, I can."

"Well?"

"As good as anyone else, I suppose."

"That's not very encouraging, Mr. Rhodes."

"Well sir," Nathan said. "In my short time upon God's green earth, I've found that it isn't how well you shoot that matters. It's how well you think when you're shot at."

Robinson chuckled softly, the sound deep and rich. "Very good, Mr. Rhodes. I don't entirely agree with you on that thought, but I can appreciate the sentiment. Let me ask you then, how often have you been shot at? To realize that pearl of wisdom?"

Nathan mulled it over. He'd been shot at quite a few times, while robbing coaches or people in back alleys. "Enough," he finally said.

"Bob says you've killed two men?"

In the silence that followed, the wind picked up outside, mustering enough force to bluster the windows again.

"He told you that?" Nathan said, slowly wincing.

"More or less."

"Through the telegraph?"

Robinson nodded.

Nathan sighed deeply, shifted, and faced the man across the table. He considered Jimmy right behind him, before returning to Robinson. "That wasn't... real smart, Mr. Robinson. The telegraph sender's just a regular—"

"Don't you worry about being reported," Robinson cut in. "Not when Lone Bob is the one sending the message. Bob has a reputation. Not all of it is earned, but once you get one, it tends to act like a weed, in that it grows. Fabrications sprout from the sides, but the main stalk is the one that remains true. The one you worry about. In any case, don't you worry about your killings becoming public knowledge. At least, not enough to summon the law to search for you. Bob will have looked after that. Guaranteed."

Perhaps so, but Nathan felt a twinge of unease. He couldn't chance going back east now. Not for a while at least.

"Let me tell you something," Robinson said, smoke puffing around his words. "To ease your mind. About the job we're planning. Jimmy, Charlie out there, and I. What do you know about the Klondike?"

A tingle went up Nathan's spine. "Only that there was a gold rush up there. Few years back."

"There was."

"Gold's all dug up now."

"Not all," Robinson said. "Still a few companies based in Dawson City. Prospectors have shifted to other places like Nome and Atlin Lake. Still a few workers digging into mountains and hills, sifting through rivers and streams. My point is, work is still ongoing. Slowed down some, but still ongoing. One company in particular—Shuster and Morris—has a sizeable workforce on its payroll. I've come into information that those people earn a regular wage. A wage that comes from Toronto, once every month, by train. About two weeks from now, that train will be going west on the Canadian Pacific. It's got a pay car with roughly three hundred thousand dollars in its safe. Maybe more. Wages for those miners and processors working for Shuster and Morris. The train has to pass through the Rockies. The railway is steep there, so for the train's safety, they built a series of tunnels called the Spirals, just opened up not two years ago. The Spirals help the train go up and down the mountain. Follow me so far?"

Nathan nodded.

"Good," Robinson said. He checked on his cigarette. He had another three or four minutes on the thing, at least. "Now, the train will be traveling slow because of the gradient. By which I mean the slope. Rail folks call a slope a grade. Think it's fancy. But I still call it a slope. Anyway, the train'll be climbing, pulling the rest of the cars behind it. It's going to pass under Cathedral Mountain, and when it comes out the other side, we'll be waiting to board her. Just haul ourselves up like a bunch of deer ticks climbing onto a dog's neck."

An attentive Nathan sat on the other side of the table, clearly all ears.

Robinson smiled through the smoke. "We board her. And then we rob her."

At that point, Nathan realized he was expected to say something. All he could think of was, "Three hundred thousand?"

"At least. Maybe a few thousand more."

"That's a lot of money."

"And it'll be potentially dangerous. There's every chance it'll be guarded.

By either police or soldiers or hired guns working security for the company. That's one thing I haven't been able to learn. So, we prepare for the worst. It's winter, and it'll be cold heading up into the mountains. That's a week's ride from here at best, but it'll probably take longer. So, we'll have to supply ourselves before we head out."

"From Eddie?" Nathan asked.

"Yes, from Eddie. The whole affair has made him a bit nervous."

"That why he was acting like an asshole out there?"

Robinson chuckled. "No, he's always like that."

Nathan thought on that for a second. "How many men are in this group of yours?"

"Ten. Eddie won't be going but he's the supplier, if you will. Lone Bob also has a stake in this, despite him being smashed up. So the cash will be divided ten ways. That fine with you?"

"What's my share?"

"Thirty thousand." Robinson smiled again. "At least."

"For a week's work."

"A week's travel, and perhaps two to three hours' work."

Nathan chewed on that. "You got an escape plan?"

"Of course. And we have guns."

"Got my own guns."

"Because of the unknown nature of the train's security, we'll get you a little more. A rifle at least."

Nathan didn't mind that. He'd already made the trip out here on Bob's word alone that it would be worth his while. It certainly looked to be worth his while.

"Well, Mr. Robinson," he said, his smile spreading. "I'll join your group if you'll have me."

"Call me Leland," he corrected, reaching across the table with an open hand as he clamped his cigarette between his teeth. "Leland Baxter."

They shook hands.

3

The Boarding

Upon hearing that eerie whistle, the men got busy.

They dismounted, their shins sinking in snow. Hands flipped open saddlebags and bandoliers of extra ammunition were looped over heads and shoulders. Those with scarves adjusted them over their faces, while those without wrapped them on and tied them. The baleful moonlight cast their shadows long over the snow, and there was no issue with seeing anything in the undisturbed white of the gulley.

"Milton," Leland said and pointed with a rifle. "Take those horses a little farther back along the trail. Get them out of sight. Tie them off somewhere and get back here. The land leading up to the railway is uneven and there could be dips. It'll be a hard walk for us, so when we get off that train, you make damn certain to cover our retreat. Shoot anything that's pointing a gun our way, until we get to the treeline. Understood?

"Give you cover, shoot anything pointing a gun at you. Got it."

"Try not to shit your britches when the shootin' starts, Milton," Eli jeered.

"Go fuck yourself, peckerhead."

Leland silenced any further retorts with a single warning finger. Once order was again established, he inspected the six long-coated wraiths standing before him. His eyes twinkled, betraying a smile underneath the scarf pulled up over his nose. "All right, gentlemen. This is what we've been waiting for. Keep calm. Collected. And do your jobs. Try not to kill anyone, but be forceful if you must. Any questions?"

"You think they'll remember me like they do Bill Miner?" Eli Gallant asked.

"Anything's possible."

"I sure as hell hope so, 'cause I hate that Kentucky bastard. 'Hands up' my ass. I was the first man to say them words. Me. Not him. Stole my goddamn words and got famous for it. Y'know they call him 'The Grey Fox' now?"

Leland didn't appreciate the distraction.

The train whistle sounded again, somewhere deep in that stone-cut tunnel, where the tracks disappeared into a black curtain.

"This way," Leland said, and got to marching through the snow. "Single file."

"Why single file?" Eli asked.

"Shut up, Eli," Nathan said and meant it.

"Make me."

But they all heard the clicking of two hammers being pulled back on a shotgun. The sound silenced the lot of them. Shorty Charlie Williams wasn't aiming at Eli, but he wasn't far off.

"All right, all right," Eli muttered and started walking. "Poor time to start shootin' your partner, but what the hell do I know."

The seven pawed their way through the drifts, toward the rail bed. Their winter clothing warmed them, but it made them wider, stockier, and just a touch clumsy. Leland trudged through snow deeper than expected, and he sank in places, fighting to move forward. Nathan wasn't fairing much better, and a quick glance over his shoulder told him the others, strung out in a wavering line, weren't having an easy time of it either. He soon wished he had a pair of those fancy Cree snowshoes that allowed a man to walk on snow. They sank to their knees and mid-thighs, and any misgivings about leaving the horses behind soon vanished. The seven men stood out against the snow, their figures lit up by the moon and their shadows stretched across fine sheets of white.

The rail bed was raised, and Leland actually fell face-first into a drift upon reaching the incline. Nathan, just behind him, reached out to lend the man a hand.

"I'm fine," Leland said.

"It's hard-going." Nathan said, the snow's deep chill penetrating his boots.

"This is easy," Eli chirped. "I've crawled through deeper in a Manitoba shithouse."

"Somehow I don't doubt that," Leland commented, getting to his feet. He pointed. They were parallel with the rail bed and the tracks and could see the tunnel mouth a distance away, perhaps some fifty yards or so.

Where a white light, just a bit bigger than a firefly, winked into existence deep inside the tunnel's depths.

"Come on," Leland urged. He double-timed it to the rail bed and freed himself of the deep snow. The others followed, grunting, their breath visible on the night air. The rail bed's shoulders were firm and frosted in only a thin layer of powder, and Leland stomped his boots to clean off his legs. He quickly wiped clear what didn't fall off.

The train whistle sounded again, closer now, and the huffing of the engine grew in volume.

Eli stumbled, went down with a grunt of "Jesus Christ," and stayed there until Gilbert kneed the man's shoulder. Shorty was behind them both and urged them on with a glare and a cocked shotgun.

The group eventually hauled themselves onto the rail bed and performed a quick dust-off, stomping and wiping at themselves and then each other.

"You three over there," Leland ordered Eli, Gilbert, and Shorty. "We'll board from either side of her. Be faster that way. Space yourselves out, but not too far or you'll risk being outpaced by her."

The group split apart and faced the tunnel mouth. Nathan felt a rush of excitement, momentarily imagining himself to be a lawman ready for a gunfight. Then the reality of what he was doing struck him full-on, and his excitement wilted just a little.

The light of the approaching train hung in the dark, a miniature moon of pure white that seemed to intensify with every passing second. The whistle sounded again, a raspy, almost breathless thing. The iron horse's wheels rumbled over the rail joints in a steady rhythm, pulling itself forward from the deep black. The beat was a minor thing, a faint percussion, but growing stronger.

"Here she comes," Leland called out some ten paces ahead.

Nathan barely heard him over the approaching din of the locomotive. He adjusted his hat, then his scarf, and took in the night sky overhead. That same blue-black field of stars lit up the heavens. It wasn't the first time he'd gazed upon the night sky with a deep, appreciative wonder. Many a time he'd camped out on a prairie, with just his horse, and simply laid back and stared at the heavens before sleep took him. But there was something about the mountain air that sharpened the stars, polished them, elevating their beauty to a level of purity that was just mesmerizing. Perhaps it was the altitude that put that final sparkle upon the sky, remembering folks said a person was closer to God up in the mountains.

Perhaps he was.

The whistle sounded again, a long-winded piping that filled the gulley before petering out. A steel beast growing weary of the dark and eager to be free of it.

"They're laying on that horn awful fierce, aren't they?" Nathan said.

"Just warning folks to stay off the track," Mackenzie explained a couple of paces behind him.

"Y'mean like what we're doing now?"

"Yeah, like what we're doing now."

"Animals, too," Leland called out, while staring at the approaching light. "You'd be surprised what wanders onto the tracks."

"At night?" Eli asked with a note of disbelief. "Up here? God-*damn*."

"Can't be any more surprising than a pack of gunslingers," Mackenzie said, hefting his rifle.

The light grew larger in the tunnel, straightening ever so slightly, as if aware of the seven men waiting on the rail bed. Even at that distance, Nathan found himself squinting at the harsh brightness. He looked back to the night sky and blinked.

The stars…

The stars were larger. More prominent. As if the entire night had dropped a hundred feet or so. Or the land had risen. The sight bewildered him so much, he arched his head to seek out the moon and found it hanging in the sky over his right shoulder.

Nathan's mouth dropped open.

The moon looked bigger by some unknown margin, but it had definitely grown, enough to notice. An eerie yet spectacular halo encircled that moon's face—a great spectral ring that he hadn't noticed before. Nathan had to blink a couple of times just to take it all in, to give his mind time to appreciate what he was seeing.

The ground beneath his feet began to tremble.

Ice and snow rattled free of the rails, as if the very tracks themselves decided to shake themselves off, revealing their dark lengths right up to the tunnel mouth.

"Hey, uh, Leland?" Nathan asked, raising his voice.

"What?" he answered, focusing on the approaching train.

"Look up."

Leland glanced a question at Nathan before doing so.

Mackenzie said it first. "Holy shit."

Mutters of disbelief came from the others, and even Jimmy Norquay's usual stoic demeanor was shaken by the sight overhead.

The whistle sounded again, much, much closer than before, and the great machine's laboring grew even louder. A mechanical, repetitive puffing then, along with a discordant, underlying screech of metal that pierced the night and rubbed each man's eardrums raw. That steely huffing and clatter distracted the train robbers. To Nathan, it sounded like a person playing the cymbals in a grand orchestra, slapping the metal plates together, while rusty pistons struggled to keep pace with the rising tempo.

And that didn't seem right to him, either.

The grade was uphill.

The train should be slowing *down*.

Before him, Leland Baxter held a hand up to shield his eyes against the growing might of the locomotive's eye.

"Awfully bright," Mackenzie declared over the rising raucous. And it was.

Incredibly bright. And becoming brighter.

Blinding even.

Enough to make one believe the great train was right on top of the group of seven, but that was far from the case. The gang still remained fifty or so yards back, but the light continued to grow from within the tunnel, until it seemed like the sun itself was emerging from the brickwork exit. The ground shook something terrible, and a rock or two tumbled down from the mountain slope to land harmlessly in the nearby powder. A blast of steam and snow whorled from the tunnel mouth, preceding the thing about to emerge.

Nathan widened his stance—out of fear of slipping, but also in wonder, utterly transfixed by the machine's headlight—until he had to shy away from the painful glare. The engine's laboring increased tenfold, becoming the breath of not a train, but a mechanical monster.

"Christ Almighty," Eli Gallant shouted, as he lifted his own hand to protect his eyes. Beside him, Gilbert and Shorty Charlie Williams turned their whitened faces away. The light bleached the color from the entire gang, rendering them as pallid figures frozen by the beam. Nathan saw his shadow stretch out behind him, and then watched as the snow shook and sparkled around it. A January blizzard swept over him, stabbing at his exposed bits, as if summoned by the train.

Mackenzie grabbed him and pulled him back.

The train rolled by Nathan, missing him by a mere foot, its ominous weight startling him with its closeness. The three men on the other side of the tracks disappeared, replaced by a ribbed profile of black iron and chrome. No longer blinded by the headlight, Nathan glimpsed the train's collection of tubular pipes, animated rods, and whirling discs comprising the profile of the great machine. The locomotive steamed by, pushing tirelessly forward, mounted atop a series of great wheels that whispered metallic whale songs. Bars of steel rowed and churned, moving that great ominous bulk along.

A cloud of steam engulfed Nathan, warm and moist and laced with a scent of engine oil and something else. A chuffing, wintry maelstrom swallowed him up and flung ice and snow into his face. Nathan again lowered his eyes as the train rolled on past, billowing coats and causing hands to secure hats.

The engineer cab flashed by, and Nathan glimpsed the glow from a single lantern through the engineer's open window.

And a hunched figure, all gone in a second.

"Come on!" Leland shouted, readying himself upon the rail bed's shoulder, searching for the stairs.

The wind and fury whipping up the snow diminished for a second, and an open car bed of chopped wood became visible. Hoarfrost partially concealed the numbers and lettering painted on the side. Nathan looked from the passing car to the dark form of Leland, closing with the moving train. A railing popped into sight, and Leland latched onto it with one arm before hoisting himself up. His struggling figure was black against the snow squall.

Then it was Nathan's turn, and he had no time to think about it.

The train, oddly enough, wasn't moving as fast as he'd initially believed, and time seemed to slow as he reached out and grabbed onto the rail. He got one foot on the lowest step, and then the other.

"Get up here," Leland's shadowy figure commanded as he climbed up onto a platform, where a single door led into the first passenger car. Lamplight shone from a glass portal set high into the door. Two drooping guard chains, hanging between the cars, were the only barrier keeping someone from falling onto the railbed.

There wasn't much room upon the platform, and there would be even less very soon, especially when Eli Gallant finished pulling himself up on the other side. Gilbert was right behind him. Leland stepped toward the wood car's platform and gripped the lip of the filled bin.

"Over here, quickly now," Leland ordered, clinging onto the bin while still holding onto his Winchester.

Nathan scrambled after him, sensing that impossible slowing of time right to his bones, where each fleeting second stretched into three. He stepped onto the wood bin platform and grabbed on, taking a huge settling breath and catching a smile on Leland Baxter's face.

"Nothing like it, is there?" the gang leader asked.

Nathan smiled back and shook his head.

Shorty Charlie Williams was the last to board. He stopped at the lower step as Jimmy Norquay did the same on the other side. Steam and snow blasted by, distorting or concealing the gulley walls. The men clung to the railing, their shoulders set, their faces lifted to the partial roof that extended from the passenger car over the platform, which provided some measure of protection from the elements.

If the elements had been coming from the sky.

In the pale light of the car door, the gang settled down while the train chugged onwards, gently rocking them.

"Hard part's over," Leland informed them all. He looked back towards the main engine. The wood was piled high, and the billowing steam all but hid the locomotive's forward parts.

"Wasn't so bad," Eli remarked, clutching his rifle in one hand while hanging on to the railing with another.

"Wasn't so bad," Mackenzie repeated, but his tone suggested it *had* been bad, as if he'd somehow been scared quite badly.

For Nathan, however, that odd sense of time had disappeared, and he was fully in the moment.

"All right then," Leland barked and nodded at the others. "There's the passenger car. Control the car and everyone on board." He glanced back toward the engineer's cab and received a face-full of stinging snow.

"The hell this snowstorm come from?" Eli asked, placing his back to the passenger car door and chancing a quick adjustment to his hat.

"Just blew in, I suppose," Mackenzie answered.

But that didn't feel right to Nathan.

"Never mind the snow," Leland said. He nodded toward the passenger car. "Get in there and do your jobs. We'll be back once we secure the engineers and stop this thing. And, Eli?"

"Yeah?"

"Just reminding you is all. Don't do any shooting unless you got to."

"Yeah, yeah."

Gilbert stood behind the man and slapped his back for encouragement, all to the rising tune of *chump, chump, chump, chump* as the train's tempo gradually increased.

"All right then," Leland said to Nathan. "Let's stop this thing before she picks up any more speed."

With that, the outlaw leader skirted toward the outer side of the wood bin. Dipping his head into the rising wind, he held onto the steel lip and shuffled along the narrow platform.

One careful step at a time.

Nathan heard the passenger door slide open behind him. The five men there went inside, one after the other.

The thing that caught his attention, just as he grabbed the rail and leaned into the rising gale, was that there were no gasps or screams of any of the passengers as the group of armed men filed inside the car. Nathan didn't dwell on it. He concentrated on threading his way along the walkway running to the engineer's cab, clinging tight to the railing.

4

"What do you want to be when you grow up, Nathan?" his father asked, drawing a forearm across his balding head and soaking up the sweat there. The August sun beat down upon the parcel of farmland that they currently worked, drying out the soil faster than the water they sometimes had to dump over it. His father pulled out a handkerchief from his stained overalls and applied it to his right temple, then left.

Squinting in the sun and getting to know firsthand how damn hard farming was, nine-year-old Nathan squinted back at his perspiring father and smiled. "A lawman!"

That was met with silence.

"A lawman?" his father asked, placing an elbow upon one of the hoe's handles. The leather reins drooped and ended at the harness of one solitary workhorse his father had named 'Amigo.'

"Yup," Nathan replied.

"Not a farmer?"

"Nuh-uh."

That answer seemed to crease his father's tanned face in puzzlement, and maybe in a touch of sadness, too. Nathan didn't want to make his father sad, however, but didn't quite understand his mistake. Then it occurred to him what he'd said wrong.

"I mean… I want to be a farmer, too," he explained, "but also a lawman."

That put a smile on his father's worn face. He chuckled, his smile missing teeth but pleasant all the same. Once he got his little laugh out of his system, he shook his head and applied his handkerchief to the back of his neck. He grimaced at the sun.

"Don't you worry, son," he said in a voice neither offended nor sad, but quietly content. "Don't you worry. Being a lawman is a fine idea. Just fine. But it's just as tough as being a farmer, don't you be mistaken."

"It is?"

"Yes, it is."

Nathan looked to his feet, reconsidering his career choice.

"But it's a fine profession all the same," his father said. "And I know you'll make a fine lawman if you become one."

That perked up Nathan's spirits mighty fine, and under the terrible summer heat, he and his father smiled at each other.

*

Snow swirled and battered Nathan's face as he shuffled his way along the walkway, boot toes to bin wall. He leaned over the upper lip of the bin, and the wind fluttered his coat and strove to rip his hat from his head. That wasn't happening, however. That felt hat had belonged to his father once, and though he had fastened the chin string, if the wind did manage to take it, well, Leland would have to stop the train all by himself.

Because Nathan would go after the hat.

Chump, chump, chump, chump… The train's pulse beat, pushing the machine forward as it let out steam.

A sheet of white powder whipped over the woodpile, conjuring up snowy demons that lashed at Nathan's face. He lowered his head and wormed his way along, peeking every now and then to check on Leland.

Who was nowhere in sight.

In fact, there was nothing in sight. It was a complete whiteout. Or, as it was night, a complete and chilling *blackout*. All that was left in the world was a bin of wood and a train robber hitched to its side. The snow subsided just a touch, and somewhere far ahead, much farther than anticipated, was Leland's dark silhouette, stopped and waiting.

Then he was gone, rounding the wood bin's corner. Nathan hurried at best speed, hampered by his rifle and wishing he'd had the sense to attach a strap. He reached the corner and saw Leland within the engineer's cab.

The engineer himself was bent over in front of the open fire box, where wood and shovels of coal would be tossed inside, feeding the locomotive's terrible hunger for fuel. A circular iron plate was pushed to one side, the surface dimpled in a pattern of riveted seams. Above that was an assortment of gauges, dials, levers, and hand wheels, all below a narrow collection of brass piping and blackened knobs that reminded Nathan of a grasshopper's face. A ratty-looking coat hung from a peg. A shelf held a pair of dented metal mugs and a smudged oil can between them. A frayed seat, the cushion imprinted over the years by a sizeable ass, lay to the right. A lamp burned on a secured perch, behind the seat and overhead. The light played off the snow streaking past the two open windows.

Despite the cold Nathan had just endured, a wall of heat radiated from the firebox and hit his face hard enough to make the cold seem like a comfortable retreat. Leland glanced back at his companion as he slunk inside the cab and righted himself. The older man had his rifle pointed at the engineer's back, who was oblivious to his half-frozen company.

"You okay? Leland asked Nathan, over the chuffing of the train.

"I'm okay."

Leland nodded and indicated the engineer, who still hadn't turned away from the firebox.

"You there," Leland ordered. "Turn around. Nice and slow."

The engineer continued looking inside the open firebox, where red coal glowed. The heat was considerable where Nathan stood, and he thought it incredible the engineer stood practically with his nose hairs upon the fire box's threshold.

Chump, chump, chump, chump…

"I said, turn around," Leland ordered.

Nathan brought up his own rifle and aimed it from the hip.

The engineer stopped staring into the firebox. He closed the small door, slowly righted himself, and then checked on a gauge.

"Relaxed old bird, ain't he?" Nathan smiled behind his scarf.

"He's relaxed all right," Leland agreed. "Probably stone deaf from working this engine. Hey. You. *Turn around.*"

The engineer's head cocked at that, as if finally catching wind of something after all. With an elderly man's grace, he took a moment to compose himself, straightening out his well-used gray uniform before lumbering around.

Chump, chump, chump, chump.

The engineer's face was completely removed of its flesh, and the nearby lamp colored his skeletal features a harsh orange. The sight stunned both men, but Nathan felt the time warp again, a sensation of turning around underwater, where the seconds stretched themselves out much longer than a pocket watch's comforting tick. All the while, the heat in the cab did nothing for the paralyzing chill of his innards that had seized up completely.

"Oh Sweet Mary and Joseph," Leland sputtered nearby, his rifle pointed at the grinning apparition. "Oh Sweet—"

The engineer considered them both, even though it had no eyes within its orbital cavities. A bony, impossibly functioning hand rose and clutched a lever, each skeletal digit enclosing the metal with foul purpose. Candlelight flickered in the deep vats that were its eye sockets.

Nathan couldn't speak.

Leland grunted a religious verse, but the words were lost upon the rising of the wind and the clamor of the engine—which was picking up speed.

"Don't…" Leland warned the engineer.

The ghost didn't listen before, however, and it sure as hell wasn't listening now. It pulled the lever, releasing a shriek as piercing and startling as a hot thumb goosing one's ass.

And despite all his talk about crowd control, Leland fired first.

Nathan fired second.

The shots ripped through the engineer's gray uniform, barely moving the figure, and ricocheted off the iron plate behind it in a sizzling stutter where each metallic ping marked a new bounce.

A miniaturized comet fired past Nathan's profile, close enough for him to flinch.

In that reflexive moment, the engineer lunged.

5

When Eli opened the passenger car's door, all he felt was warmth. All he saw were empty seats. He moved inside, nudged along by Gilbert, who wanted to get out of the weather.

"Ease off," Eli warned with a stern look.

Gilbert scowled back, soaking up the reprimand, but grateful to be inside.

Eli turned back to the empty car, walking ahead a few steps as the rest of the group entered.

"What the hell?" Gilbert said.

"What the hell, indeed," a puzzled Mackenzie repeated as he studied the interior.

The passenger car had, at a glance, about two dozen rows or more split down the middle by a well-worn aisle. Wide-berthed seats with a framework of polished mahogany gleamed softly underneath burning oil lamps. Fancy glass fixtures hung over the main aisle, three of them in total, spaced along the ceiling at measured intervals. They provided ample, if not a touch subdued, light. Frost covered the windows' exteriors, but there wasn't much to see out there anyway. A smell of spent tobacco scented the air, mixed with a complicated blend of different perfumes and a hint of rancid breath.

Eli stepped into the first row of seats and inspected the cushions of deep grassy green.

"Did someone shit in here or something?" he asked with a disapproving frown, eyeing all the empty berths.

"You smell shit?" Gilbert asked, sniffing in earnest. "I don't smell any shit, Eli. I smell pipe smoke. And maybe perfume."

"There's no dung in here," Mackenzie said, stopping in a berth and inspecting the remainder of the passenger car.

"No, there's no dung," an annoyed Eli said. "I said 'shit'. As in 'horseshit' or otherwise. Just makin' a point is all, 'cause there's sure as hell no other reason why there's no one in here."

Mackenzie looked at rifle-toting Jimmy Norquay, and the serious Metis shook his head. Shorty Charlie Williams blocked the door they'd all come through, his shoulders dusted with snow and his tall hat almost touching the ceiling. Snow covered them all to some degree, but mostly for color, and not so thick as to be a hindrance.

"So this is first class," Mackenzie said, taking in the comforts of the car. "Nice."

"What time is it?" Jimmy asked.

"Some time past nine, perhaps?" Mackenzie suggested.

"Felt more like ten."

Eli eyed both men. "Neither one of you educated peckerheads got a watch?"

Neither man answered.

"Shorty," Eli barked. "You got a pocket watch?"

"Nope."

"Thanks, Shorty," Eli muttered in annoyance.

"Leland's got a pocket watch," Jimmy said, remembering. "Though it does us no good. Not yet, anyway."

"Daresay the passengers are in the next car," Mackenzie said. "Sleeper car. Must be later than we figure."

"Doubt if it's a sleeper," Jimmy thought aloud. "If this is first class, there's supposed to be another. Supposed to be four passenger cars."

"Maybe they're in the dining car?"

"This train has a dining car?"

"Certainly does." Mackenzie said. "It's a long trip."

"It is a long trip," Jimmy said.

"From Montreal to Port Whats-his-face."

"Eight days."

"Ten or eleven in the winter," Mackenzie pointed out. "Depending on the weather."

"Long trip," Jimmy said quietly.

"Fuck the long trip," Eli rumbled with heat and walked right up the middle of the car. "Goddamn educated cocktuggers. All I asked for was the goddamn time and I get a report on traveling conditions. You bastards are in the wrong fucking line of work, that's all I gotta say. The wrong fucking kind."

Gilbert scowled at Jimmy and Mackenzie, reinforcing those sentiments.

Gilbert didn't dare look at Shorty Charlie Williams, however. Shorty secretly scared the shit out of him, and it took every ounce of courage he could muster to keep calm while around the hulking bodyguard.

Gilbert followed Eli, their boots scuffling along a clean floor.

Jimmy and Mackenzie exchanged looks, shared a consulting glance with Shorty (who said nothing) and then followed the two leading men.

Not seeing any need to hang around at the head of the car, Shorty dutifully followed them all, keeping his shotgun ready at the shoulder.

Mindful of what Leland had said, Eli stopped at the next door and waited for the others to catch up, eyeing them all from underneath an unimpressed lowered brow.

"You shit-squirts best keep up," he warned. "I'm tellin' you now. Don't dawdle on me. Don't none of you dare to fuckin' dawdle on me."

"I wouldn't dawdle on you, Eli," Gilbert protested. "Not me."

"All right, maybe not you. Sorry. But you three."

Mackenzie looked indifferent, but Jimmy and Shorty didn't flinch from Eli's gaze.

"You just mind what Leland told you to do," Jimmy Norquay warned him. "And remember, while you might be in the lead here, you *ain't* the one in charge. Until Leland gets back here, *I'm* in charge. Not you. Me."

Eli's frown deepened. "Did I say I wanted to be in charge? Just said don't dawdle on me. That's all. Quit tryin' to make something outta nothin', Jimmy. Christ Almighty."

"You just open that door and mind your business," Jimmy said with a dangerous calm.

Shaking his head, Eli did just that. He gripped the lever and pulled up, and the door slid open on ball bearing rollers. A short, weather-protected vestibule between the two cars appeared, and Eli craned his neck to inspect the enclosure. Three strides ahead was the other door. Light glowed from a single square window marred with dust. The whole area was dark, somewhat narrow, and rocked with the locomotion of the train.

"What are you waiting for?" Jimmy asked.

"Hold on a goddamn second, goddammit," Eli shot back. "Ain't never seen one like this."

"It's a vestibule," Mackenzie explained. "Think they're called gangway connectors or something of the like. They're mounted over the couplers."

"The hell's a coupler?" Gilbert asked behind his scarf.

"Ain't you ever been on a train before?"

"Yeah, but…" Gilbert shrugged and pulled down his scarf, revealing a scraggly beard, a large mole on his left cheek, and a pimpled nose. He spat cotton bits, licked his lips, and once done with all that, said, "Not recently."

"Coupler's what keeps the cars together," Jimmy informed him.

Eli was inspecting the enclosed section bridging the space between the two cars. "That roof looks like my old man's accordion, except we're on the inside."

"It keeps the snow out," Jimmy said. "And rain."

"Not the heat," Eli said and, with his rifle up, proceeded across the shaking floor, testing it as one might crossing a pane of river ice. The train wheels rolled unseen underfoot.

Chump, chump, chump, chump…

Gilbert tugged his scarf up over his nose.

Once across, Eli snorted and took hold of the next lever.

"Go on," Jimmy said to Gilbert.

"You go on," Gilbert shot back, so Jimmy went forward. The others went after him, including Shorty, whom Gilbert shied away from just a touch. Once they were all inside, Gilbert stepped somewhat uncertainly into the cramped space.

The door rolled closed behind them.

"You say this is another first-class car?" Eli said, peeking through the window.

"Supposed to be," Jimmy said. "Two total. The other's for regular-paying folk."

"Oh yeah?" Eli leered and slid the door open.

Another passenger car with the same fine adornments and comforts as the previous one. And, like the one before it, the interior was also deserted.

The train's movement gently rocked the men upon the threshold as they stared at that puzzling sight.

"What the hell…?" Mackenzie whispered in confusion.

"They can't all be in the sleeper car," Jimmy declared.

"Or the diner."

"Sure as hell can't all be in the shitter," Eli said and moved inside. The rest of the men did the same. Some twenty-plus rows back, another closed door waited. They stopped and studied the empty car.

"This ain't right," Jimmy said.

"You're tellin' me?" Eli asked, not expecting an answer.

In the lapse of conversation that followed, the sound of the moving train filled their ears.

"Well, we stick to the plan," Jimmy said after a time. "We'll go on ahead. You two," he indicated Shorty and Mackenzie, "stay around here. Wait for Leland to show up."

Mackenzie looked around. "We got no passengers to look after."

Standing a full head taller and looming behind the man, Shorty shook his head in support of the assessment.

"Maybe it's best we stick together," Mackenzie continued. "Until we find the passengers."

"Come on, then," Eli said and strode through the rows of seats. Gilbert immediately pushed his way through the other three (being quite careful with Shorty Charlie Williams) and hurried after the man.

Sharing yet another puzzled look with Mackenzie and Shorty, Jimmy sighed and walked after the pair. Mackenzie marched after him, while Shorty turned and watched the closed door behind them, mindful of the light fixtures overhead. He glanced from one row of seats to the other before finally turning around, when something lying in the middle of a green cushion seat caught his eye.

A child's rattle, round, with little noisemaking dingles on it, or what Shorty identified as little noisemaking dingles.

Shotgun held in both hands, Shorty stooped and inspected the little toy, his low brow scrunched up in thought.

Then, without another thought, he hurried to catch up with the rest of the group.

6

The engineer grabbed both Nathan and Leland by their coats before either one could react. The uniformed skeleton lifted both men off their feet, slamming their heads into the hard ceiling. The impact stunned Nathan, but he was aware of falling, his hat coming off, and Leland crashing down beside him. He realized he was on the floor, and rolled about like a man attempting to regain control of his legs.

Chump, chump, chump, chump…

The engineer turned back toward the train's controls and inspected a gauge as if far-sighted. It then reached down and opened the lid to the firebox, revealing a roaring blaze within. Only for a second, before the engineer slammed the door shut again.

Leland was slumped against the cab wall, clawing at the air as if swiping at mosquitoes. Nathan wasn't much better, but he discovered he could move his legs and arms. He winced as he pulled himself to a sitting position, and that little bit of effort spun his head like a greased roulette table. As the interior twirled and even bobbed, Nathan watched the engineer as it fiddled with a lever.

The effect was immediate. The train picked up speed.

Chumpchumpchumpchump … Chumpchumpchumpchump…

A lurch threw Nathan backwards. He pawed at air, missed whatever he was grabbing for, and clocked the back of his skull on the steel floor. Dazed and confused but fighting to sort matters out, he found himself staring at one of the cab's windows, where a tattered screen of snow and night flashed by.

The engineer strode past him, ignoring the fumbling men at its feet. Nathan lifted his head, struggling to keep the figure in sight. The engineer went to a wood box and gripped two large chunks of cut fir. The skeletal figure, still darkly smiling, turned and strode back to the fire box, where it opened the door and threw in the wood.

The click of a revolver's hammer brought Nathan back to the present.

"Nathan," Leland said weakly, gun drawn, and fighting to draw the strength to aim it.

"Yuh," Nathan answered, rolling onto his side.

Chumpchumpchumpchump … Chumpchumpchumpchump…

"We're speeding up," Leland said.

"I know."

The engineer tapped a gauge with a skeletal finger. It then slapped the metal, twice for effect, and threw up a hand in frustration. The ghostly figure then consulted two more dials before standing back and, in a pose of pure vexation, at least to the living, placed its hands on its hips and shook its head.

Nathan picked up a rifle and aimed at the thing's back.

Chumpchumpchumpchumpchumpchumpchumpchump…

The engineer cocked his head back as if remembering something.

"Hey," Leland said with deadly intent, aiming his pistol. "You."

The engineer half-turned. Those empty eye sockets spied Nathan first, then Leland. Both men pointed their guns at the thing. The engineer didn't lift his hands in surrender. It stood there, while the machine it commanded continued to increase speed.

Without warning, Leland fired, the report hot and deafening in the cab.

The engineer's head snapped backwards a split instant before the shell blew out the back of its skull and ricocheted all over the cab. Metal punched metal. Glass crinkled and Nathan cringed at the explosive scene.

The engineer remained standing, however, and when it righted its skull, Nathan could see right through a ragged bullet hole drilled in the thing's forehead. No blood came from the wound, but there was a single, haunting wisp of smoke. The engineer lowered its head, its smile still firmly in place, but taking on a decidedly darker, more menacing demeanor towards the two men, as if realizing that simply subduing the pair wouldn't do.

Or so Nathan thought. He fired his rifle at the thing's dead heart, and blew a hole straight through that old uniform and out the back in a tent punch of cloth.

Which did nothing to the engineer.

"Sweet Jesus," Leland muttered, and took aim again.

Not waiting to be shot, the engineer abruptly raced past the men, the unexpected speed startling.

"Shoot him!" Leland cried out, struggling to find the fleeing figure.

Nathan slammed himself against the cab wall, twisting, attempting to keep the ghost in sight. The engineer leaped outside the cab and landed upon a woodpile. There it stood, the escalating wind ruffling its uniform until it resembled a flag caught in a tempest. Smoky clouds streaked by, as if the very universe was accelerating around them.

"Stop!" Nathan shouted and lined up his sights. The thing wasn't ten paces away.

The engineer crouched, very much aware of the aimed rifle.

Nathan didn't fire, however, even though his finger rested on the trigger.

"What are you waiting for?" Leland demanded. "Shoot the bastard!"

"What about the train?" Nathan asked, not taking his eyes off the engineer.

Leland looked at the controls. "Jesus H. Christ, get him back in here."

His senses fully returned to him, Nathan bore down on his Winchester. "You hear that, you…" he started, but was at a loss as to what to call the crouching thing on the woodpile. "*You get back in here or I'll shoot!*" he finally shouted.

Snow and steam and wind streaked overhead, partially concealing the uniformed apparition with the bullet hole decorating its forehead. For a moment, Nathan actually thought the thing was going to do as ordered.

But then the engineer jumped clear of the train, and vanished into the stormy night.

7

Seven passenger cars deep into the train, Eli stopped at the midway point between a pair of green cushiony seats, and threw a tantrum under a set of fancy light fixtures.

"How fuckin' *long* is this thing, anyway?" he demanded with a stomp of his boots. He whirled upon his companions, who were equally mystified at what they were seeing. No one told Eli to calm down, to relax, because, quite frankly, they were increasingly uneasy themselves.

"There's only one engine, right?" Mackenzie asked of Jimmy, who stood right behind him in the aisle.

"I only saw one," Jimmy said.

"Me too," Gilbert said with a note of nervousness. "All I saw was one."

"What about the goddamn engines?" Eli asked.

Jimmy pulled down his scarf. "We've walked through seven passenger cars and no passengers. The train would need an extra locomotive to pull all this weight, but this thing's outfitted with just one."

"So?"

Jimmy paused to sift through his buzzing, spinning thoughts. "So… we're on a bigger train than expected. There should be two engines."

"So what?" Eli said.

Jimmy clearly didn't know what, but he felt the train's tempo underneath his feet. "Feel that?"

The men looked to the floor.

"We're speeding up," Mackenzie said.

"We're speeding up," Jimmy confirmed.

"So what does *that* mean?" Eli barked at them. "Give me some goddamn answers here."

"For one," Jimmy said, "means Leland and Nathan haven't stopped the train."

That struck them speechless.

"Something must've happened," Mackenzie eventually said.

Jimmy looked past Shorty Charlie Williams to the last door they entered.

"You thinking of going back?" Mackenzie asked.

"Yeah."

"Well, *shit*," Eli exploded and hopped on the spot. "What about the goddamn passengers?"

Jimmy was already moving. "Shorty, you go with Eli and Gilbert. Find them passengers. Mackenzie, you come with me. And Eli?"

"Yeah?"

"You're in charge until we get back."

That seemed to pacify the hard case.

"Shorty?" Jimmy said, now at the car door.

Charlie Williams turned.

"Don't let that brazen bastard do anything we'll regret later on."

Shorty nodded that he would indeed do just that.

Jimmy and Mackenzie disappeared behind the sliding door, which rolled closed behind them.

A clearly pissed-off Eli regarded the hulking Shorty… and his ready shotgun.

*

"What do you think's happening here?" Mackenzie asked as he followed Jimmy Norquay back into the last passenger car. The lamps, perhaps burning a touch dimmer, streaked by overhead, creating an almost dreamlike quality to the varnished mahogany frames. The green cushions were colored a deeper hue, and the air remained redolent of pipe smoke and fading perfumes.

"No idea," the man replied as he hurried through the deserted aisle. "None."

Mackenzie lowered his scarf, his face glistening. "Well, there's sure as hell something going on here."

Jimmy slowed to a stop and faced his companion. "I don't *know*, Mackenzie. All I know is we're on an empty train, with about five more cars than there should be."

"An empty train picking up speed," Mackenzie reminded him.

Jimmy nodded. "Yeah."

"You think Shorty will be okay?"

"Shorty'll be fine."

"I don't like Eli. Think I mentioned that a few days back."

"I don't like him either," Jimmy said. "Think *I* mentioned that a few days back. Nobody likes him. Maybe except Leland. Leland got him with Gilbert and wanted a couple of shit-kickers. We needed them for this job."

"What do you think happened to the passengers?"

"I don't know that, either," Jimmy said, but then he looked to the overhead compartments. Ornate walnut boxes with sliding doors and fancy designs. Varnish finishes shone. Jimmy reached up and slammed one of the boxes open, revealing an empty cavity.

"Nothing," Jimmy reported and handed his rifle to the other man. He gripped the compartment's edge and, planting his boots on a seat cushion, pulled himself up to look inside.

"Nothing," he repeated. "Like a bare ass pantry."

"No baggage?" Mackenzie asked.

"No baggage." Jimmy dropped to the floor and righted himself. He studied the berths around him. "Nothing. No suitcases, nothing."

He went from one row to the other, scrutinizing each one in turn.

"Maybe the passengers took them," Mackenzie said as he followed. "When they left the train."

"All right," Jimmy said, going along for the moment. "But then why did they get off?"

"I don't know."

They stared at each other then, puzzling things over, before Jimmy spoke. "Let's get back to Leland. Something's going on up front, and I'll bet we'll find our answers there."

"The engineers?"

"The engineers," Jimmy said, taking his rifle back. "They'll know what's going on."

8

"Well…" Leland muttered, clearly shaken by the ghostly engineer and its unexpected departure from the train. Nathan could tell the gang leader was trying his best to compose himself.

The strength returned to Nathan's legs, and he rose shakily—a little too fast as the cab seemed to tilt one way and then the other. He staggered to the box car filled with wood (and a portion of coal, he noticed) and stretched his neck to see. Freezing wind and snow attacked his face as he looked around, but the thick steam clouds streaming past blinded him.

"See anything?" Leland wanted to know.

"Not a damn thing." Nathan crossed to the other side of the cab and gazed over the edge. "Nothing."

"Too harsh out there," Leland said, raising his voice to be heard over the engine's rising clamor.

Nathan returned to the cab's considerable depths, the elements swirling and beating at his back. "The hell was that, Leland?"

The older man didn't answer, his face pale, and his eyes glassy with uncertainty.

"I mean, you saw the same thing, right?" Nathan demanded with mounting energy. "'Cause I saw… I saw a goddamn ghost. A goddamn ghost, Leland. That's what I saw. That's what I shot. Twice. Shot twice and the damn thing was just as dead as it was before. Alive, I mean. I mean—you know what I mean."

Leland pressed himself against a wall and noticed the engineer's seat. He sat down heavily, dazed as if gut shot.

Nathan wasn't unaffected by the sight. "You okay?

Leland met the other man's concerned gaze. "I'm fine. Just… you know."

"Yeah. Me, too."

Leland took a deep settling breath, as if remembering why they'd come to the front of the train in the first place. He stood and staggered to the controls, studying the levers and dials. One dial had taken a bullet to the face, wrecking it completely. There were three levers and Leland considered them all.

"One of these is the brake," he said. "One is to increase steam pressure, which will make the train go faster."

Nathan picked up his hat and put it on before joining Leland at the controls.

"He pulled that one there," Nathan said and pointed. "And the train sped up."

"You sure?"

"No."

That drew a look from Leland.

"My head was rolling at the time," Nathan explained. "But what the hell? Just leave it and try the others."

Leland looked from one gauge to the gunshot one. "I think this is the water pressure. Or steam."

"Best choose one," Nathan said. "And do it fast. Unless you figure we can back this thing up from the caboose, because it's gonna be a long walk back to Milton."

"Dammit." The leader arbitrarily gripped the nearest lever and slowly pulled it from right to left.

Chumpchumpchumpchumpchumpchump…

"Nothing," Leland said, waiting for a reaction. "Not one damn thing."

Nathan fixed his hat's string under his chin and held onto it. He then stuck his head out the nearest window and was immediately blinded by snow and steam.

"Can't see a thing, Leland," he said. "Not even the ground."

Leland inspected one gauge, the one the ghost had slapped, and read, "New York Industrial Mills."

"What's that then?" Nathan asked, pulling himself back inside.

"I don't know. I don't know any of this. Probably the manufacturer, but it doesn't say the purpose of the gauge."

Leland pushed the lever into the original position and moved to another. He gripped it, and with the same careful pressure, cranked the thing to the opposite side until it touched a dimpled iron plate.

Nathan waited, studying the floor, imagining the wheels underfoot turning, racing.

"Nothing," Leland reported, still holding the handle.

"Not one goddamn thing," Nathan agreed. "Pull the last one."

"You said that one sped up the train."

"Said I wasn't sure. My head was messed up. Could've been any one of them, tell the truth."

"Well, that's no good."

"Look," Nathan said and tried to think. "You tried two already and the train ain't slowed down yet, right?

Leland paused as if listening to the train. "I believe you're right."

"So that lever must be a brake, right?" Nathan quickly inspected the controls. There wasn't anything left, so the last two controls must have been 'stop' and 'go'. Three levers total, and Leland held the last.

Without warning, the gang leader moved the lever to the right.

And the train continued to roll.

Chumpchumpchumpchumpchumpchump…

The two robbers regarded each other over the sound of the speeding locomotive.

"Holy shit," Nathan said for them both.

9

Growing more and more pissed with each passing minute, Eli strode to the door of the next car and whipped it open with a clatter.

"Christ *Almighty*," he swore. He stormed ahead into what was yet another empty passenger car. Gilbert duly followed while Shorty Charlie Williams brought up the rear, glancing at the seats as he passed.

"Where the hell *are* you people?" a furious Eli demanded. He stopped once to check the overhead compartments. He whipped them open with mounting frustration. Each one was empty.

"You bastards and bitches jump train or what?" he yelled and proceeded to the next car. "What number is this, Gilbert?"

"Uh, number nine, Eli."

"Number fuckin' nine," Eli fumed and yanked open the door to the vestibule, where the next door waited. Like the others, a dim light flickered beyond the portal's window, noticeably darker than before, as if the oil lamps had burned themselves dry.

Eli hefted his rifle, lowered his scarf just long enough to spit at a wall, and hoisted it up over his face. "It's the heat that's gettin' to me," he confided to Gilbert and Shorty as they joined him. "The goddamn heat. It's rubbin' me all the wrong way."

"It's a long train," Gilbert said.

"It's too goddamn long," Eli snapped back, before shaking his head to clear it. "All right. Ready?"

The two men nodded.

"All I can say is, if it's soldiers or police on the other side of this door, I'm gonna shoot one. Probably two. Maybe three. Just for makin' us walk this goddamn distance. I'm gonna shoot them through the fuckin' heart. Swear to Sunny Jesus himself."

Eli stormed through the vestibule, peeked in through the window, and shook his head. "Can't see shit in there."

Gilbert glanced at the leather roof of the connecting section and teetered just a bit from the increasing rattle and roll of the train. The vestibules were colder than the cars as well. He cast a worried look back at Shorty, who didn't say a word.

"All right, here we go," Eli said.

He gripped the lever and yanked it open.

The door slid open, revealing a darker, but just as empty, passenger car. Of the three light fixtures hanging from the ceiling, only one was functioning, shining a weak cone upon the midway point. There were oil lamps, but their near-finished reservoirs created fluttering pockets of light. All that dying light put a pleasant shine to the woodwork, an almost surreal quality in fact, but it was a darker finish, a touch gloomier, as if it were well past social hours.

Not a soul was in sight.

"I'm getting goddamn tired of this shit," Eli muttered, shaking his head.

10

"Leland!"

Both Nathan and Leland turned in the direction of the voice. Leland rushed toward the wood bin and held onto his hat, attempting to peer past the supply.

"That you, Jimmy?" he shouted back.

"Me and Mackenzie," came back the holler.

"You got them passengers secured?"

"No passengers, Leland."

That dumbfounded both Nathan and Leland. "The hell you say?" the leader yelled.

"Hold on. I'm coming over."

Several seconds later, the hunched form of Jimmy Norquay appeared through the freezing, swirling veils of snow. Nathan watched the man as he shuffled along, one hand over the other while shifting his feet, all to the increasingly impatient song of the train.

Chumpchumpchumpchumpchumpchumpchumpchump…

When he got close enough, Leland reached out and pulled his friend into the cab. Snow coated both men, but they ignored the elements and hunkered deep inside the metal walls.

"Where's the engineer?" Jimmy asked, pulling his scarf down and freeing his beard.

Leland didn't hesitate. "He jumped out the side."

That visibly stunned Jimmy. "He did what?"

"He jumped," Nathan said and pointed. "From right over there."

Jimmy glanced back at the wood bin, then sized up the cab itself. "How the hell he get past you to do that?"

50

"Never mind that," Leland said, indicating the train controls. "You know how to stop a train?"

Jimmy studied the man's face before nodding. He then walked over to the controls and inspected the sparse features. "What happened here?" he asked, pointing at the shot gauge.

"Stray bullet," Leland said.

"You shot at the engineer?"

"Stop the train, Jimmy," Leland said in a stern tone, "and we'll talk about the engineer afterwards."

That cutting voice surprised the Metis man, but he just nodded and turned back to the controls. Without hesitation, he wrapped his fingers around the second lever Leland had tried, and slowly applied pressure.

The train did not stop.

Jimmy's face crunched up in confusion. He turned the lever until it could go no further, then checked the controls for alternatives. Confused, he reset the handle and tried again—to no avail.

"That's all there is," Nathan said. "Leland tried them all."

"One of them stray bullets blow something out?" Jimmy asked.

Leland faltered. "I... don't know."

Nathan came to his rescue. "How the hell could a stray bullet do something to the brakes? Most everything here is made of iron, anyway."

That got Jimmy studying the interior again. "Well, that's the brake handle. I don't know what's going on, but we're going faster. Well beyond any point we planned on."

"Milton's probably shittin' his britches right now," Nathan said.

"Milton will wait for us," Leland countered. "Don't you worry about him. He might not be the smartest in the group, but he's got common sense."

The curt admonishment quieted Nathan and made him feel a little guilty about saying anything ill about the man. Of course, Milton did indeed seem dependable to him. Nathan just spoke out of line was all—the heat of the moment.

"So what do we do?" Jimmy asked, changing subjects.

"What about them passengers?" Leland asked.

"Like I said, Leland. No passengers."

"What?"

"None," Jimmy shrugged. "We went through seven passenger cars. All high-class ones. Not a soul to be seen."

That clearly puzzled Leland, and he failed to muster a question. Nathan struggled to get a hold of his own confusion.

"No baggage either," Jimmy added. "I sent Eli, Gilbert, and Shorty on ahead while Mackenzie and I came back here, to find out why the train was speeding up."

"Where's Mackenzie?" Nathan asked.

"On the other side of that wood bin, holding onto my rifle. The walkway's covered in snow and getting slicker than cow shit."

"No passengers," Leland muttered.

Jimmy didn't bother to comment.

"No pay car then, either?"

"Not yet," Jimmy answered.

Leland thought about it. "All right. This is what we'll do. We'll finish the job. Scour the last of the train, and make our way to the caboose. We'll decouple it if we can and ride it 'til it comes to a stop."

"Why not decouple the engine?" Nathan asked.

Jimmy and Leland looked at each other. "I like that idea even better," the gang leader said.

They glanced around and stopped at the engineer's seat. Leland pulled up the cushion, which doubled as a toolbox, and extracted a hammer, a spike, and a set of tongs.

"Jesus," Nathan said, eyeing the three items.

"Don't you worry," Leland assured him with that crinkly smile of his, his confidence returning. "We'll slow this horse down one way or the other. And we'll get that payroll car."

11

Eli didn't bother waiting for Gilbert or Shorty when he got to the tenth passenger car door. He grabbed for the handle and yanked it open.

And stopped and stared.

Therein, sitting perfectly upright in their seats, under lights just a little more diminished than the previous car, were passengers. The men wore light coats and proper suits, their manes slicked and oiled and parted straight down the middle. The women were all gussied up in white traveling dresses with short, stylish coats, with their hair set in stylish poofs or covered in pretty shawls. The children were all outfitted in scuffed shoes and winter jackets. Every face lifted at the violent opening of the door, and all conversations came to a lurching stop.

Eli stared back in horrified wonder and realized he didn't have his scarf up and around his nose.

"Shit," he growled. He covered up while pointing his rifle at the ceiling, then stepped into the car and allowed the boys behind him to spread out.

With a captive audience, Eli took stage.

"All right, you bunch of sorry lookin' bloodsabitches, *hands up*. And I'm including the wives there, too. Stay where you are and lift your goddamn hands in the air. Any of you dapper bastards pull out a gun and I'll shoot you dead. If I hear your wife cry out, I'll shoot her dead, too, just because you thought to be all brave and shit. If any of you got children, get them close and keep them there. *Now do it.*"

Roughly three dozen people did as they were told. Within seconds, a forest of hands sprouted from the berths.

"Stay here, Shorty," Eli said. He marched forward, his rifle planted firmly against his shoulder and pointed generally at the seated passengers. Men and women whimpered, cringed, and lowered their gaze. The children fled the aisle and buried their faces into their parents' torsos. The weakly lit compartment appeared comfortably filled, and the sight of all them people secretly gladdened Eli Gallant's black heart. He was getting goddamn worried there for a while and hated to think he'd climbed on board the wrong fucking train. That shit simply would not do.

The floor of the aisle was nothing more than a shadow in the poor light, but Eli saw just about every seat full with someone. Some of the men watched him, calmly even, and he stopped just long enough for them to look away.

"The hell you lookin' at, peckerface?" Eli demanded of one long–nosed man wearing a light dress jacket, shirt, and double-knot tie. Two little girls clung to the mother sitting near him. The mother visibly swallowed and gazed ahead. The husband did the same a second later.

"Yeah, thought so," Eli said and turned his rifle away. "You got something to say?" he asked of another not-as-scared-as-he-should-be individual and pointed the rifle barrel in the man's face. That got results every time.

Eli moved along, verbally unloading on the more contrary-looking of the lot. "Get that dangerous look out of your eyes, darlin', and don't make me fuckin' ask twice. You too, Henry. Look away while you still got 'em. You got something to say there, Alice? Then eyes front before I knock them from your fuckin' head, and don't think I wouldn't, 'cause I would. Damn right I would, and with a smile on my face. Hey, Jedidiah, you swallow your chaw or something? Then get goddamn happy right now before I blow your greased head clear off."

Gilbert followed a few steps behind as Eli tromped down through the aisle, slinging threats and taking aim where needed.

Crowd control, Eli scoffed as he neared the next door. He was a goddamn *expert* at crowd control. When he reached the end of the passenger car, he stepped to one side to allow Gilbert to pass by. Shorty Charlie Williams stood near the front, his outline shadowy in the dark car. Eli waved and Shorty waved back.

"All right, listen up then," Eli shouted at the dark, sundown-hued collection of upraised hands and backs of heads. "My partners here are going to keep watch, so don't try anything foolish. You hear me? Any one of you sorry cocktuggers tries something contrary and I swear to Christ above you'll get a bullet either in the front of your face or in the back of your head. You all understand me?"

A flurry of nods.

The results satisfied Eli. He traded looks with Gilbert, who might've been smiling under his scarf. Then it occurred to him to get some information, so he went to the nearest gentleman sitting with his elderly wife. The pair resembled Mr. and Mrs. Santa Clause, but instead of a merry red livery, both wore fine-tailored clothing of whites and fetching grays.

"Hey, Father Christmas, I wanna talk to you."

Father Christmas stared back, his bearded mouth open in a perfect little 'o', while his wife pressed her face to his shoulder.

"How many passengers on this train?"

"I don't know," Father Christmas rasped.

"Are there more?"

"Most definitely, yes."

"Next car?"

"Yes."

"Where the hell is all them other folks?"

"Beg your pardon?"

Eli scowled. "Beg your ass if you don't listen, you cotton-chin bastard. Don't make me pull that fluff off your jaw and use it as my shit rag. You heard me. Where are they? We must've walked through nine or ten empty passenger cars before we got to this one, and not one person in any of them. So where the hell are they?"

Father Christmas swallowed and shook his head.

"You don't know?"

Another headshake.

"You actually tellin' me you don't know? Way back here where you are? You don't fuckin' know?"

"I don't fuckin know!" Father Christmas erupted into tears. The man wailed something terrible and pitched forward into his wife's hair, burying his face in her winter shawl.

Gilbert gave Eli a look of disdain.

"Don't get on my nerves," Eli warned his partner. "Just tryin' to get answers is all. Not my fault the hairy bastard took a conniption fit. Come on, then. We're on a roll."

Eli opened the door to the vestibule, exposing the short walk to a window even more dimly lit than the last.

They entered another full passenger car, the occupants oblivious to what had just happened. Once again, Eli Gallant grabbed the bull by the dangling rosebuds and wrangled the entire lot of them without a word from Gilbert.

After an opening barrage of curses, threats, and profanity-laced instructions, Eli jumped up on one green seat and took aim at each face as the passengers stood, one-by-one, row-by-row. They marched down that dark aisle with their heads down and palms up, towards Gilbert, who stood at the front, right next to the door.

"Get 'em all back into that other car," Eli yelled. "Squeeze 'em all in. I don't care if you got a dozen to a berth, just squeeze them assholes in and keep 'em quiet."

Gilbert waved, signaling he'd heard.

Eli left him then, his thoughts already on the next cattle load. Leland's voice sounded off in his head as he remembered how many people he might have to control.

About twenty passengers to each car. That seems comfortable. Roughly four cars. Say, eighty people, thereabouts.

Well, Eli figured. Seeing as how their great leader was dead-wrong about the number of cars to begin with, he was willing to bet dollars to dimes that eighty people wasn't right either. Especially considering Shorty was guarding almost thirty people in one car, and he'd just sent on nearly another thirty. Eli scoffed at Leland's information, and hesitated at the next door.

Sixty people almost.

And two gunmen to guard the works.

A tingle of unease settled into the back of Eli's skull then, right at the base, where his spine slunk up under like a snake getting out of the sun. He thought about maybe waiting for Jimmy and shithead Mackenzie to show up, but seeing as how they'd all gone to the front, who knew when they'd get back.

Hell with it, Eli decided and gripped the next door. He was equal to three men with the number of guns he was carrying. He was bad intentions walking, and willing to knock a person down if needed. What was another thirty head of cattle? Only twenty or so were adults, and of that, only ten were men, and only a fraction of that again might be dangerous and in need of watching. The children were nothing if not just taking up space. Perhaps Leland was only counting the men and women and forgot about the kids.

Didn't matter.

There was over three hundred thousand dollars on this piece-of-shit train. And Eli Gallant meant to have his share of it.

He opened the door and went inside.

12

"What the hell is that?" Leland Baxter said, controlling his horrified surprise much better than Nathan. Nathan stood next to him, on the platform extending from the first passenger car, while Jimmy Norquay remained on the much narrower wood bin. Steam and snowy gales pommeled the men and whipped up their coats. Between the platforms and a foot below, barely visible, were the couplings that kept the section connected.

Except, in the flashing dark, there wasn't any ice to hammer free of the metal, nor were there any pins to extract with the tongs.

"I can't see correctly," Leland said as he peered down between the platforms.

Mackenzie stood nearby and held the passenger door open, to allow some light onto the situation.

"I can't see any pins," Jimmy said, also staring into that flashing gulf.

Leland handed off his rifle to Mackenzie and got down on his hands and knees, being careful of the edges. Nathan got clear of the light, and took a handful of the gang leader's coat, ensuring he didn't have a nasty spill.

"Well, Jimmy," Leland said calmly. "The reason we don't see any pins is because there aren't any."

"What?"

"There aren't any. Look for yourself."

Jimmy stepped across the gap, all to the steady chugging and rocking of the speeding train. He dropped to his hands and knees, then flat on his chest, and peered below.

"Well, shit," the man gently released. "It's all one piece."

"That's what I'm seeing," Leland agreed. "Except, look at that."

The pins and links might have been separate at one point in time, but were now fused together into an intimate knob of iron. There was movement between the two cars, a constant but mild swaying, but the couplings themselves appeared like weird sculptures once subjected to an intense heat. Below that, the speeding gray-white of the ground.

"There's no way to unhitch the train," Jimmy said after a sobering moment.

"Doesn't look like it."

"What did you say?" Nathan asked.

Leland stood up and indicated Nathan take a look. The sight both confused and horrified him.

"The hell we do now?" he asked, rising to stand with the others.

"In here," Leland said. He stepped inside the passenger car. Once they were all out of the elements, Mackenzie closed the door.

"So much for that," Jimmy stated in a sour tone.

"All right," Leland said, going over the facts in an attempt to muster the troops. "We can't unhitch the train… because there aren't any coupling links to unhitch. They've been melted and hardened into lumps."

"But what did that?" Jimmy wanted to know. "I've been on plenty of trains and I've never seen anything like that out there. Never heard of it happening before."

"I don't know what did it," Leland admitted wearily. "But we can't worry about what we can't control. We can't unhitch the train from here, but we might be able to somewhere else. Maybe the caboose. I propose we continue on, meet up with the others, find out where those passengers are, and above all, get to the payroll car. We're on this horse, so we might as well get paid for riding her. Once we do all that, we can focus on getting off."

"The caboose?" Nathan asked.

"The caboose," Leland repeated. "We get there, and we see if we can unhitch the train. Let the rest of her drive off into the mountains while we drift to a stop."

"And if the couplings are melted?" Mackenzie asked. "Like the ones out there?"

Leland paused before answering. "Let's just hope that was just some strange act of nature."

Nathan picked up his Winchester from where it rested against a seat. Leland and Jimmy rearmed themselves with their own rifles.

"Leland," Jimmy said. "What happened with the engineer?"

Leland hesitated.

"What happened?" Jimmy pressed.

So Leland told him.

13

Eli burst through the passenger door and took aim at about twenty or so faces, excluding the children freezing in their tracks. "All right you bunch of sorry assholes, hands up. Get your hands up. Way up, where I can see them, and if I see anyone go for a gun, I won't shoot them. I'll shoot the person nearest and that'll be on you. So get your fuckin' hands up in the air and so help me Lord, don't fuckin' twitch unless I say so. Hands up, *hands up!*"

A multitude of hands flowered over the passengers' heads, every bit as pretty as a field of daisies blooming under a summer sun.

Hands up, Eli mentally projected. *And fuck you too, Bill Miner.*

He took aim at the nearest face. "You best hope they all listen."

The man in question looked like a banker, dressed in a fancy suit with a waxed mustache trimmed to the thickness of an eyebrow. Eli didn't like the style, believing if you were going to let hair grow on your face, you let it grow. The banker froze upon staring down the Winchester's barrel, and the woman beside him looked positively mortified.

"All right, now," Eli muttered, taking in the shadowy interior. "Jesus. Ain't the conductor been around to fill them lamps? It's darker than the crack of my ass in here. All right, then, now here's what we're gonna do. You're all going to file on out to the next car behind me, and start walking until you meet some friends of mine. You're all going to do this one row at a time. And if any of you chicken fucks try anything funny, just know I'll shoot Mr. Banker here."

That jarred the man Eli was aiming at.

"Ah, excuse me," the man said. "I'm not a banker…"

"Shut the fuck up," Eli snapped before turning his attention back to the crowd. "All right, you folks right behind Mister and Missus Banker. You stand up and walk through that door. Keep on going until you find the others and don't you goddamn dare stop or try anything funny. If you do, I swear I'll shoot someone dead."

The faces, all shaded by degrees, stared back at him.

"Move your asses," Eli ordered at the second row.

The family of three sitting there stood up and did as ordered.

"That's right, get on," Eli barked as they marched by. Then came the next row, their heads lowered and hands up. They marched by with a couple of kids following Eli's orders quite nicely. After that, the car gradually emptied of people as they left their seats.

All the while, Eli watched and urged them on, keeping his rifle trained upon Mr. and Mrs. Banker.

"You enjoy your steak, I see," Eli muttered sardonically as a portly man shuffled by. He cocked an eyebrow at some of the more attractive mothers, ignoring the children being led by the hands. "I can see why you have three kids, Ma'am," he said to one attractive lady, who kept her head down as she walked out the car door.

"Hell," he added when she was gone, "I'd be willing to go for a dozen more if'n I was married to her."

Mr. Banker didn't smile at that. Neither did Mrs. Banker.

Eli tucked away his own amusement. He didn't mind the lack of humor. He knew he was being an asshole.

"Goddamn, you're an ugly bastard," he muttered as one heavy-jowled individual waddled by. "Your folks must've called you fugly, just so the neighbors would look at you."

And he didn't stop there, taking shots at anyone that took his interest.

"Get that shit shaved off your chin there, Mister," he said to one man passing by. "I don't mind beards, but what you got growing looks like the crusty fuzz swingin' from a grizzly's ball sack."

"Fuck you staring at, you old codger?"

"Fuck you staring at, old bitch?"

"Fuck *you* staring at kid? I ain't your daddy."

And on it went. In fact, Eli had a parting thought for each passenger as they all appeared rightly upper-class to him. Well dressed, impeccably mannered (or so they liked to believe), and full of shit. Their very skittered demeanor pissed him off something wicked, and part of him *wanted* them to just try and test him.

The last few folks meandered down the aisle, and Eli glanced at Mr. and Mrs. Banker. "How you folks doin'?" he asked all nice and civilized.

"Not too well," Mr. Banker replied from between his upraised hands.

"Yeah, well, I don't give a shit." Eli slapped the barrel of his Winchester off the bottom of a woman headed out the door. A crackle of metal came from the open vestibule, but Eli wasn't worried about that. The door rolled closed, and he eyed the last two passengers passing the midway point of the aisle. Dressed in tailored wintertime blacks and grays, the couple were older, gray-haired, and not as spry as they might've once been.

"Get along there, Sweet Jesus," Eli said and backed up to the empty seats across the aisle from Mr. and Mrs. Banker. "Feel like I'm going to die of old age before you two. Hell, if'n I'd known…"

He trailed off, staring at the last approaching couple.

Even though the light in the passenger car was dim, there was still something off about the elderly pair approaching him. It puzzled him so much that he was momentarily distracted from the Banker couple.

"Don't you be gettin' any ideas over there," Eli warned Mr. and Mrs. Banker. "Just 'cause I don't have my eyes on you don't mean anything. I squeeze this trigger and there's gonna be a mess all over those fine seats. Not to mention a hole in that window that'll sound like your lady taking a quick suckle off your dingle."

A terrified Mr. and Mrs. Banker stayed as still as they could, keeping their tired hands in the air.

Eli studied the nearing couple, feeling that familiar tingle of unease at the back of his skull, like a rattlesnake making itself known. And, as God was his witness, the old folks coming his way were keeping their heads down a little lower than needed, their hands strategically placed so as to conceal their features just enough so that Eli wouldn't see them.

When he realized that, he swung the rifle barrel away from Mr. and Mrs. Banker and aimed it at the old folks.

"Hold on there," he rumbled, suspicion lacing his voice. "I swear… you two look like a couple of weasels trying to crawl up a chicken's shitty asshole. Stop right there and drop your hands."

The old couple stopped but wavered with the second order.

"I said drop them hands," Eli warned. "I ain't sayin' it again."

The hands lowered.

And Eli squinted at the two senior citizens. He blinked and even hunkered down a bit, to best use the light available to him. His mouth went dry, and he swallowed thickly. "What the hell…" he whispered, stunned at what, at *who* he was seeing.

Because even though their *clothes* had changed, there was no doubt in his mind he was staring at not-so-merry Father Christmas and his wife.

And the way they were looking at him, they knew *he* knew.

Chumpchumpchumpchump, chumpchumpchumpchump…

Eli swallowed again before speaking. "How did you…" He faltered, still not quite believing, but knowing what he saw. "How'd you get back here?"

A high-pitched scream then, like someone having a length of skin ripped from their bare back, shot up from across the way, paralyzing Eli at the worst possible time.

Just before all hell broke loose.

14

Shorty Charlie Williams stood with his back against the door, shotgun lowered but at the ready, staring down the roughly sixty or so people jammed into the once comfortably plush, first-class interior. His fingers flexed upon the shotgun's barrels as he scanned his audience for troublemakers. They looked back at him, their hands—so many hands—on the upper frame of those fine mahogany seats. Sixty people. Of them all, perhaps a dozen men potentially carrying a pistol under their coats, and maybe half of that actually thinking about using it.

Six potential shooters.

Shorty's expression didn't change, didn't falter, and he had so much beard on his face that no one would notice a twitch. He no longer felt confident with his task, however, even with Gilbert on the other end, patrolling the aisle near the last few feet of the car. Every now and again, Gilbert would raise a hand to show all was well back there.

Except Shorty was noticing something strange about all them people sitting before him, like a congregation waiting for a sermon. Shorty wasn't dumb by any means. Far from it. He knew he wasn't no genius either, but he wasn't dumb, and he certainly had plenty of what his mother and father had called—and prized—common sense.

He had plenty of that, but damn if he didn't always use it.

Not wanting to live a life of hard labor tending to a potato farm like his father, Shorty left home when he was still growing. He hooked up with the Wilson-Tarry company in Southern Ontario, just outside of Kingston, who were into shipping railway supplies and other building materials out west, feeding the ongoing ambitions of the railroad companies and migrating settlers. Shorty got hired on for room and board, and a few cents here and there for overtime. He lifted a lot and ate a lot, and as a result, grew a lot, both in height and musculature. He grew so high that one afternoon, one man remarked that he wanted to work nearby Shorty, as the summer sun was going to be a scorcher. When another worker asked why he wanted to work alongside Shorty, the man replied, "'Cause Shorty's pretty much the best shade around these parts."

And so he was.

But after four years of working for Wilson-Tarry, and only a handful of dollars in savings to show for it, Shorty believed it was time to move on.

To a circus.

Owned by one Travis "Dicky" Bailey. "Old Dicky", as his employees called him, had an eye for potential talent, and he saw plenty of potential in Shorty, who was, by that time, perhaps the biggest man around.

Having never owned a razor, Shorty's beard grew out, and that lent him a powerful fearsome aspect, one that he didn't see the need to dispel. The circus called him "The Strongest Man Alive," and "The Living Giant," and, along with a pair of boots especially made so that he was about three fingers taller, he supposed he *was* a giant. Night after night he performed acts of strength under a circus tent, wowing the crowds. Old Dickey didn't pay much better than Wilson-Tarry though, and Shorty soon questioned his life in show business. He was twenty-four at the time, which was around when he met Leland Baxter, while touring through Kingston during a particularly hot July.

Leland asked him if he'd like to earn two hundred dollars.

Shorty had said he'd like that very much. It didn't bother him that the work was holding up a private stage coach with a payroll box in it. And it didn't bother Shorty that he might have to shoot the armed guards that were riding with the coach. He'd never considered a life of crime before, but when Leland handed him his share of the robbery—close to eighteen hundred dollars and not the expected two—well, Shorty started considering. He started considering mighty hard, in fact.

Four years later, and he was still working with Leland and Jimmy Norquay, who was every bit as honorable, dependable, and, dare he say it, trustworthy as Leland. Shorty discovered that he enjoyed his outlaw life. All he had to do was look mean and ready to kill a person, without actually killing anyone. Over the years, he'd only had to fire his shotgun three times during a job, and no one was hurt because of it. It was more for shock and compliance, if anything.

Leland warned there would come a day, however, when Shorty would have to use that shortened, two-handed cannon he carried, and use it on a person. Shorty didn't mind that either. The money more than made up for the potential guilt. That time hadn't come yet, however, and part of Shorty's brain wondered if this job, the biggest one the three of them had ever attempted, might be the job.

Especially with the potential security force on board the train.

Shorty didn't dwell on that. He only focused on the present.

And presently, the hostages placed in his charge were giving off some plenty strange vibes. He didn't like the way they were looking at him. Nor did he like the dwindling light in the room. One of the nearest oil lamps sputtered and died, leaving a dark crater some five rows deep alongside the right side of the passenger car. A blight of blackness that hid the folks and turned them into faceless shades. The smell of pipe smoke seemed thicker, too, somehow, even though no one was smoking.

Gilbert paused in his patrol and stared at the section where the lamp just died. He started walking back towards Shorty, looking over folks as he came along.

Gilbert saddled up alongside Shorty, the top of his head just reaching Shorty's shoulder, and whispered, "Getting kinda dark in here."

Shorty nodded, watching all those hands, distinctly aware of those lowered faces watching him back. They were no longer looking scared, either, but rather scary *looking*.

"Everything all right back here?" Gilbert whispered.

"Mm-hm," Shorty grunted. He flexed his meaty fingers upon his shotgun.

"Well," Gilbert said in a flat voice. "If any of them give you any trouble, you have my permission to shoot them."

Any other time, Shorty might've glared at the suggestion, but not then. He understood the thought behind it. Gilbert was only saying that to keep the folks in line. That didn't make Shorty feel any better, however. All those eyes were clearly watching his every movement, gauging him and Gilbert both.

The eerie thing was, even the *children* were watching them, their little shadowed faces set and stern, glaring at him under lowered brows.

"Awfully quiet in here," Gilbert noticed. "Awfully quiet. I like that. I can hear the train."

Shorty's attention was on the round, decidedly fat faces of a pair of boys, perhaps nine or ten years old. Their hair was slicked down to the skull and parted clean down the middle. They peeked over the wooden frames of the seats, little noses resting on top, mouths hidden, and little eyes observing. The parents were right behind them with their collars drawn up high and their faces indistinct. Their mouths were dark lines that split their faces.

"Well," Gilbert announced, blissfully unaware of the mounting tension. "I'll head on back there. See if Eli needs me."

That drew a frown from Shorty. Gilbert had just fucked up by saying Eli's name, but that really wasn't what bothered Shorty. What really bothered him was how all sound had mysteriously left the car, with the sole exception of the train's brisk rattling.

Chumpchumpchumpchump, chumpchumpchumpchump.

The crowd seemed to lean forward, ever so slightly, in anticipation of some approaching signal. Shorty dreaded the thought of what that signal might be. The two boys stared at him still, and one licked his chops as if he was gazing upon one of them big lollipops with fancy twirls. Shorty stared back, turning on every ounce of his considerable intimidation, attempting to break them like he'd done to so many before. The boy didn't flinch, however. Didn't blink.

Gilbert started to walk away.

Suddenly, Shorty didn't want to be left alone. "Hey," he rumbled.

Gilbert stopped and turned, his hat almost completely hiding his eyes.

"C'mere for a second," Shorty said.

"What for?"

"Just… *c'mere.*"

But Gilbert vacillated on the spot, unaware of what was transpiring around him, and finally looked toward the distant door.

"*Now,*" Shorty insisted, wanting to throttle the man for wasting time.

"I should get back. Maybe go on ahead to see if Eli needs any help."

Just then, Shorty was distracted by movement on the left, as if one of the women had shifted in her seat. Then someone else moved, somewhere in that pocket of darkness. Ever so slightly, but he picked up on it. The two boys were still watching Shorty, as were their parents, but other heads were turning in Gilbert's direction as well, as if realizing that one of the captors was directly in the middle of the pack.

And that the passengers had far superior numbers.

A great and terrible sensation of dread sprouted from within Shorty then, of standing still in a dangerous situation. And he knew, just *knew*, a fight was about to start. He hadn't been in any gunfights, but he'd been in plenty of fistfights. He knew with intimacy the vibe that preceded the storm.

"Don't worry about him," Shorty said to Gilbert, his scarf muffling his words, and warming his face to the point of perspiring. It was getting warmer in the close quarters. "We got something to talk about. You and me."

Gilbert thought about that, still oblivious to the disturbing side-eyes from the passengers and the subtle but very deliberate rustling of fabric.

"Like what?" he finally asked.

"Just come here for a second," Shorty said.

"You're slowin' me down here."

"Just need you over here, is all."

"For *what?*"

Shorty decided he might shoot Gilbert first. "Get your ass over here now, Gilbert."

Silence then, as deep as a mine shaft. Gilbert didn't appreciate him revealing his name or the implied threat. Shorty didn't care. He waited, noticing the fluttering of one oil lamp on the far wall, its light weakening, dying. And as that light died, the seated ranks of shades and their evil eyes sparkled all the more.

"All right," Gilbert sulked and trudged back.

One of the boys, the one on the left, lifted his face just enough to bite the wood of the seat in front of him. It was a slow, deliberate bite, and somehow, despite the constant chuffing of the train, Shorty heard the sinewy give of hardwood fibers as the child sank his teeth into the woodwork, teeth that were a sinister tiara of finely wrought needles.

The nearby brother lifted his face as well and his mouth hung open, where a flood of fluid dripped and spattered.

Gilbert stopped just at Shorty's side.

"Don't appreciate you usin' my name," Gilbert stated, attempting a stare down, just as the *father* of the two boys shoved his brood aside and leaped over the seats in a startling feat of agility. The father's face blackened in mid-jump, and his mouth stretched open to twice its size, displaying a wet trap of rattlesnake fangs.

Shorty let him have both barrels, the blast shockingly loud in the confined space. The sawed-off cannon propelled the evil thing back into its berth in a halo of gore and gun smoke. The father landed in a crumpled heap, where only his lower legs and feet stuck up over the seats.

But Shorty didn't have time to appreciate the first man he shot.

Because the entire car of passengers was rushing both him and Gilbert.

15

"You get all that?" Leland said as he walked through the empty passenger car.

Jimmy and Mackenzie clearly got all that, but Nathan could tell they were having trouble believing it. Truth was, Nathan didn't think Leland should've said anything at all. When the leader started talking, however, Nathan started nodding, backing Leland's story up when needed.

"What do you think?" Nathan asked, as they strode through the second passenger car, every bit as abandoned as the boys had said it was.

"Give me a few minutes," Mackenzie said.

"I believe it," Jimmy said with a quick glance behind. "I believe."

"You do?" Nathan asked.

"Yeah."

They fell silent then, the train's pace loud in their ears, growing faster. That worried Nathan. It worried him a lot.

"Leland?" he asked.

"Yes?"

Leland slid back the vestibule door and strode towards the entrance of the third car.

"The train's going faster," Nathan said.

The four men stopped and listened, gazing down at their feet. The train rocked ever so slightly, like the prow of a boat cutting across a calm sea, but her pulse had indeed quickened.

"Sweet Mary and Joseph," Jimmy released in a whisper.

"She's picking up speed, all right," Mackenzie verified.

"That's bad, ain't it?" Nathan asked.

"Very bad," Mackenzie said. "Trains can jump the tracks if they're going too fast. They call it *derailing*. The whole thing could wind up on its ass, and if it does, we're more than likely dead."

That got them all thinking.

Leland's head snapped up. "Is that gunfire?"

Nathan heard it as well. "Holy shit."

"That's gunfire," Jimmy confirmed.

The four charged along the dreamy interior, their boots thundering along the aisle. They threw open the door to the fourth car and saw two of their number at the far end. One was Shorty Charlie Williams, reloading his shotgun while on the run. The other was either Gilbert or Eli, right behind him.

"*Get back!*" Shorty yelled as he stomped towards the others. "*Get back!*"

No sooner did he shout when the four men saw why.

The far door opened with a booming crash and a mob jammed into the portal. They didn't just force their way through, they pulled and shoved and popped through the fixed doorway, like greased-up spiders sprouting from a loose floorboard. And they *moved* like spiders, a fluid, nimble, yet nerve-twanging motion that no human being could ever replicate, but they were.

Then there was the growling.

A low, throaty gravel that originated from deep within that teeming mass. That sound frightened Nathan badly. They were *passengers*, crawling forth from that doorway, skittering over the seats, and...

A split second before he ran, Nathan crouched and released a short note of disbelief. Passengers emerged from the *upper* section of the doorway and skittered along the shadowy paneling of the *ceiling* with a nightmarish energy, their murky faces turned to the fleeing men. Their hands and fingers splayed, knees cocked, and feet clinging with supernatural adhesive.

Leland whirled and pushed the others back, wanting no part of what was coming. Nathan suddenly found himself in the forefront of the retreat, his footfalls crashing upon the floor. The door handle slipped in his hand as he grabbed it, whipping its metallic length across the inside of his wrist as if chastising him for his clumsiness.

"Hurry, Nate," Mackenzie huffed, crashing into him from behind and every bit as frightened.

Nathan whipped open the door, spun inside, and held it for the others to pile through. When Gilbert stormed past, scarf lowered and teeth bared, the sight behind him was petrifying. Mind-numbing.

Passengers continued to fill up the car in the rear. They charged along the floor and ceiling, swarming light fixtures and plunging the section into flickering darkness. A dismal gush of terror rushed through and defiled that first-class interior. The growling grew in volume, as did a disturbing mewling, the sound of worms chewing away at the edges of paper, impossibly amplified.

Nathan slammed the door closed. He hurried through the vestibule to the third car, just as the forward elements of the passengers slammed into the portal behind him, and the growling reached a peak.

"Watch out now," Leland said and pulled Nathan away. The gang leader studied the door before dropping to a knee and hauling out the very tools needed to knock ice loose from the winter-cursed couplings. Leland hammered his one and only spike into the floor, jamming the door.

"That should keep it shut," he said in a shaky voice. He reached into a deep pocket of his winter duster and extracted the tongs he carried from the engineer's cab. He tossed the tool in a nearby berth.

A weight slammed into the door, scaring the train robbers. Guns swung up and aimed.

"Get back," Leland ordered, steadying his rifle. "Make some room."

The gang retreated to the midway point of the car, where they immediately spread out across two rows and took up firing positions. The door trembled and jerked, just enough that a seam appeared, and hundreds of white fingers sprouted from it. The sight tugged free a memory best forgotten, where Nathan, in the root cellar of his parents' farm, had once picked up a rotten potato. His fingers easily plunged into the tissue-thin skin, and he remembered the writhing maggots inside.

All those clawing, probing fingers resembled energetic maggots.

The door rattled and shook. A chorus of those bone-dry voices seeped inside, almost drowning out the sound of Gilbert frantically reloading his Winchester.

"The hell's wrong with them?" Nathan said. He was crouched in a seat, his own rifle steadied by the backrest and pointed at the door.

"They're changed," Gilbert said. "All changed. Into monsters."

"Into monsters," Shorty agreed, aiming his shotgun at the door.

"Monsters?" Leland said, the color gone from his face.

"Monsters," Shorty repeated.

"*All* the passengers?" Jimmy asked, ready to blast anything coming through.

"Daresay most of them," Gilbert said and worked the Winchester's lever with a defiant snap. He immediately took up an unobstructed position among the seats. "But bullets stop 'em just fine. I shot about a dozen already."

"Only a few stayed down," Shorty pointed out.

"But they stayed down," Gilbert said.

All eyes concentrated on the door, which continued to violently tremble within its frame, barely holding in the pressure beyond. A hammering ensued, violent and powerful.

Nathan swallowed thickly and sweat slid into his right eye. He pulled away his scarf and wiped his face, unable to tear his attention away from the door and the fingers there. The glass window exploded, and a multitude of arms reached in like a bouquet of lunging snakes. Teeth snapped around the edges, or what Nathan thought were teeth. A face appeared, its mouth opened wide in a snarl of hate and hunger, a split second before it was shoved aside and replaced with another arm.

"The hell are they?" Leland asked, his rifle sure and steady.

"Damn sight flexible," Mackenzie muttered.

"Contortionists," Shorty said, surprising them all.

"Well, hell with this," Gilbert said and fired, working the Winchester with a killer cadence. The blasts exploded in the interior, as loud as cannon fire. Arms quivered upon being shot. Blood spritzed and spattered the frame. Growls became pained, piggish squeals. Ruined limbs were withdrawn but new ones replaced them. Another face appeared, howling and clearly pissed off, and Gilbert put a bullet through its nose that shoved the whole head back into the nightmarish glut of limbs.

The door lurched open an inch more.

"What do we do, Leland?" Mackenzie wanted to know.

"Hold this line," the leader ordered grimly. "Don't fire until I do. And when I do, shoot anything that presents itself as a target. But make. The shot. *Count*."

Gilbert hunkered down in his seat and began plucking replacement shells from one of his bandoliers. Nathan took a firmer grip on his own rifle.

"*Go back*," Leland suddenly shouted at the passengers, scaring the shit out of Nathan and, considering the head jerks and flinches, most the others as well. "Go back whence you came! I command you in the name of the Father and the Holy Ghost and Christ our Lord and Savior! *Go back*!"

It didn't seem too strange for Nathan to hear a train robber call upon the Almighty to help out in their current situation, but the passengers hammering away at the door didn't appear too discouraged by the mention of the Heavenly Father.

The door creaked open another inch, and more palms and forearms wormed their way through, applying more pressure upon the barrier, searching for the impeding spike. The door jolted another stubborn inch, and Nathan's guts went cold.

The passengers, or the things that were once passengers, were teeming in the narrow space beyond, filling the vestibule completely.

The door jerked open another two inches. Then it skidded open enough for one head to pop through the middle, wailing with a resounding bass, until the mindless passenger managed to get its arm and shoulder through.

Leland shot it through the face, and the entire upper torso flopped dead.

The rest of the men opened fire.

Bullets tore into that gap, exploding flesh and heads and shoulders. Chunks of meat and cloth flew. Blood sprayed in forceful arterial lines. Bone split apart and shattered. One face had an eye burst and the entire head switched off. Near the ceiling, a woman in a white dress pulled herself through the door right to the waist in a frightening burst of speed and strength before Jimmy Norquay put three bullets into her. Her form jerked from behind as the door opened almost to the halfway point, revealing an inhuman swarm of faces and limbs.

The sight damn near paralyzed Nathan.

"Leland," he said over the rapid fire and clattering of reloading weapons.

The passengers were coming through.

Leland saw it as well. "Get back, all of you! Shorty, you stay with me. Jimmy get to the door and get out your dynamite."

Jimmy was already running. Gilbert was right behind him, and Nathan didn't need any more encouragement. He bolted, retreating all the way back to the next door where Gilbert stood, and started firing.

Nathan turned around as Leland and Shorty started screaming.

Both men were tearing up the aisle, running as if hell itself was tickling their boot spurs.

And it was.

A foul, humanoid pestilence wearing the colors of the grave erupted from the distant breach, spreading, flooding the rear in an impossible surge of bodies. *Eighty passengers?* Nathan's mind questioned in a shriek. *Ninety?* Was that what Leland had figured on?

Behind the two men in full frantic retreat, there had to be *hundreds* of the things.

"*Jimmy!*" Leland roared as he thundered down the aisle. Shorty matched him as the things in human skin pursued in a thickening mass of spidery quickness.

Gilbert opened the vestibule and entered. Nathan stopped just inside and held the door back, while a crouching Jimmy worked upon the destructive sticks.

Leland raced through.

The eager hissing of lit fuses scratched the air, and Nathan didn't think he'd ever heard a sweeter sound.

Shorty lumbered inside, lowering his head as he squirmed past the men and continued onward.

"Jimmy?" Nathan said, his eyes wide and staring at the multitudes bearing down upon their position, racing along the ceiling and bounding over the seats. Berths were swamped. Heads rapped off low compartments. And the *sounds* coming from them…

Jimmy chucked three sticks of dynamite upon the car floor.

Nathan slammed the door shut, barring all those livid, pallid faces.

Both men raced to the open door of the next car. No sooner was Nathan through when Gilbert slammed it closed.

The explosion shook the train.

16

"And that's that," Jimmy panted with grim satisfaction, eyeing the closed portal.

"Holy shit," Gilbert muttered in awe. "Is there anything back there now?"

"Good question." Jimmy met Leland's gaze.

Nathan placed an ear to the door. "Can't hear anything. I mean, I can hear the damn train, but I don't hear anything like before. None of that throaty shit."

"That throaty shit was disturbing," Mackenzie said.

"Where's Eli?" Leland asked.

They looked to Gilbert.

"I don't know," the man said. "He was going on ahead, to drive the passengers back to me and Shorty. I don't know what happened to him, if those things got him or not."

Jesus, Nathan thought, remembering those bleached faces and the needle teeth. The memory prompted him to lean against the nearest wall for support. He didn't care much for Eli Gallant, but he wondered if the man deserved to be taken down and killed by those things.

"All right," Leland said after a thoughtful moment. "We're going back in there. Guns up. We'll go as far as we can, and if we find him, excellent. If we locate the payroll car, that's excellent, too. Otherwise, we go for the caboose."

"What about those monsters out there?" Mackenzie asked for them all.

Leland regarded each of his gang in turn, studying their faces. Nathan could see they were shaken up by the frightening encounter with the passengers—he certainly had a tremble in his own ticker and lower legs—but God bless their outlaw hearts, none of them had curled up into a ball, or run screaming to the ends of the train. They were strained but not torn. They were holding on, just like they were holding onto their rifles—and in Shorty's case, shotgun—and nowhere near breaking down into mindless terror. Jimmy's dynamite had helped with their morale, and Nathan had to admit that knowing the man had such power at his disposal was comforting. Knowing those things could die helped as well.

"Bullets stop them," Leland said and started reloading his rifle. "I saw more than a couple drop dead just as sure as anyone taking a bullet. As for the dynamite… we'll soon see how many were killed in the blast. Nathan, get ready to open that door."

The others reloaded their Winchesters, drawing strength from the activity.

"All right," Leland said. "You all ready?"

Nods all around. Nathan held his loaded weapon while one hand gripped the door's handle.

Leland stood about five paces back from the portal and aimed his rifle. Jimmy and Shorty stood on either side of him, while the other men took up flanking positions among the seats. All gun barrels were pointed at the door.

Leland gave a squinty-eye nod and Nathan yanked back the slab of metal with a rumble and a squeal.

Icy winds buffeted the men, carrying snow.

"Well, god…" Gilbert trailed off.

The vestibule had been blown away. Completely. The next car had its face equally blown away, wiped clean in the fearsome blast, leaving almost a quarter of its length as bare as a flatbed. In that space, the passenger car's square metal frame, beautifully constructed overhead compartments, and the comfortable seats, had disappeared. There were ragged edges, scorched wood, and twisted, upturned bars of metal some fifteen feet in, where the remaining walls and roof still held. Tatters of green upholstery raged in the wind, as if trying desperately to get free of the wreaked berths. Streamers of white flailed along the edges. It appeared to Nathan as if the Lord himself had reached down and tore a section of the car away, as if it were no more than a fistful of snow. And that wasn't all. Torn metal and blasted woodwork were now decorated with torsos, limbs, and an unmoving stew of bodies farther back in that open wreckage. A few rags of clothing stirred amongst the corpses heaped into the berths and aisle, but nothing else.

"*Damn*," Gilbert finished for them all. "We don't haveta walk through all that, do we, Leland?"

"Looks like we do," Leland answered.

"Through all *that*?"

Leland looked back at the Albertan gun runner and partner of Eli Gallant. "Yeah, through all that. I'll go first, to alleviate your mind. Just follow me a'ways back and keep your eyes open. On any of those… things. Just in case."

From what Nathan could see, none of those things looked as if they might be playing possum.

Rifle first, Leland carefully stepped through the doorway and onto the scorched iron of the platform. Wind pulled his coat one way and then the other, but somehow the elder gunman and gang leader managed to keep his hat on as he navigated the floor. He hesitated once, actually teetered, before righting himself with a quick step to the next car's floor. Leland swept his weapon from left to right and back again, ignoring the various ribbons waving around him.

Nothing moved to attack.

He advanced a few more paces, inspected the blasted floor and berths, and even lifted his face to the unseen heavens. Having ascertained all was as well as could be, he waved the others forward.

Nathan was taken off-guard by the strength of the wind. He set his stance wide and advanced. The vestibule had been destroyed, leaving only the moving plates attached to each car. At the very center was a gap, right where Leland nearly stepped. The scrunch and grind of the wheels were louder there. The couplings were fused as before, two great knots of contrary metal that the dynamite couldn't part. Below that, snowy ground streaked by, framed by two lengths of black steel. Nothing prevented him from falling over the edges, so he quickly crossed the exposed gap, despite the mounting gale.

Leland had stopped up ahead, near the thickest of the piles of dead.

"Holy shit," Gilbert said somewhere behind. "You do all this, Jimmy? Did you do all this?"

"The dynamite did all this."

"And how many sticks you used?"

"Three."

A sheet of static gray sped past the section of missing roof, already frosting the destruction of the car and the dead things filling it. The wind's high-pitched screaming replaced that of the unnerving passengers. A single oil lamp burned in the distant corner, failing to light up much. Snow and night swept over the exposed bits, and a powerful gust caused Nathan to grab onto a headrest.

He didn't look at the occupant of the seat directly—a young man with the blackened mask of dead rage. Instead, he merely made a note of how the body was missing both legs and an arm. A stink of manure and raw flesh lingered below all the dead things, but the wind kept the worst of it away.

"This way," Leland said while plodding over the bodies filling the aisle. Nathan and the rest followed. It was hard going. They stumbled and fell, staggering over detached limbs. Gilbert stumbled, thrusting out a gloved hand and having his arm sink to the elbow in a sludge of dead flesh. Nathan passed a grandmother type, splashed in inky gore but otherwise looking normal.

"Don't pay them too much mind," Leland instructed as he struggled along. "They're all dead.

"Can't be all dead," a distracted Jimmy said from further back. "This car was full of people."

"These bastards and bitches weren't people," Gilbert said.

"You know what I mean. And I'm not sure three sticks would have killed them all."

"Looks all dead to me."

"I hear what you're saying, Jimmy," Leland said, standing a few paces away from the door that he'd spiked only minutes earlier. "You're saying, you're *asking*, really, where did the rest of them go?"

"That's it."

Nathan glanced back at the whole section that had been torn away. The windows had all been destroyed the entire length of the car. "Maybe they got blasted from the train?" he suggested. "Tossed out on the tracks?"

"Maybe," Leland said.

They regrouped at the far exit, where the bodies thinned out to nothing. The only light fluttered in that right corner, as if assuring the gang it was doing its part. A few bodies littered the intact vestibule—the monsters that had taken bullets and died—right up to the closed door of the next car.

Leland led his men to the closed entrance.

"You boys ready?" he asked over the train's chugging.

Nathan was ready, and he felt the others were too.

"Jimmy?"

"Yeah, Leland?"

"Get a stick of that wonder stuff ready," Leland advised quietly. "Just in case."

Jimmy opened his coat and rooted around inside. Mackenzie was next to him, watching him dubiously. "You think that's wise, Leland?" he asked. "We can't be blowing the train apart one car at a time."

"Like hell we can't," Gilbert said.

"The train's in sections," Leland explained. "You said it yourself. Connected, but still in sections. One stick might be enough to clear the way. Certainly can't do what three sticks did. We'll chance it, but I'm not going to be overrun like before."

That silenced Mackenzie.

"All set, Jimmy?"

"All set."

"Then here we go," Leland said, and hauled open the door.

Darkness filled the train car's interior, as the lamps had all either expired or forcefully doused. Faint outlines could be seen a few feet away, but beyond that, nothing. The lack of light uneased Nathan, who'd wished they'd brought along an oil lamp of their own.

"Great," Gilbert said, shaking his head at the sight.

"All right, now," Leland said in a low voice. "We're going through. Just mind where you're walking and check the seats, in case I miss something."

Nathan's pulse quickened, and his heart hammered in his chest, reckoning he was stepping into a full graveyard at midnight. Leland slipped into that vault-like pitch, his figure barely visible, and inspected the seats on either side of him. Nathan followed, rifle at the ready.

Chumpchumpchumpchump, chumpchumpchumpchump…

And damn if the train seemed to be moving faster than ever, though rocking less. Nathan wondered if the wheels might've hit a smoother part of the tracks, but that didn't feel right to him. He focused on the task at hand and followed Leland deeper into the interior. As his eyes adjusted, dark, uneven petals protruding from the seats appeared. The fabric had been ripped all to hell as the passengers made their way through the train.

Leland walked ahead, carefully, checking each berth before proceeding to the next. The five men crept behind him, spaced evenly apart and watchful. Shorty Charlie Williams guarded the back, constantly glancing over his shoulder.

"Nothing," Mackenzie whispered.

"Seems that way," Jimmy agreed.

Leland reached the exit without incident, and he stopped and gripped the door handle. He motioned for Nathan and the others to take aim. When the gang was in position, he pulled open the door.

The vestibule beyond appeared empty, and through the window set within the next door, a weak light glowed.

"Not a sound," Leland quietly observed. He motioned Nathan forward.

Squinting, his face sweaty, Nathan forged ahead, keeping a shoulder against that flexing leathery wall encasing the vestibule. He sidled up next to the entrance but couldn't see anything inside because of the dirty glass. Leland stood behind him, while Gilbert got down on one knee and took aim.

Leland nodded and tapped Nathan on the shoulder—who opened the door.

Another empty car, with one solitary lamp flickering on a distant wall, like a torch casting a dour light over an empty dungeon.

"Nothing," Leland said. He moved ahead, sliding around the corner and taking up position just inside. "How many cars you say you went through? Before you reached passengers?"

"Nine or ten," Gilbert reported.

"All empty?"

"All."

"Damnation," Leland whispered, peering ahead. Nothing could be heard over the low ruckus of the train. Leland stepped softly, cautiously, leading the men down an aisle flooded with darkness. Light from the distant lamp outlined his head and shoulders.

The gang leader halted and cocked his head.

"Something wrong, Leland?" Nathan whispered just behind him.

Leland held up one hand, wanting silence.

The lone light at the far end continued to flicker, as if tormented by a ghost's breath.

Nathan was about to ask what was wrong, when he heard it.

A soft clinking of bottles just ahead, as if a crude wind chime had just caught a breeze.

Nathan gripped his rifle tighter.

Leland crouched upon hearing the noise repeat. Rifle first, he took another step when a knife-wielding hand whipped out from one of the berths and slashed at his leg.

Leland grunted and went down, dropping his rifle with a clatter.

Nathan fired at that twisting limb, blowing the hand off at the wrist.

A second and third arm darted out from the seat berth, their flesh as pallid as eels. They slashed for the stricken gang leader. Leland stopped one blade upon his rifle, but one steely edge took him across the ear. He screamed that time.

"*The hell is that!*" Gilbert yelled as arms erupted from the berths on either side of him and slashed his legs. He fired, blowing out a section of the ceiling, and staggered back.

Then the entire aisle became a swarm of flashing, slashing knives.

17

A blade sliced across Nathan's right knee, crumpling him. He dropped and lurched for his hidden attacker. Gunfire ripped through the dark as the men behind opened fire, but at what, Nathan had no idea.

For there were no attackers.

All there was—in front of him, anyway—was an arm, holding a large knife, extending from the center of the seat as if it was an exceptionally big shoulder.

The arm reared back, flexing at an elbow, and stabbed for Nathan's face.

He deflected the thrust with his rifle, got past the elbow, and grabbed the wrist. The limb fought back, pulling and attempting to back-slash, but Nathan, in disbelief at what was happening, held on and refused to let go.

More gunfire around him, and the flash and sizzle of a ricochet.

The arm attempted to pull away from Nathan. He leaned back, stretching the thing out like a snake, before the air overhead exploded. He fell backwards, holding a shotgun-severed arm, while a stern Shorty Charlie Williams broke open both barrels and reloaded. Realizing what he held, Nathan dropped the arm and kicked it away.

Across the way, Gilbert stood within one berth, angled his rifle over the backrest, and fired three quick shots into the seat. Jimmy Norquay hurried through, firing as well, but Nathan collapsed in his berth and watched in horror as the remaining stump in the cushion's center oozed oil.

"Holy shit!" Gilbert was yelling. "Holy shit, *holy shit!*"

"Quiet, Gilbert!" Jimmy shouted and got the silence he wanted. The shooting died away to nothing. In the aftermath of the short but unexpected fight, Nathan reached out and prodded his knee with his fingertips. He hissed at the contact, knowing full well he'd been cut.

"You okay?" Shorty asked, his torso looming over the berth behind the one Nathan occupied.

"That thing cut me," Nathan winced, eyeing the bleeding stump and then the dark floor, where the detached arm lay.

"Got me, too," Gilbert groaned while checking himself out and shaking his legs.

Leland rose, his hat fallen off his head. "We need some light in here."

"I'll get it," Jimmy said.

"Watch your legs. Goddamn things are… are in the seats."

Nathan couldn't take his eyes off the bleeding stump embedded in that grand cushion. He lurched to his feet just as Jimmy fired twice more, swearing at unseen assailants.

"More of them?" Leland asked.

"A damn nest of them," Jimmy reported. "Except…"

"What?"

Jimmy took a moment to stomp upon a seat. It took several attempts. When he'd finished driving his heel into whatever it was, he stood back, breathing heavily, and his shoulders slumped.

"It's just *arms*, Leland," he reported. "A damn nest of *arms*."

"Check under the seats," Leland said.

Nathan was already ahead of him, pulling, pushing, and finally trying to pry away the cushions. Nothing moved.

"Use the knife," Shorty suggested.

Nathan considered the blade that had cut him but decided he didn't want anything to do with that infected piece of metal. He pulled free his own Bowie knife and, composing himself, stabbed it down into the cushion.

The knife hit wood.

Nathan's hand stung at the connection, but he didn't stop. He cut away the fabric and gutted the feathers within.

"Oh," he muttered when he stopped and studied what he'd uncovered. "Oh… Sweet Jesus."

The stump grew *out* of the wood underneath the box, in a sinewy collection of roots and organic matter he didn't recognize but knew would haunt him for a very long time. There was no body, just that tough fibrous attachment that might've been the ends of an organism turned inside out. Nathan studied those beet-red tubes in mounting horror, before stabbing the base of the limb and sawing away. Halfway through, the arm stump detached itself like a leech filled to capacity, leaving a dark-stained wood.

"Sweet, Sweet Jesus," Nathan muttered again, and swept the unholy protrusion onto the floor with his knife. Grimacing, he tapped the very surface where the arm had attached itself.

Solid, unbroken wood.

Except an arm holding a very large knife had moored itself there.

Jimmy returned with the detached oil lamp, swinging it around. Leland pressed a hand to the side of his pale face, his fingers seeping blood.

"Arms," Nathan said. "Nothing but arms."

"The hell is going on here?" Mackenzie said for them all, at a loss as to explain the horrifying sight.

"I cut around one," Nathan said. "Right down to the wood. Just an arm. With a knife. Attached to the plank like a goddamn leech."

"Must be someone underneath," Mackenzie said.

But there was no one underneath. No one trapped inside the seat, impossibly contorted to fit a hidden chest's dimensions. A quick hammering of the seats showed immaculate workmanship, and no means of entry or exit. Nothing could be stored within, unless the builders had installed the seats with a person inside, but that was just as impossible as what had just happened.

A stoic Jimmy quieted everyone when he stooped into one berth and did some serious cutting. A short time later, he held onto a skinny arm dripping and severed at the shoulder.

"Oh my god," Leland whispered.

Jimmy tossed the lifeless meat away and shone the light around. "They died all the same," he said, inspecting the others. "Looks like one or two for each berth. Mostly along in the middle of the aisle. The one I stomped on? The one like a snake nest? There were five or six in that."

"Man-sized?" Mackenzie asked.

Jimmy scowled and didn't answer.

For a time, the six men stood and absorbed the numbing horror of the situation. Nathan regarded each one in turn, even Gilbert, who might've once been perceived as the jumpiest of the bunch. Not so. Gilbert held his rifle at chest-level, above the seats, and appeared very much in control and alert. In fact, no one showed even a flicker of the fear that Nathan was feeling, and he realized in a match-strike of understanding that these were not ordinary men. These were seasoned outlaws. They'd all seen and done things where blood had been spilled. And even though what they'd just experienced was definitely supernatural and beyond imagination, one thing above allowed them to keep their wits and their nerves under control.

And that was the resolve to *not* show any outward fear, to *not* break in front of the other gang members. Such a breach of outlaw etiquette would not do, under any time of extreme duress. No one wanted to partner up with a weak will and mind. If the situation were different, say, if they were holed up in some bank on the prairie and surrounded by North West police and facing a potential hanging if caught, a gang member crumbling under such pressure would be a weak link in the chain. A liability.

No one wanted to be the weak link.

And no one sure as hell wanted to be a liability.

Liabilities were frowned upon, mistrusted, and ultimately shot, for fear of endangering the rest of the gang.

So Nathan took two deep breaths, held them, and let them out slowly, all the while taking a firmer hold of his Winchester, which killed both passengers and bodiless limbs just fine. On this wavering plane of reality, he held onto his weapon like it was an anchor dug in. It kept him mentally in place, despite a killer undercurrent attempting to sweep him away. Faces were set and reflective, eyes glittered in the lamplight.

"We on the right train here, Leland?" an uneasy Gilbert finally asked.

Leland didn't reply, his face set as he continued pressing the side of his head. Blood dribbled over his fingers. Jimmy swung the light around, bathing the man's features in an orange hue.

"I mean," Gilbert continued, trying to organize his thoughts. "Passengers who become monsters? And now arms—bare *arms*—with knives, trying to cut us to *pieces*?"

Leland still didn't answer. He stood there until he motioned for Jimmy to get the lamp out of his face.

"This is…inexplicable," the gang leader admitted. "I don't know what's going on. But I'll tell you this. Nathan and I had an encounter as well. With the engineer of the train. The engineer wasn't a person at all. It was… an apparition."

"A what?" Gilbert asked.

"A ghost," Mackenzie clarified, pulling his scarf down to reveal a deadly serious expression.

"A ghost," Leland repeated. "We shot the thing, but our bullets passed right through it. In the end we managed to drive it from the train. That was the last we saw of it. The train itself, however, is a solid thing. This," he patted the seat, "is certainly real to the touch. The passengers, these things…. they all seem to bleed. To die. Suggesting we're not quite on… a ghost train."

"But a crazy train," Nathan added.

"A crazy train," Leland said, looking from one face to the other. "A crazy train that probably doesn't have the payroll car that we were looking for. So, following all that, I'd say… yes, Gilbert. We're definitely *not* on the right train."

The lamplight shaded Gilbert's profile as he warily looked from one end of the car to the other.

"A crazy train," Nathan said. "We're on a crazy ghost train."

"Fucked up train," Shorty Charlie Williams muttered.

"I don't know what we're on, truthfully," Leland said. "But if it makes you feel better calling it that, go ahead. It's certainly not what I expected. Regardless, gentlemen. The plan doesn't change. The train controls were damaged. The brakes do not work. Even now, we're speeding along faster than before. We can't unhitch the main engine from the passenger side, but perhaps we can unhitch the caboose."

"And if we can't?" Mackenzie asked.

Leland's eyes glittered in the flickering lamplight. "Then we ask Jimmy here what his thoughts are on using his remaining dynamite on the couplings. Whereupon we coast to a stop. One way or another, we're getting off this train."

"Why not blast the couplings now?" Eli demanded. "On any of these cars?"

Nathan shook his head. "You see those couplings back there? They're all melted together into one big black kernel. Same as back front."

"We'd have to blast through the floor first," Jimmy said. "And there's another risk."

That got the men's attention.

"We could derail the train," Jimmy said.

That silenced the lot of them. At the speed they were traveling, they could be shot through a window or have their heads bashed against the hardwood berths. Or simply crushed inside the cars as it compressed like an accordion.

"The caboose will have to do…" Leland reasoned, studying his companion.

"I think so…" Jimmy said and nodded in support of the plan. Nathan drew strength from the Metis man's stern expression. He suspected Jimmy Norquay had a bar of iron in his spine that went from tail to skull.

"I'm in," Nathan said. Jimmy and Shorty nodded their consent.

"Whatever you decide, Leland," Mackenzie said.

"Yeah, whatever," Gilbert said quickly, not wanting to be seen as undecided.

The gang's thoughts were known, their intent clear, and Nathan, for one, knew this particular group was a determined one.

"All right then," Leland said, looking to the next door. "Watch the shadows. And let's get ready to move."

18

Nathan and Leland sustained the only wounds from the surprising attack. Gilbert and Mackenzie both inspected themselves and were relieved to find their thick winter dusters had saved their extremities. Gilbert held up the ends of his coat and poked fingers through the slash that, thankfully, didn't cut any deeper.

Nathan doffed his outer winter shirt and cut the thing into strips. He shared the makeshift bandages with Leland, and they trussed up their wounds as best they could. Once done, the six men approached the waiting door of the next car, mindful of the nearby seats. Mackenzie took the lead, and the once cattle thief gripped the handle. He waited until the others got into position, ready to fire.

With a nod from Leland, Mackenzie pulled the door open.

The vestibule was empty.

Shorty crept forward, and the rest followed the big man to what Nathan believed was the tenth car. Shorty stopped at the entrance, gripped the handle, and squeezed his sizeable frame out of the way in case the others had to open fire.

He opened the door.

The men didn't shoot. The oil lamps within burned low, allowing more than enough light. Not a soul in sight. An eerie ambiance hung over the deserted car, however, tugging at the threads of superstitions best forgotten, and bedtime tales of things that existed only in dark places. Nathan, in particular, wondered what had changed all the passengers into such horrifying creatures in the first place.

Moving as quietly as they could manage, their rifle barrels gleaming in the soft light, they entered the car. Shorty and Mackenzie went on ahead, while

87

Gilbert trailed. They checked on the berths before passing each row, not caring to be ambushed a second time. Nathan and the others gathered behind them, casting wary glances back the way they traveled.

Shorty reached the exit door and readied himself to crack it open. "All set?" he asked the others as they gathered.

Leland gave him the nod.

Shorty pulled back the door, and a winter wind blasted the gang. Nathan's hat blew off and landed against his back, where the chin string kept it. He shied away from the gale at first, only to peer beyond the doorway.

The vestibule was gone.

"What the hell?" Nathan whispered in puzzlement.

Shorty looked around the edge of the portal as Leland strode forward and stopped upon the threshold, where his coat flapped in the wind. "Damnation," he said.

A moment later, Nathan understood why.

A roofless flatcar lay out before them, bare and forbidding. An ominous darkness swallowed up the deck's edges, and a tempest of a crosswind cut across that open expanse. No railing along the sides, and lamplight revealed a smattering of ice and snow upon the dimpled iron. Above the intimidating pitch blackness, however, the night sky shone in its full glory.

The stars caught Nathan's attention, but with all that had happened in the last ten minutes or so, he couldn't identify what bothered him about the scintillating spectacle overhead. They were still oversized and twinkled with unnerving indifference.

"We ain't going across that, are we, Leland?" Gilbert asked.

"Looks like we'll have to."

"Shit."

There were no connecting plates to the flatbed, just a foot-wide chasm that had to be stepped across. The space below was a flashing screen of lights that weren't quite sparks. The display puzzled Nathan, so he handed off his rifle to Mackenzie, and crouched at the edge of the platform.

"Jimmy," he said. "Give me that lamp."

"See something, Nathan?" Leland asked.

"Yeah, I do."

"What is it?"

"Give me a second."

Jimmy handed over the lamp, the flame protected from the wind by glass. Nathan lowered the light into the gap. Right there, framed between two sets of rails, and a pair of jostling couplings that shivered and shook, was another night sky. Deep. Infinite. And positively frightening.

Even as he looked, stars zipped across that space like streaking comets.

"What is that?" Leland asked, taking notice.

"That ice, Nathan?" Mackenzie also inquired.

Nathan couldn't quite answer, however, as his voice failed him. He looked to the right and saw no land. Nothing lay to the left, either. At first, he thought it was a trick of the dark, but the night was too bright to conceal the landscape. Then he thought they had to be on the wide flatness of the prairies, except he knew they'd all boarded the train in the Rockies.

Then there was the absolute lack of anything beneath them that defied all explanation.

"Leland?" Shorty asked plainly, filling the lapse of conversation.

"Yes, Shorty?"

"You see any mountains around?"

That was met with a resounding silence, where only the wind raised its voice, and the train continued to power its way along the rails. Nathan drew back from the gap. He held out the lamp for Jimmy, except Jimmy didn't take it. Like the others, Jimmy was trying to make sense of the missing world around them. The mountains had vanished. There were no hills, no forests, and certainly no bodies of water. Only the night existed. As far as anyone could see, the only thing surrounding the train was that vast emptiness of space. The only thing holding up the speeding locomotive was the thin set of rails beneath it, suspended in the air without any visible trusses, defying both gravity and reality.

"The hell's going on, Leland?" Gilbert asked in a low voice that wavered around the edges.

Leland didn't answer.

"There's no ground underneath us, Leland," Nathan said as that familiar nervous energy returned to his chest and lower legs. "There's nothing. Not a damn thing."

Those closest held onto the car's door frame and leaned over.

"Oh Sweet Jesus," Gilbert exclaimed and jerked himself back.

The sight was worse when the lamplight was out of the way, when their eyes could adjust and behold that endless, star-studded chasm beneath them. All the while, the wind slapped their faces.

"Get back," Leland ordered, having enough. He signaled a quick retreat inside the passenger car with his hand. Shorty kept the door open until everyone was in, then Leland motioned for him to close it.

If the raving passengers or the knife-wielding limbs didn't unnerve them, the rail system held up by *nothing* surely did. The men stood in the aisle and glowered for a few seconds. Leland sat down in one of the nearest berths and put a hand to his bandaged head. The nearby lamplight deepened his despondent expression, and one could tell he was at an utter loss as to explain the events outside the car.

Chumpchumpchumpchump, chumpchumpchumpchump…

"We're…" Gilbert whispered. "We're flying out there. I mean *here*. Wherever the hell we are."

"What the hell did we jump on?" a stunned Jimmy Norquay asked, as if he'd taken a punch flush to the jaw. He dropped his winter clad ass into the seat across from Leland.

"And how the hell do we get off?" Mackenzie demanded.

"We can't get off," Gilbert blurted. "There's nothing underneath us! Just goddamn *stars*. Oh blessed Lord Almighty."

"What the hell did we jump on?" Jimmy repeated, staring at Leland as if he'd just been gut shot.

"We jumped on a devil train, is what we jumped on," a rattled Gilbert moaned, his eyes wide and face pale. "We jumped on a goddamn devil train, and we're going straight to hell."

"Shut up," Leland told him.

"Straight to *hell*, Leland."

"Shut *up*, I said."

"And that's only if any of *those things back there don't rip us apart first*!"

Shorty Charlie Williams aimed his shotgun at Gilbert. Mackenzie also took aim in a clack of metal and rustle of winter fabric. Having been beaten to the draw and knowing it, Gilbert froze on the spot. His trembling attention flickered from one gunman to the other.

"Appreciated," Leland said to the pair before considering a distraught Gilbert. "I'm only going to say this once, Gilbert. Only once. So you listen and listen real good."

Gilbert licked his lips and nodded. He was all ears.

"Settle down. Keep your gun ready, and stay alert. But know this…I won't tolerate another outburst like that. Not from you, not from anyone. But sure as hell not from you. Understand?"

His jaw visibly clenching, Gilbert held up a hand. "I understand."

"You're not going to do anything that's going to upset me?"

"No, Leland."

"Because right now, at this juncture, we have some very serious thinking to do. And I said 'we'. That includes you. Now is not the time to unravel."

The extended lecture caused Gilbert to sigh and roll his eyes, but he kept his mouth shut.

"All right," Leland said, the relief clear in his voice. He nodded at the two gunmen. "Don't worry about Gilbert, boys. He's fine, now."

Shorty glared at the smaller man but lowered his shotgun.

Mackenzie didn't.

"Mack," Leland said.

Mackenzie's rifle remained steady for a few seconds, but then it dropped.

Gilbert released a relieved sigh as the tension in the car dissolved.

"Watch the back door there, Gilbert," Leland ordered.

Nodding, and perhaps grateful for something to occupy his mind, Gilbert aimed at the car's entrance.

"And watch the door here, Shorty, if you please."

Shorty did just that.

"Now, then," Leland began. "Let's deal with this situation, as impossible as it might seem. This car seat is real. I'm sitting here. However, you all saw what waits for us outside, and I'll be honest, I'm having trouble coming to terms with what it means. Thoughts?"

"I don't think we're getting off this train anytime soon," Jimmy said, a hand to his forehead, as if that helped the thinking process.

That statement darkened Leland Baxter's face. "We're getting off this train. I guarantee you. How many of those sticks do you have left?"

"Nine."

"All right," Leland said. "We don't go to the caboose. We get to the other side of the flatcar and use the dynamite on the couplings. If there are couplings, that is. Can you do that?"

The very suggestion got Nathan's attention.

"I can do that," Jimmy said after a time.

"You can't blow the couplings here," Mackenzie said quietly. "We're on a set of rails in the night sky. There's nothing around us. Above or below. I mean… how did we get here? To this point? Where are we going? And if you *do* blow up the couplings, what happens then? Where does that leave us? Are you even sure we'll roll back to where we came? I don't know, and I'm not willing to guess. But I'm willing to take a guess on one thing. If you separate us from the engine, there's no telling where we might stop, what might happen, or what might be waiting for us."

That stark assessment quieted them all.

Leland cleared his throat. "What do you suggest?"

Mackenzie had the floor. He looked to a dust-covered window. "We continue onwards. Get to someplace safe. Or safer than here. Maybe we can find out what happened to Eli. Maybe we *can* find a way off this train. A safer way. But let's not use dynamite on anything until we have solid ground underneath us."

"All right," Leland said. "You make very good points, Mackenzie. We carry onward. Are we agreed?"

Nods all around. Nathan nodded, simply because going forward seemed better that going back, and because he didn't know what else to do. Mackenzie made good sense, however, and he appreciated the man's cool thinking. His own mind was racing, and he took a moment to pull his scarf up over his face.

Leland stood, and the others rose with him. He went to the door. "Stay behind me. Watch your footing, and don't stray from the center of the flatcar. There're no handrails—none that I saw, anyway. Check the overhead bins for rope or something to tie us together."

All they found was dust, as if the compartments had never been used at all. This discovery only deepened the mystery of the passengers.

Ropeless, the gang members gathered at the exit. Leland pulled up his scarf and motioned for Jimmy's lamp. Once he had that, he studied them, as if gauging their readiness.

"All right, stay close," Leland told his gang. "Within arm's reach of each other. And for the love of God, don't slip over the edge. If you fall, there's no guarantee you'll *stop* falling."

Nathan swallowed, knowing the man spoke the simple truth.

"See you on the other side," Leland said.

<h1 style="text-align:center">19</h1>

That cutting, freezing wind attacked the group the moment Leland opened the exit door. Rifle in one hand and lamp in the other, he stepped out onto the platform, the single flame fluttering despite the protective glass shell. His coat rippled from the gale force, but he didn't stumble or fall. Mackenzie stepped up behind him, and Nathan after that. Jimmy followed, with Shorty and Gilbert bringing up the rear. In single file, each man stepped over that foot-wide chasm between the two platforms, their coats fluttering in the gale. No one dared to gaze down into infinity, for the very real fear that their minds, and willpower, would break.

They crossed without incident, and stopped once they were all standing upon the flatcar.

"Jesus Christ," Leland growled against the howling wind, and lowered his head.

Nathan's hat was already off and hanging from his neck. He looked around, discovering it wasn't nearly as dark as he'd thought. The night sky was stunning, however, and his breath was a release of vapor. Stars surrounded that rectangular deck, muted only by the black lines and edges of the flatcar. The snow had ceased falling, and thousands—*millions*—of stars and other celestial phenomena shimmered and twinkled in the now clear night. The six men marveled at that blue-black midnight shine, their wide winter figures easily visible against the cosmic backdrop. Even Leland lifted his eyes to that magical spectacle. As magnificent as the heavens were, Nathan's anxiety returned, reminding him that nothing existed below the train except two strips of steel without any visible means of support.

The thought was incredible. Frightening.

Yet there he was, second from Leland's back, following him across a long stage darker than anything in the night sky.

Leland stood some three feet ahead, the lamp held high.

"Mind your step, now!" he yelled, words muffled by his scarf.

The gang leader started marching.

Be strong, a woman's voice whispered inside Nathan's head, and he knew it to be his mother's. *Be strong.*

Mackenzie walked past him, nudging him with his rifle. Gripping his Winchester, Nathan got in line. His boots clattered off the flatcar planks, and the wind, while powerful, wasn't enough to sweep him off his feet. Leland was a hunched beacon striving forward, seeking safe harbor. Mackenzie was behind him, and at times their outlines meshed together. Nathan found his attention drifting away from Mackenzie's back, to the tilting, rolling universe all around them.

"Lord Almighty," he whispered, squinting against the night winds. Space spiraled around the flatcar's deck, as if the iron fabrication was the very center of a vast globe and God above had gripped it by some unseen handhold and given it a lazy whirl. Stars periodically shot across the heavens. Silky, almost ephemeral clouds masked some of the brighter points of light. Hazes of interstellar dust glowed with color.

Despite all that otherworldly wonder, Nathan was unable to identify any of the bodies of stars his mother had taught him. He couldn't see the Great Bear, nor the Bowman (which he knew wasn't the exact name, but the one his mother used) or the Jumping Fish.

Nathan scrutinized one patch of stars and then another, cringing under the wind, while checking on the men ahead. He slowed and expanded his star search by looking over his shoulder.

And saw what lay behind them.

Or rather, *before* them.

Nathan stopped and stared. His mouth dropped open. His eyes damn near popped from his head.

There, rising above the passenger car they'd just left was the unmistakable face of the moon, and the moon was *huge.* Impossibly huge. Perhaps almost double its regular size. The moon was no longer full, but *bloated.* Clear craters shone brightly, vast and shadowed and speckled, as if blasted by buckshot. Steep ridges and mountains jutted out into the black sky, as plain as looking out over the Rockies. The moon was an immense thing, battered and gouged by powers unknown to Nathan, and being so close to that scratched and dented pearl rendered him spellbound.

Jimmy halted and also looked back… and remained that way, staggered by the spectacle rising above the train. That, in turn, created a ripple effect, as the others did the same. The line of train robbers bunched up in the end… and fragmented.

That awesome lunar display charmed Nathan, until the barest thread extending from the moon's surface caught his attention. He focused on that razor-thin cut, and believed he could make out just another line, parallel to the first.

A fluttering of black rags, just above the roof of the passenger car, broke the spell.

The movement drew Nathan's eye, and as he watched, the rags appeared to grow longer and thicker. Until the unmistakable outline of a head rose above the roof, and what might've been a hand gripped the edge.

"Jimmy," Nathan said.

Jimmy glanced over his shoulder, distracted from all that wonder.

Nathan pointed.

And Jimmy saw. Gilbert and Shorty were behind him, mere silhouettes against the rest of the inky backdrop that was the passenger car. The heavens and the moon had transfixed them as well. Jimmy pushed on and pointed, breaking their paralysis.

"The hell is that?" Gilbert said, just heard over the wind.

Another head appeared upon the roof, weirdly shaped and… predatory. It took Nathan a moment to realize that the thing had its skull cocked to one side. Then a third head rose, at which point the first two nimbly crawled face-first down the sheer wall to the platform, their flesh waving in the night wind. *Clothes*, Nathan realized, and his guts went cold. The figures dropped to the deck as others followed in a ripple of heads and backs and flailing arms.

Man-sized shapes gathered at the end of the flatcar.

Many man-sized shapes.

"Shit," Gilbert whispered and aimed his rifle.

Nathan spread out to Leland's right, taking aim as well. He discovered that while the wind didn't move him so much, it did nudge his arms just a little.

"Keep moving," Jimmy said, even though he readied his own Winchester. "Keep moving."

The shapes withstood the wind, righted themselves, and charged.

"Jesus Christ!" Gilbert yelled and fired, blowing one of the shadows backwards. The things behind it faltered but swarmed over the fallen. In the background, however, a lumpy tide of knobs and heads continued to pour over the passenger car's rooftop.

Shorty fired, unloading one charge into the rush, then another. Jimmy opened up and Nathan joined in, working the levers, firing at indistinct figures clamoring forward.

"*Keep moving*," Leland shouted from on ahead.

The four gunmen continued shooting as they backed away in jerky steps, mindful of the flatcar's edges. Shorty took the longest to reload, so he hurried past Nathan and the others.

Nathan blew back a torso, the arms long and pointed and reaching, glimpsing the flash of a corpse-white face.

Jimmy fired two shots into a shape and blasted it back several steps, where it tumbled off the edge of the flatcar and disappeared from sight.

Gilbert dropped to a knee and worked his rifle, reaping a terrible toll among the onrushing force. And, in between the gunshots, a throaty, disturbing wailing grew, just as a figure rose atop the passenger car, its clothing flapping against the face of the moon.

The figure leaped onto the flatbed, disappearing behind the charging mob. *Passengers*. Nathan realized. *They were passengers.*

Crawling over the roof of the train, like cockroaches clinging to walls.

Nathan resumed firing. Then Leland was there, shooting into the mob. Spurts of ink exploded as bullets ripped into torsos and faces. A few squirts even spattered across the starry emptiness of space. Bodies dropped and a few even fell off the flatcar, twisting, clawing at the air with an eel-like fury as they vanished from sight.

Nathan worked his rifle. A head snapped back. A body twirled off its feet. He shot one white-faced passenger in the shoulder and put another bullet into its chest. One leaped over the entire pack in a frightening display of agility and power, only to be flung backwards with a thunderous blast from Shorty Charlie William's shotgun.

But like a gruesome deluge of sludge and moving offal, the passengers, a continuous *stream* of passengers, flowed over the train car's roof and dropped to the platform.

"Back away!" Leland shouted. "Go, Gilbert, go!"

Gilbert did so, clutching at his bandolier as he staggered by Nathan. Jimmy went next. When Nathan's rifle went dry, he turned and hurried past Leland.

A few steps back stood Mackenzie, taking steady aim and firing with deadly cadence into that black mass gaining ground. The outlines of the other train robbers were behind him, but Nathan could also see, with unreal clarity, the distance to the *next* car.

He'd thought a regular flatcar would've been no more than sixty feet long, and he was probably right.

Thing was, they appeared to be on the first flatcar of at least *three*.

"*Move, Nathan!*" Leland screamed as he ran past, no longer concerned with maintaining a careful balance.

Nathan turned, only to be yanked off his feet by the ankles. He crashed onto his chest as a force immediately jerked him back a step. In a burst of frantic energy, Nathan kicked and squirmed onto his back, seeing clawed hands clutching his ankles. A corpse-white face pulled itself forward, needle-smile blazing, lighting up its horrid features.

Nathan whipped the rifle's wooden butt into that maddening face. He hit it once, then twice more—hard blows that broke skin and spilled oil.

A white hand ending in talons flashed into Nathan's sights. He cracked his rifle across the arm, released his weapon, and drew one of his Colt Navy 1851 revolvers. His fingers and aim came together in a deadly display of speed and muscle memory, and he put two bullets into the passenger's head. The thing lost all life, and Nathan kicked himself free.

"*Dynamite, Jimmy!*" Leland shouted in the distance.

Nathan stumbled to his feet, abandoning his rifle, knowing there was no time to spare. He ran, boots hammering across the flatcar's surface. The noise of the train and the passengers' horrible crying engulfed him. The others were ahead, no longer shooting but running. Their shapes were well-defined against the flat darkness of the train, as well as the scintillating beauty of the star field surrounding them.

Leland was no longer shouting. No one was shouting for that matter. Nathan stormed forward, arms and legs chugging, realizing just how much weight he carried in not only weapons and ammunition, but clothing as well. He never imagined having to sprint for his life on a train.

The next car loomed ahead, the vestibule door marked by a dimly glowing window. The sight gave Nathan an extra shot of energy just as that evil chorus of voices seemed closer on his heels. Any moment he expected another set of hands to grab his ankles. Or seize his neck. Or perhaps even just tackle him around the middle and bring him down, holding him just long enough to be swarmed.

The entire gang sprinted for that narrow door—which opened. A wide figure emerged, froze upon the threshold… and started bellowing.

"Run you lazy cock-pulling sonsabitches!"

Eli Gallant lifted his rifle and opened fired.

A bullet screamed by Nathan. More bullets shrieked past, their high-pitched whines filling his ears. One of the retreating gang members reached the door and held it as Eli stepped away, widening his field of fire. The gun runner didn't blaze away, but quickly aimed, fired, and worked his Winchester's lever with fluid expertise.

Two more figures passed through the door, winking out of sight around the corners. Then the remainder. Gilbert stopped on the other side of the portal, placed his back to the wall, and opened fire, supporting Eli as he picked his shots.

The wind screaming in his ears, Nathan rushed past them and stumbled inside another passenger car. He joined Leland just a few feet away from the door, the leader's rifle raised and pointed. Nathan turned and aimed his revolver.

Jimmy stood next to the doorway, and a crackling fuse lit up his fist. Framed in that doorway was a raving, teeming frontline of passengers. An ebony current of faces and claws that filled the flatcar's framework, and shocked Nathan to his trembling core.

Eli and Gilbert retreated inside. Jimmy tossed the stick back onto the flatcar.

Shorty slammed the door closed, and everyone inside dove for cover.

The dynamite exploded.

20

The train shuddered and the door to the passenger car crimpled inwards, as if a heavy weight had slammed into it. The window remained intact, oddly enough, but Nathan didn't care. All he cared about was that the dynamite had done its job. He lifted his head, peeking out from the berth where he took cover, and inspected the door. The floor rattled underneath as the great machine continued to speed forward.

Other heads and figures rose, their attention focused upon the closed portal. Shorty lumbered to the door and inspected the damage. He reached for the handle, thought better of it, and retreated a step. A second later, a scratching rose from the metal, followed by a hammering of fists. The door quivered in its frame but did not open.

"Blast warped the door," an astonished Jimmy said, looking to Leland.

The gang leader stood and stared. "They can't get through," he whispered.

"They can't get through," Jimmy repeated.

"Not yet," Eli Gallant said and started extracting shells from a bandolier. He thumbed them into his rifle. "But the thing on my mind is, we can't get out that way."

"Why the hell you want to go out that way?" Nathan asked, getting some of his nerve back.

Eli regarded him. "It ain't that I *want* to go out there, it's that I like having the *option*."

The hammering continued, even intensified.

"We're not staying here," Leland decided. He glanced over his shoulder at the poorly lit train. "Another passenger car?"

"Empty, too." Eli reported. "I saw to all of that."

More fists rattled off the door, distracting the men.

"We better go, Leland," Nathan said and entered the aisle. "That door might not hold for long. What's in the next car, Eli?"

"Just another passenger car."

"Another one?" Leland asked with reserved doubt.

"Another one," Eli replied in a saucy tone, greeting Gilbert with a nod. "But that ain't what's bothering me, Leland Baxter. What's bothering me is that flatcar out there."

"Why's that?"

"Because when me and Gilbert and the boys were walking through here, there *was* no flatcar. Even when I went on ahead and then backtracked through the same fuckin' cars, there was no flatcar. You understand me now?"

The door shook underneath multiple impacts, distracting the stunned men.

"Come on," Nathan said, unable to wait any longer. He hurried down the aisle, towards the next door. The rest of the gang followed in a stampede of feet. The berths were empty, and the overhead compartments had all been opened. Eli had been busy, apparently.

They reached the end and glanced back. Only two lamps lit the interior, but Nathan thought he could see the distant door shiver from the constant pounding from beyond.

"There's nothing ahead?" Leland asked.

"Nothing," Eli answered.

"Open the door."

Nathan opened it with one hand, his gun held ready in the other. The dark vestibule shook with the motion of the train, but it was empty.

"What were those things, Leland?" Jimmy asked. "The passengers, I mean?"

"I have no idea."

"Maybe we just hold off on the questions," Nathan said, striding to the next door, where the window wasn't lit like the others. "Until we're someplace safe."

"Like where, shithead?" Eli barked. "There's only more passenger cars that way. This whole fuckin' *train* is nothing but a string of passenger cars."

"There must be others," Leland said. "There has to be."

"There ain't shit on the other side of that door."

Nathan grabbed the handle and opened it.

A chasm of blackness greeted him, and a howling wind much like that at the bottom of a mine shaft blasted by his face.

"Holy shit," Eli said. "The lights went out."

"Get something from the other car," Leland ordered.

But when they looked back, one lamp had already expired, while the other one flittered weakly. In seconds, the dark smothered the light.

"Christ Almighty," Eli said. "Left in the dark with a bunch of you shit flingers. I've died and gone to hell."

"Shut up," Leland said.

Nathan could no longer see their faces, but he sensed their closeness. In the dark, that steady drumming on the door seemed all the more ominous.

"Go on ahead, Nathan," Leland said. "But be careful of those knife arms. The ones we encountered earlier. We'll follow after a time."

"Be careful," Jimmy echoed.

"Careful?" Nathan asked. He peered into the gloom, unable to see anything. So he marched forward, feeling his way along the tops of the berths. Nothing tried to cut him.

"Come on then," he called back when he reached the midway point.

"We're coming," Leland said, and winter boots trudged over the floor. "Stop at the next door."

"I'll probably break my nose on the next door," Nathan muttered, forging ahead, the seat rows his only guide. He looked for windows but couldn't see any. He stopped and entered a berth. His fingers felt a window sill, but no blind. No curtains.

"What the hell...?" He trailed off, feeling the frame.

"What's wrong?' Leland asked nearby.

"There's no stars," Nathan said. "I'm at the window but there's no curtains. I'm tapping on glass." Which he immediately did. "And there's no stars. I mean, there's nothing. All them stars we saw aren't there anymore."

"The hell you say?" Eli demanded.

Nathan tapped his gun barrel off the glass. "Nothing."

"Shoot it out, then," Eli said.

But that didn't set right in Nathan's mind.

"No," Leland said. "Just... just leave it. Move on, Nathan. Perhaps the next car will have light."

"Why not blast it?" Eli wanted to know.

"The shot might alert the passengers as to where we are," Leland said in the dark.

That quieted the lot. Nathan knew their nerves were frazzled. He knew because *his* nerves were frazzled. Memories of all those faces and claws and the total absence of *fear…*

"Keep going, Nathan," Leland said.

So Nathan kept going. He returned to the aisle, his footfalls louder than the hammering far behind. Leland and the others followed, scuffling along the floor and occasionally cracking the wood with a rifle. The air smelled of varnish, familiar and pungent.

"The hell are the windows? And the night?" Gilbert asked and got shushed by someone.

"So dark," Mackenzie said, his voice barely a whisper.

And it *was* so dark. Nathan ran a hand over a seat, across a small gulf of empty space, and touched another cushion before repeating the process. He couldn't see a damn thing, as if the oil for the lamps was used up and gone.

"Keep going," Leland said, just a few steps behind him.

"Those cars you went through, Eli," Jimmy asked. "They all as dark as this?"

Eli didn't answer.

"Eli?" Jimmy asked.

"They had their lamps burning," Eli replied, sounding both sullen and nervous.

"Not anymore they don't," Mackenzie said farther behind.

"Keep going, Nathan," Leland droned. "Keep going."

Step after step, seat after seat. One hand sliding over fabric in a whisper of contact and then repeating, until he touched a fat knob which he instinctively knew was a person's shoulder. Nathan jerked his hand back and collided with a seat.

"What's wrong?" Leland asked.

"Sounds like he found something," Jimmy said.

"Yeah," Nathan got out, his thumb easing off the hammer of his revolver. "I found something. Maybe someone. Hold on."

"Anyone there?" Leland asked.

There *was* a person there, but as Nathan reached out, he was both thankful and frightened at what he might find. What he might touch.

"Wait," he said and stretched out his hand a little further. His fingers brushed cloth, clean and dry. Stitches. Seams. Thick and straight like railway tracks themselves. He explored a little further. There was a coat and he patted down a chest, a man's chest.

"Feels like a man," he reported.

"He's letting you touch him?" Eli asked harshly. "The bastard's long dead."

"Probably," Leland muttered.

Probably. The thought echoed in Nathan's mind. He reached inside the folds of the coat where fibers brushed the back of his hand, raising the hair on his neck. He located an inner pocket and a quick pat down revealed it was empty. Nathan's hand rose to a collar, to a neck, where he caressed cold skin and shorn whiskers down to the quick. Touching dead skin wasn't anything new to him, so he searched for a pulse. As expected, there was nothing.

"Dead," he said to the others. "I'm feeling the throat."

"That's too bad," Leland said.

"You search his pockets?" Eli asked.

"That's a good idea," Gilbert piped up.

"Leave his pockets be," Leland ordered, steel in his voice. "We rob trains, not corpses."

Nathan's fingers slid up from the man's lifeless neck, gliding over a jawline. He felt the lower nub of an ear, and drifted along the jaw to the face.

Except there was no face.

There was a stretched lower lip followed by an empty cavity. At first, Nathan thought he'd reached the man's mouth, except the way it was opened made it much too large. His fingers rose about an inch, then two, then *three.*

Then he grazed teeth and jerked back his hand.

"Keep going, Nathan," Leland said, but Nathan wasn't sure if he was being told to go forward, or to keep on touching. One thing was certain, he wasn't going to keep touching, not in the dark.

Those teeth, those unseen teeth…

They weren't a man's teeth. They were a dog's teeth. Or a wolf's. A very large wolf. Pointed and curved. Nathan's heart started up again, thumping at his ribs like a size-twelve boot kicking at a door. His gun came up, pointed at the dark and ready to fire. He left the mysterious body in the berth.

"Yeah," he said, half-expecting that thing to leap out of the seat and attack, only it didn't.

"Yeah," he repeated and took a tentative step forward, edging through that narrow void while the memory of dead skin and pointed teeth remained on his fingers. His breathing had quickened, his face sweaty, and he closed his eyes to compose himself. That darkness was nowhere near as deep as the one within the passenger car.

"Keep going," a voice whispered at his back.

Nathan kept going.

"You say you touched something back here?" Eli asked, sounding genuinely puzzled. "Because I ain't touched shit."

Oh Jesus, Nathan thought, his mind racing.

"You're searching the wrong spot," Jimmy said.

"Am not."

"Keep going, Nathan." Leland advised. "Keep going."

"There ain't nobody *here*," Eli said, his voice rising.

"You must've missed him!" Jimmy insisted, but there was a nervousness in his tone, as if he hadn't been able to locate the body either.

Nathan's hand went through a gap between seats and, instead of connecting with the next seat over, his hand kept right on sailing, which informed him he'd reached the end of the car.

Except there was no wall. No door. He explored the dark with one hand, holding his gun with the other.

"Leland," he said. "Leland?"

"Yes?"

"There's no wall."

"What?"

"The hell he sayin' up there now?" Eli asked.

"He said there's no wall."

"There's no wall," Nathan repeated. "No door, no nothing."

Silence greeted that.

"Keep going," Leland said. "But be careful."

A hand engulfed his shoulder, and Nathan's heart damn near exploded at the contact. He released a wheeze of pure fright, a sound one might make upon diving into arctic waters.

"Relax," Leland said. "It's just me."

"Yeah," Nathan whispered, composing himself.

"Make a chain, everyone," Leland ordered. "Take a hold of the man's shoulder in front of you."

"He said *shoulder*, Mackenzie," Eli stressed. "Not my ball sack."

"Fuck you, Eli."

"Be quiet," Leland commanded. "Keep hold of each other. And keep alert."

"The hell is that smell, Leland?"

What was *that smell?* Nathan asked himself, wondering where the bouquet of varnish had gone. Another scent replaced it entirely—a strong, viscous smell, of dampness, and of rot. Of unchecked mildew left to grow wild and steep in its own putrid juices. Nathan's boots sunk into the floor, causing him to stop in his tracks at the sensation.

"What's wrong now?" Leland asked, very close to his back.

"Floor's all wrong."

The gang leader paused. "Seems fine to me."

"I must've sunk half an inch."

"What?"

"At least."

Nathan probed the floor with a boot, feeling a solid surface just underneath that mossy softness. Nothing surrounded him, and he waved a hand around that cauldron pitch just to make sure, splitting only air.

"What are you doing?" Leland asked. "I can feel you moving."

Nathan hesitated. "There's nothing around me, Leland. Not a damn thing."

Silence, then.

"He's right," Jimmy said.

"Can't feel a thing." That was Mackenzie.

"The fuck the seats go?" Eli wanted to know.

"We keep going," Leland said. He nudged Nathan forward, even though his guts were sinking with every step.

"The floor," Leland said soon after. "You're right about the floor."

And the smell grew stronger.

"What is that?" Eli asked.

Gilbert spoke then. "Smells like your—"

"Shut up," Leland said, cutting off the man. "Just shut up."

Nathan took a step, the gang leader still holding onto his shoulder. His feet sloshed through water.

"We should go back, Leland," Jimmy advised.

"There's no going back. If we go back, there's only those things that were once passengers. They're at the door now, Jimmy. They're at the door. You heard them. Pounding away. And that was after the stick of dynamite. I don't know how many of those things are on this train, but I don't think… I don't think we have the ammunition for an extended confrontation."

That stark assessment struck nerves. Not even Eli Gallant opened his mouth.

"Forward, Nathan," Leland urged. "Into the dark."

Not willing to disobey an order, Nathan got walking. One careful foot after the other, his eyes almost adjusted to the surrounding nothingness and he was still unable to see a thing. The water however, was rising. Over his boot soles, seeping inside, and chilling his feet.

The others sloshed along behind him.

"Water," Leland said. "Up to the ankles."

"Getting deeper, Leland," Jimmy pointed out.

"If it gets too high, we'll go back."

"We could go in another direction," Gilbert said.

"No," Leland said. "And let me be clear. We're moving in a straight line. Do not deviate from the path and do not let go of the man ahead of you. If we stray, if we break up, we'll only have the sounds of our own voices to—"

"I see something," Nathan blurted. "Up ahead."

And there was.

A soft, eerie glow emanated from the end of the passenger car, roughly the width of the train. The gang studied the phenomena in the distance, which might have been a car-length away.

"What's that?" someone muttered, sounding as if he'd covered his mouth and nose to escape that increasingly offensive odor. "Smells like someone got sick."

No one answered. Nathan hitched his scarf up over his mouth and nose, but that foulness seeped through the material and polluted his eyes. Two strangely shaped objects beckoned them forward, offering a darkness not quite as forbidding as the one surrounding them. The glow fluttered, however, as if threatening to extinguish themselves at any moment. And in that unclean stench, in that damp graveyard dark, any source of light was better than none at all.

Nathan trudged forward, sloshing through water now at his shins. The others splashed along behind him. He hurried forward, the glow drawing him, able to discern walls just beyond the reach of his arms. The walls, however, gradually became a sunken steamship hue of rust, pocketed with shadow, and looking every bit as unclean as the air they breathed.

"I see something," Leland said.

Nathan saw it too.

The two glowing twins were oblong, and perhaps the size of the passenger cars' plush cushions. Each elongated shape seemed set into a wall, and beyond that, the same lighter shade of dark continued onwards, allowing them to see. Nathan stopped just before those glowing ovals, with Leland peeking over his shoulder.

"What is that?" the gang leader asked for them all.

Particles streamed past the oval-shaped aperture, some no bigger than a cluster of nail heads, some long and stringy, like the slobber hanging from a horse's mouth. They flowed beyond the glowing openings, as if riding unknown currents. Nathan leaned in closer to one oval frame, keeping his shoulder clear of the nearby wall. He sized up the queer illumination and the specks and spots beyond. When he'd seen enough, he reached out with his gun.

And tapped the barrel off what appeared to be thick glass, except the glass didn't tinkle. It thudded.

"The hell is that?" Mackenzie asked.

"Stay in line," Eli warned him.

"Let me get closer."

Nathan and Leland traded looks. "Go ahead," the gang leader said.

Mackenzie waded through the oily water at their knees and studied the set of oval windows. Then he did what Nathan was afraid to do. He reached up with a hand and spread his fingers across the surface.

"This is… amazing," he whispered. "Amazing."

"What is it, Mack?" Leland asked.

Mackenzie shook his head, uncertain as to how to explain. "It's not glass, but the texture is firm. Solid, yet just a touch damp. Like…maybe like the surface of your own eye."

"That's an eye?" Gilbert exclaimed.

"Not an eye, but *like* an eye." Mackenzie leaned in and inspected the edges before staring deep into the light. "Feels like an eye," he repeated, lost for a moment.

"What's all that inside it then?" Nathan asked.

Mackenzie glanced at him but didn't answer.

Just then, a long metallic roar erupted behind them, followed by a crashing that every man recognized as water. *Rushing* water.

"Now what?" Eli demanded, the non-light just bright enough to see his scarf-covered profile.

"We have to hurry," Mackenzie said and looked ahead. "This way."

He ran, splashing through the water at his knees. Nathan and the others broke into a run as well, struggling to catch up. The walls pressed in, becoming a narrow corridor at points, but further along, another window appeared in the ceiling, just right of center. The gang raced underneath it. The crashing water grew in intensity, getting closer, becoming heavy, like boulders shaken loose and tumbling off a mountain's back.

"There!" Mackenzie shouted over the pursuing noise.

Nathan saw it and couldn't understand what he was looking at.

The corridor ended in what might've been a door. It was egg-shaped, starting a foot from the floor, and stopping a foot away from the ceiling. Like the walls, it was an unpleasant color of deep-soaked rust, where the very touch of it might disease a person. There was a definite seam, outlining the width and height, and all manner of weird vegetable matter hung off its surface. Water sloshed at the base.

And directly in the center was a wheel, spoked and ancient, attracting the attention of all.

Mackenzie gripped that wheel, just a shade smaller than the hat belonging to Nathan's father. He attempted to turn it, but it would not budge.

Water creamed about their knees.

Nathan moved in, though there was very little room. The two men turned the wheel the other way, and the door opened with a great sucking noise that drowned out the rising thunder behind them. A gasp of filthy air blew by the men, souring their faces, but then Mackenzie and Nathan were pushing their way through. The others clambered through the portal, lifting their soaking legs and boots over the lower frame.

"Close it, Nathan!" Leland screamed. "Close it!"

Shorty Charlie Williams sped through, almost stumbling in the dark water loaming about his thighs. When he was inside, Nathan pushed but felt like he was attempting to move a train. The water pushed back, keeping the door open. Nathan sputtered, grunted, and finally screamed with the effort.

Shorty's great hands shot past either side of Nathan's face and slammed into the metal. He pushed, and together they slowly shut the door. Water spewed through the diminishing crack until it receded in a series of dark jets and oily dribbles, before abruptly dying.

Gasping, Nathan spun the wheel, locking the portal.

Then something massive slammed into the door with enough force to startle them all. The door whined under the pressure, but held.

"We're saved," Nathan gasped, spent from both the effort and the fright. "We're saved," he repeated.

"You think so?" Eli Gallant asked from behind him.

Nathan struggled to turn around and when he did, Shorty had to get out of his way.

The gang stood, silent yet dripping, within a chamber perhaps the width of a train car, but they were no longer on a train. That much was clear. That same rusty hue extended along the walls, and more oval-shaped membranes fluted the entire section from stem to stern. Light spilled through those membranes, the kind of light seen within halos, or sun beams penetrating deep within an ocean's depths. At the center of the narrow chamber, a singular cone of that peculiar light shone down from the ceiling several feet, illuminating what appeared to be a chair.

The back of a chair. A throne, in fact, that nearly filled the center of the room.

And the unmoving figure occupying it, leaning back as if sunning himself.

Nathan rubbed his face and drew away a handful of water. A quick lick informed him it wasn't entirely water, but a viscous string of unpleasant matter. He quickly spat and wiped off his face.

Leland was at the forefront, eyeing the seated figure as well as the light stemming through those dense portals. Patterns of watery light fluttered over awestruck faces and rust-flavored surfaces. A gentle swaying underneath rocked the gang members, as well as a barely noticeable undulation of the walls. Moisture dripped from the ceiling, but the water had drained away until only the men's feet were submerged.

"What is that?" Leland asked, stopping underneath one of the glowing portals.

Mackenzie approached the seated figure. He drew up alongside and, with an uncertain expression, moved past the chair to gaze upon the hidden face.

Mackenzie's breath hitched in his chest.

Nathan moved past the stunned men, hearing another whine again, much deeper that time—a disturbing, sonorous note that sounded both sad and majestic. He slipped through the light emanating from the walls and reached the chair with Mackenzie.

"What is it?" Eli asked from where he stood, dripping, holding his rifle at arm's length across his thighs.

"What, indeed," Leland asked, stepping in to get a better look.

The throne had the outward appearance of polished obsidian but pulsated like a living organism. The material shone wetly under the cone of light and paled the upturned face. A man's face, clean-shaven, eyes closed, and seemingly at rest, even though the throne he sat upon didn't really support him—it rose and engulfed him, like a huge leech of shining black glass attempting to suck him down. The throne stopped at his chest, where his clothing began, and his arms hung over the sides.

Clothing that resembled those of a conductor.

"Is it… eating him?" Jimmy asked, as moisture continued to drip from the ceiling.

"Looks that way," Mackenzie answered, taken in by the sight.

Nathan frowned and, upon impulse, leaned in closer to the fellow's profile, whereupon the conductor opened his eyes.

"What's that I smell?" the man asked.

21

"The end," Nathan's mother said with a contented smile, and closed the storybook with a soft clap. She stood up from his bedside and moved to the oil lamp, perched on a small chest. Eight-year-old Nathan watched her every movement. He was in bed, thick handmade quilts tucked under his chin, while his head rested against a feather pillow. Blowing snow scratched at the window, but his room was warm.

"Did you like the story?" she asked, picking up the lamp.

"Yes."

"Alice in Wonderland *is my favorite,*" she told him. "My mother gave me this book. I think I read it in two days."

Nathan's eyes drooped.

"What an imagination Mr. Lewis has," she said, her voice laced with pleased wonder. "I've read this book five times since, and every time, I wonder if there are places where... if you crawl or step through them, there's a chance you might find yourself in another place. Another world. Where everything is... very different. Where the animals talk, and up is down, and down is up. That sort of thing."

"Mm-hm," Nathan agreed, struggling to stay conscious.

His mother held the lamp by her side, the light as bright as a captured star. Her face was dimmed somewhat by the shadows filling the room.

"Mother?" Nathan asked.

"Yes?"

"If you... had a chance..." a deep yawn broke his thought. "Would you... want to go..."

"To a place like this?" she asked with a smile, and held up the book. She sighed, long and dreamy, and that nudged Nathan just a little more to sleep.

"I don't know," she said. "A story is one thing, and I daresay I wouldn't be as brave as Alice. But you know something..."

Nathan didn't answer.

"I do think…" she began.

But by that time, Nathan had fallen asleep.

*

"What's that I smell?" the conductor asked. He spoke in a tired English accent, but Nathan had no idea from what region.

The man opened his eyes, and they were utterly black—as black as a freshly polished boot toe. That sight alone caused Nathan to tense, and Mackenzie and Leland drew back.

The conductor wasn't an old man—he looked to be in his late forties, with thinning hair on top and a scar above his right eyebrow.

"What is that?" he asked and twitched his head to the left, in Nathan's direction. "Ohhhhh." The conductor let out in wary surprise. "Oh my, indeed. How did you get here?"

That struck the men speechless, to see this person, nearly swallowed by a throne, actually able to speak. The throne itself appeared embedded in the floor, though it was difficult to tell for certain as the water sloshed at their ankles. The cone of light sparkled off the conductor's eyes, and though he possessed no pupils, the men could tell he was scrutinizing them.

"Oh my, oh my. Three of you. Oh dear."

Worms of light squirmed across the ceiling. Water drops trickled into the pools around their feet. The conductor released a sigh and slumped forward. "I don't know what I did with my hole punch," he muttered.

"Who are you?" Leland asked, regaining his wits first. "What is this place?"

The conductor's scarred brow hitched in a question.

"What's all of this?" Leland asked, indicating the throne and all surrounding it.

The conductor's black eyes narrowed in confusion, and the man's mouth dropped open as if about to pose his own questions.

"What's all of what?" he asked in return.

"This," Leland persisted. He pointed to the throne and ceiling. "All of this."

The conductor inspected himself, struggling to take breaths. "Oh, this," he muttered. "It's my uniform."

That silenced the lot of them.

"Yes, my uniform," the conductor said. "Bit ragged right now, but I'll clean up well enough."

"What's your name?" Nathan asked.

"My name?"

"Yes."

The conductor stopped to think about it. He thought about it very hard. "Archie. Willmoore."

"Archie Willmoore?" Nathan asked.

"Yes," Archie confirmed, his black eyes unsettling and his mouth never closing at the end of a sentence.

"You're the conductor."

"Yes."

"Of this place."

"Oh, yes." Archie smiled, flashing black and barren gums.

"What *is* this place?" Mackenzie asked then.

Archie turned his head slightly toward the new speaker and took a moment to study him. "You lot certainly have a good many questions. I might ask a few of my own, if you don't mind."

"How about you just answer our questions first, you pinched-off piece of shit," Eli cut in. "Else I put a hole in the back of your head the size of a goddamn wagon wheel."

That caused Archie's eyes to pop. He became quiet for a few seconds, absorbing the words, understanding Eli's threat quite well.

"Shut up," Leland ordered Eli. "We'll do the talking."

"The man's mind is gone, Leland," Eli protested.

"I said shut *up*."

Eli settled down.

The train—or the chamber they were currently in—creaked and whined. Nathan noted that he could no longer hear the familiar *Chumpchumpchumpchump* anymore, and that both puzzled and worried him.

Archie the Conductor sized up the men in his field of vision. "You have guns," he finally whispered. "Oh dear. Do you mean me harm?"

"No," Leland said with a shake of his head. "Just answer our questions."

"Do you mean my passengers harm?"

Leland didn't answer that.

"Just answer the questions," Nathan said, stepping in.

"I see. Oh dear. Well, then, ask away."

"Very good, Archie," Leland said. "Now, where are we?"

"You, sir, are on board the Majestic 311."

That familiar bone rattle and building of nervous energy crept back into Nathan's lower bits.

"The 311?" Leland repeated after a time.

"Yes, sir. We call her 'The Majestic'. Not a finer locomotive travels these tracks. A dream on wheels, she is. All the finest materials available cover her bones, to ensure the most luxurious ride, the most decadent travel experience this side of the great pond."

"We're on the 311?" Mackenzie asked.

"You are indeed, sir."

"What happened to the 5409?" Leland asked.

"Excuse me?" Archie asked back.

"The 5409. What happened to her?"

"We're looking to get aboard the 5409," Nathan explained.

Archie looked from one man to the next. "I see," he finally said. "You mean to board her? And rob her?"

Leland didn't answer. They studied each other for a time before Archie spoke. "Well, sir, I have no knowledge of a 5409. This is the Majestic. The 311."

"You don't have a payroll car?" Leland asked.

"We have a mail car," Archie replied in a helpful tone. "Containing registered mail destined for stops all along the way to the West Coast, but not exactly a payroll car."

"He's lyin', Leland," Eli said.

Leland silenced the gun runner with a look.

"You don't have any cash on board? To pay miners way up north?" Nathan asked.

"No, sir. That we do not."

"No safe?"

"Well," Archie said, thinking it over. "There is a safe, but I can assure you there's no great amount of cash inside of it."

"The money we want," Leland said, "is a considerable amount of cash. Well over three hundred thousand dollars, Archie. And you're right. We intend to rob her. We won't harm anyone who stays out of our way. That includes you."

Archie's inhuman black eyes stared at the gang leader. "Very kind of you, sir."

"The money is supposed to be a secret," Nathan said. "Maybe he doesn't know about it."

"That so?" Archie asked. "So how is it you came into this information?"

"That's our business, Archie," Leland said softly, with a hint of a smile.

"I suppose it is, sir. Not meaning to pry. My apologies if I've overstepped my bounds. In any case, you're looking to be aboard *another* train. This is the 311. There's no such sum of money on the Majestic, sir."

Archie's mouth hung open at the end, as if exhausted by the effort.

"This is the 311," Mackenzie stated.

Archie shifted his head ever so slightly to address the man. "It is."

"A train."

"Yes sir."

"This… is a train?" Mackenzie waved a hand, the very wet environment Archie currently inhabited.

The conductor followed that hand, studying the walls and the ovals of subtle light. A crease formed between his black eyes as if he realized his surroundings for the very first time. "Oh dear," he muttered, taking in the sights.

"Oh fucking dear," Eli echoed.

"What's all this then?" Archie said, his mouth drooping in a horrified panic. "What's all *this*? Oh my Lord…"

The conductor whimpered as he inspected himself, his head turning left to right and back again with growing urgency. Archie's face pinched and darkened, as he clearly saw what had become of himself but did not understand in the least.

"Oh my sweet, sweet Lord," he exhaled and looked directly at Nathan. Archie took a breath as his panic came to a boil.

"*What's happened to me!*" he screamed.

22

The throne remained steady, but everything above the chest line, everything that was *Archie*, shivered as the conductor's terror seized him.

"What's happening to me? What's happening to me, oh sweet Lord Almighty *what has happened to meeeeeee!*"

The conductor's uncorked fright and frenzy unnerved the three men standing about him, prompting them to withdraw in horror. Archie thrashed one way and then the other, screaming, emptying his lungs before reloading and screaming again. He tried moving his arms, but failed miserably, and when he realized he *couldn't* move his arms (as demonstrated by checking each one and grunting forcefully), he *truly* began to whistle.

Until Eli, having quite enough, stepped up and smashed the butt of his Winchester into the back of the conductor's skull.

Archie slumped forward before settling back, mouth gaping wide as his black eyes closed.

"Jesus Christ," a disgusted Eli swore, poised to hit the conductor's head again. "That boy could—"

The train lurched sharply downwards at a gradient of perhaps forty-five degrees, throwing the men off their feet and sending them into terrified screams. Nathan clawed for purchase and latched onto the base of the throne, hanging on for dear life. Putrid water splashed across his face. The whine became a deep bass groan, a sound of injured fright, and the walls flexed and moved.

"This ain't no train," Mackenzie said through a grimace, struggling to hold onto the other side of the throne and looking Nathan straight in the eye.

Fifty degrees, and Nathan felt the same rush as when his mother and father had taken him for his first sled ride, down the side of a frozen hay bale.

There was a lump of motion sickness, and it kneaded his guts as if dithering to worsen or to leave everything intact.

The other gang members were no longer howling, but Eli was certainly swearing. Hot lines of profanity and blasphemy fired from his mouth, scorching the very air.

Sixty degrees, and that lump of sickness didn't relent. Mackenzie had bared his teeth, and his eyes were tightly shut as if waiting for the inevitable crash. Leland was nowhere in sight. The light in the chamber diminished as the train continued to dive.

But then … it leveled out. Just like that.

Nathan and Mackenzie exchanged overwhelmed looks, just thankful to be alive.

"God Almighty," Nathan released as a wave of water slopped over him, jolting him to his senses. Mackenzie sputtered when a second wave splashed over his face. Both men rose to their knees and clawed at the throne to get to their feet.

"The hell was that?" Jimmy demanded.

"*You!*" Leland barked, flinging the word in Eli's direction. "You're responsible for this."

Untangling himself from a soaking Gilbert and a sullen Shorty Charlie Williams, Eli stood and glowered.

"Don't you strike anyone ever *again* without my say so," Leland yelled. "Understand?"

Eli resembled an oversized drowned rat still capable of delivering a wicked bite. He scowled and nodded once, shaking out his rifle as the men behind him got up.

Overhead, the groaning lessened to the whine of a mournful violin.

"I don't know what you did," Leland said. "But you did something just then. And as God is my witness—"

"Leland," Mackenzie interrupted. "You should see this."

"See what?"

Mackenzie pointed to one of the oval windows, no longer glowing as brightly as before.

"What, Mackenzie?" Leland asked, having lost his usual patience.

"Just take a look. All of you. Whichever's closest."

"What's out there?" Jimmy asked as he went to the nearest window.

Nathan stepped to the one on his side of the throne. He peered outside. "Oh my," he whispered.

Fish.

An entire wall of fish sped by, just beyond the portal, a dark silver ripple of shapes and sizes, zipping past as if shot from a cannon. Entire species, it seemed. The school darted left, then right, a flittering mass of confusion yet in a tight unity.

"There's fish out there!" Gilbert exclaimed.

"A whole fucking school of fish!" added Eli.

And as the watery spectacle bewildered and excited them all, Nathan rubbed a hand over his face and knew that Mackenzie had spoken the truth.

This was no fucking train.

Maybe one time it was, but not no more.

So, the question was… *what was it?* And how the hell did they get out of it?

Another whine came from overhead, slow and ponderous, a note sounding of singular sadness and… something more.

"What is this place?" Leland asked.

"He knows," Eli said, nodding at the unconscious Archie Willmoore.

"And you knocked him out cold," Jimmy Norquay said before returning to the underwater wonderland outside his portal.

"You might've killed him," Leland said.

"Hold on," Nathan said, and sloshed over to the throne to examine Archie. The man didn't appear to be breathing. Worse, disturbing rivulets of inky blood ran down the back of his head, where Eli had brutally clubbed him. The pallid skin was broken, and Nathan loathed touching the wound.

"Well?" Leland asked.

"I don't know, Leland," Nathan replied. "He's not breathing. Not as far as I can tell. He's sure as hell bleeding, though. Just like a butchered pig. Right here."

Leland and the others could see. "You did that," the gang leader shouted at Eli.

"Didn't mean to kill the bastard," Eli shot back. "Only meant to get him talking, is all."

"He didn't know anything," Mackenzie declared. "Not with all that screaming he did. He wasn't even aware of what happened to himself. Far as he knows—or knew—we're all still aboard the 311."

"The Majestic," Nathan provided.

"The Majestic." Mackenzie nodded, appreciating the support. "He still thinks we're aboard a train."

"That sounds familiar," Jimmy Norquay mulled.

"It does," Leland said.

"It should," Mackenzie said. "The Majestic. The 311. I'm not exactly sure of the dates, but she was a luxury train out of Toronto. One of the first to go through the newly opened Spirals. The same tunnels we were waiting outside of. Remember now?"

No one did.

"Well, you're not going to like the next part, then," Mackenzie resumed. "The Majestic disappeared in one of those tunnels. The longest one. I mean, she entered the tunnel mouth and was never seen or heard tell of again. Didn't come out the other end. The tunnel just… swallowed her whole. I even think there were people waiting for her on the other side. A platform of fancy dignitaries or such. Story goes, they didn't even hear a whistle."

"Horseshit," Eli Gallant said.

"You say that a lot," Nathan told him.

"That's 'cause I hear a lot of it."

"And they never found her?" Leland asked. "The train?"

"You never heard about this?" Mackenzie asked.

"News doesn't travel as fast as you think when you're in the country."

"I've heard about it," Eli said. "And I still think it's all horseshit."

"Yeah, horseshit," Gilbert threw in.

"Just a goddamn ghost story to tell around the fire while you're out on the trail," Eli continued. "To scare the shit outta some young green bastard. Disappearing train my ass."

"Well," Mackenzie shrugged, not bothering to debate. "That's all I remember. This happened some nine or ten years back. She went into one end of the tunnel and didn't come out the other. I think there was a search party involved. Lamps and torches. They scoured the tunnel length, searching for clues. All they found was a lady's fancy hand fan. An Oriental one. Opened wide. And I'm not sure, but I think there were reports of… of the workers hearing a train's whistle in the tunnel. But no train."

"She disappeared," Nathan said.

"Vanished," Mackenzie said. "From the face of the earth."

"So what's this then?" Eli asked. "A fuckin' ghost train? You saying we're on a ghost train?"

"He said we're on the 311," Mackenzie said, pointing to Archie. "When I think of ghosts, I think of a white sheet. This is all solid enough. Nathan and Leland got cuts from real enough knives. So I don't think we're on a ghost train, but… something else."

That sobered them all then, and a well-timed whine of haunting indifference rattled the length of the chamber. The light had greatly diminished, but they could still see enough. Nathan stepped back and studied the ceiling, where the cone of light had also lessened.

What he saw through the overhead opening robbed him of words.

More fish swam, clearly visible through that membrane keeping the water out. What stunned them all, however, was a long serpentine length, impossibly huge, coiling over itself, encircling a huge section of the surrounding fish. As the unexpected leviathan passed overhead, the light from the ceiling lessened even more.

A second later, the whole length of the chamber turned, in the very same direction as the thing gobbling down the fish.

"We've gone down a rabbit hole," Nathan whispered. "A very wet rabbit hole."

"What?" Mackenzie asked.

That brought Nathan back to his senses. "Nothing."

"You said wet rabbit hole."

"I know."

"You said a *very* wet rabbit hole."

"I know what I said. Just forget about it."

The walls curved ever so gently, but the men eyed the flexing sides with worried expressions. The bountiful aquatic life fled from the windows, and some light returned, but nowhere near as bright as before. Mackenzie returned to his window and stared outside.

Leland and Jimmy approached the throne.

"Wake up, Archie," Leland said, smacking the back of his hand across Archie's cheek. "Wake up, I said."

Archie, however, did nothing of the sort.

"All right," Eli said, tearing himself away from a portal as if clearing his head. "So… we're in the belly of a whale? Is that it? We're in the goddamn belly of a whale?"

"Surprised you even know what a whale is," Nathan said.

"Go to hell, Nathan Rhodes, lest you want your ass kicked and then stomped on."

Nathan left it at that. He peered out the window, spacing his feet apart to better roll with the gentle movement of whatever it was they were inside of. *Inside a whale.* That surely had a ring to it, but it wasn't quite right. Close, but not quite. Not if what they'd just witnessed feeding on all those fish was… a part of the chamber they currently occupied. The very thought made his head hurt.

A heavy weight slammed against the door they'd closed, startling everyone. Eli immediately aimed his rifle at the door, and Gilbert did the same. Metal creaked but held, and a gentle tapping creeped into existence from the other side. More importantly, however, nothing came through.

"Now what?" Eli said. "I'm gonna lose my mind during all this."

"No, you will not," Leland ordered and regarded each man in turn. "None of you will. We're in strange company, guaranteed, aboard a very strange… vessel, that's certainly not a train. But we're alive. And still capable of thinking. So don't any of you even *consider* going insane during all this. Because if you do—and by doing so, unknowingly endanger the rest of us—I will put a bullet in you myself and not think twice."

An unfriendly silence ensued, as that familiar whine drifted in from all sides.

Nathan looked out his window. Shapes still swam alongside. All manner of fish, even though he had no idea what they were. There were long ones, and huge ones. Fish shaped like garden rakes and ones shaped like canes. Some appeared fat like full umbrellas, while others were serpentine. He recognized the sharks, having learned about them from his parents, but they looked odd, with several dorsal fins along the back instead of just the one. Those predators stayed away from the train-thing, and eventually vanished into blue-black depths.

"Where are we going, Mack?" Nathan asked.

"I don't know, Nate. Somewhere, I suppose."

"Awful lot of fish out there."

"There are."

"Sharks, too."

"I saw some of them."

"Never thought I'd see a shark outside a train."

A pause then, as Mackenzie considered that last thought. "We're not on board a train anymore. No sir. Forget about that right now. You all hear me? Forget about it. Like Leland just said. I mean, if thinking we're still on board a train helps you accept what's going on, then go right ahead. But if you think you got a firmer mind for things, then listen. We're not on a train. Or a missing ghost train. I'm not sure what we're on, or *in*, but we're here. We're presently safe. And until Archie there wakes up, if he ever does, we might as well… accept what it is."

The gang quieted then, taking the necessary time to process the little speech.

"Well said, Mackenzie," Leland said.

"Thank you, Leland."

"If you have any more thoughts on all this, let us know."

"You sure some of us can handle that?"

"You talkin' about *me*, shitbird?" Eli yelled. "'Cause if you are—"

"Will you shut *up*, Eli!" Leland shouted over him.

Looking poisoned, Eli turned back to the window that he shared with Gilbert.

Nathan glanced over at Mackenzie, who smiled back, careful not to show such a brazen display in Eli's direction. That little exchange boosted Nathan's spirit just a little, enough to let him return to looking out that oddly organic window. He checked on Jimmy and Leland, their faces drawn and tense, but determined. Shorty Charlie Williams lurked nearby, shotgun in hand and his hat tickling the ceiling. The soaked rug that was his beard dripped relentlessly onto his coat. Then there was Gilbert and Eli, two gun snakes if there ever were a pair. Nathan studied them all, but not too long as to draw attention. They were his partners in crime, trustworthy to a point, but right at that moment they were all each other had in the present world. The present reality.

He remembered the nighttime stories his mother read to him, and as far as he was concerned, they had indeed gone down a rabbit hole, some cosmic ball twister of a magical passage, leaving the Albertan Rockies far behind. He hadn't a clue as to where they were going, but if the people in the stories could find their way home, then he sure as shit figured he could find his way back home as well.

All he needed to do was keep everyone alive. There was strength in numbers. Leland knew that, which was why he stressed order and discipline.

Nathan figured they were going to need a lot more if they were going to find their way home.

23

"This all seems like one piece," Jimmy said, causing Nathan to turn away from the oceanic wonders outside his window. Jimmy and Leland remained by the throne, examining the chair and how it appeared to fuse itself to the conductor.

"All one piece," Leland murmured, deep in thought. "Yet, the upper bit is still a man."

"Yes."

"And poor old Archie was talking to us, right up until he couldn't."

"He was."

They quieted then, and Nathan went back to gazing out his window. Fish of an extraordinary range of size, shape, and color swam by the train-thing, and all he could do was marvel at every one. Some were incredibly ugly, consisting of teeth and particles that resembled worms, while others were simply beautiful. And the *colors*. Whatever sea they were under, whatever ocean, the blazing colors that popped from the depths were of a variety and richness that shamed the great mountains of Alberta, and tarnished the golden prairies of Saskatchewan. Oranges, yellows, greens, and blues, and the magical thing about them was the *light*. As rays of light penetrated the clear membranes through which Nathan peered, the creatures above and especially below somehow produced their *own* light. Nathan had heard of how the Chinese were able to light up the heavens with dazzling displays of fireworks. Nathan hadn't seen anything like that, even though he would dearly love to, but what he was witnessing in those ocean depths might very well rival those fireworks.

Backs and limbs, spines and fins, speckled and lined. All lit up and shimmering by some magical property that he didn't know or comprehend.

They simply *were*.

"You guys seeing this stuff?" Eli Gallant asked, sounding equally impressed and mystified.

That drew Leland and Jimmy over to see. And they saw.

"Good Lord," Leland exclaimed softly.

Below them, more shapes swam along, lit up in striking shades of blue-green bioluminescence. Ghostly swarms of glowing mushrooms flowed through the waters. Beyond them were lines and shading that hinted at mountains and valleys. Trenches of sand and stone lay like crude roadworks upon the ocean floor, while twisted coral rose up in spirals and noble minarets. Entire populations of radiant creatures moved throughout the deep. Sea greens, dark and mysterious, waved at them from the peaks of submerged highlands, while clusters of shining fish darted in and out of tunnels with all the speed of a comet.

Good Lord, indeed, Nathan thought, pressing his shoulder up against the walls and heedless of the contact.

"What are we looking at, Mack?" Leland asked.

Mackenzie hesitated before answering. "I don't know. I don't know."

Nathan didn't know either, but he knew it was beautiful.

"Glorious, isn't it?" Archie suddenly asked.

The world outside was forgotten then, as all attention flew toward the recovering conductor.

"What happened?" Archie asked as he righted his head, cracking his vertebrate while doing so.

Leland licked his lips. "You were struck," he finally said. "By one of the boys."

"He struck me?"

"He did."

"He certainly did a job."

"You were… hysterical, Archie," Leland explained. "He thought it best to subdue you."

"No worries, sir," the conductor said and blinked. "Quite all right. There've been plenty of times when the missus has done the very same thing to me. I tend to lose feathers quickly, I'm told. I do endeavor to try better in the future."

Leland gripped the conductor's shoulder. "You did fine. As long as you're not hurt."

"Just a bit of pain in the old head. Nothing to worry over."

Leland smiled.

"Enjoying the sights, are we?" Archie asked.

"We…are," Leland replied.

"Lovely, aren't they?"

"What are we looking at," Mackenzie asked. "Exactly?"

Archie took in the open portal right above his debilitating throne. "I can't rightly say. I mean, I know, and yet I don't."

"Best tell us what you do know," Leland said.

Archie became silent then, composing his thoughts. "We're underwater. Under a great sea. A great and wondrous ocean, filled with all manner of breathtaking delights."

"What is this train?"

"The train?" Archie asked with a confused look. "Ah yes, the train. The Majestic. This is her. And it's not her."

"What do you mean?" Mackenzie asked.

"We are part of the serpent now," Archie reported. "A great and wondrous creature that inhabits these waters for many, many years."

"A part of the serpent?" Mackenzie asked, needing a little more explaining.

"Yes. I… I don't know the name. I just know what it is."

"And how is that, Archie?" Leland asked.

"Why…" the conductor turned his head to face the gang leader. "Because I'm part of the serpent as well. I know what it knows."

That was met with shocked silence.

"What's happened to you, Archie?" Mackenzie probed. "And the other passengers? What's happened to the Majestic? Before… you became part of the serpent."

"I don't know. I remember moving through the cars, before entering the tunnel. I remember holding my, my ticket punch. And then darkness. Total darkness. I mean, we had lamps, but even they seemed to expire. At the same time. That was worrying, let me tell you. After that, I remember people talking. Screaming. And I recall helping passengers leave their cars in droves. I don't know why. In any case, I strove to maintain order, and directed them onwards, to the next car, while I moved forward."

Archie stopped then, his black eyes staring. "I remember opening one of the car doors and seeing… light. Then darkness, and becoming incredibly weary. And then… and then *swimming*, you see. Under the water. Going deep. Seeing sights you wouldn't believe. And I was part of the serpent then. Seeing things through its eyes, yet my eyes as well. It all had a…a dream quality, you understand. Until I felt a pull, and opened my eyes to all of you."

The conductor studied himself then. "All of this."

"Steady now, Archie," Leland said, holding the man's shoulder.

"Oh, I'm all right. My apologies for losing my composure earlier. My memory comes and goes. The serpent—and let me be clear, I don't know its real name, it's just what I call it—the serpent is, or has, made me its conductor of sorts. Of all of this. Even now, a part of it calms me. Somehow. As we swim through these waters."

Nathan looked from Leland's concentrating face to Mackenzie's and saw not a trace of disbelief.

"We're inside the serpent?" Mackenzie asked.

"We are," Archie said. "You most certainly are. But if I close my eyes and allow myself to drift, and by which I mean relax, as if to fall asleep, then I'm at the front. With the great creature. It doesn't mean to hurt us. It won't hurt you. Not with me aboard. My job is still the same, to ensure the welfare and safety of the passengers."

Another round of stunned silence. Shorty Charlie Williams took off his hat and massaged his face and forehead. Gilbert stood speechless as if he'd taken two hooves to the skull. Eli said not a word, perhaps not wanting to be told to shut up again. Jimmy, Leland, and Mackenzie all remained calm and contemplative. It wasn't so hard to believe in Nathan's mind, once you accepted it and dealt with it.

"Where are the other passengers now?" Nathan asked.

Archie frowned. "Gone. I don't know where, or what's become of them."

Nathan had an idea where they'd gone. He'd shot enough of them just a short time ago.

"Archie," Leland asked. "Where are we going?"

That question seemed to confuse the conductor. "Why, anywhere we like. Anywhere you like."

"We'd like to go back," Leland said. "To our rightful place."

"I see. That's understandable."

"Can you help us?"

"I'll certainly try, sir," Archie answered. "It's my job, after all. Even though you were looking to rob a train."

"Not this one."

"Any train, sir," Archie said. "Though I do sense a rather… crooked nobility about you. For the sake of the world you left behind. The one I left behind. And shall never return to. I'll see what I can do… to get you back."

Leland patted the man's shoulder. "Thank you, Archie."

"Allow me to consult with the serpent's memory," the conductor said. "Perhaps she has seen something."

"You can do that?" Leland asked.

"I most certainly can," Archie smiled. "In the meantime, enjoy your journey aboard her. Us. You'll not have this opportunity ever again."

Nathan didn't doubt that.

24

The men gathered just beyond Archie's throne, their demeanor downcast. They didn't even look at Leland anymore, but glanced at the watery world outside the numerous membranes. Curls of light played upon the walls, and the smell of wet clothing and body odor overwhelmed all else.

"You all heard what Archie said," Leland informed them. "We're aboard the serpent."

"I guessed it first," Eli said.

"You said 'whale'," Nathan corrected.

Eli scowled at him as if taking a whiff off a shithouse door.

"None of that matters," Leland interrupted before more words were exchanged. "We have an idea of where we are, and Archie's going to help us get on our way."

That produced a series of harsh looks, wondering if the conductor could be trusted, especially since he knew they were train robbers.

"We don't have a choice," Leland said, reading those faces. "Not really. So keep calm. Stay alert. And try and enjoy the ride." He ended that with a smile.

"Look outside," Archie suddenly exclaimed. "You'll see a *plethora* of underwater flowers underneath us."

"The fuck's a goddamn plethora?" Eli muttered.

"An abundance," Mackenzie explained. "A wide variety."

"Why the hell didn't he say that, then?"

Mackenzie didn't answer, and the other men became much more interested in what was transpiring beyond those clear membranes, if only to occupy their minds.

They weren't disappointed.

Refracted sunbeams lit up a garden of colors spread out across the ocean floor. All manner of alien vegetation covered mounds and shallow valleys in a diverse and awesome display of life. Tall pillars of stone and coral held up orange streamers that swayed with the currents, reminding Nathan of parades in the summertime. Nebulae of purple and gold expanded and contracted as if possessing a life of their own, and perhaps they did. Fish darted throughout, in galaxies of silver and pink. Along the seafloor, white things scuttled and fed among pillowy swards of green.

"Are those crabs?" Jimmy asked.

"Those are crabs," Mackenzie answered. "Big crabs."

"And they're incredibly delicious," Archie announced from his throne. "The meat is as succulent as… as… well, anything, I suppose."

"How the hell do you know?" Eli asked.

"Well, I've eaten them, obviously. We, I mean. The serpent and I."

As accepting as Nathan could be about their predicament, he found the idea of Archie and the serpent being one and the same absolutely mind-twisting.

"Have you discovered anything about finding the way home?" Leland asked.

Archie became silent then. "Not yet, I'm afraid," he replied. "Oh look… the lava flows!"

The vast garden had ended, replaced with more ominous sights in the distance. Bubbles of fiery orange burped from a concealed fissure as great blue-white plumes of smoke churned and coiled with an intestinal life. Magma flashed to the surface as water underneath heaved up the molten rock, resulting in a series of explosions resembling underwater cannon fire. Bubbles and smoke clouded the waters above it all.

"What's this?" Mackenzie asked.

"Underwater volcano," Archie said. "I've seen several in my time with the serpent. You have no idea how hot the water is issuing from those cracks in the planet's crust."

The conductor sighed then.

"So…" Leland asked. "You've known that you're part of this creature for some time now, Archie?"

"Yes… and… no." he answered, suddenly inspecting his person.

Nathan shared a look with Leland, and they both suspected the same thing. Archie's mind had become more than a touch unstable, perhaps because of his predicament, or simply to better cope with it.

"This is incredible," Mackenzie whispered, his hands planted on either side of a portal, studying the event.

"Isn't it, though?" Archie said and brightened.

"What ocean is this? The Atlantic? The Pacific?"

"I'm sorry, sir. I'm afraid I don't rightly know."

Nathan didn't quite like that. He quickly lost interest in the volcanic show.

Archie and the serpent took them over a world the men had never dreamed existed. Most had never seen an ocean for that matter, and the numerous species of plant and sea life were lost upon them. Only Mackenzie seemed to fully appreciate the wonders of the deep, as he rarely appeared to blink.

Nathan only wished they were headed home.

The oceanic bottom receded then, and the floor tilted at a sharp incline, causing the men to grab onto organic knobs and other solid fixtures offered by the walls.

"What's happening, Archie?" Leland asked.

"We're ascending," the conductor said. "We need to take a breath, it seems."

"The serpent needs air?" Mackenzie asked in a voice of wonder.

"She most certainly does. She's capable of holding her breath for a very long time. A very long time. Tens of minutes upon a full breath. We believe that it might be best to get you to land. Any land. And from there you might best find your way home."

Nathan didn't quite agree with that. In fact, he was growing aware of a subtle tug, like one from a very weak magnet, drawing him towards the rear of the chamber.

"How would we get out of the serpent?" Mackenzie asked.

That befuddled Archie. "Good question, sir. Haven't the foggiest. Seems to me, however, you have two options, and neither one especially pleasant. You may exit through the rear of this chamber, or exit through the front. However, exiting through the front might cause us to… ah… forcefully eject you. If you gather my meaning."

"You mean vomit?"

"Precisely, sir."

"Hold on," Eli said, "so we have to get *thrown up* to leave the front of this thing? That mean we're going to get shit out if we go the other way?"

"Crudely put," Archie said. "But accurate enough."

Eli looked at Leland. "I ain't crawlin' out of some snake's shitty asshole,

Leland. I'll cut my way out before that."

"You'll do nothing of the sort," Leland shot back. "Disregard that last thought of his, Archie."

A pause from the conductor. "I'll try, sir. And I'm glad. Any, ah, cutting, would greatly hurt us. Not to mention allow the water inside. Whereupon you'd surely perish. I'd suggest you focus on whether or not you wish to disembark from the front or the rear."

"I vote for the front, then," Eli said.

"Me too," Gilbert added.

Leland, however, glanced to the rear. Nathan realized then that the gang leader felt that same gentle tug.

"I don't understand any of this," Eli muttered, as wild lassos of light swept over his features. The higher they ascended, the stronger those beams became. Outside, the water gently shifted from blue to green.

"We were walking through a *train* before we got here," Eli stressed. "Now we're caught in the guts of this thing?"

"It's incredible," Mackenzie said.

"It's goddamn insane, is what it is."

Nathan ignored the debate, hearing that deep note stretch overhead, sung by an immense creature. Archie had bent his head back, his expression hidden, but he appeared to be gazing at the portal above him.

"We're almost there," the conductor whispered with a smile. "Once we surface, we'll make for the nearest land. We'll head for the shallows, as I'm not sure how we'll fare on dry land. We don't wish to beach ourselves."

"Land," Mackenzie said. "That could be anywhere."

"And it could be Port Moody," Leland said. "Or nearby."

"It would take a lot of luck to—"

Sunlight streamed in through upper portal membranes, throwing back most of the shadows. Light entered through some of the side portals as well, only briefly, before the rise and fall of the surface obscured the view.

"We've reached the surface," Archie informed them, sounding pleased.

The men crowded the nearest windows.

"Can't see a damn thing," Jimmy said.

"We're floating," Nathan said, "but not quite above the water line."

"Probably only the back is showing above the water line." Mackenzie said. "Like a whale. Or eel."

"Give us a moment," Archie announced. "We'll be taking a breath. Out with the bad air, in with the good, and all that."

"Do you wish to come with us, Archie?" Leland abruptly asked.

Archie didn't think long upon it. "Thank you but no. That's quite all right, sir. I actually enjoy this. When I drift, my… consciousness becomes one with her. I see what she sees, but in a dreamy way, as I mentioned before. In fact, once I've seen you men to safety, or what I hope is safety, I'll probably go right on back to, well, drifting. It's so wonderfully peaceful, you see. And time holds no power. And certainly no meaning. Regardless, I'm fascinated with what I've seen, and genuinely look forward to seeing more. So, once again, thank you for the offer but—"

A shudder went through the great beast then, and the once indifferent but sadly melodious whine became a frightening screech.

It took Nathan a second to realize it was Archie doing the screaming.

Two more shudders passed through the chamber, prompting the men to hug the walls despite the unhealthy rust color. Leland hurried to Archie's side, who paused only to reload his chest before screaming again. The gang leader reached the conductor's shoulder when a mighty force yanked the entire chamber sideways.

The unexpected lurch slammed Nathan against the wall. He collapsed, and cold water immediately soaked his coat and chilled his ass. The others floundered, slipping and sliding as they struggled for firm footing. Men grunted and called out. Another quake rumbled through the chamber, however, heaving them all into unyielding walls.

Archie screamed again.

"What is it, Archie?" Leland yelled, grabbing the conductor's shoulder. "What is it?"

But Archie only continued to shriek, great wheezy peals of pain that might've frayed his capacity for speech.

"Look," a horrified Jimmy said. "Out the window."

Nathan did and balked.

Against the serpent's membrane, beads of water had turned and foamed into a bright spawny red.

25

"What's going on?" Leland shouted over the cacophony erupting from Archie and the great serpent.

Nathan struggled to see outside, but couldn't see past the bloody water smearing the membrane. The serpent's mass dipped underneath the waves, clearing the gore off, but only for a second as fresh color sprayed the portal. A mighty force hauled the entire chamber sideways, pushing waves up and over the membranes and washing away the blood. Nathan leaned forward, discovering he had greater balance in doing so, and strained to see outside. Beyond the watery smears was a violent plane of blue, where a great black mass bobbed, and long heavy lines extended from its side and stretched towards the crippled serpent.

Then the mass was gone in a cleansing wave, and the whole of the interior tipped again. The men yelled out before crashing into walls in a sharp list. Shorty Charlie Williams tipped forward, mashing his face against the rust-colored confines in a grunt of pain and a spurt of red. Gilbert and Eli were on their backs, thrashing like a couple of pond trout feeling the heat of a frying pan. The others were behind Nathan, but he could hear Jimmy and Mackenzie fighting to steady themselves.

"What's happening out there?" Leland yelled, holding onto the throne.

Archie was no longer screaming.

"I can't see," Nathan shouted back. "I think there's a ship out there."

"A ship?"

The floor leveled out and Nathan sprang to the portal, bracing himself for any other surprising rolls. Water dribbled in thick rivulets over the membrane, distorting the outside world. There was a powerful undulation then, from the struggling serpent itself. The force drove Nathan to his knees while his face pitched into the portal. A spasmodic shiver ripped through the entire length of the room, further impeding the men. Darkness doused light, only to be beaten back again. Nathan swore, grabbed onto meaty protrusions on either side of his window, and pulled his face to the transparent membrane.

There *was* a ship out there, disappearing at times behind the onrush of water.

"I can see it," Gilbert yelled as he stuck his face up to a portal—a split second before the serpent shook itself and plastered the gun runner against the window's firm surface. He slumped to the floor, stunned by the blow.

"Could be a whaler," Jimmy suggested while the floor steadied itself somewhat.

"We're not in a whale," Leland yelled back.

"Is it a whaler?" Jimmy asked.

"Can't rightly see what it is," Nathan replied.

Mackenzie staggered to a portal and gazed outside. "It looks like a whaler. Three masts. Black sails."

That struck Nathan as odd, but he soon saw that Mackenzie was right. The sails fluttered above the ship, as black as pitch and matching the hull. The entire vessel rocked and rolled upon the waves, glimpsed just above the surging waterline slapping against the serpent. There were at least four lines running from the whaler, connecting ship to serpent. Lengthy strands that were perhaps chains, ending at points in the great beast's hide.

"Black sails?" Jimmy asked.

"What manner of ship is that?" Leland added.

But no one answered him.

The four lines seemed strange to Nathan and he couldn't understand why. No sooner did the thought enter his head when the whaler fired a dark bolt of lightning in their direction. Nathan scowled in puzzlement, a split second before a harpoon punched a hole through the serpent's side in a startling explosion of meat and scarlet streamers.

Into the very chamber the men occupied.

"*Goddamn!*" Eli exclaimed, diving for the floor even though the weapon was feet above his head.

Upon the harpoon's impact, Archie convulsed in his throne as if stabbed through the guts. Ichor bubbled and spilled from his mouth.

Nathan threw himself to one side and stared at the weapon impaling the great beast. The spear was a long narrow shaft, wickedly barbed, and dripping dark matter. As the men gazed upon it, the weapon's head split open like a bare umbrella, into five separate lengths of metal. A tremendous force jerked the harpoon back, and those lengths sank deep into the serpent's flesh.

The whaler then began to pull.

The men again stumbled about, off-balance by the whaler's irresistible force. A mournful groan erupted throughout the chamber, from the wounded serpent itself, and the very sound of it wore on Nathan's heart.

"We're being towed!" Jimmy shouted.

"Back to the whaler," Mackenzie added.

"That's a good thing, then," Eli said.

A flow of bloody matter poured into the chamber from that grievous wound in the serpent's side, mixing with the water at their ankles. The sight caused Nathan to doubt the goodness of it all. Even poor old Archie had slumped forward, as if Eli had once again smacked the conductor's head.

"Is he dead?" Nathan asked Leland, clinging to the throne.

The gang leader appeared lost for a second, before remembering who and where he was. He examined the unconscious conductor. Jimmy moved closer and did the same.

"I don't know," Leland reported. He actually cracked open one of the conductor's eyes with a thumb. "I don't think so." He leaned towards Archie's face, cheek to mouth, searching for a breath.

"What's the whaler doing?" Jimmy asked, as the harpoon lines pulled the beast sideways across the waters.

Nathan checked on the vessel. Waves lapped over the portal, obscuring his view, but he caught glimpses of the ship, much closer and stark against the blue backdrop of the sky. Though he knew about whaling ships, he was far from being an expert on them. The rigging appeared to be a neat webbing spread between the main masts, but the hull's solid black rendered the ship forbidding. Menacing.

"Have no fear, boys," Eli crowed. "That whaler will pull this goddamn worm up to her side and pitch into her. Don't worry about crawling out of this thing's asshole because they'll cut open her guts. All we'll have to do is climb on out."

"That so, Eli?" Gilbert asked, soaked from splashing around in morbid red waters.

"That's so. You just wait. Pull your ass up out of that slop, Gilbert. Jesus Christ. You look like the world's bloodiest piece of shit."

"I feel like the world's bloodiest piece of shit."

"Just don't go acting like it, is all," Eli told him and looked to the ceiling.

"*Whalers*. Saved by whalers. God*damn*. Ain't that a yank on the weasel? Hey, Leland! When we get out of this thing, you want to try being a pirate? Huh? How's that sound? I bet some of them boys up there have got some dollars on them."

"They might be Americans," Leland said, looking up from Archie's unmoving face. "Or British."

"I don't care," Eli said as if he were talking to a child. "Yanks or fuckin' otherwise. They all got cash. Hell, I prefer an American dollar anyway if'n I have to head south. Just in case."

"Regardless," Leland said, focusing on the gun runner. "You'll do nothing of the sort. If those men help us get back to the mainland, that'll be reward enough."

"Awww *Leland*."

The ship loomed closer, rising and falling upon the waves, though as the serpent drew closer, the less the waves obscured Nathan's vision.

It was a huge vessel, bigger than he'd expected.

The water fell away from the portal, providing a clearer view of figures moving along the railing high above. *Sailors*, Nathan initially thought, but then he got an even better look.

And his guts clenched into an icy knot.

The figures gathered at the ship's railing were indeed sailors, but their three and four limbed torsos didn't belong to any human being. Their oddly shaped heads, like square melons, possessed eyes where the chin would be, and the mouth…

God Almighty.

The mouths were vertical cuts that chittered and gnashed in excited conversation. Fangs and nests of unnaturally long snake tongues flickered and darted forward.

Sailors, perhaps, but not men.

And what was not quite as frightening but equally disturbing was that the crew, jostling and leaning over their ship's sides, wore sailors' *clothing*. Some wore collared shirts that were opened and fluttering in a wind. Others wore dashing handkerchiefs about their necks. Some of the sailors were bare-chested, showing off torsos as white as the underbelly of an eel.

A pole lifted above the animated line then, the end crowned with a number of hooks. Other implements of butchery came into view, a gleaming array of spears, barbs, and blades, all for stabbing, hooking, and cutting the great serpent up.

"The hell is that?" Mackenzie muttered nearby, also absorbed in the ghastly sight of the assembled sailors.

The hull loomed, a black embankment of tightly fitted ribs that didn't look like wood at all, but rather a glossy material that might've been bone. Then the light faltered and grew dim as the serpent was pulled hard to one side. Again the interior lurched.

"We're going to hit," Nathan said and braced himself. *"We're going to hit it!"*

The serpent hit the whaler broadside in a brazen clap of iron-tough flesh and unyielding hull. Nathan stayed upright, but some of the others slipped in the bloody waters. The great beast wailed one final time before going quiet. A new sound could be heard, as if from a great distance, an angry whining that might've been from a cloud of mosquitoes. Nathan didn't have time to think about it, however, as the floor jerked upwards in an unexpected heave. Nathan pitched face-first into the wall, smashing his right cheek against muscle, and ended up on the floor. A mouthful of bloody water attempted to choke him and left him sputtering.

Old Archie released a pained moan, as Leland started shouting.

"Grab onto something, grab anything!"

Nathan tried grabbing anything but raked only the serpent's inner walls, leaving his fingertips buzzing with pain. The water drained away as the serpent's bulk was hoisted further up alongside the whaler. Nathan slid past the throne and slumped over Archie, past Leland and Jimmy clutching onto the sides. Mackenzie flashed by and then Nathan was sliding deeper into the serpent's innards, towards the rear of the cavernous beast. The walls became a fluted tunnel of light and shadow, where the day glared through numerous membranes as if the chamber had been riddled with cannon fire.

Nathan noticed the oval doorway a second before his feet slammed into the unyielding surface with a muted *gong*. The landing sent a shiver of pain up his legs, and he rolled to the side, searching for a handle. Their rifles littered the floor, released by the men when the world had tilted.

"Coming through," Eli Gallant shouted as he slid to a stop, landing in a half crouch with his shoulder to the door. "Christ Almighty, floor's slipperier than a fish's shithole."

Nathan ignored him as he checked on the others, all further up the incline. They were clinging to unseen protrusions, looking about a chamber and waiting for whatever came next.

They didn't wait for long.

Chopping. Stabbing. A ravenous melody of meat being hacked into, swelling into a frenzied clamor. The walls shuddered overhead as those alien whalers chopped away at the serpent's flesh.

"We'll be free in a few seconds, boys," Eli yelled out, delighted with the turn of good fortune.

"I don't think so," Nathan told him.

Eli fixed him with a questioning look.

"That's not men out there."

"What?"

"You heard me. They're not men."

"What's that you say, Nathan?" Leland asked from above.

"He said they're not men," Mackenzie said. "And they're *not*. I got a look at them. They're something else entirely. Sure as hell not people, I can guarantee you that."

"We gotta get moving, Leland," Nathan said. "Before those things cut their way through."

No sooner did the words leave him when something punched its way through the inner wall of the serpent. The chopping grew, sounding like a line of railway workers being whipped into a killer pace, driving home spike after spike.

"Archie?" Leland said, holding onto the throne's base.

Archie didn't answer. Showed no sign of having heard.

More spear points perforated the ceiling, withdrawing only to penetrate deeper. Bits of metal flashed as tips and blades worked themselves into the meat and muscle of the serpent.

"Leland, come on," Nathan shouted. "He's dead. Let him go."

The gang leader drew back, scrutinizing the conductor, whose frame rattled with every weapon beating into the serpent's body.

Leland let go and slid downwards.

"Wait," Eli yelled with a glare. "The rest of you hold on."

"The hell for?" Nathan asked as Leland slid to a hard stop beside them.

Eli pointed and Nathan immediately understood. He pushed Leland aside to get a better look at the skewed floor beneath their feet, now at a sharp angle.

The chamber narrowed at the last few feet, leading, *ending* in the door deeply embedded in a surrounding musculature. There was a bony projection that resembled a wheel, and Eli shooed the two others away a heartbeat before he grabbed it.

He pulled with mighty effort… and failed.

Eli unleashed a venomous glare at the nearby men. *"Get your fuckin' feet off the door!"*

The man was right. Nathan and Leland dug their fingers and heels into the walls, lifting themselves off the barrier. Eli tried again, his grunts loud but not enough to drown out the chopping and stabbing overhead.

"Hurry up down there," Mackenzie shouted in a worried tone. "They're coming through."

"Shoot them if you have to," Leland yelled back.

"I can hear them," Gilbert cried out. "Oh shit, Leland! *I can hear them!*"

No sooner did Gilbert say the words when the butchery overhead stopped for long considering seconds. Nathan knew the reason why. The alien whalers had heard *them* as well.

"Get that door open, Eli," Nathan said, feeling that familiar pang of anxiety swelling in his chest while his lower legs buzzed with energy.

Eli groaned loudly in reply, pulling then pushing upon that bony wheel, only to pull again.

"C'mon you sack of shit," Nathan urged as, overhead, the hacking resumed with renewed vigor. *"C'mon!"*

"I'm *tryin'*," Eli blurted back before, with an exhausted gasp, releasing his grip.

"Get up here," Nathan said and slid down as Eli got out of the way the best he could. Nathan grabbed the wheel, feeling the smooth, rounded surface, and pulled with his arms and back.

Nothing.

A huge spear broke through the wall overhead in a spurt of gore. The blade wrenched one way and then the other, widening the incision before withdrawing. Alien voices sounded through the perforations above, their excitement needing no translation.

"Hurry *up!*" Gilbert shouted, fidgeting from where he held on.

Nathan pulled again without success, as if the door was nailed into the floor. The edges looked flush with the surrounding musculature.

A pair of broadswords smashed through the serpent's side in a splash of blood and water. Metal groaned, and the sound of escaping steam filled the chamber as a much wider blade of light penetrated the interior.

A round of frightening cheers went up from the whalers.

"Hurry, Nathan," Leland urged.

Nathan filled his lungs, gripped the wheel, and dug his feet in at the edges, free from what he thought might be the hinges. Once his footing was secured, he bent over and tried the wheel once again.

The whalers continued to cut through the layers of fat and muscle tissue, eager to discover what was making those curious sounds inside the great serpent. Dark matter rained down, spattering the men. The serpent's body quivered and swayed against the vessel's floating mass but its eerie yet peaceful voice was long gone. Nathan bent his knees and remembered a time years ago when he and his father struggled with a stump that plagued the development of their cornfield.

"Take a breath," his father told him, their shoulders brushing, their shirts soaked with sweat. "Take a breath and on the count of three. I'm helping you, here, not you helping me."

The sun peeked around his father's profile as he smiled at him, just before his expression became a stern thing.

Nathan took a breath and heaved.

The door snapped open at an angle, flinging into Leland. The gang leader immediately held onto the barrier while Nathan peered inside, seeing only the familiar walls of the serpent's digestive tract, walls that faded into a vat of darkness.

"Go!" Nathan said, grabbing Eli by the arm.

The gun runner needed no further encouragement. He grabbed for a nearby rifle and plunged through, not knowing what lay beyond. Eli vanished into the blackness beyond with a peal of evil glee. Only the foul smell of his saturated winter duster remained.

"Door's open!" Nathan yelled at the others while grabbing for a rifle. "You go on, Leland."

Leland glanced up and hurried around the door. He dropped below as the others slid down the sharp incline.

Mackenzie went through, followed by Jimmy Norquay. Shorty barely fit and Gilbert glanced back before committing.

Nathan did the same.

A great sheet of sunlight blazed through a rip in the serpent's side, some fifteen feet beyond Archie, who drooped from his throne like some off-kilter pendulum frozen in mid-tick. A multitude of hooked poles latched onto the wet edges of the opening and widened the horrific gash even further. Flesh snapped and tore, resulting in a morbid drizzle. That mosquito whine reached a fevered pitched, and a misshapen hand, swollen and long of finger, reached inside and dug into the soft sides. A second hand followed, one possessing even longer fingers as well as a gruesome assortment of claws that were pearly white in the sunshine.

No such appendage belonged to a living, breathing person.

But the face that followed didn't belong to a person.

With a whimper, Gilbert turned and bolted through the open door, leaving Nathan behind.

That sound whipped the whaler creature's head around, and eyes on either side of a vertical mouth locked onto Nathan, who stared back at the abomination. More of those clawed hook hands appeared, and the daylight leaking into the great serpent darkened with a collection of shadows and torsos. The whaler's mouth opened, and a nest of whip-thin flagella waved madly. The whaler screamed—or Nathan thought it screamed—and a serrated spear was handed to him through the opening.

Nathan didn't wait around. He rushed through the portal and yanked it closed with a slam.

A second before the spear smashed into the barrier.

26

The dark engulfed Nathan, and for seconds, his attention was centered on the ceiling where he'd closed the door. He wondered whether the alien whaler would pursue them. He readied his Colt and pointed the weapon at the ceiling.

He waited, tensed, shaking from the recent rush of activity and trying hard to steady himself.

Nothing.

In time, he became aware of a panting, and realized it was his own. He eased off on the trigger and eventually lowered the gun. He rose and the murky fluid soaked into his clothes pattered onto dry ground. Nathan backed away, mindful of the unseen door, and wondered what might be happening beyond it, if those monstrous whalers had taken Archie or were somehow gathering their numbers, forming up a hunting party of sorts.

He wouldn't wait any longer to find out.

Turning around, he stopped and tried to listen to the still air around him. His breathing slowed but water continued to slap the dry floor below him.

That last thought stayed with him.

Nathan dropped to a knee and touched rock, or what felt like rock, and the moist grit covering it. He rubbed his fingertips together, puzzling over the wetness before staring ahead into a starless night.

"Gilbert?" Nathan finally whispered and waited for a reply. "You there?"

No answer.

Nathan held his peace for a moment longer before glancing left and right. He reached out for the wall.

No wall.

On either side.

Just empty space, even ahead of him, and not a sound to be heard.

"The hell is going on…" Nathan whispered. "Gilbert? Leland?"

Again, no reply. He took off his father's hat and gave it a shake, freeing the last few drops clinging to the material. He then ran a hand over his duster, grimacing at the feel of his soaked clothing underneath. He'd need a fire to dry out, that was for certain. That got him moving, shuffling forward, testing each tentative step as if inching his way across uncertain ice. The ground seemed solid enough, however, but he took his time, not wanting to march off a cliff or fall victim to an unseen pitfall. He paused several times, listening to the dark, wondering where the hell the others had gone, or if they were even still alive.

The air tasted dry, a glaring contrast to what'd he been breathing in a few minutes earlier, and the dark didn't relent, nor did his eyes adjust to that absolute pitch.

Footfalls and the squishing of saturated boots and socks were his only companions as he forged ahead, rifle lowered but ready. He glanced over his shoulder, expecting any number of those whaler weapons to start hammering upon the door behind him. No such thing happened, however. He didn't call out anymore, for fear of giving away his location if the others had been captured or killed. Then he wondered if he was walking towards the same fate.

What did they do? Nathan thought, slinking along in the dark. *And what happened to them… because of what they did or didn't do?*

Boot heels clicking, he trudged on, stopping every now and again and reaching out for a wall, touching only air. He actually extended his entire arm and felt nothing. He felt very much alone at that point, but not lost. Not in the least. As long as he could put one foot down, in front of the other, he figured he was walking towards *something*.

The notion that he was no longer in the belly of a sea serpent took root in his mind.

A pinpoint of twilight caught his attention, a knot of non-dark far off in the distance. Nathan stopped and listened, noting that he wasn't dripping so much anymore, and that the air had become much warmer and drier. That gloomy, not-quite light grew increasingly more distinct as he drew closer, and he hefted his rifle to his shoulder just in case.

Voices stopped him in his tracks.

"So what do we do now, Leland?"

Eli Gallant.

No mistaking that man's long tongue, and Nathan even caught the sound of Leland Baxter's reply, but failed to hear the exact words. Knowing Leland's temperament, however, he was probably asking if Eli understood the meaning of being quiet, or something of the like.

Nathan started running.

"*I'm here,*" he yelled. "I'm on my way out!"

The voices ceased.

Nathan continued racing until the ground became more uneven. His boots hooked in a rocky protrusion and he tumbled. The opening ahead was no longer a neat pinhole, but rather a crooked gash, with a figure standing before it.

"It's me!" Nathan shouted again while rising.

"It's Nathan," Leland informed the others. More figures crowded in, dimming the light even more.

Nathan hurried forward, feeling the land gently rise beneath his feet. In time, he slowed down, seeing the familiar outlines of his fellow gang members. It remained twilight, but there was a hitch that Nathan couldn't identify just yet.

"I see him," Leland said.

"Hell, ain't no need to see him," Eli grumped. "I can smell the shit stain."

Nathan let that one go, being too glad to see his outlaw companions.

"Hello, boys," he said with a relieved smile. "Don't think I've ever been so glad to see your ugly faces."

That was met with a resounding silence.

"That was only a joke," Nathan explained, close enough to see their grim expressions. "Hell, why didn't you wait for me?"

"Wait for you?" Eli grumbled with an air of incredulity. "The hell you talking about, Rhodes?"

Nathan stopped not five feet away from the opening—a cavern mouth, which was no taller than his shoulders, and just a bit wider.

"Why didn't you wait for me?" Nathan repeated, giving back as good as he got. "What part of that did you not understand, peckerhead?"

"Watch your mouth, Rhodes," Eli said with a narrow-eyed glare. "'Cause let me tell you something, you're about as funny as a stitched-up asshole."

"Bet you know all about them."

Leland held up a hand, calling for a truce. "What do you mean, Nathan? Exactly?"

"Took me ten minutes at least to find you sonsabitches," Nathan said in an offended tone. "Those things might've come straight through the door and—"

Leland held up his hand again. "Ten minutes, you say?"

"At least."

"From the time we left you?"

Nathan studied the gang leader's face, then the wary looks of the others. "What?" he finally asked.

Mackenzie stood just behind Leland. "We only just got here."

"What?"

"Only just."

Nathan was speechless for a second. "That's not right. How the hell could you just get here? I was walking in that tunnel for at least ten minutes. Heading towards this." He indicated the tunnel opening.

"We all came through no more than thirty seconds ago," Mackenzie said with this usual scholarly patience. "Been standing here ever since."

"Figured you were right behind," Leland added, "but we didn't hear anything from inside the tunnel. So, we were going to form up a defensive line in case you were being pursued when you came out."

"Well, why didn't you?" Nathan asked, still sore about being left behind. "Form up that defensive line."

"We were distracted," Leland said, and pointed. "By the sky."

"And the sand," Jimmy Norquay threw in.

"The what?"

"Get out of the way, boys," Leland said before removing himself from the tunnel mouth.

Nathan saw then, and the sight left him thunderstruck.

The sky was an apocalyptic shade of sundown, a deep velvet purple that encompassed the entirety of the heavens, and not just an evening coloring of an errant cloud. It was purple, with distinct, almost fibrous lines of orange and pink arched across that great expanse as if unraveling. Stars twinkled throughout and that seemed well enough, but some of the stars were overly large, disturbingly so, in fact. There was a horizon beneath it all, as black as the whaler's hull that had captured and killed the great serpent, but not a shimmer of water in sight. In fact, the air was bone-dry and still, and carried not a sound except the thumping of Nathan's own racing heart.

Unblinking, he stooped to clear the tunnel opening, his mouth hanging open as he took in the scope of the scene before him. His feet sank into black sand that sparkled in places as if sprinkled with ice. The sand stretched out before him in all directions, meeting the heavens in a distant but easily discernable horizon. He checked on the tunnel behind him and saw how it was located in the face of a mound.

"My Lord," he whispered, once again transfixed by the sky.

"No moon, either," Mackenzie pointed out. "Nothing."

"So what does that mean?" Eli asked.

"I don't know," Mackenzie admitted with a shrug, studying all that moody color overhead.

"Maybe we got here just after sunset?" Jimmy suggested.

"Maybe we're on that beach?" Leland added.

Word of the beach broke Nathan's wonder-induced paralysis. He took it upon himself to trudge up the side of the mound, climbing to the top. Once there, he steadied himself and gazed out over the heads of his fellow outlaws, looking one way and then the other, ignoring their upraised faces.

"I don't see a damn thing," Nathan declared. "Except that black crest of hills or mountains or whatever the hell it is on the horizon. Sure as hell ain't no water in sight. Not even a shimmer."

"That means no beach, then," Leland said.

"One thing's for certain," Nathan said. "We're not in the Rockies anymore."

"We haven't been in the Rockies for the last hour or so," Eli scoffed, "in case you forgot the train we were on, on a set of tracks where the goddamn ground was missing."

"Or the sea," Mackenzie added as an afterthought.

"I know one thing, we're in a goddamn steam bath," Eli grumped, opening his winter duster and plucking at the upper buttons of his inner shirt. "This ain't natural."

Mackenzie dropped to a knee and placed a hand to the ground. "It's the sand. Hot to the touch. Not burning, but close."

"Where in the world do we have sand hot to the touch?" Leland asked. "Black sand?"

No one answered.

"And purple skies," Mackenzie said with a nod. "Ain't never seen a purple as deep and fine as that. No place on God's green earth has a sky like that. Least, not that I know of. But I know someone who does… or who has an idea."

"Who?" Leland asked.

"Him." Mackenzie gestured at Nathan, still standing upon the mound.

"Him?" Eli snorted. "And here I thought you were the smart one, Mack."

"Say what you will, but Nathan has an idea of where we are. He already said it once, back when we were riding the serpent."

"So what is it?" Leland asked.

"Go on, Nathan," Mackenzie said. "Tell them what you said. What you told me. Back when we were underwater there. When Leland warned us not to lose control else he'd put a bullet in us."

That earned a frown from the gang leader.

Nathan sighed and rubbed at his own overheating neck. "I said… I said we'd gone down a rabbit hole."

Against the black sands and purple skies, no one said a word.

Then, Leland spoke. "What?"

"A rabbit hole," Nathan said.

"You actually said wet rabbit hole," Mackenzie reminded him.

"I know what I said," Nathan snapped. "That was because we were under water. That's all. Nothing more. But… we've gone down a rabbit hole. A place that leads from one place to another."

"In this case," Mackenzie interjected, "one world to another. Or many worlds."

The men traded looks, mesmerized by the revelation.

"How do you know this?" Leland asked. "This rabbit hole?"

"My mother," Nathan replied. "She used to read to me. Bedtime stories. Where people go from one world to the next, through holes in the ground. Or other such things. They leave their own world and walk into another. Weird places, sometimes dangerous, sometimes not, but always different from where they left. Where people aren't really people at all, but maybe… talking animals. Or, Jesus, I don't know, people who sound like people, I mean talk like us, but they know different things. Different ways of doing things."

"Jesus Christ," Eli scoffed under his breath, but Leland put a stop to anything more with one stern look and a raised finger of warning.

"Continue, Nathan," Leland said.

"That's it. I don't know anything more. I mean. It was just a bedtime story. Something to put me to sleep. That was it."

"That's probably the best possible explanation we have right now," Mackenzie said. "All things considered. We've gone down a rabbit hole, or in this case, climbed aboard a ghost train that's been missing for years. The Majestic 311. The very train that disappeared upon entering the Spirals. The one we mistook for the 5409. Maybe… just maybe…that train, for whatever reason, went through a rabbit hole—that was the tunnels—and disappeared. And now it's come back, just in time for us to climb aboard, fumble about searching for a payroll, whereupon it…" Mackenzie faltered, attempting to make sense of his own speculation, "…traveled *back* into the rabbit hole, or some other tunnel. Or portal. Or opening. Taking us with it. Completely unawares."

The scholarly outlaw waved at the surrounding landscape. "To this place. And the ocean before it, and the… place where the train traveled upon steel rails but nothing but empty air beneath that. Places no mortal man has witnessed."

For once, Eli Gallant didn't say the word horseshit. Or goddamn.

"How does the bedtime story end, Nathan?" a surprisingly reserved Shorty Charlie Williams quietly asked, holding his shotgun in the crook of an arm.

"I don't remember."

"Doesn't matter," Mackenzie said. "Not really. The story's only an analogy. To make our present situation easier to understand."

"The fuck's that mean?" Eli asked.

"What?"

"An *analogy.*"

"I just said, something to make our present situation easier to understand."

"Well, why didn't you say that?" Eli complained. "Instead of making my head hurt, you fucking dandy. I swear, I'll shoot you yet for using them big educated words."

"All right," Leland said. He swallowed thickly. "So if what you say is… true. If we have gone down a rabbit hole, or whatever, aboard a train…"

"The 311," Mackenzie clarified.

"…then where are we going?" Leland questioned. "For how long? And will we ever return to the Rockies? I have matters to attend to back in our world. Matters of great importance. Urgent, even."

Mackenzie shook his head. "All that, that reality—our *world*— is behind us somewhere, Leland. And the only way I know of reaching it is by marching straight back through that tunnel. Back into the belly of the great serpent, where Archie Willmoore is no longer a man even though he called himself a conductor. Where the passengers intended to do us harm, and we stood upon a railcar that rode upon air. Considering all that, I'd strongly suggest you accept what this place is. Until further notice."

Nathan came down from the mound. "Archie said that we were part of the serpent. That the *train* was part of the serpent. What does that mean. For us?"

Mackenzie considered that. "*He* was part of the serpent. About the train? I don't know. I mean, we *were* on the train. We walked into the serpent's belly after going through a passenger car door. And we got back out. We're not underwater anymore. Not in the serpent's belly. We're someplace entirely different, and yet… I suspect, somehow, yes, we're *still* aboard the 311."

On impulse, Nathan turned and stuck his head into the tunnel mouth. He walked inside a few steps, before a low-hanging mantle of rock swept his father's hat off his head and onto his back. Nathan took it off and held it while he skirted a few more paces forward. He soon discovered that the tunnel was narrowing instead of widening.

Before coming to a dead end.

"See anything, Nathan?" Leland called.

Nathan didn't answer.

"You all right in there?" the gang leader asked.

No, Nathan thought. *I most certainly am* not *all right. I'm as far from being all right as anyone can expect.* He suddenly felt a very long way from home, from anything remotely as comforting as his own bedroom way back in his parents' house.

But what he told Leland was, "The tunnel's gone."

"What's that?"

"You heard me, Leland. The tunnel's gone. Come see for yourself."

He did. They all did, squeezing inside, each having a go at prodding the rocky ending to a corridor nowhere near the length that Nathan had passed through. Once they'd confirmed that, yes indeed, the door they'd dropped through was no longer there, they'd returned to the sandy desert and stood in shock, gawking at the unchanged sky. Their winter clothing, soaked and dripping, weighed heavily upon their shoulders, and the kiln-like heat pressed down upon them with equal force.

"We're fucked," Jimmy Norquay said quietly.

No one argued that assessment. Not even Eli Gallant.

Yet somewhere, at the back of Nathan's mind and just above the base of his skull, underneath bedrock layers of silence, he thought, just for a second, he heard the constant, pulsing *chump chump chump* of a train…

27

"All right," Nathan said, having his fill of the moody silence. "We can't go back that way. But that doesn't matter. If the way is gone, that means those whalers can't come after us. So, look…" he waved at the horizon. "We got all this open space. All we need to do is decide on a direction and get walking. If we opened a door to get here, maybe all we have to do is open another door to leave."

That idea was met with resounding silence.

Mackenzie took off his hat, twisted up the felt, and wrung out water. "Nate's got a good idea there. We can't stay here. Nothing here, anyway. The 311 disappeared years ago only to come back right when we showed up. Maybe… maybe the train came back more often than that. Maybe we just have to get back on a part of the train, at such a time when we can get off. When it's back in our world."

"So you think we can get back?" a hopeful Leland asked for them all.

"After all this? Possibly. One thing's clear to me, we won't get back if we stay here. As Nate said, maybe all we have to do is open another door."

"That's just a guess."

"That's the best I got right now."

That quieted the whole bunch.

"The caboose," Leland finally said. "At least that part hasn't changed. We get to the caboose."

Nathan supposed that part of the plan hadn't changed at all. Not yet, anyway. But what concerned him more was the slight trembling to Leland's once rock-solid voice, a barely audible waver that suggested this whole nightmare had affected the gang leader to his core.

Perhaps even his mind.

Leland Baxter was the glue that had held the gang together. The authority within their lawless ranks. Nathan didn't want to think what might happen if Leland's confidence started to crumble.

Jimmy Norquay threw off his winter duster, distracting the men from the purple skies overhead and the black, starry sand underfoot.

"The hell you doin'?" Eli asked.

"What's it look like?" Jimmy said as he unbuckled his belt and pulled up the tails of his doubled-up shirts.

"Looks like you're strippin'."

Jimmy didn't bother commenting.

"Goddammit, Leland," Eli complained. "Tell your henchman to keep his fuckin' clothes on."

"In this heat?" Leland asked, his features just barely visible in the awesome twilight. As answer to his own question, he shrugged off his coat and went to work upon his wet clothes underneath.

Eli looked away in annoyed disgust. "Knew there was something off about all of you. Not you, Gilbert, so keep fuckin' quiet."

"We start walking," Leland explained as he undid his belt buckle. "I don't care which way you all want to go. But anywhere's better than here. I don't know if the sun's going down or coming up, but if it's this warm now, we'll fry when it's daylight."

Nathan couldn't argue that bit of logic, so he got to removing his winter gear as well. He stripped off his duster, two shirts, two undershirts, and two pairs of rough cotton pants. The material around his knee was filthy with dried blood, from where he'd taken the cut from the knife-wielding arm. Just seeing the wound made him aware of the dull ache he'd been carrying around there. He kicked off his boots to remove his pants, but wasn't sure what to do with the doubled-up stockings. A quick glance around informed him to take those off as well. Once done, the sand was uncomfortably hot under his bare soles, so he hip-hopped from one spot to the other.

"Like I'm on a frying pan here," Nathan said, taking the burn.

"Sand's like coal just coming to life," Mackenzie noted, already stripped down to his red long johns.

"Couldn't agree more," Nathan said. He pinched at his own cotton unmentionables, pulling the white material off his chest. They all stood around in their winter undergarments, and Nathan grimaced upon seeing Eli stripped down to his dirty white drawers, but with half of the exit hatch in the rear unbuttoned and hanging, exposing one shadowed ass cheek.

"Cover yourself up, Eli," Nathan grumped. "God Almighty, no one needs to see that."

"Then quit staring at it," Eli said and, with deliberate slowness, fastened up his back flap.

"All I need is to see your ass crack in my sleep."

"Stop talkin' about my ass, willya? I know how sweet lookin' it is. The ladies tell me all the time. 'That's a damn sweet ass you got there, Eli,' they say. 'Damn sweet ass'. 'I feel a touch jealous of how sweet that ass of yours is'. Women have been pinching my ass since I don't know when. I might not have the goods up top, but goddamnit my ass is damn near perfect."

"It's true," Gilbert supplied as an afterthought, already down to his own gray underbits, and opening his shirt to his navel, revealing patchy chest moss. "They say that."

"Gilbert," Nathan said, "does Eli pay you to back him up like you do?"

"Nope."

"Then maybe he should. 'Cause you do a damn fine job for nothing."

"He does," Mackenzie agreed.

The seven train robbers stood about in their soaked unmentionables.

"Hell with this," Eli said and stripped that final bit of clothing off as well.

The others reluctantly did the same, and soon the seven stood with their arms full of about thirty pounds of wet clothing and gear. Bandoliers were slung over naked shoulders, while belts and gun holsters hung off bare hips.

"Christ," someone muttered. "What a sight we are."

"I feel better already," Eli announced, taking a deep breath and filling his sinewy chest. "Everything's feeling free-like."

"Which way we going, Leland?" Nathan asked, ignoring the gun runner holding his gear at waist level. They all did so, carrying their possessions in untidy clumps. They balanced their rifles across the top of their clothing, along with their boots. At least with his clothes off, the heat was tolerable.

"That way, I think." Leland pointed toward a craggy line where purple sky met black earth. "You all fine with that?"

They were.

Nathan noticed that the direction Leland pointed in seemed to be in line with the tunnel exit. "Any reason you chose that way, Leland?"

The gang leader thought about it. "No."

"No?"

"The man said no, Jesus Christ," Eli said.

"Because," Nathan stated in a voice loud enough to drown out Eli's. "That direction seems to be in line with the tunnel here. Or what was the tunnel. And, if we're still on the train, and we're making a straight line, it would go to the door of the next rail car."

Leland's shadowed face crunched up at that.

"Interesting find there, Nate," Mackenzie said. "I was thinking about that way myself before Leland even mentioned it."

"So did I," Jimmy said.

"I was thinking it," Gilbert admitted.

Shorty Charlie Williams held his peace, as did Eli.

"I was feeling a tug," Nathan finally revealed, "for that direction myself."

"That way it is, then," Leland said and started walking.

The others followed in a loose clump, as disheveled as the clothes they carried.

Shorty Charlie Williams, as so often as before, was the last to follow. He stood for a few seconds, taking in that vast royal hue of the sky with all its trappings. He turned one way, then the other, holding his gear before him like a tub of freshly laundered clothing.

"Pretty," he murmured, struck by the beauty of it all.

Then he, too, got to walking.

*

Under purple skies where cloudy streamers stretched to the point of fraying, the seven men marched. The black sand became tolerable underfoot, and Nathan wondered how the ground could maintain such a heat without a sun. That little mystery picked at his mind every now and again, distracting him from the growing ache of his arms, and the disturbing events ever since they'd boarded the Majestic. Memories of the passengers scrabbling over the seats and ceiling tormented him. The knife-wielding arms. The nightmarish faces belonging to the whalers. Even poor old Archie, made part of the great serpent, bothered Nathan more than he cared to admit. Whenever those pictures threatened to overwhelm him, he squinted and dug his feet a little deeper into that hot sand—just to get his mind back on track.

"Where's the sun?" Gilbert asked. "Where's the goddamn sun? How long we been walking?"

"About an hour," Mackenzie answered.

"An hour."

"About that."

"And the sun ain't rose or set yet," Eli said. "Goddamn if that ain't queer."

"No more queer than being in the belly of an honest-to-God sea serpent," Jimmy Norquay rumbled.

"And all them passenger folk," Gilbert added.

"And all them passenger folk," Jimmy agreed. "Compared to that, all this is pretty damn peaceful."

Their feet shuffled through the hot sand, the grit caked to their soles sloughing off as it dried.

"In the belly of a sea serpent," Leland Baxter said with a hint of wonder.

"Wasn't that something?" Jimmy said.

"I'm thinking about Archie," Mackenzie said. "How he came to be like that."

"Didn't seem to bother him."

"It did at first, when he saw that the serpent had… absorbed him."

"That was disturbing," Leland said. "As if he was… awakening. From a dream. But once he was aware, he eventually settled down. Damn if I'll be thinking about that in my sleep."

"I'll be thinking about them whaler things," Gilbert said. "Those bloodsabitches made me shiver, I ain't too proud to say."

They gave Nathan a shiver as well, especially those weird vertical mouths.

"They didn't speak English," Nathan remarked.

"They were monsters," Gilbert said. "Monsters don't speak English."

That quieted the bunch.

They continued shuffling along, glancing around, studying the shadows for signs of pursuit and seeing none.

"This shit reminds me of a desert," Eli said. "A goddamn desert. Ain't there a desert out your way, there, chief?"

Leland took his time answering. "No desert. Some parts like a desert, I suppose. In and around Fraser Canyon. And along the Thompson River. But those places aren't like this. This is fine sand. Dust almost. And not a rock to be felt underfoot. I haven't stepped on a rock or pebble or jabbed my toes since we started walking."

Nathan stomped a few steps, spraying sand before him. Mackenzie, who walked alongside, frowned a question. Nathan shook his head. "You're right about the sand," he said, not needing to raise his voice. "This place is flatter than the whole of Saskatchewan. Not a lick of grass, even. Or a prairie dog hole. Just sand."

"Just keep your eyes open," Leland warned, his frame a silhouette under the deep purple overhead. "After the things we've seen, a healthy dose of caution would not go astray."

"The hell that mean?" Eli asked.

"I mean just what I said, Eli. Be on guard. We're in another place we have no right to be, far and away from the Rockies, walking upon sand that's close to burning our feet. I wouldn't be surprised if there's predators about."

"Like what? Coyotes?"

"Rattlesnakes?" Gilbert asked.

"I don't know," Leland replied. "Possible, however. Or worse."

"Or worse," Nathan said under his breath, surveying the horizon.

"Just be ready to drop your gear and grab for whatever's handy," Jimmy Norquay told them. "Winchesters or pistols."

"We got bigger problems than what might be worse than coyotes," Nathan said. "And that's water. I don't know about the rest of you, but I'm getting thirsty."

"Me too," Mackenzie said.

"I'm already thirsty," Gilbert said.

"I could gargle my own piss right about now," Eli said. "If I could squeeze out a drop."

"You win, Eli," Leland said in a tired voice.

"I always fuckin' win."

The rolling seam of sky and land stayed right where it was an hour before, informing the men that the desert of black sand was a very big place indeed. Nothing stirred around the seven men and, in time, Leland stopped, halting the procession.

"What is it?" Eli asked.

"Shush now."

So Eli shushed, which impressed the hell out of Nathan. The sky was the same shade of purple, not getting any darker or lighter as the evening (or morning) wore on. He stopped and gazed across the unnatural sprawl of the desert, hearing nothing but the breathing of the men and the clatter of their gear. Nothing darted across his field of vision. No wind blew.

Then it hit him—the enormity of the silence surrounding them.

"Jesus," he whispered, suddenly very conscious of the lack of noise.

"You hear anything?" Mackenzie asked.

Nathan didn't answer right away. "Nope," he finally said after trying to squeeze a note out of the air.

The others listened, straining to keep quiet, to better gauge the desert silence.

"Holy shit," Eli finally let out, unable to contain himself any longer.

"Figured you'd be the first," Nathan whispered.

"Go fuck yourself, Nathan Rhodes."

"I said *shush*," Leland ordered in an urgent whisper.

So they did once again. Nathan's ears buzzed, creating their own sound in the absence of any other. He strained to hear, a distant caw, a chirp of an insect, or even just a breeze, but got nothing. Mackenzie's expression was one of thoughtful attentiveness, and he shook his head when Nathan questioned him with a look. And after a few long seconds, Nathan's imagination began to spark and burn, envisioning things like the whalers hanging back in the deeper parts of the dark, studying the seven strangers with interest, all the while readying spears. Or flexing misshapen claws.

"This ain't right, Leland," Eli murmured. "This is goddamn eerie."

Leland didn't answer, his shadowy profile set and alert.

"When might the sun come up?" Nathan asked Mackenzie.

"No idea, Nate."

The hush in between that exchange seemed all the deeper now.

"None?" Nathan pressed.

Mackenzie leaned in close. "We've been walking for more than an hour. The sun should've cracked the horizon but it hasn't. The moon should've come up but it hasn't. We're just walking along in this twilight."

The others didn't speak, but Nathan knew they were listening. "So what's that all mean?"

"I don't know, Nate. Don't know. It's beyond me. Maybe Jimmy might know."

"I do not," Jimmy said quietly.

"God Almighty, Jimmy," Mackenzie said in controlled dismay. "Rest of you hear that?"

"Everyone heard that, dingle wood," Eli muttered.

The men quieted again, gazing around in growing unease. The stringy clouds, or what they assumed were clouds, didn't cross the sky or diminish, and that was damn peculiar.

Then the sound of someone taking a piss got Nathan's attention.

Shorty Charlie Williams, no longer able to contain himself, stood back from the group and cut loose. No one admonished him for taking a leak, although Nathan thought the sound was as loud as a flooded river. Eli kept his smartass remarks to himself, however, and for that, damn near everyone was thankful.

Shorty's stream dribbled to a stop. There was a sigh, and the stream resumed, sputtered, then stopped. Only to start up again.

"God Almighty, Shorty," Leland whispered from on ahead.

The voiding tapered off. "Can't help it," the big man whispered back. "Held it as long as I could."

"Anyone else need to relieve themselves?" Leland asked, and lowered his load to the sand. "Do it now."

No one did, however, but they did put their gear down, and that little bit of relief did them all good. In the minutes that followed, the men decided to sit. In ones and twos they spread out their damp dusters and planted their bare asses. Leland remained standing, turning one way and then the other as he studied the skyline.

Roughly ten minutes later, the men stood again.

They picked up their belongings and rearranged their weapons. Leland trekked off and Jimmy was only a step behind him. The others carried on as before, a little refreshed from the short rest, although the sand and air remained only just tolerable.

Purple sky, an unending, never changing portrait missing its centerpiece.

Two hours later and nothing had changed overhead. The silence was just as awesome. Sweat coated them all when they halted for another rest, and that time Leland plunked himself down as well. He drew up his legs and stared at the way they'd yet to travel, studying the mysterious landscape for clues as to where the end might be. Nathan didn't see one. He'd once feared the whalers might've followed them, but that notion had perished entirely. Now he wished they'd find a marker of some sort, anything that might reveal where they were in the world.

"Nothing," Mackenzie said in a low voice. Nathan didn't think he had to whisper anymore, but the lack of noise imposed its will upon the men, compelling them to speak in hushed tones.

"Not a thing," Nathan agreed.

"What do you think of it all?"

"I think we'd better find some water soon. I'm parched."

"Yeah. Me, too."

Just ahead, a sitting Gilbert bent over and pulled his foot up to study the sole. He brushed off the bottom and picked at his feet.

"Never been in a desert before," Nathan admitted. "Only prairie. So all this is… new to me."

"I don't think anyone's been about a place like this before," Mackenzie said.

"No, I suppose not."

"Be different if the sky did whatever it was going to do. That being either light up or get dark."

"Right now, I'm fine with all this."

"Why's that?"

Nathan stared at the darkness just below the skyline. "Because, if there is something out there, maybe it can't see us. Because there's no light. Sunlight or moonlight or whatever, I mean."

Mackenzie didn't say anything to that.

Leland rose then, signaling the end of the rest period, and that was the end of the conversation.

28

If Nathan had been parched before, he was truly in want of a drink when Leland and Jimmy, walking side-by-side, both staggered and dropped to their knees.

Leland keeled over onto his right while Jimmy flopped forwards, landing flat on his chest like a discarded saddlebag. The collapse of both men froze the others in a fluttering state of paralysis.

Broken only when Gilbert screamed. *"Holy fuckin' shit Leland and Jimmy's been SHOT!"*

They all dove for cover.

Seeing how there was no cover to dive for, however, all Gilbert really did was splash down face first into the sand. He did so with great conviction, however, as it convinced Eli to kiss the dirt as well, who'd been looking away when Leland and Jimmy fell.

That prompted a quick, better-safe-than-dead flurry of activity among the remaining men. The loudest still came from Gilbert, who Nathan knew, just *knew*, was ready and waiting to unload his Winchester at the first thing daring to cross his sights.

Nathan lay upon his naked chest, heaving his gear before himself and establishing a wall of cover. Mackenzie did the same, and his rifle sprouted over the top, aimed and ready to spit lead if needed. Shorty Charlie Williams had dropped to one knee behind them all, hunched over but considering the scene before him.

"Get your ass down, Shorty," Mackenzie urged. "Before someone pops a shell between your eyes and blows out the back of your head."

"I will not," Shorty replied tersely, taking stock of the situation.

"Oh Jesus! Oh Jesus! The boys have been shot! Oh Jesus!" Gilbert continued to

wail, loud enough to shake the heavens.

"Shut the hell *up* for Christ's sake," Eli barked right back. He lay on his belly with his head lifted above his own mound of gear. His self-proclaimed sweet ass gleamed with perspiration in the twilight.

"But the boys've been shot, Eli!"

"I said *shut up*!"

So Gilbert shut up, frantically worming around behind his winter duds and armaments, his head spastically rattling as if he'd taken two hard hooves to the face. Nathan checked on Mackenzie, who was peering off to the right, rifle raised and ready.

"I didn't hear a shot," Nathan whispered.

"Neither did I," Mackenzie whispered back.

"I sure as hell didn't hear no shot," Eli declared.

"You hear a shot, Gilbert?" Nathan asked.

That was met with resounding and sobering silence. "Well…"

"There was no shot," Shorty Williams grumbled. "Not even a hiss of wind being split."

"So what are you saying?" Eli asked.

"It's obvious what he's saying," Mackenzie rasped in dehydrated annoyance. "No one's been shot. And your little buddy over there missed his calling with a Kansas City chorus line. He's got quite the set of pipes."

"You be careful, now," Eli fired back. "I ain't decided you being on my Christmas list just yet."

"Shorty's right," Nathan threw in, scanning the unlit horizon and unable to discern any movement. "I didn't hear a shot either. But I did see them both drop."

"Just keep quiet for a bit," Mackenzie advised, eyes narrowed and piercing. "Can all of you do that? Just shut up and keep quiet."

Nathan fought to get his own thoughts in order, attempting to ascertain what had just happened. His constricted throat distracted him, feeling like a dry well steeped in salt. The purple sky gave no clues, and the shadows kept their secrets. So they all stayed there, feeling the seconds stretching out. Mackenzie was all still and watchful. Eli as well. Gilbert squirmed as if he'd dove directly on his quirt.

All that wiggling in the sand was getting on Nathan's nerves.

"Stop moving," Eli finally warned in an impatient tone. "Christ, Gilbert. You diggin' for gold over there?"

"Just tryin' to get some cover is all."

"The man said be *quiet*."

"That was a minute ago."

Nathan rolled his eyes. "Sweet Mary and Joseph, shut the hell *up*, Gilbert. And stay *still!*"

Gilbert did as told, but Nathan didn't think the man would stay put for long.

Jimmy moaned then.

"The hell was that?" Eli asked.

"That was Jimmy," Mackenzie answered.

"You okay, Jimmy?" Nathan asked.

But Jimmy didn't answer.

Leland released a gasp then, as if the life was being choked from him and he'd only just managed to break his attacker's stranglehold.

"Shit, Leland, you all right?" Nathan asked and waited, watching the two men over the brim of his gear.

"They're alive," Mackenzie observed.

"They're making noise, anyway," Nathan said. "Not much else."

"You been hit, Leland?" Gilbert asked since everyone else was talking.

Leland didn't say a word. He did roll over onto his side, however, and one pallid arm flopped over and back, as if he were feebly combing his hair away from his face.

"Leland?" Nathan asked.

"I don't think he's all right," Mackenzie said. "Gilbert, go check on him."

"I ain't getting my ass shot off."

"You ain't gonna get your ass shot off."

"How do you know?"

"There's been no *shot*," Mackenzie insisted. "Listen to me. You listening? No one heard a shot; ergo, no shot's been fired. No one's shooting."

Gilbert thought that over. "Well, they both ain't right."

"Which is why I'm telling you to go check on them."

"I don't wanna."

"Christ," Eli said in disgust and lifted himself into a low crouch with the help of his rifle. "Stay put, Dorothy, and keep quiet. I'll check on them poor bastards."

Jimmy groaned then, and tried moving.

"Best get going, Eli," Nathan said. "We'll watch the hills for you."

"What hills?" Eli asked. "There ain't no hills around. There ain't shit around."

All the same, the gun runner crouched low and waddled over to the two groaning men. He scuffed up sand while releasing the occasional huff and foul expletive, which Nathan would forever associate with the man.

Eli got within two feet of them before dropping his rifle and toppling over onto his side without so much as a word.

"The hell was that?" a startled Nathan whispered, unable to take his eyes off the fallen man.

"Oh shit!" Gilbert released in a squeal of barely suppressed terror and a quick working of his rifle lever.

"You stay quiet, Gilbert," Nathan warned without taking his eyes off the newest victim.

"Eli?" Mackenzie called out. "Eli?"

"Say something," Nathan added.

Eli didn't say a word, however.

"Something sure as hell ain't right," Mackenzie muttered.

That comment surprised Nathan, and not in a good way. "That's all you can say? Something sure as hell ain't right?"

"I'm man enough to admit when I don't know what's going on."

Leland groaned again, and to the remaining four's surprise, he actually struggled to rise to his hands and knees.

"You okay over there, Leland?" Mackenzie whispered. "You get shot with something?"

Leland planted his head into the sand and stayed there, ignoring the question. Then, "Just… be quiet. For a minute."

"Be quiet?" Mackenzie repeated in confusion. "He just say that?"

"That's what I heard," Nathan said. "The boss wants quiet, so we be quiet. You hear that, Gilbert?"

"Uh-huh."

"That means no shooting. At all. Until Leland says otherwise. Got that?"

"I got it," Gilbert answered in an anxious tone that suggested Leland better say something otherwise pretty damn quick.

Jimmy rolled over onto his side. He moaned, sounding like a man who just had his balls kicked up into his throat.

"Go on over there and help them out, Gilbert," Mackenzie said.

The nervous gun runner's head did a double take. "Now?"

"Right now. They aren't dead. And they haven't been shot."

So Gilbert stood, hunched over and bare-ass naked, with his rifle firm against his shoulder. He crept towards the fallen men.

Nathan had an idea. "Hold on, Gilbert."

That stopped him in his tracks.

"You take your time, you hear? Go—go slower than Eli, if you can. And let us know if you hear or see anything."

"Hear or see anything?" Mackenzie asked.

"What for?" Gilbert asked.

"Just do it, all right?"

"All right, Nathan," Gilbert replied uneasily, knowing full well he was being sent to the slaughter. Or the next worst thing to being slaughtered, which had obviously laid out three men more than capable of defending themselves. Gilbert crept ahead, well aware he was closing in on an unidentified danger.

"See anything?" Nathan asked.

"Nothing," Gilbert answered. "But… but something weird's goin' on."

A chill enveloped Nathan then, despite the hot sand he lay upon. "What?"

"Heart's beatin' real hard. And my teeth are achin'. Real bad."

"Jesus Christ," Mackenzie whispered.

Without another word, Gilbert dropped as if all his limbs suddenly became boneless. He landed in a heap as twisted as the winter gear he'd left behind.

"Well, that was interesting," Nathan observed.

"What was interesting?" Mackenzie asked, more than a little annoyed. "'Cause right now all I see are four of ours face down in the sand."

"That *was* interesting," Shorty said from behind them, agreeing with the assessment.

"What?" Mackenzie asked again. "Tell me for Christ's sake."

"Well, for one, they aren't being shot," Nathan said. "Or anything else for that matter."

"But something's dropping them," Shorty said from behind.

"Right around where Gilbert and Eli fell," Nathan said. "That's the marker."

Leland lay back down and became silent.

"Leland?" Nathan asked and got no reply. "You okay? Leland?"

But the gang leader failed to answer. The next few seconds were hard ones to wait through. "All right," Nathan finally decided. "I'm going on ahead."

That nearly twisted Mackenzie's head off his shoulders.

"I think that's unwise," he offered, staying right where he was. "Something's still laying them out."

"Yeah," Nathan said as he hefted a Colt. He held the weapon before him, not at all confident.

"You really going over there?" Mackenzie asked.

"Gonna have to," Nathan said, and took one step forward. "Can't ask you to go over. And Shorty sure as shit ain't gonna take an order from a hard case like myself. So it's me or no one."

"Just wait," Mackenzie said. "Jimmy looks like he's coming around."

Jimmy was stirring, but didn't sound as if he was capable of doing much.

"I'm going," Nathan said. "Stupid as that sounds. Just pay attention to what happens."

"It's damn obvious what's going to happen, Nathan," Mackenzie said. "Just *wait* a few minutes."

Nathan couldn't wait however. Ignoring Mackenzie, he started forward another cautious step, followed by another.

"You stubborn bastard," Mackenzie scolded then. "Let us know what's happening."

"Nothing yet," Nathan said as he passed the two dark lumps that were Eli's and Gilbert's gear. Four steps from that, both men were sprawled out as if shot in the head. Leland's right hand waved weakly, but Nathan wasn't sure if that was a warning or an invitation.

Two more steps, and his heart was pounding in his chest.

A step away from Gilbert's unmoving ass and Nathan's teeth started aching, as if someone were driving nails into them. The pain bloomed so quickly that it enveloped his head. A buzzing flooded his ears and forced him to squeeze his eyes shut.

"Teeth are achin'," Nathan growled, as the sensation flowed downward in a shocking gush.

And the last thing he heard before an unexpected blackness overtook him was "You okay—"

Then the sensation of falling and he knew no more.

29

A hand slapped his face—then another—quickly evolving into a more frantic version of patty cake.

"Christ," someone said. "Ease off, Mackenzie. That ain't a set of ass cheeks you're slapping."

Nathan fended off the attacking palm with two of his own. "Lord almighty," he winced and saw a headless face looming above his chest.

"He's coming around," Leland said, and a shadow behind the headless face straightened.

"You okay, Nathan?" the headless face asked in Mackenzie's voice.

"Huh?"

"Asked if you were okay?"

Nathan took a moment to process that. "Yeah."

"You were out cold."

"I was?"

"Like us all."

"After we crossed over," Jimmy added. "That haunted place."

"You still going on about that haunted place?" Eli demanded.

"I like it better than your explanation."

"I don't have an explanation," Eli grumped. "All I know is that I walked a few feet then got knocked out."

"For about twenty minutes," Jimmy said.

"What?" Nathan asked weakly, struggling to sit up. Mackenzie moved back to let him do just that.

"About twenty minutes or so," Leland said. "Senseless for most of it myself, but the boys were watching over us."

"That's me and Shorty," Mackenzie said. "Nervous times."

"You waited that long?"

"Waited and watched," Mackenzie replied. "Like I said we should in the first place. Next time, listen to me."

"Leland was moving. So was Jimmy."

"Senseless. Out on their feet. Like a man reeling from a solid uppercut to the jaw."

"Don't remember a thing," Leland said. "Started in my teeth, and before I could say a word, all I remember was waking up and spitting out sand."

"We're across now," Jimmy said. "So that's a good thing."

"We're across?" Nathan asked and looked at Mackenzie and Shorty. "You fellows, too?"

Mackenzie's darkened face nodded. "Tried to go around, and Shorty walked right into it. Dropped dead on the spot. I stayed back, and by that time Jimmy was conscious and Leland was coming around. They sounded fine enough. I figured that whatever had knocked them down was only temporary, so I decided to try for myself but at a different point."

"He fell like the rest of us," Jimmy said. "Not like that one, though," he said, indicating Shorty. "The ground shook when he hit."

"The ground did not shake," Shorty said, unamused.

"How the hell would you know?" Eli challenged. "You were as dead to the world like the rest of us."

"So where are we now?" Nathan asked.

"On the other side," Leland said, facing the unseen boundary that had rendered them unconscious. "Your gear is over there."

Nathan saw that it was, along with the other men's winter clothing, guns, and ammunition.

"So how do we get it?"

"Walk on over there and get it," Jimmy said with a sad smile.

"But that means crossing that line again."

"So it does," Leland said.

Nathan's thoughts were still muddled, but he was coming to his senses fast. "You mean one of us has to go back?"

"One of us already has."

Nathan realized Gilbert was missing.

Shorty Charlie Williams glanced ponderously over his shoulder.

There, just a few feet away from his belongings, was the crumpled form of Gilbert.

When Gilbert regained consciousness and was fully functional, he tossed across whatever items the men had left behind that invisible pitfall. They gathered up their belongings, and once organized, encouraged Gilbert to return, who was none too pleased about the prospect of being knocked out for a third time.

"Maybe it won't happen," Eli said.

"It's gonna happen."

"How do you know?"

"It's gonna happen."

"Well, maybe it won't. Stop fussing like an old woman."

"Mack?" Gilbert pleaded. "It's gonna happen, ain't it?"

"Probably."

That was met with a deep silence, which Eli filled with a quietly put, "You shithead, Mack."

Gilbert slung his belongings over and held his face for a few seconds, as if contemplating a mad dash across the mysterious line.

"Do it and get it over with," Jimmy said.

"Catch me if you can, Eli."

"Sure, Gilbert, sure," the gun runner said with impatience, and placed his stuff on the sand. He waved Gilbert on with both hands. "C'mon then. I'm damn well waitin' here."

Gilbert charged.

And crashed headfirst in a spray of sand.

Eli dropped his arms and took in that deep royal sky.

"You didn't catch him," Shorty said.

"Gotta tell him something to get his ass moving," Eli muttered before studying Gilbert's heap. After a few seconds, he selected one outstretched arm and dragged the unconscious gun runner a safe distance away from the sinister border.

"That was an asshole thing to do," Nathan said in an accusatory tone.

Eli released Gilbert, letting the limb flop to the ground like a length of riverboat rope. "Guess I've been called one enough times that it comes natural to me, now. And before you all get bitchy about this, just remember, we got bigger things to worry about. Like finding our way back to that goddamn train."

"We've got something bigger to worry about," Leland said quietly, drawing the men's attention to himself.

"Yeah, what's that?" Jimmy asked.

The gang leader's shoulders heaved as he took a deep breath. "Like who put that invisible wall there? And why…?"

*

Two hours and three rest stops later, the sun still hadn't made up its mind on whether it was coming or going. The heat didn't intensify, however, so that was all fine, but the gang was powerfully thirsty, and the desert was an unending carpet of sand, scrolling towards a featureless horizon that didn't seem to get any closer. No breeze blew, so there was no relief from that quarter either.

"Where the hell are we?" Eli panted, and he almost staggered to his knees. Gilbert stopped beside him, ready to help his companion if necessary.

"Still in a desert," Nathan said.

"An alien desert," Mackenzie added. "Another part of your rabbit hole, Nate."

Nathan was beginning to wish he'd never heard stories of other worlds and the secret passages to them.

"I ain't never heard of a desert like this before," Eli rasped.

"Well, now you have," Shorty said.

"Fuck off, Shorty."

Nathan sensed Eli was one hour past the end of his rope.

"How long we been walking now?" Mackenzie asked.

"Five or six hours," Leland said up ahead, where he and Jimmy walked side-by-side once again.

"Milton's long gone by now," Mackenzie said.

"Maybe," Nathan said, the damp weight he carried slowly stretching his arms.

"What's that?"

"I said 'maybe'. I've been thinking. When you guys were outside of that tunnel, you said you were only there a few seconds, right? To me it was much longer. Like ten minutes or so. I think time is just as warped as this damn desert we're walking across. I don't know why, but if doorways can appear and disappear, if we can go from a train to a sea serpent and then to a desert, well, anything can happen. Including time being stretched out. Or shortened. So maybe, just maybe, if we've been here for five or six hours, maybe it's only been a few seconds for poor old Milton."

"Maybe it's been longer," Jimmy suggested. "Like days."

"Maybe," Nathan granted.

"Interesting thought, Nate," Mackenzie allowed. "Interesting."

"Yeah," Nathan said, not seeing that way at all. If time was so unstable in such a manner, he wondered what it would mean for them—or what it might do to them.

Mackenzie scanned the sky and slowly stopped in his tracks.

"Something wrong?" Nathan asked, noticing his companion.

"Maybe," Mackenzie said. "Look over that way."

Nathan did. "Yeah? So?"

Shorty stopped behind them and did the same, while the others trudged onwards.

"The sky seem darker over there to you?" Mackenzie asked.

"Yeah, it does," Nathan answered, taking a moment to gauge the difference in colors. The shades *were* lighter along the skyline, signaling an approaching dawn.

"Sun's coming up," Shorty said quietly.

"So we got here during the night," Nathan said. "Or what passes for night."

"Looks that way," Mackenzie assumed.

Nathan, however, wasn't entirely certain it did look that way, not after his assessment of time.

"Best tell the ones on ahead," Mackenzie said. "We better find someplace with shade. I don't want to be caught in the sun if it's this hot during the night."

"I don't either," Shorty added, his voice wasted and dusty.

Nathan looked from Shorty's grim features to the surrounding desert and wondered where the hell they would find such a place. Without warning, Mackenzie hurried after the four men on ahead, and Nathan and Shorty followed. Nathan noticed that Leland and Jimmy were already looking to the east, or what he assumed was the east.

"Sun's coming up," Mackenzie announced, pointing to the light creeping along the skyline.

"Saw that," Leland answered, sounding bone-weary and very much wanting a drink.

"Might be a good idea to get out of it," Nathan said when he caught up to them.

"Where we gonna do that?" Eli snapped in a tired voice, running on spirit alone.

"There's no place in sight," Jimmy said. "Nothing."

"We keep walking then," Leland said as if freshly risen from the dead.

"Not much else we can do. And I'm certainly in no condition to run."

Nathan winced. "No, I don't suppose I am either."

"None of us are," Jimmy noted. "Unless we all pile onto Shorty's shoulders and let him carry us."

The comment momentarily distracted Shorty from the horizon.

"Come on then," Leland said. He started plodding ahead yet again.

"At least we'll get a good look at this place," Nathan said.

"Haven't seen enough, lawman?" Eli muttered.

The poke didn't brighten Nathan's spirits, and he let that be known with a glare in Eli's direction. A hard case himself, Eli didn't back down.

"I said come on," Leland barked at them as he led the others away.

Eli and Nathan continued glaring.

"What's it gonna be, lawman?" Eli said, narrow-eyed and willing. "If I had a choice between walking and kicking the shit outta you, well, you can see I ain't walking."

Nathan scowled, the horizon brightening in the background. "Eli," he finally said, "you've been on my ass like a saddle boil ready to pop, but I ain't gonna fight you while you're bare-assed. That might be what you do out your way, and probably the reason why you are the way you are. But with me, that just ain't gonna happen."

With that, Nathan turned and hurried after the others.

He didn't have to check to see if Eli was following.

So they marched, double-time, making tracks in that black sand which was becoming increasingly finer. The sky continued to brighten, promising a smoldering dawn that unnerved Nathan and lent him a little extra strength. He carried his weapons and wet clothing before him while casting fearful looks at where he expected the sun to rise. His skin glistened in a sheen of sweat that he didn't think possible. There simply wasn't enough water left in him to sweat, by his reckoning.

"It's coming up fast," Mackenzie observed.

And it was, much faster than it should, or so it seemed in Nathan's mind. He blinked away stinging rivulets of perspiration that smeared his vision, hefting his load in one arm at times so that he could wipe away the annoying moisture. The morning was on its way, and the rising temperature warned of a very hot sun. Nathan believed that when the sun did break free of the horizon, he wouldn't have to worry about sweat in his eyes anymore, because he figured his own flesh would be sizzling like bacon hitting a frying pan.

"I see something," Jimmy Norquay gasped. He pointed ahead of him.

There, still a good march away, was a milky patch stamped upon the land, sticking out like a polished eggshell.

"The hell is that?" Gilbert asked for them all.

"A rock," Jimmy said.

A rock wasn't going to help them, but there was something odd about it. Still, hope drained from Nathan's chest, his mind fabricating all sorts of fiery demises once the sun cleared the distant ridge. A sound caught his attention and he swivelled to the left. Mackenzie did the same, having dropped back from where he walked with Shorty.

"The hell is *that?*" Eli stressed, hearing the noise as well.

Nathan scanned the nearly flat plain and located the disturbance. His mouth dropped open at the sight.

Perhaps a hundred yards away, a black fin bulged upwards and broke free of the surface in a puff of sand. At first, Nathan thought he was staring at the broad side of a big old bass violin, the kind he saw people play at town dances. He couldn't see the details, but he knew that something wasn't quite right. Grit fell away from the thick curvature, but a lot still coated the thing. More of the sand bulged and crumbled away as the shape continued to rise, taking great effort to free itself from the desert's clutches before pausing as if recovering its strength.

The spectacle captivated the train robbers.

The bass violin pushed again and more of its bulk came free, just as a *second* bass violin breached the grainy detritus that marked the wake of the first.

"The hell is that, Leland?" Eli asked again.

"No idea, Eli."

"It's big," Shorty noted. "And alive."

No sooner were the words out of his mouth when the lower section of the violin came free of the desert. The thing lifted itself into the morning air like a flower searching out the sun. Thick, gnarly stalks supported the mass, appearing like several stumps of old cedar or the like, all connected.

"We better get moving," Nathan said in a low tone, fear doing the talking for him.

The violin shape split apart in the middle.

"Lord Almighty," Mackenzie said, realizing what the thing truly was.

It was a claw.

A great pincer flexed its length with an energetic *clap clap*, the sound loud and startling and carrying across the empty space. The pincer snapped three times more in lively succession. The significance of the larger disc underneath the claw suddenly became much clearer. A substantial ridge popped free, creating a billowing dust fall. The dense outline took shape within that cloud and turned around.

The men didn't wait. Nathan was running with the rest of his companions.

"Oh Jesus," Eli was panting as he chugged along.

"*Oh Jesus, oh Jesus!*" Gilbert stressed in even greater volume.

Oh Jesus, indeed, Nathan thought, his fright giving him all the energy he needed as he ran away from the emerging crab thing.

But all around them, other crabs were rising, near and far. In fact, everywhere he looked, points and shapes were emerging, summoned by the approaching dawn. Claws erupted from once flat planes, some slow, some popping forth with vigor. Some claws shot straight up like fat, serrated Vs while others shook off the sand's weight with great vibrations. One section of the sand exploded forth in a pile of black grain, not a dozen yards away, and that one frightened Nathan worst of all.

That claw was attached to a mass perhaps the size of a fully-grown cow, black and disc-shaped like a crab, but covered in a shaggy coat that might have been hair. The thing turned, rotating itself on a multitude of legs that Nathan didn't count. A second claw came into view and flexed—*Clapclapclap!*—snapping out a code as clear as an evening dinner bell.

"Oh *shit!*" Gilbert shouted, still carrying his gear.

"Run!" Jimmy shouted.

They ran—as best as they could given the loads they carried—charging the glowing green line brightening the horizon.

A flicker of movement to the right caught Nathan's eye. Then his left, and he felt his bowels loosen.

There were hundreds of the things. In fact, sand clouds were erupting as far as the eye could see, meaning there were *thousand*s of the creatures pulling themselves free of the earth. All around. Even in their direct path.

Leland and Jimmy veered around the violent breaches of the enormous monsters. By the time Nathan and Mackenzie rushed by them, the beasts were flexing their claws, sending up even more sand. Grit pelted the men, covering their skinny-assed frames and sticking like an unpleasant dew.

Nathan heard a moaning and realized it was himself.

The crabs scurried after them, their legs obscured by dust clouds. They nimbly kept pace with the fleeing men, skittering sideways in parallel lines, as if studying the curious creatures in their midst. The crabs were hairy things, the strands clotted with sand and filth. Their bodies were round and meaty, and as big and bulky as cattle. Claws snapped out that hungry code while a few remained open and were held at guard, protecting alien faces.

Dozens of black, soulless eyes the size of fists tracked the men.

A shot rang out, causing Nathan to flinch.

Leland fired his Winchester a second time, and the cattle-sized crab beast that approached him cringed as if it had been stepped on and skittered back a few paces. It went no farther, however.

Leland—who had dropped all his gear except his rifle—stopped and fired at another crab darting forward. The bullet zinged off the hairy shell of the beast, driving it back. But Nathan wasn't sure if it was the impact frightening it or the sound of the shot itself.

He dropped everything except his Colts and aimed at one crab coming too close. He fired, parting a patch of weedy hair the size of a pine knot. The crab retreated in a flurry of legs and sand, but didn't go far.

More of the creatures gathered around the fringes, while hundreds more filled the land beyond that, attracted to the confrontation. There were far too many to count, and certainly too many to fight. The tallest of the things were chest height, with smaller ones no higher than a man's waist.

And they were closing in.

A metallic hammering distracted Nathan, and he saw Jimmy slamming the butt of his rifle into that milky plate that they'd seen earlier from a distance. Over Jimmy's head a green line of dawn trembled and fattened upon the horizon, flaring to life like the first flames taking to kindle. And, though Nathan had been preoccupied by the monster crabs, a hot and ferocious heat engulfed his face—the searing temperature spike of an inferno.

"Get around him!" Leland bellowed.

The men encircled Jimmy Norquay as he hammered that odd-looking plate.

All the while, the very earth trembled from an awakening army of crabs.

Shorty roared as he stood fast and leveled his shotgun at the monsters edging closer, their claws poised and ready. Shorty fired both barrels, hitting the nearest one square in a hot spatter of lead. The blast drove the creature and the ones behind it back in a flurry of legs and claw claps.

Jimmy dropped his knees and fanned the surface of the door-sized plate, clearing it of dust. There were markings upon the metal skin, fat scrawls that shouted out a mysterious message. Nathan didn't know what they were, but he dropped alongside Jimmy and felt the hot exterior.

"Steel?" he asked.

Jimmy shook his head.

"Shoot anything that gets too close!" Leland yelled overhead. "*Anything!*"

The rest of the gang surrounded Nathan and Jimmy, marking the borders of that little island of metal. Naked-ass cheeks and an assortment of skinny and broad backs—complete with dimples—shone in the growing morning light. Beyond that, the crabs orbited the little circle of men, coming closer in arcs, as if daring them to do something. Claws snipped and flashed like well-oiled scissors, while those black orbs that had to be eyes studied the little gang and wondered how they tasted.

Eli shot one crab square in the face. The monster took the blast, its legs tensing up upon impact, before scuttling away.

Not far enough, however, as the number of crabs behind it was too thick to allow it to go any farther.

And that started the shooting in earnest.

The men screamed as they unloaded into the black-haired crustaceans, and all the while Nathan and Jimmy bent their heads and readied themselves for another round of gunfire. There was no cover, nowhere to run or hide. The little island of metal would mark the gang's final stand—before they were overwhelmed and devoured.

Shorty reloaded and fired again at a crab that was becoming far too brave. The shot scrubbed the hair from the creature's face and burst open one of those can-sized eyes in a spray of pink jelly, splashing the rest of the shell in a thin lather. The crab didn't retreat, however; rather, it darted forward and grabbed Shorty's leg. Shorty went down with a scream, his leg suddenly gone below the knee. The crab scuttled backwards, holding the severed limb in one claw while the other one snapped excitedly.

A screaming Shorty writhed on his back, holding onto his lower leg that whipped and flung dark gushes at the desert. Jimmy latched onto him and pulled him into the circle.

Another crab had a different idea, however, and charged. Its claws snapped at Shorty and neatly snipped off his right arm at the bicep. The big man shrieked, a piercing note that paralyzed Nathan. A great eye flicked one way then the other, birdlike, and focused on Shorty's bloody bits. Shorty thrashed under the life-stealing procedure. Gunfire erupted, blazing away at the black-haired shell where lengthy strands of hair drooped and hung, spattered and clingy with sand and other dried matter. Men screamed. Gunsmoke burned the men's eyes and lit up their sinus cavities.

Eli hammered the attacking crab with the butt of his Winchester and that backed the creature up on its legs. The monster withdrew, but a claw clamped down on Shorty's *other* leg and dragged him free of the circle of men. Jimmy tried to hold onto him, but Shorty's blood-slicked limbs and shoulders rendered it impossible to maintain a grip. Shorty continued to howl. He crunched himself in close to the attacking crab and drove his remaining fist into the space between its eyes. The men fired at the beast, hoping to free their companion, but another crab barreled into their midst and promptly snatched up Shorty's severed arm. Leland fired at the thing point-blank, and a piece of shell flew out of the creature's hide. The crab scrabbled off while stuffing Shorty's dead fingers into its mouth. Meanwhile, other crabs converged upon Shorty's weakening frame, and one quick snip separated the big man's head from his shoulders in a shocking burst of tar.

"*Shorty!*" Leland shouted, before a crab reached in and cleanly pinched his foot away from his ankle. Leland fell screaming. The men whirled about, firing as they did so, facing the chest-high monstrosity scuttling up their leader's spine.

"*Christ Almighty!*" Eli screamed and fired, feverishly working his Winchester's lever like a punctured bellows.

The crab didn't flinch under that barrage, even though pieces of shell split apart and spun off into the dying shadows. Leland half turned, coming up with a pistol, and planted the gun square against the soft underside of the beast—when another crab darted forward, emboldened by the success of its brethren, and snipped off Leland's gun arm at the elbow. The gang leader fell, his stump spraying a jagged line across Nathan's chin and neck. Mackenzie was screeching. Gilbert was reloading. Eli hammered his rifle's shoulder butt into the face of the attacking crab. Sand and grit salted the air, while jets of blood snaked throughout. Gunsmoke also added to the chaos, rendering all as apparitions.

Gilbert joined Eli and pounded the monster with his rifle, as did Mackenzie, but the crab did not release Leland. In fact, the other claw belonging to Leland's captor came around and sheared off the top of the gang leader's hairy head in a crackle of bone, and that was that.

Like a starter's pistol, that unmistakable, gut-clenching crunch attracted the rest of the crabs.

Hundreds, *thousands* scrambled towards the growing melee, drawn by the noise or the blood or the violence. Perhaps everything. In that fleeting glimpse of certain death, Nathan's mind and blood went cold, despite the rising temperature.

We're dead, he thought. He clawed at the metal beneath him.

When his fingers dug into something.

He glanced down and saw that he was no longer upon the large metal plate he and Jimmy had tried to clear away. His animated retreat from the attacking crabs had uncovered a distinct curve along the thing's surface, as well as a groove that his fingers had hooked into, an indentation with a bunch of black markings, partially uncovered, pointing at the inset.

Above the screaming and the gunfire and the blood, Nathan jammed his hand into that inset.

His fingertips sank into a pliable material, shockingly cold.

There was a ponderous click of metal, then a great prolonged scream that might've come from a storybook giant. The sound paralyzed Nathan.

Just before the world rose beneath him in a gush of white.

30

The white nose of a whale rose up from the desert depths in a long groan of metal, turning the very air into an unbreathable tempest. Nathan rolled down along the side of the emerging monolith in a cloud of grit and dust before landing at the bottom—except the bottom was expanding as the white cone at his back continued to rise. The other men fell as well, damn near frantic from the deaths of Shorty and Leland. The crabs withdrew as a black tide, their claws held up in a defensive posture, their thick legs barely visible through the dust clouds of their rapid retreat.

The shell at Nathan's back stopped moving.

He twisted around, wrenching his attention off the carnivorous multitudes not twenty paces away, and squinted at the milk-bone whiteness of the thing behind him. It resembled a revolver's spent shell, the tip flattened as if it had smashed itself against a slab of pig iron.

And it was the size of a house.

Sandy ribbons snaked off its heights as Nathan checked on the surrounding crabs. Those multitudes were no longer retreating, but rather tensed with a predatory readiness.

"What is it?" Mackenzie was shouting, his face lifted and staring at the heights.

Nathan couldn't answer because he didn't know. The crabs didn't seem to like it, however, but they were getting used to it pretty fast.

Then he noticed the heat.

Searing, scorching heat, and the alarming smell of his own cooking skin.

Nathan glanced over his shoulder, at the skyline, where the distant hills or mountains or whatever they were blazed with the approach of a killer sun.

The crabs didn't seem to notice.

A whine of unseen gears and machinery whipped Nathan's head around, and a sphincter- like hatch opened at the base, some two feet above the desert sand. A green light snapped on from the inside, illuminating a roomy chamber within.

Nathan didn't need a proper invitation.

"Get in!" he yelled and plunged through the opening, clanging the barrel of his Winchester off the frame. The others followed as the heat—that terrible, terrible heat—singed the hair of their ass cheeks.

Mackenzie pushed his way through, tumbling over Eli's heels, as Nathan threw himself at the door's side. He searched the frame, locating an oddly shaped picture just above eye level. He slapped the symbol, fingers becoming desperate claws, searching for a similar groove that had opened the door from the outside. There was no such thing, however.

Jimmy was through, and Gilbert was right behind him, shoving the buffalo hunter through the doorway.

The crabs were behind Gilbert.

A *world* of crabs.

The door chirped unexpectedly, and Nathan glanced up as one huge pincer shot out for Gilbert's naked neck.

Except Gilbert ducked inside a split second before the crab could get him.

And the instant Gilbert cleared the threshold, the outer door spiraled shut with a slam and a soft hiss of air. The green light became a bright ring around the ceiling, illuminating them all, while much cooler air flooded the chamber. Claws slammed into the door, seeking to pry their way inside and failing. The remaining gang members pressed themselves against the rounded walls, staring in wide-eyed horror at the sealed entrance and wondering if it would hold.

"Do something, Rhodes," Eli said.

"Hell you want me to do?"

"Get rid of them things."

"I don't know how."

"You got the goddamn door open."

"I was lucky."

A heavy force slammed off the metal, but failed to do anything except scare the living shit out of everyone inside. Rifles and pistols were aimed at the door, but were eventually lowered when the men realized they were safe from the creatures.

And that blistering sun.

Nathan slid down the wall, panting, sweat and grime coating his face, and let his Colts fall to his hips. He drew up his legs for modesty's sake, realizing that he hadn't a stitch on him. The other men were likewise without clothing, and only a few held weapons, though they still wore their ammunition belts and bandoliers filled with their remaining rifle and pistol shells.

"Well, goddamn," Eli swore and rubbed his face, then his scalp. "This is a first. Almost killed by a bunch… of fuckin' *crabs*."

"*Giant* fuckin' crabs," Mackenzie added, inspecting first himself, the bare empty area they all occupied, and then the green lights overhead. "The hell are we, anyway?"

That got looks from all of them.

"At least it's cool," Nathan said. "I was roasting out there, just before the crabs started… well…"

Images of Leland and Shorty being graphically nipped apart by huge pincers silenced him. He sighed, taking relief from being out of danger for the time being, but sad about the loss of Leland. He was even a little sad about Shorty, too, for that matter, but not in the same degree as the gang leader. Though an outlaw, there was a nobility about Leland Baxter.

"What do we do now?" Mackenzie muttered, placing his gun across his man-bits.

No one answered.

Crabs continued to probe and search for a way inside the chamber.

"We're stuck here," Jimmy said. "That's the way I see it. We can't open that door because of the crabs. And even if they weren't around, the sun would've been too damn hot for us, anyway."

Too damn hot, Nathan echoed. He focused on the door. "Just keep your hands off that picture up there. That weird one."

"The one that looks like a whirlpool?" Mackenzie asked.

Nathan realized it did look like a whirlpool. "Yeah, that one. It closed the door when you were all through it. This is just a guess, but if you touch it again, it might open."

"All right. Got it."

"What if the crabs open the door from the outside?" Gilbert asked.

"Then we're dead," Eli said smartly, and smiled at his companion. Gilbert didn't return the gesture.

"Then we're dead," Nathan repeated with a whisper. They would indeed be dead. Picked apart by pincer and devoured, just like poor old Leland Baxter and Shorty Charlie Williams.

"What is this place?" Jimmy said, studying the interior.

"No idea," Nathan replied. "But I'm thinking… maybe… this place is here to protect whoever built it, from the crabs and the sun."

Silence met this observation.

"Why do you say that?" Mackenzie asked.

Nathan's eyes came to rest on the symbol far up the wall, on the left side of the door. He had to reach for it. He had to reach for the groove that opened the door outside as well. Two controls that were placed well overhead, and that made him wonder why.

He was still wondering when he fell asleep.

*

A loud buzzing rattled the bank of controls, and the Vog herdsvog sleepily opened its horizontal eye stalks. Compound eyes located the flashing light upon one console jammed among an intricate wall of others, prompting the Vog herdsvog to draw a shallow breath through its neck gills. It thought-controlled its bunk to recess back into the wall, and the slab of metal rotated until it tipped eighty-five degrees, whereupon the creature stepped away. The Vog herdsvog was almost eight feet tall by human measurements, while its shoulders were three feet across. The Vog was bipedal, its arms and legs skeletal and lengthy, its torso no thicker than a grown man's thigh.

The console light continued to flash, bouncing off chrome-colored flesh that appeared shrivelled and pocketed. The Vog herdsvog thought-manipulated a control, which opened a window in the air before its eye stalks. A flash of annoyance then, as a number of reports flared across the ethereal screen. A two-fingered hand rose to its mouth, a horizontal proboscis, and rubbed one side of the rigid extension. The proboscis equaled its eye stalks in length and was situated a few fingers directly beneath them. The Vog's head was no bigger than, say, that of a human child in its middle years, and its chrome-colored flesh was otherwise featureless.

A crisp image of the bayak herds filled the center of the screen, complete with scrolling numerals and symbols. The Vog herder studied the information for a lethargic moment before dismissing it. The eye stalks parted then, in a display of surprise, before drawing close together. The proboscis beneath lifted, almost touching the Vog's eye stalks and completing what could be interpreted as an angry or pensive expression.

In this case, it was a pensive thought.

A tube emerged from a nearby wall and floated toward the Vog herdsvog, stopping just before its face. It coupled with the Vog's proboscis, and the creature took in the first of several feedings throughout the day. The Vog drank, slowly, ingesting both fluids and information, eye stalks wide and unwavering.

The screen flashed a group of alien lifeforms before the Vog, causing it to cease feeding in mid-stream. The Vog lifted its hand and split the two digits wide, enlarging the recorded images. It thought-pressed points of interest upon the screen, absorbing the finer details, documenting age, sex, body temperature, size, and height, as well as other biological readings of interest. The body fluids filling and comprising a significant percentage of the aliens' overall mass greatly interested the Vog. The plasma was an enticing mixture of oxygen, proteins, and other nutrients both known and unknown.

This data was accurately gathered, as each figure passed through the energy field that separated the numerous bayak herds. An energy field that kept the bayaks within, yet took precise analytical readings of whatever had passed through, either by accident or intentionally.

The energy field was an exceptional analyzer as well as cage.

The Vog twirled a finger, and miniature images scrolled as directed. The alien lifeforms were inside a bayak ranch capsule, a multiple sleepaway unit used at night or heat of the day. That the aliens managed to take refuge within the shelter interested the Vog herder very much.

The Vog resumed drinking, switching camera angles to an outside source, locating the sector the capsule was located within before zooming in and replaying the moments before the shelter's door had been opened. The distance was great but of no consequence to the Vog surveillance systems. Images were displayed as if the aliens were mere strides away. The Vog checked the time. All events had taken place several krons ago.

Aliens, trudging across the desert, wilting under the oppressive heat, and then fleeing the waking bayaks. The bayaks catching a pair of aliens and dispatching them. Life fluid spilled from the aliens then. Screams.

That irritated the herder, knowing the bayaks' digestive system would reject any food that wasn't a part of their normal diet.

The Vog wasn't about to sift through any bayak excrement.

The herder's eye stalks widened at the interesting discharge of weapons. Primitive weapons, but weapons nevertheless. The repeating sound and fury of the sticks brought the Vog herdsvog to an even greater level of attention. It replayed the violence several times, slowing the fight down and examining every minutia of information.

The Vog watched one of the aliens inadvertently locate and activate the front door of the capsule. They all fled inside and sealed the shelter, much to the displeasure of the bayaks who had sampled the aliens.

The Vog resumed studying the creatures inside the shelter, as invisible beams further analyzed their genetic makeup without their knowledge. They appeared lethargic, eventually becoming inert, though still managing to make a rattling noise the Vog herdsvog found annoying.

Tapping a finger against its head, the Vog made a decision. It stopped feeding and switched off the screen, as the footage could be viewed again at any time.

The Vog herdsvog walked through a rectangular frame, and chrome armor belts immediately fitted to the Vog's body. It held out a hand, projecting a mental image, and a .50 kor blaster materialized from a pocket of netherspace. The Vog took the weapon, the stock immediately wrapping itself around the sinewy bicep of its upper arm. The weapon's energy level was instantly known to the Vog. A second thought summoned a long starsteel knife from another pocket of netherspace, the blade long and serrated. The hilt wrapped its length around the Vog's upper-right thigh.

The tall creature plodded to the exit, but before it left its home and office, it stopped at a closet and opened the storage space with a thought. A vest flew from the interior and wrapped itself around the creature's shiny chest. A thought later, and a second sheet of material dropped from the vest, unraveling itself the full length until it resembled a sleeveless winter duster. That wasn't all, however. The creature reached inside and pulled forth a black felt hat, with a ring of serrated fangs decorating the rim.

The Vog herdsvog placed the hat upon its head, adjusted it just so, and thought-opened the door.

31

"The end," Nathan's mother said with a contented smile, and closed the storybook with a soft clap. She stood up from his bedside and moved to the oil lamp, perched on a small chest. Eight-year-old Nathan watched her every movement.

"Did you like the story?" she asked, picking up the lamp.

"Yes."

"*Alice in Wonderland* is my favorite," she told him. "My mother gave me this book. I think I read it in two days."

Nathan's eyes drooped.

"What an imagination Mr. Lewis had," she said, her voice laced with pleased wonder. "I've read this book five times since, and every time, I wonder if there are places where... if you crawl or step through them, there's a chance you might find yourself in another place. Another world. Where everything is...very different. Where the animals talk, and up is down, and down is up. That sort of thing."

"Mm-hm," Nathan agreed, struggling to stay conscious.

His mother held the lamp by her side, the light as bright as a captured star. Darkness crowded her around the edges, however, dimming her face.

"Mother?" Nathan asked.

"Yes?"

"If you... had a chance..." a deep yawn broke his thought. "Would you... want to go..."

"To a place like this?" she asked with a smile, and held up the book. She sighed, long and dreamy, the sound nudging Nathan just a little more to sleep.

"I don't know," she said. "A story is one thing, and I daresay I wouldn't be as brave as Alice. But you know something..."

Nathan didn't answer.

"I do think..." she began.

But by that time, Nathan had fallen asleep.

*

Chumpchumpchumpchump … Chumpchumpchumpchump

Nathan awoke with a lurch.

It took a moment, but he slowly realized he was still inside the mysterious chamber that had saved them from the crabs. He relaxed, wiped the drool from his mouth, and realized that he was a pale shade of green. Light from the glowing rings set into the ceiling had colored him, and he smiled faintly at the result. The temperature remained cool inside, but he had no way of knowing if the sun was up or not.

Nathan glanced around the smooth, featureless interior, and a shock ripped through him.

Thin blue wires extended from the walls and had attached themselves to his arms and chest. One had even slithered up into his neck. In a panic, Nathan jumped to his feet and ripped the cords away. Jimmy and the others awoke to see him freeing himself of the wires, only to realize that they were similarly afflicted.

"What the hell?" Eli exclaimed before he plucked away four of the things. There was no blood, just a pale discoloration that was noticeable even under the green light.

"Leeches!" Gilbert said, frantically examining his arms, his legs, and then, with an absolute terrified look, his manhood. "Oh thank you Jesus," he sighed in relief, seeing all was well south of the border.

"They aren't leeches," Mackenzie said, studying the dangling wires. "But damn if I know what they are."

"They're moving," Jimmy pointed out.

That quieted the lot of them, as, sure enough, the wires withdrew into small holes within the walls. Once inside, the holes sealed up without a sound, to nothing more than a small nail head.

"The hell was that all about?" Eli wanted to know.

"No idea," Nathan said.

"Nate," Jimmy said. "Weren't you cut?"

Nathan glanced at his knee, the one cut by the knife arm back on the train. The wound had healed, the scar barely noticeable. Nathan probed the patch of skin, stretching it one way then the other, before letting it go. "The hell happened there?"

"Mine's gone, too," Gilbert declared in wonder, inspecting his legs and seeing only faint traces of wounds.

"How long have we been sleeping?" Jimmy asked.

"Not long enough for that to happen," Eli said.

"Well, it did," Nathan said and looked puzzled, suddenly aware of something else. He felt good. He pawed at the back of his neck and inspected his arms, but couldn't feel anything resembling the painful tightness of sunburn he should've had.

In fact, he felt fully refreshed.

"You boys feeling all right?" he asked the others.

The four men thought about it and went about checking themselves out.

"I feel pretty good," Mackenzie said. "Despite where we are."

"Same here," Jimmy reported.

"Yeah," Eli said in a suspicious tone.

"Me too," Gilbert added.

"I don't hear any of them crabs trying to get in either," Eli said and nodded at the door.

It was true. In the silence that followed, all seemed quiet enough.

"How long were we asleep?" Jimmy asked.

"No idea," Nathan said.

"We got bigger problems," Eli said. "And that's getting out of this shitter."

"It's a pretty nice shitter, Eli," Gilbert said, whereupon Eli silenced him with a scowl.

Nathan moved to the door and located the picture of the whirlpool. He studied the symbol and wondered if the thing would indeed open the door if touched.

"This might do it," he said. "It closed the door before. There's nothing else around that I can see."

"So that's it?" Eli asked. "We push that, it opens, and we go?"

"I ain't goin' back out there," Gilbert said fearfully. "Not if them things are out there."

"It's quiet," Nathan said after a listen. "Maybe they gave up when they couldn't get in. If the sun's gone down, now might be the chance to get away."

"Get away to where?" Mackenzie asked.

Nathan didn't answer right away. "Same direction we were going before all this happened."

"Not sure I like that direction," Eli countered in a surly tone.

"Well, that's the only direction we got."

"Maybe I got another direction to go in."

"Yeah?" Nathan asked, feeling the rapid rise in tension. "Where's that?"

"Maybe I'll decide when I get out of here."

"You thinking about leaving, Eli?"

"Leland's gone. Might as well."

"Go on, then," Nathan dared in a calm voice. "Leland's idea was still a good one. Find the caboose."

"Leland's dead," Eli said. "And we're sure as hell nowhere near a train. I don't think we'll ever find that train again, so it's best we look elsewhere. See just what else is out there."

"Nothing else out there. Not for us, anyway."

"Yeah, well, I'll be the judge of that."

"You do what you want," Nathan said. "We'll do the same."

"So you're takin' over for Leland now, Rhodes?" Eli asked, his eyes narrowed. "You seem to be doin' a lot of talkin' for these boys. Maybe they'll want to stick with me."

A distinct silence fell over the interior then, one which Nathan was familiar with. He needed to be extra careful with his next few words, because he knew, just knew, Eli *was* thinking about taking over the gang.

The men heard a loud click of a hammer then, and Eli didn't so much as flinch at the sight of a rifle barrel not three inches from his profile. An unwavering Jimmy Norquay eyed the gun runner with disdain.

"Got a question, Jimmy?" Eli asked, apparently unfazed that the buffalo hunter had a gun to his head.

Gilbert didn't have his rifle on him, but Mackenzie had his revolvers still hanging off his naked hips. Mackenzie glared at the other gun runner, making it clear that if Gilbert was stupid enough to try anything, Mackenzie would draw and fire.

Despite the cool air filling the interior, Nathan felt the temperature rise.

"Got a message," Jimmy said after a solemn moment.

"Yeah?" Eli asked. "What's that then?"

"I'll let Nathan talk for me before I let the likes of you talk for me."

"That so, now?"

"That's so."

"Huh," Eli stated, mulling over the situation. "You know about him, right? 'Member that conversation we had about the lawman here? Huh? How he tried for a job with the North West police? And during the sit-down with the sheriff he got called on to back the sheriff up? Real life test, see if'n Nathan had the nerves, the calm, to settle things down without firing a shot. Remember that?"

"I remember."

Nathan remembered as well.

Going with Sheriff Parkinson just as Eli had said, to confront a couple of horse thieves spotted in town by a bystander. An unexpected shootout in a stable, and Sheriff Parkinson going down on one bloody knee. His shooter bleeding out on a mat of hay, done in by Parkinson's bullet, fired at the same time. The sheriff screaming at Nathan not to let the other boy get away, so Nathan, carrying only a rifle, chased the boy out through the back, into the prairie town. He remembered the thrill of the chase, until the bastard he was chasing realized there was only one on his tail, and decided he'd had enough running. The boy, an eighteen-year-old brute with a baby face and a few hairs for a mustache, smiled in a dirty fashion when he realized he was being chased by a kid perhaps the same age as himself. And about fifty pounds lighter.

"You don't have the guts to shoot me," the bigger boy had said, balling his fists up and walking forward. "I'm gonna put my boot up your ass."

"You're…" Nathan tried to say 'under arrest', *but the other boy didn't give him a chance. The other boy started swinging. The two youngsters traded blows, and while the bigger boy was stronger, Nathan was faster, and he had more sting to his punches. Still, ruddy cheeks were bruised on both, as were eyes and noses. They swung for the fences for a good minute, before the fight went to the ground and they wrestled for a bit. After that brief tussle, they broke off and stood up, and Nathan thought he could* win *this thing, really* win *it.*

Until the bigger boy pulled out a boot knife and cut Nathan's cheek.

A lawman was supposed to uphold the law, his father once told him. To the best of his ability, and to protect the people. A lawman was supposed to keep calm during challenging, stressful times, especially when bad blood was boiling, and the need to spill some blood seemed unavoidable. A lawman had to stay in control at all times.

Nathan had told his father he could do that.

But when the bigger boy opened up his cheek with one flash of a knife, smiling when he did so, well, Nathan discovered he had something no lawman should ever have.

And that was rage.

A killer rage.

"That one right there killed a boy no older than himself with his bare fists," Eli said, nodding at Nathan. "Broke open the boy's head like it was a melon. Only stopped when the fury left him and his arms felt like goddamn lead. In the rush of the moment, neither one of them noticed the crowd following them. About a dozen of us. Me included, though young Nate there didn't recognize me. I remembered him, though. Won't forget that sight. Him all ferocious and bloody, bent over the other one with his goddamn face smashed in. That the one you're looking to let speak for you, Jimmy?"

"Rather him than you, Eli," Jimmy replied quietly.

"That says a lot."

"It does, don't it," Jimmy agreed.

"Hell with this," Eli said after a few seconds. "You coming, Gilbert?"

"Yeah, I guess." Though, Gilbert didn't sound so happy about it.

And Eli picked up on it. "You sound like you'd rather be stuck in here, with them."

"Strength in numbers, Eli," Gilbert said with a touch of shame, knowing full well he might look like he was betraying his friend. "And, anyway, I think we were on the right path. Until all them crab fuckers jumped on us."

Eli studied him, then the rest, branding each as if warning them to be on guard later, when he made it back to the Rockies. "I'm leavin'."

"That's a mistake, Eli," Nathan said, exchanging looks with Jimmy and Mackenzie.

"You don't tell me what to do."

"You're right. Go on then, if you're that stubborn."

"I am. Goddamn right, too. Let me outta here."

Nathan shook his head and located the whirlpool picture. Jimmy lowered the rifle, and surprisingly, Gilbert stood aside. Eli noticed and his jawline twitched at the betrayal.

"Let me out of this shithouse," he grumped and snatched up his rifle. He adjusted the bandolier across his chest and pushed his way to the door.

When he looked ready, Nathan reached up and paused, fingers poised over the whirlpool.

He touched the picture.

And the door opened.

The sun had indeed dropped from the sky, rendering the desert in shade. The sky was cloudless, however, and a wonderfully clear and startling deep hue of purple. The air remained warm and uncomfortably humid, the first breath of it clashing with the cooler stuff already in their chests.

"Christ," Eli muttered. "Like breathing in steam. Or worse."

Nathan and the others gazed out into the night. The green light extended a few feet outside, offering a glimpse of the desert. The crab hordes were gone, leaving tracks half-filled by some long-spent wind. Bits and pieces of clothing were scattered everywhere, as well as bits and pieces of gear the men dropped while fleeing their attackers. There was no sign of Leland or Shorty, however.

"Looks like a herd of cattle ran through here," Mackenzie said.

"One that'll take your damn head off," Nathan added. "I don't see Shorty or Leland." *Which was a good thing*, he didn't add, knowing he did not want to see their remains. A pang of sadness resurfaced in Nathan's craw. He'd liked both men. Especially Leland, almost in a favorite uncle kind of way. They'd only known each other for a week and a bit, but still, Nathan was already thinking about asking to stay on with Leland's gang a little longer if he needed an extra gun hand.

"Any of them crabs around?" Jimmy asked.

"Not a sign," Nathan replied, grateful for the question. "Some clothes out there, though."

"Good."

It was good. No one needed to be walking around with their bare asses hanging out. Or their bird's nests on display. Nathan studied the land, and before he could give the okay, Eli pushed by him and started searching for his gear.

"I'll give him one thing," Mackenzie said under his breath. "The bastard don't scare at all."

"You got that right," Jimmy added.

They watched for a bit, then Gilbert shoved his way through the portal, earning a few scowls. Gilbert caught up with his partner, and the two gun runners searched the sands, collecting what was theirs while discarding what wasn't.

"Hey," Gilbert exclaimed softly. "My drawers are dried. Everything's dried. Little hot, though. And dustier than your mother's hooch, Eli, but everything's warm and dry."

"Shut up, Gilbert," Eli fired back as he dug out his own possessions. "You insult my mother's memory again and I'll put a bullet in your hairy ass without thinking about it."

"Awww, Eli. I was only joking."

"Joke about how goddamn small your pecker is then, but don't you be sayin' shit about my mother. That's all I'm saying."

Burned by the scolding, Gilbert returned to picking his things out of the sand.

"Well," Nathan said in defeat. "Might as well go out and get our things. Just keep an eye on the hills. In case those things decide to show up again."

They stepped outside, and Eli stopped and studied them. "Grew some balls, didja?"

"Go to hell, Eli," Nathan replied and began searching for his own possessions.

"Anything with a yellow shit stain on it is yours," Eli said.

"Said go to hell, or you and I are gonna take up where we left off, and if that comes to guns, Lord knows what it might attract."

"Thought you might say something like that," Eli said with a hint of sly sauciness, but when Nathan didn't take it any further, the gun runner returned to searching the broken surface of the sands.

They collected what they could, identifying who owned what by the green light from the shelter. Nathan managed to pick up most of what was his. His father's felt hat had flattened in the crab skirmish, but a fist rectified that problem. The others' hats weren't so fortunate, as many were trampled and pocked with ragged holes, as if punctured by the crabs' legs. And everything was indeed dry, if not on the side of steamy, and dusty. They discovered the bloody tatters of Leland and Shorty's dusters. Jimmy picked up Shorty's undamaged shotgun and placed it on his load of gear. They pulled ammunition belts and bandoliers from the sand, still holding most of their shells. They each had a rifle for themselves now, as well as the Colts. Of the remaining dynamite, however, they could find only five sticks. The box of matches was still in the inside pocket of Jimmy's winter duster, so that was good… but most had been snapped, leaving very short sticks indeed.

With every passing second, Nathan grew a little more nervous, scanning the nearby shadows.

"We gotta get going," he finally said.

"Which way?"

Nathan settled on a direction. It wasn't just any random choice. It was directly past the green-lit shelter that had saved their lives. Something tugged him that way.

"Follow me," he said.

To his surprise, Eli didn't argue, and both he and Gilbert followed the rest. The man might be dangerous, but Nathan was glad to see he wasn't stupid.

They marched, and as they passed the shelter, Nathan reached out and patted its alabaster side.

Nathan wasn't the only one to do that.

Mackenzie did his own thankful pat upon the shelter's rump, as did Jimmy

Norquay. Gilbert slapped the side a little too loud, enough for him to sputter, "goddammit" at the resulting twang. Even Eli Gallant took a moment to nod at the thing, offering his own way of thanks for saving his miserable hide.

They only marched so far, when Nathan slowed in his sandy tracks and squinted up ahead.

"What's wrong?" Mackenzie asked.

"You don't feel that?"

Jimmy stopped beside Mackenzie, and both men waited. The others halted a few strides behind, wondering what the hold-up was.

"Feel what?" Mackenzie asked.

"I feel it," Jimmy said somberly and turned around.

"Yeah," Nathan whispered, turning to look back at the shelter, its shell gone somber under the purple night sky.

"I feel it, too," Gilbert said, and one look at Eli confirmed it.

That gentle tug they were feeling, like some unseen magnet, was pulling them back.

To the white shelter.

"We already been there," Mackenzie said.

But Nathan was already walking back. Jimmy was behind him, which turned the others around. Mackenzie's head drooped in resignation, and he eventually trudged after them.

They returned to the shelter and circled its substantial girth. Fallen sand piled against the base, but the exterior was unblemished, which seemed remarkable considering the pounding the structure had taken from the crabs.

They stopped at the door. Which was closed.

"You close that?" Jimmy asked.

"Did no such thing," Nathan said. "It was open when I left."

"Yeah, it was," Gilbert agreed. "It was. I remember."

"So who closed the goddamn thing?" Eli demanded.

No one had an answer.

Until Mackenzie said, "Maybe it closed itself."

Such a thing wasn't so hard to believe.

"You know," Gilbert said. "That whole door? Where it's round and all? It kinda looks like a nipple."

"Everything looks like a nipple to you," Jimmy muttered without turning his head.

"Being on the go for a week and a bit will do that to a man," Gilbert explained with a shrug and a little smile.

Nathan dropped his gear onto the sand. He located that odd indentation and rubbed his fingertips over it. "I'm gonna open it."

"Then do it," Eli softly urged. "Because something's coming."

That turned them all around, and the gun runner pointed, though there really wasn't any need to point.

There, already descending from the purple sky, was a light. A *green* light, shining like a crashing comet. It dropped beneath that far-off horizon of mountain peaks and seemingly hung in the shadows like candlelight in a dark window.

"It's coming this way," Mackenzie realized. "Nate, that damn thing is coming this way."

And it was.

Just in the few seconds they took to watch it, the light had grown considerably. It was miles to those mountains, perhaps even hundreds of miles, but the light was buzzing towards them much faster than any train. Much faster than a bullet, even.

The men fidgeted with unease.

"The hell you waiting for, Rhodes?" Eli said in a low tone.

Nathan faced the door. He located the groove and slipped his fingers inside that odd-looking bullseye. Once again, that pliable material of unknown origin chilled his fingertips.

A whine of unseen gears and machinery started up, and ended with that circular hatch whirling open.

Except the interior was no longer the bare, green-lit interior they were expecting.

Directly before them was a dimly lit passenger car of the 311, gently rocking with the train's movement, the rows of windows reflecting pale lamplight. Light fixtures swayed from the ceiling, directly over that familiar aisle running through the center of the car, dividing the seats. A scattering of passengers rode in some of the berths, though their faces were hidden in shadow and they showed no inclination of having seen the gang members. Even that smell of fading varnish, ghostly perfume, and spent tobacco, wafted past them.

The sight of it all rendered the men speechless.

Except for Eli Gallant.

"*Get in there!*" the gun runner shouted, exasperated by the lack of movement. And the man was right.

Nathan grabbed up his gear and rifle. He stepped through first, staggering into the aisle and righting himself with his armload.

The shadowy passengers didn't react.

The others came through, piling in behind him, forcing him a few steps up the aisle. He stopped at the third berth, where he heaved his stuff into the nearest seat and brought up his rifle, aiming it at those still, dark figures. There were two lamps in the car, one lit at either end, in a corner.

"Close that door, Eli," Mackenzie yelled.

The gun runner dumped everything he carried to do exactly that. He slammed the train car door shut on that weird speeding light.

Eli straightened and placed his back to the wall. An oil lamp burned on the opposite side. He snatched up his rifle and aimed at the door.

Nathan and the others did the same.

*

The Vog herdsvog parked his lander and slowly got out of the transport amidst spurts of troubling fumes and a clattering of rotors. Its eye stalks parted in a way suggesting it was bored, or weary from the long trip to this particular sector. The creature straightened, looked around without moving its head, and lifted its kor blaster. Out of habit, the Vog reached up and adjusted its black felt hat so that the lip hung just over its eye stalks, creating a shady scowl.

The Vog sized up the capsule. One eye stalk swung to the right before slowly returning to line up with the left eye stalk. The proboscis beneath them drew up, closer to its eyes, creating the Vog equivalent of a scowl.

The herder marched up to the closed capsule. Standing before it, it readied its weapon with that same weary attitude and inserted a finger into the activation slot. The circular door opened wide with a motorized buzz.

To reveal an empty interior, illuminated by green light.

<h1 style="text-align:center">32</h1>

They waited, guns at the ready, poised for violence.

Mackenzie shifted so that he was in the next berth, aiming at the unmoving figures seated farther back in the passenger car. Nathan was aware of the man's movements, but he was more aware of that car door and the orange glow coming from its window. So they waited, for the green light, and whatever it might bring.

And they waited.

And waited.

Eli had his head pressed up against the wall, eyeing the door, in position to blow the face off whatever might come through. His mouth was a tight button and his eyes narrowed to slits. Gilbert was only a seat back, taking cover in a berth while aiming his Winchester at the door. Jimmy had Shorty's shotgun—now his shotgun—leveled and waiting for whatever might appear.

The seconds stretched on.

Until, finally, growing impatient, Eli huffed and leaned forward, much to the others' piggish grunts of protest. He placed an ear to the door and listened, frowned, and shifted just a little.

"Well?" Gilbert asked, over the soft clatter of the moving train.

"Well…" Eli said. "If there is anything out there, it's being awfully goddamn cute about it. Can't hear a goddamn thing."

"Maybe it don't make any noise?" Gilbert asked.

Eli pulled back to the wall and faced his companion. "Or maybe it ain't there. Maybe something else is there."

"Like what?"

"I don't know, Gilbert," an annoyed Eli stressed. "I ain't educated like them cocksuckers."

That put a scowl on Nathan's face, and Jimmy wasn't too impressed either.

"How's them passengers, Mack?" Nathan asked.

"Good as gold," Mackenzie stated. "Tell the truth, I think they're dead."

That distracted the others.

The passengers hadn't moved an inch, nor had they made a sound. They were perfectly scattered around the center of the car, just outside of the lamp's fluttering glow.

"Go check on them," Nathan said. "Make sure they understand… our resolve."

That was one of Leland's words, and Nathan thought it meant attitude. Or determination. Or both.

Mackenzie hesitated before getting out of his berth and marching back.

Nathan returned to watching the door. "Jimmy, you got that dynamite?"

"Yeah."

"Why don't you fix us up a stick. Just in case."

Jimmy opened his winter duster, still holding the shotgun, and rummaged about.

Nathan checked on Mackenzie. He was standing back there, a shadow among his own kind, inspecting the passengers. He carefully stepped into one berth and sized up the situation before moving on to the next.

None of the passengers moved or squeaked from fear.

"This is some peculiar shit, if I ever seen it," Eli whispered nearby.

"I'm in agreement with you there," Nathan said.

"I don't think there's anything behind this door."

"Why don't you open it and check?"

Eli's stuck his jaw out. "Maybe I will."

"I'm serious," Nathan said. "Jimmy's got a stick there."

Mackenzie's boots clomping on the carpeted floor distracted them. "They're all dead," he reported quietly.

"What?" Nathan asked.

"All dead. Corpses. I mean… corpses. Like something left in the desert sun and dried up like lizards. Parched and gone."

The rolling of the train filled the considering silence that followed.

"We're gonna open that door," Nathan said, to which Mackenzie decided to take cover in the berth behind Jimmy.

"You think that's wise?" Mackenzie asked.

"Fuck wise," Eli spat, and reached for the handle. "And fuck whatever's in there. You all ready?"

Grim nods all around, except for Mackenzie.

Eli opened the door, revealing a passenger car filled with patrons, chatting and carrying on, while a few well-dressed children no higher than one's waist bolted up and down the aisle. There was no vestibule, and that didn't seem to bother the gang members. All there was, was a full train car, the clueless passengers sitting with their backs to Nathan and the rest. A pleasant chatter graced the air while all those smells noted earlier wafted through the car. A conductor with a sizeable mustache straightened and handed something back to a gray-haired couple, underneath a fancy fixture that gently swayed with the train's motion. Smoke curled around those lights and the two others like it, creating a comfortable haze that clung about the ceiling and obscured the overhead compartments.

So surprised by the seemingly natural scene of an ordinary train's interior, the five outlaws were dumbstruck. At that moment, the train lurched enough to make Eli stagger. He released the door's handle. The door slid shut, just as the conductor looked up with a rather dignified expression of puzzlement.

"Goddammit," Eli swore, regaining his balance and gawking at the others.

"The hell was that?" Nathan said and went for the door. He stopped just beside it and gripped the handle.

"The hell's going on, Nate?" Jimmy asked.

"Down the rabbit hole," Mackenzie said. "We're down the rabbit hole."

"Get ready," Nathan said, meeting the eyes of each gang member.

He opened the door and a set of black tentacles exploded from the rectangular opening. Several fat limbs lashed out with whip-like precision, wrapping themselves around Nathan's waist, his limbs, and his neck, while an ungodly screeching pierced his ears. The attack transfixed the train robber, immobilizing him with a frightening strength, and lifted him off the floor. Nathan floated in that muscular knot, the thigh-sized cord slinking around his throat and jaw, tightening, bulging his eyes and dispensing with his shock, convincing him that he only had seconds before the thing…

Nathan's breath shot out his nose, onto that vile textured flesh that smelled like rancid meat a vulture wouldn't touch. The others were screaming around him, all the while the train's ominous *Chumpchumpchumpchump, Chumpchumpchumpchump* returned with all the might of booming thunder. Or, perhaps that was the blood pounding through the tightening vice of Nathan's neck, forcing it upwards and stretching his temples.

With his head held fast, Nathan could not move. He stared at the inner folds of the tentacles, and an ebony face materialized deep within that fetid rose-petal cluster. A frightening expression of displeasure with flesh the color of oil. Obese features puffed and narrowed as if taking a deep breath, and yellow eyes blazed hatred. That fat face turned ever so slightly one way before oddly elongating towards him. A mouth unzipped at one corner, revealing not teeth, but a bony serration that resembled scissors cut from obsidian.

That slick otherworldly thing pulled Nathan forward, toward its off-white limb chopper of a mouth, while the irises of the creature's eyes split into two and the pupils therein became slits.

A spurt of frothy spit spilled over that ever-widening maw.

Nathan panted and fumed and squeezed his eyes shut when a gun barrel jammed itself through those tightening appendages and fired. That obscene alien face disappeared in a blast of black and green filth, and a mass of organic muck as thick as coffee grounds spattered Nathan.

Just before the other guns opened fire.

Bullets ripped into that mass of tentacles, taking huge chunks from its writhing hide. Several punched through to the creature's destroyed face, blowing holes into the blushing meat. A smell not unlike cooked corn filled Nathan's nose then, and the appendage holding onto his neck convulsed, coming only a fraction of an ounce away from crushing his windpipe completely.

But then it relaxed, as did all the other limbs holding him.

Nathan crashed to the floor, no longer held aloft in that mighty grip. Hands grabbed his arms. They pulled him away from the deflating mass that was retreating back into the doorway as if hauled from the other side. The tentacles slid free of Nathan, leaving him sputtering in green blood as thick and rancid as pea soup.

Jimmy fired another salvo of shotgun shells into the creature's collapsing front, and the entire beast sucked itself back inside the portal. It passed over the threshold with such violent force, the door slid closed with a noisy rattle.

"Jesus H. Christ," Eli Gallant breathed, staring in wide-eyed wonder at the closed door.

"Did you… get it?" Nathan rasped, holding onto his hurting throat.

"Think so," Jimmy Norquay said, popping open the shotgun and shucking the spent shells. He immediately reloaded, fishing fresh ammunition from his duster's pocket.

The men had pulled Nathan back in the aisle, covered in that offensive green slop, but very much alive. They aimed their weapons at the closed door, waiting, seeing if the creature would try to attack again.

"Nothing," Mackenzie said. "It's gone."

"We killed it," Gilbert said from behind his rifle.

Without a word, Eli went to the door and yanked it open.

An empty train car lay beyond.

"The hell's going on here," he muttered and closed the door. A second later, on impulse, he opened it again.

A flatbed, with the slow turning car some fifty yards ahead, and a green sun hanging in the distance.

Eli closed the door, ran a shaking hand over his face, and licked his lips. "God..." he started, but couldn't finish, perhaps leaving the Almighty in a state of confusion, wondering if the mortal was about to ask a question.

Nathan lay on his backside, leaning against one of the berths while Jimmy and Mackenzie flanked him. Their weapons faltered upon witnessing each successive change of what lay beyond the door.

"Can't be..." *real.* But Eli didn't finish that thought, because he yanked the door open again.

Outside. Nothing but flatbeds, perhaps dozens of them, many more than the one before. Each rectangular plane was stretched before the other, all the way to the rear of a distant car, barely visible and no bigger than a postage stamp. Overhead, green lightning crackled across a pink sky.

Eli shut and opened the door again.

An empty passenger car, filled with the same hardwood berths, and polished to a fine finish, all under plentiful light. Spiders the size of dogs hung from the ceiling, their webbing crisscrossing and smothering the overhead compartments with dewy, glistening strands in the lamplight.

Eli slammed the portal closed, took a breath, and yanked it open.

Passengers in a car without seats at all. They stood, dressed in the fashionable styles of the day. Some had their heads down, reading newspapers, while others stared out their windows. A few of the closest passengers tensed, sensing they were being watched, and slowly turned around, revealing alligator eyes, toothy, lipless maws, and surprised faces.

With an uncharacteristic cry of fear, Eli threw the door closed. He rasped, his shoulders shivering, and glanced over at his outlaw companions who saw everything he'd seen, and were equally at a loss.

The gun runner opened the portal a dozen times in rapid succession. Each time revealed a different setting. Sometimes the car's interior was slightly off; red velvet instead of green, no seats, passengers without faces. Passengers *with* faces, but possessing multiple arms and legs. Passengers utterly alien, with the bulbous eyes of house flies yet with human limbs. Once, a massive shape shot by the doorway like a ravenous bird picking at gnats.

"See!" Eli yelled and closed the door again.

"See?" he insisted, gesturing at a now ordinary interior again.

"*See?*" Again he whipped it shut, straightened his shoulders, and hauled the door open yet again.

"*S—*" he was about to say, when a blast of turquoise water erupted from the doorway, dousing them all, and actually bowling over Nathan, Mackenzie, and Jimmy. The water hit with all the force of a heavy mallet, rudely shoving the lads along the aisle until they recognized both Eli and Gilbert were protected by the berths. The jet of water, however, filled the doorway completely, quickly spreading along the floor of the passenger car as if it were a fine underwater grotto.

"Close the door!" Jimmy was shouting. "Close the door!"

But Eli Gallant could not close the door.

And Nathan saw why. When he had whipped that portal open, the infernal gush of water filled the doorway completely, cutting Eli off from latching onto the handle. The force of the water slapped away the gunman's hand, so he gave up and urged Gilbert to start climbing over the berths.

Towards the rear of the train.

"*Come on,*" Nathan roared, forcing life into his pinched limbs. Water sprayed him, splashing off the wooden frames of the seats, dousing his eyes. Once again it felt like they were back under some mysterious sea. He looked, his face dripping and his vision partially skewed, and saw the closed door at the end of the car.

Some fifty feet away.

The water was already to their knees, filling the aisle completely and frothing like creamy jade. The rising water impeded their speed. They flipped themselves over the seats with loud cries. They landed with splashes and rose with shocked sputters, all the while the water climbed to their thighs. The lit lamps flittered over the green waters, once again bestowing a dreamlike quality that mystified and terrified Nathan.

Thirty feet away from the exit door, the aisle was already submerged, but that mad gush continued to roar behind them.

"Christ Almighty," Eli panted, fear infecting his voice.

They waded now, *kerplunking* up to their chests before rising, staggering forward in an energy-sucking hurdle chase. Mackenzie slipped and went under completely, becoming a ghostly oil slick within those green depths that dimmed but never darkened. Jimmy stopped and hauled him up. Gilbert cracked his head against the underbelly over the overhead compartments, and cursed a blue stream.

Twenty feet, and the water didn't sound so furious anymore.

Nathan glanced back and noted the exhausted faces behind him. The water still poured into the railway car, except much of the noise was smothered by the rising levels. Great ripples rolled over the water's surface.

It was then when Nathan saw the dorsal fins.

"Oh Sweet Jesus," he released, his verbal prompting and dismay luring the others to look.

"Holy *shit!*" Gilbert exclaimed and started pawing through the waves, pulling himself towards the final door.

"Stay out of the aisle!" Jimmy shouted.

Ten feet, and a curving, snaking log of… *something* filled the middle of the car, submerged some two feet down. It investigated the aisle at leisure, oblivious to the men. The sight of the thing doubled the train robbers' efforts, and they hurried over the seats, splashing down to their collarbones before attempting to rise again, but crouching so that they didn't rattle their skulls off the overhead compartments.

A great hissing of water jerked Nathan's head around. Back at the other end, the rising level hid the continuing flow. More dorsal fins cut the surface, creating smooth lines that seemed to intersect each other as they approached.

Nathan reached the door just as the water touched his chin. His father's felt hat lay against his back, and of all the other men, he was the only one who still had a hat. He stood with his head angled up and sucked down air. Gilbert was the next one to reach the end, looking like a tomcat knowing he was about to drown. Eli was right behind him, but he was watching what was below his chest.

Nathan looked and wished he hadn't.

Two of those logs swam towards them, their little fins fluttering their unnerving girths through the water.

Leeches, Nathan realized. The damn things looked like giant leeches. Or eels. Or, God forbid, a weird merging of the two species.

Jimmy and Mackenzie crowded in behind him, pushing him a little more to the door which was a finger's width away from being completely submerged.

"Quit pushin'!" Nathan roared as the two leech things came right up to his underwater belly, clothed in a ton of wet winter clothing. The creatures snaked away uninterested. Nathan swallowed, watching the things zigzag through those shockingly clear waters, where the bodies of the creatures didn't seem to end.

"Oh Jesus," Gilbert panicked in a little boy wail and pulled out a nasty-looking knife used for skinning buffalo. "If one of those things fastens on to my pecker, I'm gonna *scream*."

The leeches circled off, leaving the men alone for the moment, but Nathan's nerves were raw and crackling in those warm waters.

"Get the door open," he said. "Gotta get the door open."

Nathan got in position while Gilbert's fingers scrabbled along the top. The two men faced each other.

"One," Nathan said. "Two. Three—"

He yanked down hard on the door latch and pulled. A second later, Gilbert pushed.

And under that pressing weight of water, they opened the door just a crack.

The leeches changed course, right back toward the men. They coiled their undulating lengths and made lines for the gang, as if sensing they'd missed an opportunity.

"Pull, goddammit!" Gilbert screamed.

"I'm pullin'," Nathan squealed and drew breath to refuel his efforts.

Jimmy moved in, but there wasn't much room to work unless…

Without another thought, Nathan dove underwater. He went to the floor, gripped the doors edges, and braced his boots against the nearest berth, just to the side of Gilbert and Eli. Nathan stretched his legs all the way back and heaved himself with a watery groan of effort.

Through bubbly green waters, one of those eel-leeches moved in, zeroing in on Nathan's contorted face.

The door opened with a lurch, and the sudden rush of escaping water flushed Nathan through the opening in a fury of green-white. Nathan screamed. Heard screams. Things hit him, one even hard enough to greatly hurt his shoulder. A hard ridge slapped past his arm and he reached out and grabbed a wooden base. Someone rolled over him, clutching at his duster, but failing to hold on. Nathan fought for his bearings, realizing he was on the floor, and got to his knees.

The door was still open and water was pouring in, but not like the storm surge of the previous car.

The eel-leeches were nowhere in sight.

His clothing weighing a saturated ton, Nathan flipped himself over the berth and got to his feet. The other men rose around him. He pushed forward to the door and gripped the handle. With all his remaining might, Nathan shoved the door closed, decapitating that watery rush.

"Oh Jesus," Eli Gallant was panting, lifting himself up from the aisle. Others did the same, flopping weary limbs over seats and staring at Nathan's shivering figure with worn gratitude. Mackenzie's chest was heaving, his eyes rolling, but he lifted a hand to signal all was well. Jimmy and Gilbert collapsed in a couple of empty berths.

Unwilling to relax just yet, Nathan felt for his guns. His rifle was gone, but his Colts remained. Drawing deep settling breaths, he studied the interior of what seemed like a deserted passenger car, with three lit oil lamps shining brightly.

"See anything?" Jimmy croaked and coughed water.

Nathan shook his head.

"Nothing?"

"Nothing."

That prompted Jimmy to stand and look around.

"Hold onto your weasel for a second," Eli groaned. "Goddammit. We just almost *drowned*. Give me a second. To get my strength back."

Jimmy nodded in weary agreement.

"The hell was that, anyway?" Eli asked.

No one answered him.

"Nate," Jimmy finally said.

"Yeah?" Nathan asked dreamily, realizing that he'd gone into a morning daze.

"The hell is that?"

33

Nathan looked and wished he hadn't.

The passenger car—the rear half of the passenger car—shimmered like a desert mirage. The fabricated walls faded into the background but were still there, along with the car's pair of oil lamps. Within the center of that distorted screen of reality, however, slabs of stone materialized like rocks hauled to the surface from the deepest waters. Grainy tones of black and white gave the images a degree of depth, and a flourish of ghost gray misted a huge stone face. Nathan realized then he was looking at a mountain—an enormous wall of weather-clawed rock, wearing trees and greenery like pocket flowers on a wrinkled suit.

But if you looked *past* that scene, if you focused on one point, it was enough to see that the passenger car was still back there, behind that fantasy mountain.

Behind Nathan, the others rose from the watery floor, watching those flowing images as they played out before them.

"The hell?" Eli Gallant said, eyes narrowed and staring.

A drenched and equally mesmerized Gilbert stood nearby. He wiped his nose in a soaking coat sleeve and gave a mighty snort. Mackenzie lifted his hands as if completing some feat of sorcery, while Jimmy simply stood and watched, Shorty's shotgun held by his thigh.

"What is that?" Nathan asked and expected no answer.

A multitude of white-tipped rocks gathered at the base of the mountain. It took Nathan a moment to realize he was looking at hats—hats with heads underneath. The hats resembled a mass of tiny, rounded pyramids. No, a mass of tiny *cones*. The image remained coarse and at times flickered to reveal the berths behind it, reminding the gang members that they were still aboard a train.

The figures worked a line, and before long, arms gradually came into sight, connected to torsos that bent and straightened. It took Nathan a moment to identify them.

"Those are…" he started.

"Chinamen," Jimmy finished quietly, watching the men labor over something.

A few seconds later, the black and white masses parted. Two narrow strips of metal were laid over much thicker chunks of wood. A railroad. The beginnings of a railroad.

"They're laying rail?" Gilbert asked.

"Who you think built this damn thing," Eli Gallant muttered, still soaking wet. "Or at least most of it."

The Chinese men bent their backs, setting down railway ties at measured intervals and passing along sledgehammers, pickaxes, and timbers. Hundreds of men worked the railway, bent over under a pale sun—a sun that as coincidence would have it, was right over one of the distant wall lamps. Time sped forward, resulting in the ghostly men working at five times the pace. Forests were magically cleared, and hollows filled, right up to the mountain face. There were others working with the Chinese men as well. Men both black and white, though the black men appeared the worse for wear. They wore cotton shirts and pants of varying shades of gray, often with suspenders that formed an X across their backs. Groups of six or seven workers pulled up whole sections of rail and fitted them to black timbers, one after the other.

Hundreds worked on the line, but it seemed the Chinamen had amassed closer to the mountain wall. Gray-uniformed official types came into view then, as the scope of the operations panned outward. Where the men worked over the rails, swinging sledgehammers or carrying building materials, that all became the background. In the foreground were faceless figures riding horses and gesticulating with curt chops of their hand. There were others, engineer types, set up on nearby hills, with tables filled with all manner of engineering instruments. One faceless man was bent over a telescope, while another held up a fancy pair of those new binoculars. Two more individuals were bent over their table, pointing at matters while indicating the mountain.

"They have those binoculars," Gilbert noticed. "Hear you can see like an eagle with a set of those."

"You think one spyglass would be enough," Eli scoffed. "Only an educated smartass would want to put two of them together like that."

"Much better than a single spyglass," Mackenzie said. "You have two distinct images, which offer—"

"Look," Nathan said, quieting the discussion.

A group of well-dressed dignitaries approached the engineers, interrupting their work. They wore black suits and black hats, their shoulders covered in what might have been white scarves. They stood around the table and seemed to be discussing something of importance. At one point, one of the dignitaries pointed at the mountain wall, and took a decidedly confrontational stance. That seemed to anger the engineers, who placed their hands on their hips and proceeded to give as good as they got.

All the while, workers cobbled together the railway in the background. Snow eventually fell, whitening the mountain. The snow was shoveled away, the rails cleared, and the work continued. The tracks shone against the frigid landscape, the iron glistening like polished marble.

The dignitaries were gone, but the engineers remained, fussing over a crate. One of them extracted a pair of sticks from the crate with great care.

"Dynamite," Jimmy Norquay whispered for them all.

The image zoomed to the mountain base, where several two-man teams drilled holes into the ground. The machines they used were hand-operated and crude, resembling smaller versions of southern oil towers, except more complicated-looking. Once finished, the drilling crews retreated, replaced by smaller groups of men who carefully filled the holes with dynamite. Fuses were set.

A second later, multiple blasts caused the entire picture to tremble, and that world became a dust cloud.

"Blasting the rock," Mackenzie explained. "First charges. They're starting on the tunnel."

The workers moved in, consisting of a great number of Chinamen. They loaded rubble onto horse carts and repeated, slowly removing the blasted debris.

"Goddamn," Eli muttered. "What a life."

"And all for cents," Jimmy added. "If that. And treated like dirt."

"How do you know?"

Jimmy glanced over his shoulder. "Oh, I know."

The images flowed faster in a watery flutter, showing an ant's nest of activity. Men swarmed over the blast site and with each passing second, a hole formed and deepened in the mountain.

"Well, well," Mackenzie whispered. "Look at that."

"What?" Nathan asked.

"That. Right there. Recognize it?"

Nathan did not.

"I do," Jimmy stated flatly.

"So what is it?" Eli blurted.

"That's the tunnel," Jimmy replied. "From the other side. No mistake."

Eli scowled and switched from the Metis man's profile to that yawning pit of pitch.

Time continued to rush by in a rapid replay of history. Snow melted, dark greenery blushed—or what Nathan assumed was greenery on the mountain—followed by snow again. The seasons rolled by about five or six times, seemingly in a loop, yet all the while, an army of men worked away in the shadow of the mountain, gradually burrowing into the side of that mighty rock.

There was an almost tidal quality about the history lesson, as men surged in and out of the tunnel. The blasts continued, several times through the passing seasons. Time after time great billowy gouts of rocks and dust heaved forth from the tunnel mouth. At times, men raced from the tunnel preceding a blast and immediately rushed inside after the explosion.

Sometimes, men went in, and they did not come out.

Usually, those men wore cone hats.

And on and on it went. Men would go into the tunnel, then leave, and an explosion would follow. At times, men were carried out upon horse carts, escorted by Chinamen. Nathan wasn't sure of what was going on, but it occurred to him that there were a lot of men dying in the construction of the tunnel. He didn't know if they were regular folks or not, but judging by the Chinamen hauling carts with their heads lowered, he thought it was a fair assumption it was their fellow countrymen.

"Lotta them dying," Gilbert observed, perhaps not having blinked for several seconds.

"Lotta them," Mackenzie said solemnly.

"You think they'd be more careful."

"I think they were as careful as they could be," Jimmy said. "But their employers just didn't give a shit."

"Because they were Chinamen?"

"Yeah. Because they were Chinamen."

That didn't sit well on Gilbert's conscience. "I might be a lot of things, and had a lot of things done to me, but none of them involved any Chinamen folk."

"Nor me," Nathan admitted, feeling more than a few embers of anger at how damned… *disposable* those poor bastards were to the railway people.

Then, as before, a huge surge of workers marched triple-time into the tunnel, on what seemed to be a summer day. Hundreds of cone-wearing individuals that went inside the tunnel… just before a mighty expulsion of dust was coughed back out. Then the stream of images went into a frenzy.

Men rushed to the tunnel mouth. Some figures staggered from it. Chinamen helped their companions out, men with broken arms or legs or head wounds that blackened their featureless faces. More activity around the tunnel, and the arrival of a train itself, and several more workers. The train stayed just outside of the tunnel mouth, but the workers all disappeared inside. All the while, the dignitaries and engineers watched on a nearby hill, waving and pointing at each other.

"The hell was all that about?" Eli wanted to know.

"Cave-in," Mackenzie said. "Or something of the like. Maybe some unstable dynamite going off."

"Killed all them poor bastards?"

"Mm-hm."

Eli didn't say a word after that. As hard a case he was, he clearly didn't like what he just saw. None of them did.

"Sent them to their deaths," Jimmy said. "Those sonsabitches."

"I've heard stories," Nathan said. "Of cruel things. Being done along the line."

"You just saw one of the cruelest," Mackenzie said. "Sending workers into an unstable cave. Like Jimmy said, they were sent to their deaths. Most all Chinamen."

"Good chance it was all Chinamen," Jimmy said.

"Why?" Gilbert asked.

"Because there were plenty of them, I figure. And the suits just didn't give a shit."

That stark assessment stunned the others.

"Sonsabitches," Gilbert finally whispered with heat. "And they call us criminals."

"All right," Eli said. "So what does any of that—"

The seasons blurred ahead again, where the previous mess of the cave-in (or whatever mishap had killed so many hard-working people) and a small stage decorated with ribbons was being constructed a ways back from a cleaned-up tunnel mouth. Workers wearing suspenders and overalls hammered away at the stage, while others buzzed nearby. Chairs were set up facing the tracks.

Then it was night.

A clear night, with a full moon in all its glory. A solitary figure, wearing heavy robes and with his hair tied back in a long ponytail, walked up to the tunnel mouth. Words were spoken, harsh words, filled with emotion. Filled with vengeance. Nathan didn't understand the language, but he understood fury, and the individual facing the tunnel was practically bursting with it.

"The hell's he doing?" Eli asked in a dead tone.

Nathan traded looks with Mackenzie and Jimmy Norquay.

The figure raised his arms to those brilliant heavens and marched into the tunnel mouth, where the blackness swallowed him up without a sound. Then he was gone, without any sign of having existed in the first place.

"So?" Eli asked with a shrug.

"Shut up, Eli," Nathan warned. "This is important."

"What's so damn important about watching a bunch of poor bastards being worked to death?"

Nathan silenced him with a look.

Night turned to day in that surreal sequence of events. Well-dressed people appeared and crowded into those seats, while many more filled the space before the decorated stage. Suited individuals stood upon that platform and waved their hands at the tracks.

A second later, in a dreamy locomotion, a train, a long train, rumbled along those shining tracks much to the adoration of the assemble crowds.

That iron horse rumbled right into the tunnel mouth, vanishing within its dark, dark depths, and all the while a chill of horror flared up and along Nathan's every nerve. He expected an explosion. A cave-in. Perhaps even the mountain itself collapsing upon the doomed train.

What he saw, however, was the caboose, filled with a handful of people waving handkerchiefs back at the audience. Just before they winked out of sight within the tunnel.

"Never to be seen again," Mackenzie marveled in quiet awe. "Never again."

The audience in that mystical mirage grew agitated then, as if something unseen was greatly upsetting. Horse riders arrived on scene, plunging into the tunnel, bearing torches and oil lamps. People crowded the tunnel mouth, obstructing it, until railway men pushed them back. The horsemen rode deep inside the cavern's depths, their light sources held high in the deepening dark.

"Never again," Gilbert repeated.

"So, what?" Eli said. "The train disappeared because, what? All those men died working on the tracks?"

"Maybe something like that," Mackenzie supposed. "But we're missing something."

"That man who went inside the tunnel," Nathan said.

Mackenzie nodded.

"Christ Almighty," Eli whispered.

"Who was he?" Nathan asked. "What did he do?"

"And was he responsible for all of this?" Mackenzie asked.

Eli shook his head. "You shitheads really surprise me. To think one man did all this."

"Well—" Nathan started.

But Eli cut him off. "Well, nothing. All I saw there was a bunch of Chinamen, black men, and whites working to an early grave on a railway. And one bastard walks into the tunnel at night and gets you all thinking of *shit*? I mean…"

He trailed off, staring ahead. "Now what?" he finished.

Nathan and the others looked. That ghostly retelling of history was diminishing, collapsing in on itself, and rebuilding the windows, walls, and berths around them once again. When it reached half its size, the whole picture faded away like heat shimmers off a desert just before sunset. The train rattled along, and it was night outside the windows.

Nathan didn't really want to look outside, for fear of what he might see.

The frightening smack of steel colliding with steel rooted the gang to the floor.

"Now—" *What?* Nathan was about to say, when the section where they'd just escaped crimpled inwards. An unseen pressure popped nails and bolts free with alarming force, while the lamps practically jumped off the wall.

There was a second's peace, then a growing yowl of collapsing metal.

"*Run!*" Mackenzie roared.

They did, stampeding up the aisles, every step a hard splash in ankle-deep water. The door at the far end was only a five-second run away. Five seconds. Even with his soaked clothing, it was a feat of strength to pound out those last few yards. All the while, a *scree-scraw* yowling of the train losing something important clawed at their ears and urged them to move faster.

"*RUN!*" Eli Gallant barked.

They ran. Powered by pure flight reflex, fearing for their lives.

Mackenzie reached the passenger train door first. He hauled it open to reveal a black screen and plunged through without a second thought, promptly vanishing. Jimmy was next, charging through without pause.

Nathan glanced over his shoulder and felt his blood crystalize in his veins so fast, his breath hitched in his throat.

Behind the frantic faces of Gilbert and Eli, the train was collapsing from the rear onwards, straight up the aisle, in a rush of exploding windows and wooden berths. It became an accordion squeezing out multiple notes of destruction. Cushions went up and over like soft planks. Light fixtures fell to the floor. Overhead compartments dropped and were shoved ahead with a rising tidal wave of debris as whatever the train had hit drove everything backward.

Nathan checked on where he was running—and leaped straight through the waiting portal.

34

They stood in a room.

An ordinary bedroom one might see upstairs in a hotel—or a saloon. A double bed was the centerpiece, and a thick, handsome quilt with frilly patterns covered it. A pair of lit oil lamps rested upon twin end tables, as well as porcelain wash basins that glowed under the light. A wardrobe against one wall had dark designs etched into the surface, and a mirror was set into the door. A pleasant smell of wood smoke drifted throughout, while water pattered from winter clothing onto a floor cleanly swept.

Mackenzie and Jimmy greeted Nathan with wide, questioning eyes just as Gilbert slammed into Nathan from behind, sending both men onto the bed with a thump and creak of timbers. Pillows flew onto the floor, and Nathan immediately shoved Gilbert away from him.

"Sorry," Gilbert drew out, but he was smiling, hitching up that unhealthy beard of his, while that mole rose high on his cheek and twitched with a life of its own.

"The hell you two think you are?" Eli Gallant puffed. "Down in Kansas?"

"Just happy to be alive is all," Gilbert explained as he sat up. He squeezed water from his sickly chin whisker before placing one finger against his pimpled nose and blowing, sending streamers over the blankets.

Though exhausted, Nathan still found the strength to get up from the bed and frown at the gun runner.

He looked to the passenger car door.

Except there wasn't one. Only a wall with paper on it, the showy kind covered with swirly designs, suggesting a lady's touch. There was even a second full-length mirror there, on its own legs.

As Eli was the last one through the now non-existent door, he stepped

211

over to the wall and rapped it with his rifle. He knocked all over, finding the studs, but nothing of a door.

"Well, then," he said and regarded the others. "Should I say it? Or will one of you smart asses do the goddamn honors?"

"This is some crazy shit, Eli," Gilbert muttered.

"Thank you, Gilbert. Though, I'd feel better hearing it from the three goddamn Wise Men here."

Mackenzie traded looks with Jimmy, who didn't say a word.

"This is crazy shit, Eli," Nathan said and meant every word.

That actually took a lot of steam out of Eli Gallant, who nodded, sized up the room, and walked across a solid floor to a rocking chair situated in the corner. He plopped into the thing and began rocking, placing his rifle across the arm rests and closing his eyes as if meditating. Nathan had to admit, he had to admire him for even making the effort.

"Well, we got this," Mackenzie said and went to the only door in the room.

"Not even a window here," Jimmy pointed out.

"Don't care," Nathan said. "Looks like we're back home. Somewhere at least."

"Taking this all calm-like."

"After all the shit we've seen, Jimmy?" Nathan asked, too weary to care about manners. "I don't care where the hell we are, as long as we're off that train. We just escaped a—an honest-to-God *crash*, and jumped through a door into… *this*."

Gilbert collapsed on the bed and closed his eyes. Jimmy Norquay rubbed his chin and mouth, squinting at the only door, directly across from where they escaped the crashing train.

"Wonder what's behind this one," Mackenzie added. He ran a palm over the door's surface.

Nathan joined him at the door. Then he cocked his head and frowned. "Not a thing," he said.

Then Mackenzie met Nathan's gaze.

Chumpchumpchumpchump…

So very faint, a fleeting ghost of a sound, except there, underneath the press of skin and bone.

"We're still on the train," Mackenzie whispered. "It's official."

"I'm feeling the pull," Jimmy said and indicated the door with a nod.

That was met with a round of wary agreement.

"Catch your breath," Nathan said. "And check your guns."

Nathan had lost his rifle, but he still had his bandoliers of ammunition. He unslung those from his wet shoulders and handed them over to Eli and Gilbert, who, along with Mackenzie, managed to hold onto their Winchesters. Jimmy didn't have his rifle either, but he carried Shorty's sawed-off cannon and had managed to find a dozen or so shells for the beast while searching the sands.

Nathan checked on his Colts, actually flicked them a few times to dry them, before returning them to their holsters.

And Jimmy still had his dynamite. Hidden in the folds of his heavy winter coat. Considering the amount of water they'd all just been through, Nathan wondered if the shortened matches would work.

"All set?" Nathan asked them.

Another round of nods.

"Can't we just camp out here for a while?" Gilbert asked. "I'm damn near done."

"We're in a hotel room," Mackenzie informed him. "Best get out of here while we can, before someone opens that door and finds us here."

"This place ain't right, either," Eli Gallant declared in a voice of disdain.

And it wasn't.

It was solid enough. Even comfortable. And certainly of a higher standard Nathan had never before encountered in all of his relatively short travels. But there was a feel of wrongness here, like a splinter driven into one's finger— not enough to hurt or bother, mind you, but lodged in the shallow portion of the skin just enough to be felt, especially when relaxing. Nathan wasn't sure what was setting him off about the room. Perhaps it was the lack of a window, or maybe it was the knowledge that they had just entered the room by passing through a now-solid wall.

"Yeah," Jimmy said. He squeezed at the scarf hanging loosely around his throat. Water dribbled down the front of his shirt.

"Jesus, Jimmy," Eli observed. "You drown back there or something?"

Jimmy only smiled.

Nathan watched them all before gripping the doorknob, wondering, hoping that some unholy mass of tentacles wasn't waiting for him on the other side. He pulled one of his Colts, just in case.

Then he opened the door.

And damn near had his hat blown off his skull by the force of *BOHM-BOHM-BOHM-BOHMBOHMBOHM*.

That tremendous roar staggered Nathan into the others, but the sight beyond the door amazed them even more. There was light and shadow, but the light was in blazing tethers, streaking, shining through clouds of smoke. Searching, strobing, in lines that swept over everything in perfect unity. There was a stout-looking railing that materialized within pinkish clouds, and a significant drop beyond that. The lights changed color in beat with the boot-stomping BOHM-BOHM-BOHM, but jigged and jagged over everything like wingless birds with their tail feathers on fire.

And there were *people* down there, beyond the stout railing, two levels below at least. Silhouettes drowning in a stygian cloud—figures that lit up for the briefest moments as the lights flashed over them. There was a damn town meeting below, townsfolk numbering perhaps in the hundreds, all packed in tight and jumping around as if walking barefoot over scorching coals.

"Holy shit," Nathan said, and he realized he couldn't hear his own voice.

He glanced back at the others, who were gawking at the scene beyond their room. Circles of light found Jimmy and Gilbert's bearded expressions of shock and flickered over them. The explosions of noise continued to hammer their eardrums, but there was an energy about them, a toe-tapping, boot-stomping goodness therein, almost like… *music.*

And then there was the air…

Three seconds, from opening the door to the earth-shaking booms of sound and the aimed bolts of lighting, from taking in the multitudes thrashing below to the very air they breathed.

Nathan gasped, and his nervous energy dissipated.

In fact, he felt like he might've downed half a bottle of rye whiskey. His mind swam, leaving only a very contented, extremely good mood in that drunken sense of awareness. The lights didn't bother him so much. The not-quite cannon shots were no longer frightening. And the people below…

A figure walked by the open doorway, because Mackenzie had pulled the thing as wide as the hinges would allow, and Nathan didn't have any recollection of that happening. But that didn't matter, because what just walked in front of them *did* matter. It mattered very much indeed.

It was a woman. Perhaps seven feet tall. Wearing only wisps of clothing that were goddamn inappropriate in Nathan's mind. He only thought that in a micro-second, however, before the notion dissipated like a hand poo-pooing away curls of smoke. The woman's… white-colored clothing—ribbons really—only covered her female parts—*barely*—and displayed an eye-popping amount of blue skin. Honest to *Christ* blue skin. She had a figure that was damn fetching, sleek and athletic, with hips a man just wanted to grab onto and hold for dear life. A black jet of hair flowed over her back in a thick tail, but in a single mane, while the sides of her head had been shorn to the quick.

But what really got Nathan's attention… were her breasts. The most obvious indicator of her being a female.

She had six of them.

He clearly *saw* she had six of them, because, as Nathan stood and stared—as they *all* stood and stared—she had actually stopped and sized them up in turn, turning herself about to face them.

Well.

Those wisps of material barely covered the breasts' areolas and prominent nipples, coating them like the finest fancy cake sweet frosting. The material hefted them, as well, giving gentle support, but leaving very little to the imagination. A crisscross of fabric accentuated the cleavages, which wasn't deep, but notable. Everything bounced. And below, deep into the valley of her female-hood, her lady parts were, as her breasts, covered in a sliver of silver.

Nathan lifted his eyes to hers.

She had four. Long-lashed and flashing. Her face possessed no nose, just an empty space that didn't seem very empty as all, and quite fetching to tell the truth, and a mouth twice the size of his. A mouth that smiled at him, in the coyest way, instinctively understood across the universe. *Any* universe.

"Hello," Nathan said, still not hearing his own voice, yet feeling just fucking fine off the very air he breathed.

She cocked her head, and her multi-fingered hand that resembled a spider on its back—which didn't bother Nathan much at all—rose to the side of her shaved head, to the place where her ear should've been, but wasn't. That didn't bother Nathan, either. She reached over her shoulder and pulled that enticing length of ebony hair back, letting it tumble over her amazing chest.

Nathan very much liked women with long hair.

Her mouth, which didn't have any lips at all, *rippled*, in a line, and exceptionally fine teeth peeked out. But her eyes—all four of them—were painted the deepest, seductive, shade of brown.

She reached down and took Nathan's arm, feeling her way to his hand, taking his five fingers into her eight. Nathan didn't resist. Her touch was as soft as the fluff on a baby chick, and her grip was as snug as snug could be.

She led him out of the room and onto that dark, smoky shelf of a walkway, half-turning and flashing her muscular back, the enticing dimples just above her waistline, and the jaw-dropping curves of her buttocks. Bare and salaciously on display. That strip of silver emerged at the top in a criminally small triangle, held in place by two silver strings that were only noticeable when one searched for them. Identical strings crisscrossed her back.

Light dazzled Nathan as he walked along the upper deck. He floated on his boot heels, and he looked down into the pit below him, taking in all those people jumping and shivering and flailing, all in beat with that mechanical thunderstorm that was no longer overpowering. In fact, the damn sound was… music to his ears.

"What's your name?" he asked plainly.

The lady giant merely smiled back at him. Her mouth rippled again, but damn if he could understand any of that, not that it stopped him from smiling right back at her.

How the hell could you *not* smile?

As if waltzing through a dream, they passed other figures on the walkway. Those individuals were either lounging about, leaning on the railing, or standing before closed doorways. Some were man-shaped, while others most certainly were not. Some had slick, thick torsos of muscle while others had no definition at all, or limbs for that matter, appearing as piled up gobs of substance Nathan didn't quite understand but was quite at ease with. Those wondrous individuals greeted Nathan with boneless waves of purple tentacles, or flutters of multi-fingered hands. Neckless knobs that might've been heads dipped with welcoming warmth, while a few of the males reached out and warmly gripped Nathan's shoulder. His female guide spoke to them, her mouth rippling in their direction, and the males produced their own smiles—or at least the alien equivalents.

They nodded at Nathan, and he nodded back, smiling all the while, not detecting a flicker of danger from any one of them, nor a trace of *fear*.

It was as if those emotions had up and vanished.

As he was led along, Nathan glanced over his shoulder to check on his boys. They were all there, strung out behind him, greeting and smiling at the creatures on the walkway, as those astounding examples of otherworldly life greeted them in turn. Mackenzie positively glowed, his face lit up with a rare combination of awe and overwhelming joy at the plethora of assembled species around him. Even dour-faced Eli appeared to have a considerable change in attitude, and he was, in fact, holding onto the hand of a female much like the one leading Nathan along.

Except she was… of all things… *rose*-colored, with bovine splashes of black covering her skin.

Not that it bothered Eli Gallant, who was obviously quite taken with the lady.

Then they were descending, over ebony steps that were filled with stars. More creatures, on the stairs and at the base, where the crowd thickened even more. Smoke obscured everyone in a dreamy gauze, but that didn't bother Nathan from spying a few well-endowed males—or what he deduced was the male *equivalent* of the species leading him along—dancing around that gyrating mass. They wore perhaps just as much clothing as Nathan's lady friend, and that wasn't saying much. Well defined to an almost Adonis-like quality, physically gifted, with male members that would make a horse jealous.

But that was fine with Nathan. Just peachy, in fact. And he turned back to his lovely guide with an incredulous shake of his head. The music rumbled away, getting in three beats to every one of Nathan's relaxed heart. All manner of creatures parted for them, multitudes of them, but not before offering warm nods, smiling faces, or even a fond pat on the back, shoulders, or top of the head.

The lights overhead continued to thunder, drenching faces in shadow and flashing them in split-second flares.

The lady led him to a bar. A huge bar. In fact, the bar was, without question, the biggest one Nathan had ever seen. A pyramid of multi-colored cylinders rose up from the center, as magnificent as an oversized pipe organ. Circles and waves of color rippled over the metallic bulk. Standing before this shining, sometimes glittering, spectacle was what *had* to be… the bartender.

Two dorsal fins covered the top of a neckless head the size of a boulder. The thing had multiple brows, as if another boulder had landed squarely on top of his skull, permanently mashing both bone and skin into several dense folds that bore down on a set of eyes—narrowed, of course. A jutting jaw sprouted two lower incisors rising above a thick lip-line, touching the upper bone structure of angular cheeks. The flesh might have been purple, or some similar hue. It was difficult to tell with the current lighting. The shoulders were muscular, immense even, as were the four arms folded across its chest.

The four arms fell away.

Nathan should have been surprised. Mesmerized, in fact. But with all the different shapes and sizes all around him, and sucking down that wonderful air by the lungful, all he could do was smile and chuckle as if he'd met a dear old friend gone missing for twenty years.

The bartender had a *second* face, set *into* its chest. And that alien face, complete with eyes, nose, and mouth, was aiming a *look-what-we-have-here* expression of delight at Nathan and his companions.

Nathan's lady friend led the gang to the edge of the bar, which was a scratched and well-worn hardwood counter, with a respectable coat of varnish applied to its grains. Interesting clusters of valves and spigots crenellated sections of the counter. The lady placed an elbow upon the bar's edge, hitching up a number of breasts as she did so, the fabric stretching enough for Nathan to get his hopes up. She motioned Nathan closer, which he did. The lady spoke to the bartender, her lipless mouth working in that fascinating way that Nathan couldn't stop watching. The head simply watched, a fleshly, impassive watchtower that neither approved nor disapproved, but the non-human face set within the creature's chest listened intently to the speaking lady.

Then they finished conversing, and both switched their attention to Nathan, who only then realized that the rest of his boys were crowding him. They stood there like a small island of humanity rooted to the wildly undulating floor of the universe.

The lady paused, considered the men, then resumed talking.

The face in the chest continued listening, and while listening, the head above it slowly turned to the right, uninterested with the conversation.

Finally, the face in the chest hitched in an expression of *well*, and one of the four arms reached underneath the bar. The bartender stepped in closer as the face in the chest brought up a metal box, opened it, and gave a shake. He placed the container on the counter and pawed through the contents, all while sizing up not only Nathan, but the other men nearby.

The face in the chest stopped searching and motioned Nathan closer, while the bartender pressed its bulk up against the counter edge.

With a nod from his lady friend, Nathan leaned in.

The face in the chest reached out, one of its five fingers stuck out while the other hand gripped Nathan's chin, turning his head to the side. There was an audible rustling in and around his ear, then both ears, as those alien fingers grazed the outer edges of Nathan's canals.

Then the barest contact, like a hair falling across one's lips, quickly gone and only just noticed.

"How's that?" the face in the chest inquired hopefully.

"Yessir," Nathan said.

While the head up above remained vigilant, the smile upon the face widened. "You hear that, Channy? He called me 'Sir'."

The lady nodded.

"I like you already," the face continued. "I mean, I liked you *before*, you understand, but I like you even *more* now. And you're right, Channy, they *do* look like Faknahts."

Channy stretched out a hand, in a gesture of '*See? Told you.*'

"Fak… what?" Nathan asked.

"Faknahts. For you, that's as close to those sounds as the translator I just installed is going to get. Some words aren't going to convert, so they're just going to come out as we say them. But everything else should be fine. Regional colloquial equivalents included. Now, just get in close to Channy there. I'm sure you won't mind that. I gotta get the rest of your pack outfitted."

Nathan looked at the dreamy lady who'd brought him here. "Channy?"

"*Mm-hm*," she said, her mouth rippling as if cutting the cutest snore. She placed an arm around his shoulders and drew him in affectionately, pressing one row of breasts up against his arm.

Nathan wished he wasn't wearing a winter coat.

Mackenzie was standing before the bartender, who repeated the procedure. The face in the chest fished around in the box, pulled out something unseen, and seemingly only touched Mackenzie's ears.

"Blessed Sacred Heart of Mary," Mackenzie said, and Nathan heard him over that thumping and the crowds.

"You're hearing me?" the face in the chest asked him.

"I most certainly am," Mackenzie answered.

"All right. Next. I'll do you all before I explain anything. Save me some time."

Which he did. Mackenzie stepped aside so the other men could have their ears twiddled upon. Jimmy stopped before the bar, warily so, but a smile broke out when the whole thing was over. Gilbert was next and looked every bit as inebriated as a cowpoke who'd downed far too much hooch. Eli Gallant was the last, every bit as cautious as Jimmy was.

When the face finished with him, the gun runner actually cracked a smile.

"All right, that's done," the face in the chest announced, putting the box away. "So, it's like this. You may think I just touched your ears there, but no. What I just did was install, in each of you, a set of third-generation translator implants, known and used across the known galaxies."

"Third gen, Nex?" Channy asked with a trace of disapproval.

"It's all I had in the box."

"*Third* Gen?"

"It's all I had in the box, Channy," Nex insisted. "This isn't business, here, Channy. It's free. *Free.* Compliments of the house, so we can communicate with these guys. Let them know the basics so they don't go taking leaks or dumps in the corners or some other place they're obviously not supposed too, right? Seriously. I'm doing this as a courtesy. I'm not having another repeat of what happened with those sloths from Klo-Seven. We were cleaning that shit up for days and the smell is still in some parts, no matter how much I sanitize. I'm not going to install any of the newer stuff and just stand back and hope their heads don't explode. You weren't around when *that* happened. Third gen is fine and, look…"

He gestured at the men with a hand. "Working just fine."

"And you get to empty your junk box," Channy said, her eyes narrowing.

Nex was offended. "Hey, if it's in that box, it ain't junk. I keep it because it still has some measure of worth, you understand? Some measure of worth, and guess what? Just guess? Yeah, that's *right*, those three-G dust bunnies finally have a home and we have new friends who can understand what we're saying. You don't want another fucking Mongloid incident. I *sure* as hell don't."

Right then, a huge alien walked by the group. It wasn't dressed at all, and it's oddly milky, yet jellied flesh was translucent in places. It stopped at the bar, swaying on three legs and swinging four arms. It held out one of those limbs to Mackenzie, inserting itself into the conversation, and Mackenzie had no issues with extending a hand and shaking it.

Channy lowered her head and shot a strained look in Nex's direction.

"This is… amazing." Mackenzie said, shaking the arm.

"Pleasure to meet you," the alien said in a giddy voice.

"Pleasure's all mine," Mackenzie said with a noble dip of his head and a broad smile.

"Ah, yeah," Nex said. "Listen, ah… that's not his hand you're shaking."

Mackenzie frowned.

The alien, however, scowled at Nex.

The upper part of the bartender, the *guardian* half, scowled back, releasing a frightening glare that far and away trumped the alien's.

"Get away from the guy," Nex warned and shooed a hand at the alien. "All right? Before I get mad here. Should be ashamed of yourself, taking advantage of lifeforms like that."

Mackenzie jerked his hand away and inspected it, before studying the being before him.

"I thought he knew!" the alien blurted at Nex.

"Yeah, right," the bartender scoffed. "Get outta here before I throw you out. Y'fuckin' interspecies pervert."

That earned a black look from Channy.

"Hey," Nex said, quick to apologize. "Sorry. I'm sorry. I didn't mean you. Only him. You're obviously going slow. Making sure folks understand. That depraved pudding bastard? 'Oh hi, how you doing, here, shake my dick. Shake my dick, you uneducated intergalactic monkey.' Sickening. Right in front of the bar, too. Like I can't see that shit. Or act like I'm okay with it. I swear…."

The upper part of Nex glowered, showing red eyes and more teeth.

The alien—who was standing right there—finally backed off. It muttered "sorry" to Mackenzie, and disappeared among the other patrons.

"Sorry, my ass," Nex said after the alien had gone. "I'll have to keep an eye on that one. Every week there's one trying to fuck an unaware species. Or get a free hand job. I mean, the *gall*. No manners. None, I tell you."

A disbelieving Mackenzie wiped his palm on his pants leg, slowly at first, but with growing urgency.

"Take it easy, partner, take it easy," Nex soothed, while his upper half still tracked the offensive alien. "No fear of infection there. None of that shit. Everyone in here's clean. They're all scanned the moment they enter the bar. The door would slam shut on them and holograms would be recorded in case of any lawsuits. You're good. Okay? Still with me? Look, forget about that guy. Forget about him. You didn't know what you were grabbing there and that's on him. He'll try the same thing to the wrong biped one night and have his cock ripped off. Or worse. Like a Medusoloid, and I don't even wanna think about that. So, don't worry, he'll get his. All right, so, about the translators. Right now, you're able to understand pretty much anyone in this saloon. Got that? You can speak your language, and anyone *not* like you will hear the translation in their language, and so on. You'll hear only the translated phrases in your heads, and the alien language will be filtered out. Well. Unless they're screaming. That'll overpower what you're hearing, but you understand what I'm saying. They'd probably have to be screaming right in your ear anyway. So, yeah, third gen is good. *Real* good."

Nex said that without looking in Channy's direction.

The face in the chest continued. "You have access to most of the known languages as well as an extensive database for commonly, uncommonly, and even some obscure expressions, okay? You're covered for analogies, similes, and metaphors, no worries there. So, you're pretty much good to talk and understand just about everyone in here. Advance warning, though. Translators do nothing, and I mean *nothing*, to help you understand and scan alien *organisms*, okay? Nor do they help you interpret any body language or facial expressions—if applicable. No temperature readings, mannerisms, or customs."

"That's twenty-first gen," Channy slipped in without looking in Nex's direction.

"That's twenty-first gen," Nex resumed without missing a beat. "And, frankly, that's out of your price range and probably detrimental to your overall health."

"Innuendos covered in those units?" Channy asked.

"Yes."

"Pitch and intonation?"

"Yes."

"Telepathy?"

"Fuck off," Nex warned her, his top half suddenly watching her closely. "That was uncalled for. You know that's not in there."

"Just asking is all."

"You were mocking my attempts at helping them and it's not appreciated. Hey, if you want, why not march them to the nearest shop and pick them up five sets of prime twenty-first gen. See how that works out. For them and you."

Smiling, Channy dipped her head and didn't say word.

Nex took a second to compose himself. "Okay. Like I was saying. What you got right now was on hand. And from a features point of view? The safest for you. No hemorrhaging. No aneurisms. No strokes and no exploding heads. You got all that?"

"Risk of any mental impairments or misfunctions?" Channy asked.

Nex didn't answer her right away. "Not that I'm aware of."

"Long-term effects?"

The guardian above the face in the chest scowled again.

Nathan raised a hand, and Nex's smile return. "Y'know, I like you more and more. Plus, you're not shaking every alien dick being stuck in your face. What's your question, son?"

Nathan exchanged looks with Mackenzie, who had slowed down his efforts to clean his hand on his coat.

"Stop that," Nex told him, glancing around a little uneasily. "Make him stop doing that. Seriously. Told you everyone's clean in here. You're gonna make everyone think something contagious got through screening."

"That ever happen, Nex?" Channy asked.

"You're really starting to get on my nerves here, Channy. Really starting to get on my nerves."

Channy lowered her head and hugged Nathan a little closer, pressing her exceptionally soft breasts further into him. Nathan didn't mind the cuddle at all, considering how the rest of his day was going.

"Anyway, what was your question?" Nex asked him.

"Uh… I don't rightly understand a lot of what you're saying."

Perhaps it was the genuine innocence in that statement, or the absence of any guile. In any case, a warm smile spread across Nex's alien features as his head went back into watchtower mode and scanned the room.

"You really do resemble Faknahts," the bartender told him. "Really. Skin tone is a little off, but, what's that anyway, right? Seriously? Just packaging for the goods. We're all green underneath."

Jimmy leaned into the bar, gaining Nex's attention. "Where are we?"

"Where are you?" Nex asked back. "You don't know?"

Jimmy shook his head.

"You are standing on the main floor of the best intergalactic saloon this side of Om-Cent Five. And when I say the best, I mean the *best*. I have the best grok, the best hillak, the best legal Covike. The best *illegal* Covike. And between you and me, the Kravs come here all the time. Not today, mind you. But—" At this point Nex winked. "They come here."

He tapped one finger on the bar.

Mackenzie stopped cleaning his hand and wanted to ask a question. Nex pointed at him.

"Why are we feeling this way?" the man asked.

"What way?"

"Like we just downed a bottle or two of Albertan Rye," Eli Gallant got out.

Nex took a moment to process that. "You mean drunk?"

Mackenzie pointed a *you got it* finger at him.

Nex chuckled. "Because of the *Vem*, of course. In the atmosphere. Finest Vem around. The *finest*, I tell you. Much easier than, say, charging everyone coming into the bar and serving them individually. No fuss, no muss. No spills, no spray. Just spike the atmosphere. Not too much to make a mess, but enough to cause smiles all around. Much easier. And with this—" he jerked one lower arm free and, with a thumb, indicated the pipe organ at his back,

"—I can change it anytime I want. Whenever the mood hits me. You name it, I got it on cylinder. Even got the Covike in there."

That piqued Channy's interest.

"Yeah, thought so," Nex said, seeing her lift her head. "Not right now. Maybe later."

Jimmy raised a hand.

"Yes?" Nex asked.

"Who… or *what* are all these people?"

That tickled Nex. "People. *Ha!* You know, if you weren't three-parts fried on Vem right about now, I bet that question would have come out with a lot more hysterical energy. Anyway, all these people? All of *these* people? They are…"

Nex thought about it and shrugged.

"They're most everybody. Everybody and anybody that you would want to meet in a saloon, that is. *My* saloon. With the exception of a few single-celled myclopic fuckers taking advantage of symbolic gestures of friendliness *for a quick handjob! Yeah, I see you lookin' over here you Ameboid piece of shit, I see you.*"

That turned a few heads, and the Ameboid alien from earlier immediately stepped back into the crowds.

"I'm gonna have to kick that milky piss stain out of here. Ameboids. Fuckin' hate them semi-protoplasmic bastards. Can't trust them. *Don't* trust them. Just a minute."

Nex pulled out a device from the counter. He thumbed one section, and a floating blue window appeared before him. His fingers rapped the surface, manipulating items in ways most mysterious to Nathan, until he abruptly ended with one decisive tap.

"There," Nex said. "Gone."

"Gone?" Mackenzie asked.

"Yeah. 'Ported his three-colon ass out into the street. Everyone who comes in here agrees to give up a little genetic code in case of situations like these. All I gotta do then, if I don't like the guy, is look him up, find his code, and issue the commands to teleport him out of here. No fuss, no muss. No spills, no spray. Just gone. Exactly how I like it. Excuse me. Another customer."

With that, Nex turned to move… before facing the men with an afterthought. "And be on your best behavior here. That's your first and only warning. Shit in my Vem-injected bubble and I will 'port your single-colon asses into the street.

Or into the Void if you really piss me off." Then he lightened up. "But I truly hope you have a good time. You Faknaht-lookalikes, you."

With a smile (that did not extend to the head) the bartender moved to another part of the bar.

*

The teleported Ameboid materialized in an alley behind the saloon, which smelled of alien excrement. It took the Ameboid—whose name was Snut-Snut— a moment to realize … to realize where he was. And he wasn't happy about it.

"Well, *fuck!*" Snut-Snut released in a fury, overpowering the Vem still in his simple system. Unlike several species, Ameboids had something of a tolerance to Vem, and several other euphoric-inducing chemicals. They didn't reveal that immunity to other species, however, for reasons that were purely procreative in the worst predatory way.

One of his many limbs was actually Snut-Snut's neck and head. And if one looked close enough, one could, in fact, see the same single pupil smack-dab in the center of the appendage. The eye resembled a saucer-sized indentation that blended in near-perfectly with the rest of the surrounding tissue. Ameboids were often mistaken for Echinoloids, who also resembled star-shaped, many-limbed creatures. And they were damn near identical in physical appearance. Echinoloids did not, however, share the same raging sexual appetites. Or the genetic urge for the propagation of their species.

Didn't matter what manner of organism an Ameboid mated with—as long as it was flesh, the game was on.

In short, Ameboids would fuck pretty much anything.

And since Snut-Snut was thrown out of the only place around for some serious infectious fun, he was notably pissed off.

"Oh, no you *didn't*," Snut-Snut rumbled angrily, reaching into his chest and pulling for a communication device. "No you *didn't*. No one drop 'ports Snut-Snut into some back-alley shitter and gets away with it. *No one.*"

The mitten tip of a limb manipulated the keypad, and he lifted the device to his mouth, which was covered by a permeable membrane.

One ring went through.

Two rings.

"Drop 'port me out into the cold," Snut-Snut fumed, his milky flesh becoming a deep shade of pink. "Don't know who you're messing with. No sir. Wasn't my fault the guy shook hands with my dick. I just put it out there. That's all I did. Not my fault in the least."

Five rings now.

Then a click.

"Yeah," Snut-Snut said, in a tone best described as tattle-tale bitter. "Um, is this the Vog Apparatus? Yeah? Excellent, excellent. I was ringing for a while there—what kept you? Oh. Sorry. I'm so sorry. My mistake. I mean, who has the time, right? So, yeah, anyway, sorry to be bothering you with this but I have some information I think you'll find interesting. I think there's a saloon pumping uncut Vem into its ductwork. Yeah. Oh yeah. And I'm pretty sure I saw some hot Covike as well. Yeah. Huh? Sure, I'll stay on the line."

One of his legs tapping impatiently, Snut-Snut looked around, sizing up the alley. It wasn't a bad place, actually.

Then, "Oh, yeah, *hi*. Yes, I did. Well, thank you. That's me, responsible citizen. Just tying to keep the cosmos clean. Oh, and one more thing, I'd like to report some *aliens* that look like star-bleached Faknahts. What's that? Oh yes, you heard me. Faknahts. Oh, I'm sure. Oh yeah, I got images."

Snut-Snut's communication device was always on and recording when he was on the bar-circuit. That way, he could replay any successful mating attempts for personal stimulation and gratification at a later time. Or just show that shit off to other Ameboids.

"Yeah, hold on a second," Snut-Snut said, and uploaded whatever footage he had of his short encounter with the lesser Faknaht. Damn alien wasn't *really* a Faknaht—the coloring was all wrong in his opinion, but Snut-Snut didn't care about that. He was feeling spiteful, and he wanted spiteful revenge.

And the best way to do that? Alert the Vog about the saloon. To be fair, the Vog probably didn't care about one saloon and its shady activities, but— and at this point, Snut-Snut mentally shrugged—the Vog *would* be interested in Faknahts. Very much interested.

Whether cloned or some undiscovered sub-species, the Ameboid didn't think the Vog would be picky.

35

Channny pulled Nathan a tad closer, mashing her breasts into his side. In his drunken state, Nathan didn't object.

"You always this wet?" she asked him.

"Excuse me?"

"Water. Just coming out of you. You're like a… deep-sea sponge."

Now, her mouth didn't say deep-sea sponge—didn't even come close to even forming those syllables—but that's what Nathan's Third-Gen translator provided.

"Just my coat," he said. "And my clothing."

Channy took that moment to feel his chest, her eyes flicking all over his body. Nathan didn't object to the pat-down. Not one bit.

"So many layers," she said, as she cupped one of his man-breasts and leaned in close. "I bet they peel right off, however."

Perhaps it was the Vem—no, it was *entirely* the Vem—but Nathan didn't need a translator to understand her meaning. Or how her fingers were stimulating him in ways he never thought possible.

Eli Gallant stopped at the bar and drunkenly eyed Nathan. He leaned over it and sized up one of the ubiquitous, yet weird clusters of valves and spigots spaced along the hardwood counter.

"Can I get a drink here?" he demanded, trying to be heard over the thumping—which was now layered with a serious horn section. Or what sounded close to a horn section.

"What are you looking for?" Channy asked him, while still working on Nathan's receptive chest.

"A drink," Eli yelled. "A goddamn drink. Some honest to Christ pig-piss. Something. I might look like a wet sheet-stain stripped off a whorehouse bed, but I'm plenty goddamn thirsty right about now."

Channny released a delightful giggle into Nathan's ear. "You're *swearing*. I can almost understand most of it. You'll have to do that for Nex when he comes back. He loves to hear profanity. The more vulgar, the better."

Eli screwed up his face. "I don't give a—*huh*?"

"Good, inventive profanity is an underappreciated artform," Channy went on. "Highly prized in the Cosmos. Indicative of a creative mind."

"A what?"

"A creative mind. Imaginative. Intelligent."

That positively disarmed Eli Gallant. The gun runner's normally snarling face slackened at the compliment. Nathan would not have believed his eyes unless he wasn't there to witness it first-hand.

"You're saying… I'm smart," Eli slowly got out, "because… I swear?"

"Yes. It's one indicator. Usage of profanity is also positively correlated with verbal fluency."

"What's that now?"

"It means you speak quite well."

If the first compliment took the snarl off Eli's face, then the second one slapped him cold. He studied Channy, before slowly, almost good-naturedly, turned and smirked at Nathan. He then looked for Mackenzie, who was ogling the many lifeforms packed into the saloon.

"You hear that, Mack?" Eli said and slapped him with the back of a hand, getting the man's attention. "Lady thinks I'm goddamn educated. And that I can speak well. Just because I can swear."

To his credit, Mackenzie didn't comment and went right back to his Vem-induced staring of the masses.

"You're all right," Eli said fondly to Channy and then regarded Nathan for only a second before returning to her. "You, uh, got a sister around? Or a friend?"

"What are these things?" Gilbert asked, leaning back so that he could be seen over Eli's shoulders. The gun runner was pointing at the shiny metal piping along the bar that practically sparkled in the saloon's light storm.

Channy leaned slightly forward for a look. "Those are the food and drink dispensers."

Again, not what her lips were saying, but what the translators provided.

"Food and drink?"

"Yes. Just hold one for a second."

Gilbert did, grabbing onto one of the protruding spigots.

Channy smiled. "Now hold on while it analyzes your bio-makeup."

A light over the spigot flashed purple and then remained on.

"Good God Almighty!" Gilbert exclaimed, but he was smiling, and he held on.

Channy pointed at the cluster. "It's delivering what you need. Don't take your hand away just yet. It's injecting whatever sustenance matches your physiology, directly into your circulatory tract."

"Huh?"

"Wait until the light turns green," Channy informed him, while still working over Nathan, to a point where he wanted to ask if she wanted to go find a room.

"Channy?" Mackenzie asked, despite Nathan's not-so-subtle frown and headshake. "Where are we, exactly?"

A look of puzzlement wrinkled her expression. "You don't know?"

Mackenzie shook his head.

"The Vem is affecting you more than you know," she smiled gently.

Jimmy Norquay placed a hand upon Mackenzie's shoulder, distracting him. The Vem *was* affecting them, with every breath. Jimmy focused on Nathan, sized up his predicament, and reached for his coat. He took a grip of the wet material and pulled.

Nathan resisted.

Jimmy pulled harder.

Nathan resisted harder.

Channy broke out into a delightful peal of laughter. "Go on with your friend. I'll wait. Don't worry."

She released him as she spoke.

Nathan, however, didn't want to go.

So Jimmy dug his heels in and hauled him away.

"What's wrong with you?" the Metis man demanded, red-eyed and annoyed.

"What?"

"Leave him be," Eli Gallant said, joining the huddle. Mackenzie leaned in as well.

"He's drunk," Jimmy said, his fist still holding onto the wet coat.

"We're all drunk," Eli declared. "Without taking a single drop. I swear, every breath I take is finer than the last. And, by the look of you, all of you, you're all feeling your oats. So don't be giving Nate a hard time."

That got a round of blinking stares from them all. Including Nathan, who swayed on his feet and wondered if he just heard correctly. Did shit-flicking hard case Eli Gallant just defend him?

It stunned them all, until Jimmy rattled his head and leaned into their little circle.

"We have to leave," he said, making himself heard over the music, because that's what it was… music. Nathan realized this in a soft balloon-pop of clarity. Saloon music from the *future*. From the very *stars*.

"Right now," Jimmy explained with roving side-eyes, watching the saloon crowd. "I'm feeling a pull."

"I am, too," Mackenzie said.

Eli nodded in agreement. And Nathan felt it as well. Nowhere as powerful as Channy's touch, but it was there and easily recognized, once mentioned.

"So what?" Nathan asked.

"So we go," Jimmy said and nodded. "That way."

Past the gyrating crowds mashing together on the saloon's main floor, all in sync with the booming music.

Nathan's head rolled on his shoulders in a gesture of *aww do we gotta?*

But the others were already in agreement.

"Yeah, we gotta," Mackenzie said.

Nathan sighed softly and glanced back at Channy, whose glorious legs crossed enticingly at that precise moment.

"Goddammit," Nathan sighed again.

"I'll tell her," Eli said.

"No," Nathan stepped away. "I'll tell her. You get Gilbert."

Eli looked at his friend, who was talking to an emaciated-looking alien, bipedal, but with orange skin, no nose, and three bulbous eyes, and wearing bright clothing of a fabric unknown to him.

Without a word, Eli stepped over to his partner's back and slapped his shoulder.

"Oh, hey Eli," Gilbert said. He released his hand from the green-lit spigot. "This is Buddy, here. I call him Buddy. Can't rightly say his real name."

At that, Buddy opened a mouth shaped like a sphincter and festered with rattlesnake teeth. An odd chuffing noise came from that opening, and all three of Buddy's eyes narrowed in Vem-intoxicated amusement.

"You know what he just said about us?" Gilbert said.

Eli didn't know.

"He said, he said…" Gilbert studied his saloon acquaintance. "You tell him."

"I said you really do look like Faknahts," Buddy said, his mouth moving as if he were ravenously gnawing at a corn cob. "Without question."

Eli, neither fearful nor angry but comfortably numb, stared at the alien, absorbing the creature's words.

"I've been hearing about these *faulkners* a couple times now," he finally rumbled. "Mind pointing them out?"

Buddy's eyes fluttered with mind-fried surprise. "Well, no. I can't point them out."

"None of these *faulkners* in here?"

"No, none at all."

"Why's that, then?"

"Well...." and at this, the creature plainly looked troubled, as if the matter of which he was being asked about was some disturbing public knowledge.

"Because you can't," Buddy simply said.

"Buddy," Eli said, leaning in. "I asked you... very nicely, I might add... why's that?"

Buddy fidgeted, no longer so happy. "Because they no longer exist."

"No longer exist?"

"They're all dead."

Eli shrugged. "All right. So what? That's it? That ain't so bad. So why are they all dead? Something kill them all?"

Buddy's three big eyes became sad. "Something *ate* them all."

*

The Vog teleported in with a crackle of energy that flared and fizzled out along each member's frame, as if they were absorbing the far-reaching brunt of the universe's cosmic rays. There were ten of them, all tall and chrome, and armed to their toothless proboscises.

Snut-Snut involuntary shifted back to the alley wall at their sudden appearance. *Riot suppression squad,* he realized. He bristled at the thought that they hadn't sent a more intimidating force to deal with the Faknaht lookalikes. Then again, Snut-Snut's fragmented spinal column still felt a shudder of fear when they appeared.

He waited until the leader addressed him.

There were plenty of intimidating alien species in the known universe. Far too many, depending on who one asked. It was inevitable. Some were even quite dangerous and warlike. The Vog, however, and their insectoid hive mindset, which some ridiculed as being no greater than a virus, was without question the most frightening, the most sinister of them all.

And, even though he was expecting them, the Vog terrified the lone Ameboid.

Though Snut-Snut was impervious to the chemical Vem and its effects, this was one time he wished he could partake of its mind-numbing qualities. His moment of anger and offense had up and vanished in the Vog's alien presence. Color was as absent from the Vog as a conscience, except for chrome, which was the only color associated with the aliens. Their flesh was chrome, as was their armor and weapons. Even their blood.

The Vog held their fearsome weapons at guard—an organic, bio-metal that no other race could wield, or would want to. The squad didn't move for seconds, and Snut-Snut stood and stared at the formidable aliens. Not even the creatures' eye stalks or proboscises moved. They remained motionless with a discipline that was both military and robotic.

One of the ten stepped forward then, stepping out of that solid wedge and distinguishing itself from the formation at its back.

The Vog commander stopped three paces away from the waving Ameboid. The eye stalks, protruding from an armored head, studied the informer alien impassively.

"Where is the Faknaht?" the Vog asked in its own language, which Snut-Snut's embedded translator immediately deciphered.

If the Ameboid had lips to lick, he would have done so right then. Instead he pointed to the solid metal wall across from him. A dark, imposing section of the outer, fortified curvature that was Nex's saloon.

The Vog continued to study the Ameboid as one eye stalk aimed itself at the indicated wall. Seconds later, the head turned, bringing the appendage back into alignment with the other one.

Snut-Snut waited, but dearly wanted to be on the other side of the known cosmos.

"Thank you for your assistance," the Vog said, turning its body to face the wall. It stopped once in position as if some internal braking system was engaged. Without warning, the other nine troopers turned as well, all the while maintaining formation.

"Do you—" Snut-Snut started to ask.

"Leave the immediate area," the leader interrupted, cutting off the Ameboid. "Now."

Snut-Snut swallowed, or did the human equivalent, and thought the Vog had a grand thought indeed. He immediately backed away from the squad, not taking his eye off the bulky chrome of the armored lifeforms, who all faced that reinforced wall designed to repel any legal task force associated with enforcing Cosmic Law.

Once he was a good twenty paces away from the motionless squad, Snut-Snut turned and ran.

36

Nathan didn't like leaving Channy so soon.

And, even as her lovely face disappeared among that energetic crowd, Nathan knew he wasn't going to see her ever again. That made him even sadder.

Jimmy Norquay pushed his way through the fantastic collection of living, breathing oddities populating the floor. There were lifeforms of all shapes and sizes, but Nathan wasn't moved. He was still thinking about the lovely Channy. And her six tits.

Mackenzie grabbed his arm, leading him along like a common drunk having downed far too many whiskey shots. Nathan scoffed at that. He was shitfaced on a far more potent drink than mere alcohol. He was, God help him, in *love*.

He stumbled upon a long snake of an appendage that ended in a multi-limbed thing the size of two cows. Mackenzie picked him up, apologized to the alien, and moved on. Eli and Gilbert were right behind them both, and they all moved in the direction where they felt the pull.

Music assaulted Nathan's ears, pounding upon his Vem-charged brain. Light shafts burned overhead, dazzling, flashing over faces and torsos, or what Nathan assumed were torsos, in some cases. Creatures parted for the still wet figure of Jimmy Norquay. Some patted the man on the shoulders. Some patted his back. Mackenzie was there, no longer so eager to shake any hands, but accepting of the back and shoulder pats. There wasn't an angry face among the masses, but more than a few of outright shock, as if the train robbers were the unusual ones.

"My heavens," Mackenzie said, marveling at all those crowding around. "My sweet, sweet heavens."

"Where are we, Mack?" Nathan asked his friend's ear.

"No idea. But I think it's a good place."

Nathan agreed.

The music rose to new crushing heights, demanding all those upon the floor to dance. Nathan noticed they were walking across space. Stars and nebulae and all other manner of galactic phenomena lit up the polished glass surface underfoot. And he couldn't recognize one star cluster. Then the crowds pushed in again, and the night sky underfoot dimmed while the light continued to flash and awe. Faces lit up and winked out, but their outlines danced onward in an incredible barn burner of a town dance.

Nathan, still holding onto Mackenzie for support, glanced ahead before looking hard to his left.

There, in the crowds, stood a man.

Or at least it *looked* like a man.

Dressed entirely in black, with what appeared to be cloth bands tied near his elbows and knees. His face was draped in black as well, a form-fitting head mask that covered everything except his eyes.

Those were hard and staring.

Nathan stared back before Mackenzie pulled on his arm, distracting him. When he looked back, the man in black was gone.

Jimmy Norquay stopped just ahead. He stood before some black doors whose edges were aglow in thin lines of fiery orange. There were other doors spaced out along the wall as well, but the lights outlining them shone in different colors.

The image on the door's surface, however, resembled a man.

A head, two arms, and two legs.

"That's the boys' room," Jimmy yelled. "We go in there."

"I don't think that's the boys' room," Mackenzie said. "But we still go in there."

Jimmy placed his hand against the door… and extended a hand to push.

It slid opened, parting down the middle.

Nathan fully expected to see the interior of a train car. He did not. Inside was a well-lit space, divided up into walled sections. The floor was polished marble and pocketed with grates no larger than a person's fist, and one wall was nothing but a mirror, the length of the entire chamber, from floor to ceiling. The Vem circulated in there as well, in great cotton swirls that were pink under the ceiling lights. Aliens were present, either going into stalls or emerging from them, whereupon doors would slide open or closed.

The image on the door had resembled a man.

The creatures occupying the washroom—or what Nathan assumed to be the washroom—were not.

They all possessed two arms, two legs, and one head, but that's where the similarities ended. Creatures, tall and short, wide and narrow moved through that floating ghost world of pink. Like outside, some of them were curious to behold, while others were downright frightening, if not revolting. Nathan believed there were two dozen lifeforms or more in the chamber, but his sense of time warped, and the plane of reality shifted.

The Vem, he thought.

They were breathing in straight whiskey shots, or at least the alcoholic might of whiskey shots, and right then Nathan's senses became as star born as the floor he walked across. With a dream-like quality, they trudged across a twinkling, lilting plane of stars, ignoring the things along the edges. The clouds parted for them, and just ahead was an unlit sliding door that remained shut while others opened and closed.

Jimmy walked towards that door.

Nathan and the others followed, drawn by that gentle but guiding pull.

On impulse, however, he glanced back. Through a gap of bumping shoulders belonging to an inebriated Eli Gallant and Gilbert Butler, a figure followed.

The man in black.

*

Two of the Vog worked on the saloon wall, summoning alien instruments especially designed for their two-digit hands. The others took up position around them, four of which watched the alley from opposing ends.

Lines of green light flared into existence, covering a surface area upon the wall just big enough to allow passage to an armored Vog.

Thoughts were projected, and instruments adjusted.

The Vog leader watched impassively. He recalled the uploaded playback of the sighted Faknahts. He wasn't certain the creatures recorded were indeed the race of old, but it warranted an investigation. Especially since the outerwear matched that worn by another group of mysterious creatures that resembled Faknahts. Outerwear that had a distinct, roughshod style that had been the subject of debate among Vog historians for Vog years.

The fascinating thing was, the herdsvog who collected the original recordings and physical data had been on another planet entirely.

Yet the creatures at that time, Vog years earlier—the facial expressions, physical build, body temperature and genetic make-up—perfectly matched those uploaded by the Ameboid. The lifeforms recorded by the Vog herdsvog had disappeared in curious fashion, vanishing from a shelter upon one of the herder worlds. Not a trace of them could be found anywhere, however… upon investigating the shelter's interior, there were trace amounts of what the Vog called *gilmus*.

Sparkling flickers of dissipating matter often found in ruptured dimensions.

What was also fascinating was that the bio-readings of the alien lifeforms were actually *superior* to those of the long extinct Faknahts.

That greatly interested the Vog, enough to muster a riot squad on relatively short notice to investigate.

For twenty-eight Vog years, no one had sighted the lifeforms since the herder world recordings, yet the Vog had hard documented proof of their existence.

The Vog leader very much wanted to locate these lifeforms, and determine for itself the genetic connection to the Faknahts of the past.

Those long extinct creatures were a prized delicacy.

These elusive, and genetically superior cousins to the Faknahts might very well be even *better* to eat.

The green lines upon the wall flickered twice, then thickened, drawing the attention of the Vog leader. A red line ran from the top to the bottom of the circle, perfectly dividing it. The Vog leader thought-projected a command, and the other Vog on point collapsed back upon the main group. Menacing .200 kor battle blasters were lowered and aimed forward. Eye stalks were focused.

The leader gave a thought, and the tech working with the wall opener obeyed.

The red line flickered. Became green. Thickened.

Then it parted.

The circle opened from the center out, the edges of that dividing line dissolving into nothing as if ravenously devoured by a swarm of unseen hull eaters. There were no sparks, no heat, just the smooth, focused, disintegration of a forced entry.

Music reached the Vog.

Lasers pierced the alley. Then the way was opened.

A tunnel lay before the Vog, cut through construction material some four feet thick.

The leader entered first, ducking through the tunnel. The others followed, single-file. The leader emerged on the other side, to a single blaring note. A few of the nearest lifeforms saw the Vog emerge from the wall and staggered back in horror as other Vog invaded the saloon.

Strobe lights swept over the leader's chrome armor and exposed flesh. The leader's diagnostic scanned the atmosphere and confirmed that an exceedingly high level of Vem was present in the atmosphere. There was also a highly toxic mixture of other debilitating mind-warping gases. The nearby creatures retreated from the sparkling line forming at the leader's back, but he didn't need diagnostics to know the Vem was suppressing their fear.

The Vog was aware of Inter-Planetary Cosmic Law, and now possessed evidence that this public venue was violating vapor regulations. The leader also suspected that there was enough illegal and unregulated contraband on the premises to shut it down for good.

Not that any of that mattered to the leader.

What was about to happen wasn't because of illegal activity.

What was about to happen was because they were Vog.

And the rest… were not.

On a mental command, the Vog commenced firing.

*

"Hold on," Nathan said and pulled away from Mackenzie, whose grip was as drunk as the rest of him. Equally smashed and distracted by their surroundings were the two gun runners. Nathan cleanly split the pair without so much as a dirty look from either, especially Eli.

Pink cloud matter swirled and thickened, but the man in black was back there, standing rigid, a shard of dusty volcanic rock barely glimpsed through that otherworld fog.

Nathan pushed through that pink haze and found himself standing three feet away from that mysterious figure. As close as Nathan was, he could see the finer details of the man in black. The fabric he wore resembled a bulkier pair of long johns but with a full hood and mask. There was one slit across the eyes, just wide enough to see from, and Nathan didn't quite understand what he was looking at.

The fabric was cut there, that much was obvious, but the flesh around the eyes wasn't the color of skin. The pink swirling hues hindered that determination, but the haze didn't obscure the eyes. The eyes were dead black, without any whites at all, as if coated in shoe polish. As Nathan stared and studied, the man in black did the same. The man in black's chin lifted ever so slightly, his brow scrunched up in unchecked bewilderment, as if Nathan might've been a twin of a long-lost relative or friend.

A hand came up. A three-fingered hand, bare, corded, and thick. One of these fingers resembled two of Nathan's pressed together. That inhuman paw wavered in the pink clouds surrounding them, and reached out…

And caressed Nathan's cheek.

The fingers traced the outline of his jaw, down to his chin, then slid back all the way to his ear. There, the fingers actually flicked his lobe, before pinching and feeling strands of his hair.

All under the soft scrutiny of those black eyes.

There was no breach of decency, no sense of danger or malefic intent… just a profound curiosity. And Nathan was smashed enough on Vem to allow it to happen.

"Who are you?" he finally asked, still aware enough of minding his manners, especially with the man in black, who was clearly not a man but some other creature entirely.

The question stopped the alien. It eventually withdrew its hand and reached for its waist. The man in black reached inside the folds of its clothing, felt around, and pulled something free. It raised its arm high enough so that it could release the item.

A chain dropped from the hand, the silver twinkling in the soft light.

And at the end of that length was a locket. A piece of jewelry fabricated by human hands, without question.

The man in black gestured for Nathan to take the piece. When he didn't, the creature offered it again.

"Nathan," Jimmy Norquay called out.

Nathan half turned.

"Nathan, get back here," Jimmy called out. "We gotta go."

At that, the man in black gripped Nathan's shoulder, and again, dangled the locket from a fist.

Lost in wonder, Nathan took the jewelry.

The man in black motioned for him to open it.

"Nathan!"

"*Wait*, dammit!" Nathan shouted back, meeting the man in black's eyes again as his fingers fumbled with the clasp.

Then Eli and Gilbert were there, hands on Nathan's shoulders, pulling him back.

Which was right about when all hell broke loose.

*

The snap and crackle of ten .200 kor battle blasters ripped through the saloon. Green spears of killer light lanced through the unsuspecting crowds in a rapid-fire stutter, exploding whatever unprotected flesh it hit. Dancing as they were, oblivious and chemically impaired by the miasmic fluff of Vem, the saloon's patrons were helpless. Heads burst apart in meaty sprays. Torsos were sliced in halves and uneven quarters. Arms and legs were severed in spurts of dark matter. A veritable stew of alien innards and life blood splashed onto the floor, smothering the brightly lit galaxies underneath. All the while, the saloon's strobing light systems transformed the killing into a flickering, thought-freezing horror show, leaving patrons staring in wide-eyed disbelief at their dead partners a second or two before they themselves were murdered. Some aliens near the center of the killing spree realized what was happening, but were blown apart before they could muster their Vem-addled bodies into fleeing. Their deaths gained the seconds needed for the creatures on the fringes of the dance floor and the saloon to run for cover.

Not that there was much.

The green bolts punched through smoke, wood, and metal alike, scorching gaping holes through the material. Pillars toppled, some crashing over the dead or dying. Screams cut the air, made worse when the music stopped playing.

The Vog leader's implanted tracker scanned the area, sweeping a cone of blue threads left and right.

A handful of blue pixelated bipeds appeared in that cone, behind a wall. The leader locked on to the lifeforms and thought-commanded four of its squad to follow.

The others received commands to level the saloon.

*

A series of green spears blasted through the walls, razoring through half the creatures inside and driving Nathan, Eli, and Gilbert to their knees. Another wave of green light spat through the outer barriers, twisting the pink clouds into poisoned whorls. One man-thing took a blast straight through the head, neck, and a good portion of its upper chest, dropping the creature in a contortionist knot of limbs.

"*Jesus Christ!*" Nathan heard someone scream and immediately thought it was Eli Gallant.

In truth, however, it was him.

The shots split the air overhead and anyone not already splayed out on the floor. Voices were cut horribly short with startled *gurks!* and expulsions of breath.

A cringing Nathan glanced to his left to see a smoking body crumple flat on its backside as if sitting on a front deck, a split instant before a second shot blew through its chest and whisked it away.

Hands clamped down on his still wet coat, keeping him in place.

"Get back here," Jimmy Norquay shouted, cowering somewhere back in the haze.

"We gotta go," Gilbert said, and Nathan realized then that the music had stopped, replaced by frenzied alien screams.

Nathan peered ahead.

The man in black was there, eyes narrowed, spread out over the floor like a tensed rock spider. He drew in his arms and pushed himself up and into a low crouch. The gun runners pulled on Nathan, dragging him back a whole step.

The man in black glanced over his shoulder, appraising the situation, and nimbly shuffled towards Nathan. Those thick paws hooked the stunned man under his armpits and hoisted him into a low crouch. The alien pointed at the back of the room, where Jimmy and Mackenzie were, and the pack of them hurried towards the two men. Bodies littered the floor, dead and leaking colors that sparkled in those rolling pink clouds.

"Who the hell has pink clouds in a shithouse, anyway?" Gilbert demanded, and no one answered.

Two human ghosts emerged, standing against the one sliding door that, if Nathan recalled correctly, no one was using when they had entered the room. There were other doors, opened, and only steps away, but the pull—that mysterious magnetic draw that they all felt—wanted them at *that* door.

Except that door would not open.

Mackenzie waved his hands over the barely visible seam. He scratched at what might've been a lock to no avail. In the end, he lifted a booted foot and stomped at the door.

"Can't open it?" Jimmy asked.

"Can't open it," Mackenzie huffed, pink-faced and no longer looking drunk.

Nathan looked back towards the main saloon. "Channy's back there," he muttered.

Eli Gallant grabbed him by the collar and pulled him close. "Channy's a big girl. She'll take care of herself."

Eli held on, until Nathan plied his hand away.

The man in black was behind them, crouched as if about to sprint, watching the men. The snapping bolts of green light had ceased for the moment, and there was movement along the floor, as perhaps half a dozen aliens had the sense to flatten themselves and hope the shooting stopped.

"Get back then," Jimmy Norquay said. And with that, he flung open his winter duster, blowing the pink clouds apart. He reached inside for the dynamite stashed within.

Screams nattered at Nathan's ears, coming from outside.

The man in black watched him. Watched Jimmy pull out the dynamite.

Then, as if arriving at a decision, the alien did something that caused Nathan to blink twice.

He reached inside the folds of those long black drawers of his and pulled out what appeared to be a four-pointed star. He flicked his wrist, and the star became five. Nathan's eyes narrowed at that instant of card trickery, mighty impressed.

But then the stars' edges lit up with purple light, while their centers swirled like moonlight upon glassy water.

37

The man in black met Nathan's gaze, and that one look conveyed a message, an emotion, that no embedded translator need decipher.

Then he rose to his feet, except Nathan didn't see him rise. One second he was crouching, and the next he was standing. Pink smoke curled about his shadowy frame, and then the man in black was hurrying towards the main saloon and the extreme violence therein.

"Light a match, Jimmy," Eli said, holding onto Nathan's soggy coat.

"I'm trying to," Jimmy replied.

But the matches were not only broken and short, they were also wet.

*

The leader Vog stopped just to the side of the chamber entrance, where the Faknaht beings were clustered in the back. His tracker ignored the other creatures completely. His four underlings gathered at his back. Two stepped to the other side of the closed door.

Behind them, on the main saloon floor, blasterfire erupted.

The Vog back there attended to the resistance in kind.

The leader glanced back and saw his troopers take cover, holding their battle rifles at the ready. The mass shooting had devolved into a more selective fire. Aliens hid behind the bar for cover, firing projectile weapons and low-power energy beams. The projectiles merely bounced off the chrome Vog armor in bight orange flickers of contact while the energy beams struck and did nothing.

As expected.

The Vog armor would deflect or absorb most attacks, unless the shooters had access to much more powerful weapons. The leader doubted they did, but he assumed they would know otherwise in short order.

The leader Vog turned its attention back to the main door. He readied his .200 kor battle blaster and stepped before the closed portal.

Which immediately slid open.

*

The clouds had diminished enough for Nathan to see the man in black rush ahead just as the doorway opened.

There, towering in the doorway, was a creature that resembled polished silver. The alien was tall, standing upon spindly legs, and possessed spindly arms, but its main body was bulky and powerful. It brandished what Nathan knew was a rifle of some kind, and things that looked like a snail's eyes sprouted from what he figured was the creature's head.

Everything was silver—shining, blazing, silver.

And then an amazing thing happened.

The man in black rushed the silver alien head-on. The alien aimed its weapon a split second before the man-in-black *threw* one of his stars—which became a fist of spinning energy that cleaved the silvery alien's skull in two.

Liquid silver spurted from that clean division of skull, and the spindly legs gave out. The alien dropped to the threshold. The doors refused to close.

The man in black stopped at the entrance, placing his spine to the doorframe, and looked back.

Then he did another incredible thing.

He disappeared.

*

"Jesus H. Christ," Eli Gallant said in unchecked awe, mirroring Nathan's earlier sentiments.

"The hell was *that*, Eli?" Gilbert wailed.

"The hell I know, you moron," the gun runner fired back before pulling on Nathan's coat. "Come on, you stubborn shit flinger. He's doing it for *us*."

That took all the fight out of Nathan, and he felt that silver locket in his fist.

The unmistakable sound of a fight reached them all then, and silver figures staggered through the open portal. Some fired their weird rifles faster than any Winchester, and killer light split the air.

Nathan allowed the men to pull him back.

"Can't light the fuse," Jimmy reported loudly, digging through a soggy match box and flicking away most of what he brought up. The men stood around, weapons out, but still too damn soupy in the head to properly use them.

"The hell we do then?" Gilbert asked, dropping to a knee and taking unsteady aim at the distant door.

Jimmy leaned against the stall door, with the stick of dynamite in his hand.

Then, an alien—one of the many bar patrons—stepped in close to Jimmy. The alien inspected the destructive stick in the outlaw's hand, and plainly asked, "What do you need?"

Jimmy hesitated only a second. "A light."

"Where do you need it?"

Jimmy held up the dynamite and indicated the fuse.

The alien touched the end with a single long finger, unleashing the sparks signaling a lit fuse.

Jimmy's expression was one of *oh shit!*

He jammed the stick against the door's base, grabbed the helping alien's shoulder and leaped away. The other men did the same.

Two seconds later, the dynamite went off, and smoke of a different color filled the chamber.

The booming explosion visibly frightened the assisting alien, and that was fine by the men, who quickly clustered about the rent in the door. The seam had opened just enough to poke a few fingers in there, and between them all, they forced the doors apart enough to slide a body through.

Inside, however, was the most incredible thing of all.

Right there, before them all, was an empty, early 1900s passenger car.

38

One after the other, the men pressed through that narrow gap, until they were all inside the passenger car. The helpful alien cautiously peeked around the corner of the door, at which point, Nathan, who had a hand on the car door on this side of reality, hesitated and met the creature's gaze.

"You coming?" he asked.

The alien inspected the area beyond and shook his head. "Not my reality," he said simply, and gripped the door's edges.

Whereupon he slammed the door shut from the other side.

There was a curt clap of metal, and a pink line up the middle winked out into darkness. Then, nothing.

Nathan stood there, watching that rectangular portal with unease.

"Shut it," Mackenzie urged.

"Huh?"

"Shut it before those things can come through."

Nathan thought about the silver aliens. He slammed the door shut.

"And don't open that damn thing," Jimmy warned him. "Unless you forgot the last time."

The tentacles. Nathan remembered.

With a weary look about the interior, which was indeed empty of people, Nathan wandered to an empty berth, checked the seats, and planted himself. The others did the same, with Gilbert facing the rear of the train, while Eli took it upon himself to watch the door they'd just come through.

The train car was lit up by four lamps, their light weak but burning. Nathan held up the silver locket the man in black had given him. Now that they were clear of the saloon and its Vem gas, his head was clearing by the second.

He hooked the tiny clasp with his fingers, peeled open the locket... and stared.

"What is it?" Mackenzie asked, watching him from a nearby berth.

"It's a face. Of a woman."

A particularly striking Chinese lady, in fact, with long hair tastefully done. A dress shirt was frilly in the front, with a high, buttoned-up collar. Her high cheeks were unblemished, her smile faint but there, all captured in black and white.

"Fine-looking lady," Jimmy noted.

Which brought Eli and Gilbert in for a peek. They all agreed. She was indeed a fine-looking lady.

"So why did he have it?" Nathan asked after they'd all had their look.

No one could answer.

"Maybe that's why… he helped us," Eli said in an unusually thoughtful tone.

"We ain't ladies," Gilbert scoffed, screwing his nose up at the suggestion.

"No, we ain't," Mackenzie said. "But, we resemble her. 'Course, there are subtle differences, but when looked at from, say a distance… we're pretty much the same."

"How did he get his hands on it?" Nathan asked.

"I don't know."

"I know," Eli said, getting their attention. "How else could anyone have a piece of jewelry like that in their goddamn possession? I'll tell you how. It was either *given*… or it was *taken*. And seeing how that black pajama'd bastard bought us some time back there, time enough for that other pleasant enough so-n-so to lend a goddamn burning finger—and who the hell has a light at the end of their nose picker anyway? Where was I? Oh right. I'm thinking it was given. As a gift. For reasons we'll sure as hell never know."

"So… he was repaying that gift?" Mackenzie asked. "By helping us?"

"I don't know, Mack," Eli groaned. "You're the goddamn educated one. I'm more smart for other shit n' stuff."

The train rattled on, gently rocking them where they sat.

"I wonder…" Nathan said, looking at the closed door. "If they're all okay back there."

No one offered an opinion on that.

Until Gilbert said, "Hey. Listen."

They did.

"What, peckerhead?" Eli asked.

"The train. Sounds like that music in the saloon."

Nathan met Mackenzie's eyes in a shared look of *holy shit*. They remained seated then, listening, waiting, feeling their still wet clothing, yet not suffering from it. Nathan thought of Channy, then Nex, and hoped to God above that they were all right back there.

Especially Channy.

The train rattled on, and Nathan's attention drifted from the locket in his hand and the face there to the dark window on his left. He saw his own face looking back. Ragged. Bearded. And tired beyond words. Still, he shuffled to the glass and pressed the edge of his hand up against it, to shield against the nearby lamplight. There, he stared at an empty landscape, and the stars shone above with a purity that momentarily lifted his worries, and made him think of his mother.

And those memories eventually spread a smile across his face. Sometime later, he remembered to close the locket and tuck the piece away in his inside pocket.

The train continued to rock back and forth, lulling the men to sleep, one by one.

They woke up some time later.

Nathan came awake with a lurch, scratched at his neck and chin, and looked out the windows. Clear-headed as well, as if the saloon's noxious fun gas had cleansed him entirely.

It was daylight, with a green sun shining through the dusty glass.

Nathan sighed at the picture, wondering where the hell the train was, and where the mechanical beast was going. He stared at that rising sun and realized it was coming up over a plain of tall flowers, miles long and wide, and of a bright shade of pink.

"Pretty, ain't it?" Jimmy Norquay asked quietly.

Nathan glanced over at him, sitting across the way in the other berth. The others weren't in sight, but their snores were easily heard.

"Yeah."

"Been watching it most of the night."

"Most of it?" Nathan asked.

"In and out," Jimmy's eyebrows shrugged. "Somebody had to keep watch. Might as well be me."

"You didn't sleep at all?"

"Slept a little, but when that thing started to rise," he indicated the green sun with a nod of his head, "not a wink after that. Look at that, Nate. Just look. That's a green sun. And… an ocean of flowers the likes I've never seen before in my life. Which makes me wonder where we are, and I don't have a clue."

They shared a morning silence then, only their eyes moving, looking past each other, to the window just behind the other. The only sounds were snores and the moving train.

"Think we'll ever get back?" Nathan asked.

Jimmy thought about it for a long time before slowly smiling. "Don't know. But I know one thing. Orange sun. Green sun. Any sun I get to see over a plain of flowers as fine as that, then all I need is a cup of coffee, a chair, and a porch. Maybe a smoke. Then… life is good."

Nathan smiled back. "Easy to please, ain'tcha?"

"The easiest, I know."

A mighty yawn interrupted them and Eli asked, "Anyone got any tobacco?"

Jimmy and Nathan exchanged amused looks.

"No tobacco, Eli," Jimmy said.

Eli's head and shoulders popped into view from a berth as he struggled into a sitting position. He was looking haggard like them all, but instead of swearing about the lack of cigarettes, he took a deep breath and stared at what the morning had brought them.

Nathan thought the man looked right thoughtful.

"We should get moving," Jimmy suggested.

"Anything to eat?" Mackenzie asked, still out of sight.

"Wasn't supposed to be that kind of trip," Jimmy said. "All the food is back with Milton."

"Wonder what Milt's doing right now?" Nathan asked as Gilbert roared out a yawn, and earned a dirty look from Eli.

"Milton's probably on his way to Big Mud Valley," Jimmy answered. "We've been gone way too long."

"Suppose," Nathan said and rubbed his sleeve before patting down his shirt and pants. Dried to a clingy dampness, but certainly not the ton of water weight they carried before.

Eli stood up and lifted his rifle. He gave it a quick check and frowned before inspecting the overhead compartments. Without a word, he started searching them.

"The lamps are out," Mackenzie noticed.

"So they are," Jimmy said.

"I wonder who lights them at night?"

That question stopped them all.

"We should get moving," Jimmy repeated. "I have a feeling… we're in for a long day."

As expected, Eli didn't find a thing in the overhead compartments, and neither did anyone else as they walked through the aisle. They left the door they came through well alone, not wanting to see what lay beyond, and the plan of reaching the end of the train still made sense to them.

So they gathered up their weapons, their wits, and got to marching.

The next car was a passenger one, empty, with that green sun shining in from the eastern side, coloring the interior in a hue that resembled summer leaves along Lake Huron. The men walked along the aisle, strung out in a watchful line, inspecting the berths as well as the overheads.

The car after that was identical to the previous ones.

"How many cars you think we've been through?" Nathan asked Mackenzie's back, who walked behind Jimmy.

"I don't know now. Maybe two dozen or so?"

"Not that many," Gilbert said from behind Nathan. "Surely not. There was that desert place. With the crabs. That was…"

"That wasn't a car," Mackenzie said. "That was a world. Same as the saloon."

"But we were still on the train."

Jimmy reached the next door and opened it. No vestibule, like before, just the next deserted car, and a smell of dust. The sight of the empty berths was a little disappointing, but also a relief. Nathan wasn't sure he'd want to meet any passengers now. Not after what they'd been through.

The plain of flowers lay on either side of the windows as the train sped along, and the green sun lifted itself clear of the horizon.

They continued onward.

The train was moving fast, speeding along at five or six times the normal pace, but the familiar *chumpchumpchumpchump* remained constant.

The next door they opened revealed yet another empty passenger car, without a connecting vestibule.

The next dozen cars were the same.

The men marched along, aisle after aisle, door after door, the steady sway of the locomotive as regular as a pulse. No one spoke during that time, perhaps weary from the night before, and the sights, and wondering just what in God's creation they'd stepped onto once they boarded the train.

"Feel like using some of that dynamite?" Eli asked at one point.

"On what?" Jimmy asked back.

"On one of these windows. Or the next vestibule. Maybe blow a hole outta this iron pig and jump for it. Take our chances."

"You ever jump from a train moving this fast?" Mackenzie asked.

That quieted Eli.

"He was only sayin', Mack," Gilbert muttered.

"I know. But jumping from a train moving this fast will only break your neck if you're lucky. Your legs if you're unlucky. Besides. Look at it out there. There's nothing but flowers. No animals, nothing."

And he was right.

Another dozen cars, and Mackenzie was at the front. Marching through and pulling open doors like a soldier tending to boring guard duty. After he'd opened a dozen more, Nathan took his turn, not even bothering with pulling out one of his Colts. There didn't seem to be a need. The train was empty, and the sun… the lower edge of the sun could only be seen when he dipped at the waist.

Nathan pulled open a door and stared at the enclosed vestibule before him.

"Well, now," he said, "haven't seen you in a while."

The space was different however, as there were two doors on the right and left walls, each with a small square window at eye level. Mackenzie moved to check on one, couldn't see a thing, so he went to the other.

"Anything?" Gilbert asked from behind, his rifle at the ready. He was the only one.

"Nothing."

"Haul it open then," Eli said.

Mackenzie didn't see no harm in that, so he drew back his duster, not so damp at all now, and drew one pistol. He took hold of the handle and, with a ready nod at the others, opened it.

"Well, thank you Lord," Eli exclaimed in wonder.

Behind the door was a wooden toilet, with the seat cover down.

"Holy shit," Gilbert added. "I was ready to drop my drawers ever since the crabs!"

Smiling, Nathan leaned in and, with the barrel of his gun, lifted the seat cover. A breath of fresh air blew by, and when he leaned further, he saw the ground below, speeding over a blur of railway ties.

"Go on, then," he said to Gilbert. "Do your business."

A happy Gilbert stepped inside the cubicle and closed the door. Eli went to the other side and opened the stall there. An identical toilet waited.

"Finders shitters," he remarked and went inside. When he closed the door, Nathan considered the next passenger car at his back, before turning to Mackenzie and Jimmy standing upon the threshold of the last.

"Who else needs a moment?" he asked.

The two men glanced at each other before raising their hands.

"There's no paper in here!" Gilbert yelled in horror. "Not a single goddamn square!"

"Then don't pinch, you dummy," Eli shouted from the other side.

"I just did, Eli, I just did. Oh God. Oh *Christ*! It smells, Eli! It smells real *bad*!"

"Shut up Gilbert and let me shit!"

Nathan drew a hand over his face, but the others didn't attempt to hide their smiles. And a short second later, Mackenzie started to laugh. Jimmy joined him.

It wasn't Channy's giggle, Nathan thought, but it was a good sound to hear all the same.

39

After the men had all relieved themselves, they buttoned up and moved into the next passenger car. On impulse, however, Nathan, who was guarding the rear, opened and closed the last door.

Empty car. Daylight flooding the interior.

He left the door open and walked away, but midway up the aisle he glanced back and saw the door had closed anyway.

Onwards they plodded, car after empty car, expecting to see someone but hoping less and less. When they reached what was perhaps the two hundredth one that day, the green sun was no longer visible outside, but somewhere overhead. They stopped for a rest, marveling at all that empty space outside and in.

"I've been thinking," Mackenzie started and gestured at the interior. "About all this. We boarded the train at night. That's when we had most of our encounters. It's daytime now, and we're not running into anything. Or anyone."

"So?" Nathan asked.

"So, I'm saying that maybe, when the sun finally goes down, things might start happening again."

A glance around at the men's expressions and one could see that the thought had sunk deep into their minds.

"All right," Jimmy said. "So, if it does, assuming it does, maybe we should camp out for the night. In an empty car."

"Sounds good to me," Nathan said.

"Hell yeah," Eli threw in. "Getting sick of all this walking anyway."

"We won't have to do it much longer," Mackenzie said.

"Why's that?"

The man shrugged. "There's no water here. Or food. It's all gone. If we had water, we might last a week, but without it? No more than two or three days. After that, whatever car we're in, whatever berth, that'll be our grave."

Another tombstone of information they didn't really need to know. Nathan took in that shit nugget of news and found it distasteful, as did the others.

"You mean we could die on this train?" Gilbert asked. "Just from a lack of water alone?"

"Engine's got water," Eli said.

"And how do you suppose we get to that?" Mackenzie asked. "Even if we did walk all the way back there, through everything. If we could get there, how do we get water from the engine?"

Eli didn't answer.

"We're in a pinch here," Mackenzie continued. "And the way I see it, nowhere to go but forward. Maybe with a little luck, we can find something to drink. If not, we're looking at dying of thirst. On a train."

That thought dropped on them like a five-hundred-pound weight.

"Jesus, Mack," Eli finally said. "You sure as hell can fuck up a nice afternoon walk."

*

When they hit the two hundred and fiftieth passenger car, they were tired. When they hit the three hundredth one, they took another break, and sat without a word. The day was perhaps two or two thirty in the afternoon, but no one had a pocket watch, so they only had their sense of time to go on.

Regardless, the sun was past its zenith overhead, and sooner or later, it would be sinking into a horizon of unending flowers.

"Flowers," Nathan said at one point. "Nothing but flowers. Not a hill or mountain or squat.

"Maybe we're still in Saskatchewan?" Mackenzie asked.

"Not there," Jimmy said. "I've been all over Saskatchewan. It's flat, but not like this. And not covered in flowers like that."

Which was true. The pretty plains outside the windows were unbroken sprawls of a single hearty color. An ocean of carnations that covered everything.

They trudged on, hefting rifles over shoulders, but keeping their winter clothing on. Despite all the walking inside, the temperature remained a cool ten degrees or so. Still, the sweat seeped out of them, and that water wasn't replaced.

"What car is this?" Nathan croaked as he stopped at the door.

Mackenzie had to think about it. "Three hundred and… thirty-four."

"Don't ask that question again until it's four hundred," Eli warned.

"It'll be dark then," Gilbert said.

"Yeah, maybe."

Nathan hauled the door open. The runners were getting crankier, it seemed, and certainly took more strength.

"We're gonna haveta stop soon," he said, gazing ahead into the next car.

Empty. Like all the others before them.

They forged onward.

Hours later, on the west side of the train, the lower curvature of the green sun finally began to show itself, and the sky, still blue, began to wan.

"Look at that," Mackenzie said, stopping and resting his rifle across one of the berths. "We've been hiking along this thing all damn day."

"What number is this?" Nathan asked.

"Four fifty-six or fifty-seven. We stopped a few times."

The passenger car gently swayed with the number, but it was enough to ease Eli and Jimmy into nearby berths.

"I'm done," Eli said, glancing towards the window and making a face. "This'll do me just fine for the night. Hey, Jimmy. Why don't you get started on supper? Cook us up something nice."

"Why don't you cook us up some beans?" Jimmy retorted wearily from his seat.

"Beans it is," Eli said and forced a fart into the air. "There you go. One order. Hope you wanted gravy with that."

"Not now, not ever."

Still, they were smiling when he said it.

"I'll have some beans too, Eli," Gilbert said, standing in the aisle.

"Sorry. Kitchen's closed. Come back in the morning. Though I don't think the menu will have changed much."

Nathan collapsed in a berth. He crossed his legs, propping his feet up on the green cushion across from him. He doffed his father's hat and tossed it on the seat nearby.

"Gilbert's still standing," he said, glad to be off his feet. "He's got first watch."

"Awww."

"Hush," Eli warned him. "You'll do it. You're the only one with strength still in his legs."

"That's from that thing I held onto back at the saloon," Gilbert explained. "I don't know what it did, but it topped me off without me taking a bite of anything."

"Wish I'd grabbed on to one of those," Jimmy whispered.

"Wish I'd gotten to meet another Channy," Eli said.

"I ain't watching all night," Gilbert warned.

"I'll take over when you're tired," Mackenzie told him.

"Tell me a bedtime story, Eli," Jimmy asked.

"You're a peckerface. The end."

Soft laughter at that.

Someone spoke again, but Nathan didn't understand a word of it. He was already falling asleep, his head pressed against the window.

40

Nathan awoke to a groan and pop of iron. A deep-sea wailing of metal being placed under terrible stress. The sound jolted him awake, and by the wild bird flurry surrounding him, it got the others as well. He stood and looked around, seeing the others rising to their feet, their faces and forms black with shadow, but a single oil lamp burned at either end of the car.

Who lit it? Nathan was about to ask.

When the rear of the car bent upward. The oil lamp on the wall shivered, and the glass cover fell away with a sharp tinkle upon the floor. Like a gigantic conveyor belt, the end of the train crinkled into a perfectly impossible ninety-degree angle. The bending iron screeched at being worked so, and the roof became a wide chute that quickly vanished from sight. A cliff formed there, upon the *roof,* and the overhead compartments crackled and puffed dark clouds of dust but did not break as everything rolled up and over that inverted precipice, where the light shimmered and swayed and diminished.

The sight ripped a panicked gasp from Nathan's throat.

He realized he was the last man standing. The others were already fleeing, charging along the aisle, their boots stomping over carpeted floor, their coats and guns slapping out a clatter against the edges of the seats. Nathan took one last look at that cheeky defiance of reality and launched himself into the aisle. He lurched to a stop, gasped with fright, grabbed for his father's felt hat still on the seat when his periphery vision registered a great looming wave of berths being sucked up into that gapped mouth. Now that the berths were being bent and rolled upward, the whole nightmarish scene resembled a gigantic Dutchman's watermill.

The train was going *up. Straight* up.

Nathan had no intention of going with it. He clutched his father's hat to his side as he pounded up the aisle after his boys. A great watershed growling and twisting of fibers screeched over the bending of metal. The floor trembled underfoot, but he stayed on course, stayed upright.

Twenty feet from the dark door to the next car, which was open and filled with black. Nathan knew just from the sight of it that something waited for him on the other side. He was being *forced* into the next reality, and expected the worse.

Or at least, worse than the bending train bearing down on his heels as he ran out of the aisle.

Nathan panted, winced, his limbs afire and charging, and he felt the hard pull of carpet underfoot as it was *yanked* upwards just as he dove for the open portal—

And crash landed into at least two sets of legs.

Threads of light ran along and brightened a red floor, and the seats—from what Nathan could see on his chest—were made of sculpted bone, a light brown bone, that rose up into… legs. And cushions. And a person sitting with an open mouth, bright red skin as if stricken by a serious disease, and a single wide-open eye the size of an apple.

Nathan screamed.

The one-eyed red man screamed with him. His one-eyed wife with blonde hair screamed as well, and their two children, one to each lap, positively *bawled* and buried their one-eyed faces into their parents' clothing, only to sneak peeks, point, and smother their screeches again.

In fact, the whole car was screaming.

Gilbert got a hold of Nathan's shoulder as Eli and Jimmy were struggling to stand. Mackenzie was nearing the center of a car crammed full of passengers—a very long car—the likes of which Nathan had never seen. Threads of light ran along the floor and ceiling of the interior, while the overhead compartments were beige with leather finishes and opened on a slant. Under those compartments were more lights, whole *panels* of them, which illuminated the full terrifying reaction of the passengers to the train robbers. The passengers wore clothing that was both familiar yet different. There were collared shirts of a material Nathan didn't recognize. The men wore short pants that stopped mid-thigh, and some of their shirt sleeves were practically cut off at the mid-bicep. The female clothing was even more scandalous, showing off more blistering red skin that both shocked and, oddly enough, intrigued Nathan. Cleavage was in abundance, and hairstyles were positively—

Mackenzie fired his rifle into the ceiling, cowering the passengers into silence. He worked the lever and spun around, glaring at the masses who bent over into their seats with four-fingered hands clasped over their heads. It got quiet so fast that the soft plucking of some string instrument was momentarily distracting.

"All right," Mackenzie shouted, whirling around in the aisle and watching for heroes. "Stay just like that. No one makes a move and no one goes for a gun. Just be real quiet and…"

While he talked, Mackenzie looked around, sizing up not only the alien passengers but the strange signs filled with odd stick figures and warnings of accidents he struggled to interpret. Nathan saw them as well, and the written characters accompanying the illustrations were unknown to him.

But then he saw outside the great sloping window, which resembled a regular full-size window except, somehow, it was squished to one side like a rhombus, and extended outwards oddly enough.

Beyond the glass was yet another surprise.

The flowery plains had vanished, and a charcoal grayness colored the earth. Mountains rose up. Stony colossuses that sped by faster than anything Nathan had ever experienced, and up until then, he'd experienced quite a lot. The upper portions of the mountains scrolled by, their snow-capped heights unseen, but the further the eye drifted to its base, the faster the land moved.

There was none of the gentle swaying as the train shot forward, but a rock-solid gliding that beguiled the hell out of Nathan.

And there was something else.

The train was *curling* around a mountain, and, as it turned, sunlight blazed through the windows. Except the light was diffused somehow, lessened by a gray coating upon the glass.

Some of the passengers chanced looking up, their single eyes near bursting from their faces, wondering what their fates would be.

"We robbing these people?" Eli demanded, finally standing and with his rifle ready.

That turned the gang members' heads.

"*Are* we robbing these people?" Jimmy wanted to know.

"I don't think we should," Gilbert threw in.

They waited on Nathan, who was watching Mackenzie. The man was bent over slightly and staring out the window, gripping the high cushiony seats, the material dimpled where folks had rested their heads. The cushions gleamed as if slathered in hair slick.

"Mackenzie?" Nathan called out, drawing his gun.

Mackenzie didn't answer.

"*Mack!*"

That got him, and the bearded man turned his head. He looked none too happy about their present whereabouts. That would be a conversation for another time. Right now, however…

"Yeah, sure," Mackenzie said. "But *hurry.*"

With that, he raced to the far door, which was made of black glass and framed in metal. Nathan looked over his shoulder as Eli and Gilbert started pointing guns in faces. They grabbed shoulder bags from the womenfolk and patted down the men. Nathan turned around and saw that the door they had dove through was now a plane of wide, dark glass, where he could see the ghostly image of himself sizing up matters. Above that, a white box blazed nonsense red characters across its face with flashing urgency.

"The hell are we now?" Nathan muttered.

"You doing crowd control, Nate?" Eli asked as he pushed by, working the right side of the train.

"Uh, yeah."

"Good boy."

Gilbert almost barreled him over then, clamoring after Eli and working the left side of the aisle.

Nathan ignored them, listening instead to the whimpers of the women folks, and catching a few glares from the men folk that chilled him to his nuggets. Motion from beyond the glass door distracted him then, in the area that should have been the old passenger car instead of this fancy modern bullet of a train. Beyond that black glass and his own stupefied image, he saw heads leaning out into the aisle and above the berths all looking at him.

"Best hurry up, boys," Nathan warned as he drew his second Colt. Two-fisted now, he held them above the surrounding seats and glared his most poisonous back at the more defiant passengers.

That blinking urgent message kept on flashing over the back door, however. A second later, figures charged up the aisle of the adjoining car, and the passengers there got out of the way. The figures were faceless, wearing bulky clothing, and carrying—

Nathan blinked.

Rifles. Not rifles like the venerable Winchesters the boys carried, but shorter, fatter, and much more ribbed than regular weapons. The man who once wanted to be a lawman didn't like the look of those guns.

"Time's up boys, we got company coming!" Nathan warned and took aim at the glass doors.

Beyond which, an inner set opened, allowing in light and a single charging line of the soldiers. They rushed through the vestibule, towards the second set.

"*We got company boys!*" Nathan yelled louder.

The doors opened and he shot the first soldier not twenty feet away. The man blew backwards, crashing into the others and disrupting the charge. In that tumble of faltering bodies, however, there were more soldiers. At least a dozen.

Nathan continued firing at that twisting, flailing nest of limbs and torsos. A faceless head resembling a polished bucket leaned forward out of that writhing mess, and Nathan snapped off a shot, placing it perfectly in the center of the bucket. The impact straightened the figure, perhaps even dazed him, but he did not go down.

In fact, he pawed at that wash bucket helmet and rattled his skull as if just being kicked by a mule.

Nathan fired four more shots, thumbs working the Colts' hammers, each bullet slamming into the soldier. The final hit sent him down, while that red flashing sign over the doorway actually started shouting.

Two things happened.

All at once, the passengers bent over in their seats, jamming their heads to their knees as if checking on their posteriors. Children were clutched close and forced down as well, just as a secondary line of gibberish blared out overhead, distracting Nathan from his gunfight.

A green light flared to life in the center of the head rest and formed a shimmering dome over each berth, no higher than Nathan's lowest ribs. Gilbert cut loose a short yelp of fright, holding up a bag by its straps, except the bag had been cut free upon the light field extending over the passengers. The charred ends of the straps smoked as if severed by flaming scissors.

A horrified Gilbert held up those smoldering strands before throwing them down.

"Ahead of you!" Eli Gallant shouted.

An angry burst of gunfire punched bullets into the ceiling. Nathan flinched as those shots were only a step away from him. He raised his guns and fired—but got only the harmless clicks of spent chambers.

"Get down, Rhodes!" Eli commanded just as he opened up on the soldiers, spinning around the one who'd fired.

But the soldier didn't release his weapon.

Nor did any of the soldiers Nathan had shot. In fact, those men were back on their feet, and looking very much alive.

One in particular stood just inside the open doorway, attempting to bring up his short bulldog of a rifle.

Eli fired at that figure, a measured tempo of working the lever, taking aim, and squeezing the trigger as toe-tapping as any drumbeat.

Nathan retreated, crouched low and staying out of that line of fire, moving up the aisle towards Eli. Behind the gun runner was Gilbert, shouldering a number of oversized pocketbooks and readying his own rifle. Jimmy was already at the other end, standing side-on to the glass door, and Mackenzie with him.

Nathan went by the gun runner.

"All yours, Gilbert!" Eli shouted as he ducked and turned to follow Nathan's tail.

Gilbert opened up.

Say what you will about the unkempt gun runner… call him dirty or unmannerly, or even as stunned as your ass…

But the man knew how to shoot.

And could place a shot, without a doubt.

Which Gilbert presently demonstrated.

The man quickly realized that body shots didn't have the effect he desired. Head shots were far more effective, but even those didn't seem to put the soldiers down and keep them there.

So he did the next best thing.

He blew out a leg, which produced a scream heard above that white box shouting out gibberish. The soldier flailed and went down, but the others behind him teemed forward, their body language poised and impassive.

Gilbert shot an ankle out from one, pitching the guy forward in a heap. The gun runner aimed high and cracked back the head of the second soldier as if he were hooked on a clothesline. A third shot blew apart a hand and that soldier yelled out before cringing and dropping away. A fourth was hindered by the unexpected retreat, and Gilbert spun him round with one shot to the shoulder, before dropping him to that writhing mat piling up on the open threshold.

The fifth soldier, however, fired back—an uninterrupted stream of death that flashed over Nathan's left shoulder, shredding a few of the head rests above the glowing light line in startling explosions of cottony tufts.

Nathan passed Gilbert's position and could feel the vibe of concentration surrounding the gun runner.

Gilbert dropped to a knee and fired, giving back his reply and hitting the fifth soldier in the neck. The soldier dropped his weapon and clutched at his fountaining throat as his knees unlocked and dropped him.

"*Move your ass, Gilbert!*" Eli yelled.

But Gilbert did not. He continued to fire, keeping those faceless harbingers of the train at bay, working a punishing spell of devastation. They were screaming now, the soldiers, while others were barking commands. Some were even crawling along the floor, worming their way to a better firing position.

Ten shots. Maybe twelve.

Gilbert would soon be dry.

"*GILBERT, MOVE!*" Eli barked, emptying his lungs on the order.

The black mass of soldiers choking the vestibule broke apart. One figure lunged from the doorway, over the writhing bodies below, and landed on his chest.

Gun up.

Gilbert shifted his aim and his Winchester clicked empty. That single note broke the gun runner's spell, and he turned and ran.

Streamers of light screamed past him, missing his shoulders by inches, then missing his head by hairs. The ceiling above Gilbert burst apart in peppery punches of smoke and electricity as the line of fire went from right to left.

Eli tossed his rifle at Mackenzie, drew his pistols, and immediately turned and started blasting at the soldier inside the train. Jimmy exited the passenger car. The door of black glass simply opened for him when he approached it, and he ducked into the well-lit vestibule behind it.

Nathan raced after him, cringing, waiting for his skull to blow apart like that pillowy head rest. He got through the doorway with a peal of excitement.

Mackenzie stepped inside after him and leaned back out, working his rifle as Gilbert narrowly hauled his smoking ass over the threshold. He ducked inside and planted his frame up against the wall.

Eli turned and ran, lopsided, trying to give Mackenzie enough room to keep the soldiers busy.

Ten feet. Five.

Behind him, the glut at the far end became untangled. Two soldiers raised their awesome rifles and took aim. They moved in a haunting slow motion, lining up optical sights that simply made no sense. Twin strings of red light beamed from those sights, waving through the air until centering upon Eli's retreating back.

The gun runner stomped over a white line and kept on running when those rifles fired upon him, transforming the glass doors closing on his heels into a lightning show.

Gilbert yelled and ducked. Eli threw himself against a wall and stayed there as the soldiers continued blasting the closed doors. Spidery holes flashed across the outer layer of the glass but somehow remained intact on the gang's side. Through those jagged markings, the main mass of soldiers entered the train and advanced, firing at every step.

"They mean business," Mackenzie said, as the glass door thrummed with multiple impacts.

"I mean business," Jimmy said as he swept open one side of his winter duster, revealing the last of his dynamite.

"No time for that," Nathan said, sighting the advancing soldiers and then switching to the next door not ten feet away. Passengers could be seen beyond that as well, and they were very much aware of the approaching gun battle.

Nathan ran for the door.

The glass doors opened, dispensing with the illusion of sitting passengers, instead revealing a vertical plane of tar that shimmered like water.

Nathan plunged through it.

<h1 style="text-align:center">41</h1>

And rolled into an empty train car more akin to recollection and upbringing. He tumbled upon a dusty floor, and came up with his empty pistols aimed at, of all things… a bespectacled old man well on in his years.

The twin Colts aimed at his head no doubt shaved a few more years off him.

"Freeze!" Nathan growled through clenched teeth.

The old man huffed, puffed, and raised a pair of the scrawniest wrists Nathan might've ever seen. The old man continued to jerk and twitch, as if he were in dire need to take a breath or a piss, or both, and was on the verge of choosing one over the other.

"I said *freeze!*" Nathan repeated, knowing the old bastard would drop dead any second.

Except the old bastard did not.

With a determination that had to be commended, the old man buckled down on his spiking anxiety, and became as still as a tree. Wide-eyed and distressed, however, as if the tree realized there was a dozen sticks of dynamite strapped around its base.

Nathan heard the others coming into the car behind him, but he kept his sights upon the old man. He had a long beard, as long as Father Time himself, and rounded spectacles that were in need of cleaning. His facial hair was white, as was the poorly cut turf topping off his head. The uniform he wore was blue, with black stripes up the pants' legs. Suspenders held them up, going over the shoulders of a white shirt greatly stained yellow around the armpits.

The old man's clothes looked two sizes too large for him, as if he'd lost perhaps fifty pounds at least, and he quivered like a Sunday evening dinner bell just struck.

All got quiet then, except for the hard breathing of the gang. The sounds of reloading commenced, as the men scrambled to make use of the time they had and the ammunition they carried. At one point, Eli tossed one of his emptied bandoliers onto the floor, where it landed with a whip's crack.

The sound made the old codger jump.

"Well, look at this," Mackenzie said.

So Nathan did.

They stood in a mail car, and three oil lamps supplied the only light. With several discarded mail bags in one corner, and a solid wall of shelving units containing a rat's nest of paper and twine within. More paper and twine littered the floor around the units. A significantly sized safe was also against the wall, opposite the loading door—shut and barred. Next to that was a clerk's desk with a load of paper, quills, and ink wells upon its surface. Dust and that familiar pungent smell of unwashed flesh wrinkled Nathan's nose, and it originated from the old clerk.

"Sacred Heart of Mary," Jimmy said, lifting a wrist to his face. "You taking shits in here or what?"

The old man blinked, then flicked his bespectacled gaze to Nathan.

"Answer the man," Nathan ordered, distracted by the sight of the safe.

"I move my bowels over there," the man answered with a forced display of indignance by lifting his chin. "I have the necessary facilities inside this car."

Nathan saw the half-opened door of an onboard shitter.

"You have paper for wiping your ass, old man?" Eli asked as he thumbed shells into his Winchester.

"I ... do not."

"Any rags? A corncob, even?"

A reluctant pause. "No."

"Figures."

The gang relaxed, realizing that no one was pursuing them through the closed door at their backs, which was no longer black glass, but the familiar design of a regular train.

"This the mail car?" Nathan asked as he climbed to his feet.

The old man didn't answer, which was answer enough. Nathan holstered one gun and went about reloading the other. "Don't get any ideas," he said. "If I don't shoot you, one of my partners will."

The old man didn't say a word.

"What's your name?" Mackenzie asked, coming forward.

The clerk watched him.

"What's your name?" Mack repeated.

The hairy jaw quivered again, debating on a reply it seemed, when he finally said, "Festus."

"Festus?"

Festus nodded.

"All right then, Festus," Mackenzie went on. "This is the mail car, right? And that's the safe?"

"It is."

"Can you open it for us?"

"Are you…"

"Gonna rob you?" Mackenzie finished. He glanced at his companions scattered around the car. "Yeah, I guess we are."

Festus shook his head. "Are you… from my time?"

That silenced Mackenzie.

"We are," Jimmy answered.

Festus lowed his hands, and his trembling increased, as if he'd just suffered a heart attack. Or was shot in the back. He cleared his throat and shook his head as if coming awake from a dream.

"Sweet Lord Almighty," he whispered and clamped his lips shut, and Nathan knew, just knew, that old Festus was just about to cut loose with a downpour of tears.

"You're from my time," Festus trembled. "My *world*. Oh my Lord. My sweet, sweet Lord. I don't believe it. I *can't* believe it. I'd given up. Given up for so long. So damn long."

"Yeah," Nathan said, distracted by the emotional display. "You just… take it easy old-timer. Catch your breath."

"Oh." Festus released and pulled a yellowed hanky from his pocket. The sight of that colored cloth caused Nathan to grimace as the old clerk buried his face in it and drew a mighty breath in through the material.

Gilbert and Eli, aware of the clerk, moved to the safe all the same. Gilbert dropped the half-dozen or so fancy handbags he'd grabbed from the lady passengers of the last car, as did Jimmy. The safe however, that was the prize.

The secondary prize, seeing they weren't on the train they wanted, but the damned 311.

"You can open this safe, old timer?" Eli asked, studying the five-by-five black bulk tucked against the wall.

Festus didn't appear to hear, however, as he continued to blubber away in his filthy handkerchief. Nathan met Eli's gaze, then Gilbert's. Jimmy walked over and inspected the safe. His brow furrowed as he noticed it wasn't locked. He reached for the lever and pulled the door open with a low whine from a hinge.

Wads of paper notes slid free of the safe's interior, revealing bundles of cash still inside.

"Oh my," Eli whispered, while Gilbert took on that familiar look of crazy prospector who just discovered gold.

Mackenzie grabbed up mail bags from the shelf and tossed them at the two men. They dropped to their knees and began stuffing away notes.

"Dominion of Canada." Gilbert smiled at Eli, then Nathan. "God save the Queen."

The rush of activity caused Festus to lower his moist handkerchief. He adjusted his glasses and watched the men pack away the safe's riches.

"How much is in there?" Nathan asked.

The question surprised the old man and it took him a moment to reply. "Hundred and thirty-five. Thousand. In bills. There's a bag of change in there as well. Quarters. Silver dollars. A hundred and twenty dollars worth total."

"Leave that," Eli said.

"I ain't leaving that!" Gilbert barked. "That's more'n a few royal evenings back in town."

"You can carry it then."

Gilbert stopped for only a split second before hauling out the coin bags and inspecting their strings.

"Not what we were looking for," Mackenzie said to Jimmy and Nathan. "But better than what I was expecting."

"After everything we've been through?" Jimmy countered.

Mackenzie acknowledged that with a shrug.

Nathan continued to watch Festus, and soon enough, Mackenzie joined him.

"How you doing, old-timer?" Mackenzie asked.

Festus's red eyes glared out from behind his dirty glasses, but he didn't answer.

"Don't worry," Mackenzie said. "We won't hurt you."

"Hurt me?"

"That's right."

"About what? That?" Festus gestured the safe and its contents. "I don't care about that shit. Take it. Take every damn nickel for all I care. I just…"

he shook his head. "I'm just so glad to see you. I'd given up… after so long."

Mackenzie frowned. "How long you been here?"

"Me?" Festus stared. "You'll think I'm crazy."

"Not after what we've seen," Jimmy Norquay said, placing Shorty's shotgun against one shoulder.

That actually sobered the old clerk. "Yes. Yes, I suppose you know. But, tell me, how did you get here? I don't remember you."

"We climbed on," Mackenzie said. "While the train was going up a grade. Charging up a grade, really, but we got on her all the same. We were looking for another train, mind you. Boarded this one by accident… and daresay we got the surprise of our lives."

"One surprise after the other," Nathan added.

"Right after the other," Mackenzie carried on. "Found out we were on the 311 from a man called Archie."

"Archie?" The name lit up Festus's hairy features. "You met Archie? He's still alive?"

That quieted the men.

"Not anymore," Jimmy reported. "He died."

"Oh, you didn't shoot him, did you?" Festus moaned.

"No, not us," Mackenzie said. "But he passed on all the same. Not before he told us we were on the 311."

Festus took a moment, looked around as if in a daze, and pointed at a chair tucked in behind a desk.

"Go ahead," Nathan told him.

The old clerk pulled the chair out and plopped down. "Archie was a good man. Pleasant as a… as a sunny day. He was my friend."

Nathan could believe that, despite the fact that the Englishman had somehow become a part of a sea serpent, as goddamn crazy as that sounded.

"Poor old Archie," Festus muttered.

In the background, Eli and Gilbert continued to push fistfuls of cash into mailbags. Jimmy watched them for a moment, before turning his attention back on the two doors leading into the car. Nathan noticed that the mail car had windows, but they were bolted shut.

"But he's the lucky one," Festus finally declared in a rattled tone. "God above, yes. He's the lucky one."

Nathan didn't have the mind or will to debate that.

"Don't worry," Festus said to Jimmy, noticing him watching the doors. "They're shut. Nothing is coming through them once they're shut. Opening them is another matter, but I'm sure… you know about that."

That got their attention.

"What's going on here?" Mackenzie asked quietly. "It's damn obvious this is one weird train."

Festus barked a laugh. "You said it, sir. You *said* it."

"We've seen things," Nathan heard himself say.

"Oh, I imagine you have," Festus took up. "I imagine you have. Incredible things. Horrible things, and things that defy all logic. All belief. And all common sense. I know. I know all too well. I've been on this train for…"

He stopped, a look of fear on his face.

"How long?" Nathan pressed.

Festus gazed at him. "I… eventually measured days by sleep. Counting them as days. I had no other way of gauging a day as, some days, the morning never seemed to end. Worse still, there were times when the night just went on and on. And those were the worst, even though the lamps never diminished. Never had to fill them once. Not after it all happened."

"How long?" Nathan said, getting annoyed at not getting a straight answer.

Festus paused, then gave it up. "A hundred and twenty. Years. Five months. And fifteen days, today. By my reckoning."

That quieted them all. Even Eli and Gilbert's efforts slowed to a stop. The train, however, continued to roll on.

Chumpchumpchumpchump…

"Bullshit," Eli swore, looking at the old clerk as if a horse had clocked him upside the head with both rear hooves.

"It is not…" Festus shot back. "Bull *chips*. I assure you. I've been here long enough. To know." He ended with a glare at Nathan. "I know how long I've been here."

Mackenzie was shaking his head. "But this train has only been missing ten years or so. Give or take a year."

"What?" Festus asked.

"Ten years," Mackenzie continued. "I forget the exact time now, but it sure as hell hasn't been over a hundred."

"Ten years?" Festus asked.

"If that."

That caused the clerk to grip the arms of his chair, as if trying to keep a hold of reality. He then pulled out a drawer from the desk, making Nathan reach for a Colt. Festus ignored his caution and extracted a picture from within. He turned the frame around, showing a black and white photograph. There was a collection of men, in the company uniforms of the railway, standing before the 311, perhaps before she took her first journey across the great plains. They were smart-looking, standing ramrod straight in front of the train, with fists on their hips or holding onto their hats.

"See him here?" Festus tapped a pudgy figure.

"Holy Christ," Mackenzie whispered.

Nathan recognized the man at once, when he was obviously still a man. "Archie Willmoore."

The conductor who had become part of a sea serpent, and who had died along with it. He was younger then, but there was no mistaking the man. The hair only beginning to thin, the scar still above his right eyebrow.

"Yes," Festus said. "That's him. Now see here. This is me."

Not a man spoke afterwards.

Because right beside the proud conductor stood a much younger man, no older than twenty-one if that. With a head of light hair and the smile of someone who had found his purpose in life and was supremely happy because of it.

That young man was, of course, the mail clerk before them.

"That ain't you," Eli scoffed.

"That *is* me, I tell you," Festus shot back. "That's me. I don't mind if you don't believe me because I know what's what. If you're here, you should know what's what, too. Everything happens on this train. Everything and… and more. The train ain't right, and then it's everything right. It's haunted, and it's not haunted. It's even beyond haunted, at times. And, try as I might, I can't explain it any more than that."

"Festus," Mackenzie said, keeping a level head. "Why is the train like this?"

"You don't know?"

"No."

Festus sighed. "I don't know. I figure… the closest I can figure, is when we went into that first tunnel. That's when everything went bad. Everything went dark. Just like the sun going down. Except it never did go down. And it never did come back up. It stayed dark. And, as the Lord above is my witness, that was probably the worst of it. That… eternal dark. That tunnel that just went on and on. You won't believe it… but it stayed dark for almost a year. A *year.* Not that it mattered. People… the passengers… became anxious after ten minutes. Most were insane by the end of the day. Then… things got worse."

If Nathan had been unnerved by the train before, he was positively chilled to the marrow now, and even more aware of the ghostly pulse of the great machine.

"Why?" Mackenzie quietly asked.

Festus focused on him. "Because we couldn't stop the train. Riley was the engineer. The best of his time. He couldn't stop the engine, no matter how hard he tried. He applied the brakes but that only generated this fearsome… spectacle of sparks. The train wouldn't brake and, in fact, only sped up. The light at the front shone only a great empty void on ahead, and the rails she— *we* rode. The only connection we had with reality. When the ground disappeared…"

Nathan swallowed at that point, knowing the feeling.

"Well, people truly became disorderly. We couldn't control them. Couldn't settle them down. It was mutiny. Windows were opened. Doors. The screaming. Oh the screaming. Women, children, and men. I'm not too proud to admit I howled at times, when my despair sought to rob me completely of my senses. I *screamed*. And that was *only* the first day, I'll have you know."

Eli Gallant lowered his head, his fists clenched tight around his Winchester. Money bags lay at his feet.

"The ground eventually returned, mind you. Which was welcomed at first, but then people tried to get off. Not only the people, but the company hands as well, you understand. They tried to get off the train. Some jumped, into that flashing dark, never to be seen again. Whole families. Mothers and fathers holding children. Man and wife holding hands. Stepping off the train where they could and disappearing into the dark as quick as a wink."

At that, Festus snapped up a fist.

"Some even tried… going to the caboose and hanging a rope from it. That was most disturbing. Most disturbing. As the line hit the rail bed… it suddenly came off the ground, and went tight. No one could pull it back in. No one. It was as if it was towing another car entirely. It eventually snapped. No one tried jumping off the train after that, but we'd lost a quarter of our passengers already by then. Then… it only got worse."

Nathan fidgeted from one boot to the other, glancing around. Only Jimmy and Mackenzie were keeping their faces neutral. Eli was scowling, as if hearing a story not to his liking in the least. Gilbert stood slack-jawed, holding his rifle in one hand.

"How did it get worse?" Mackenzie asked.

"We couldn't get off," Festus replied. "And the dark was constant. Then the train changed. Things passed by the windows in flashes. Ghosts, we figured, enough of them to make the disbelievers believe. Never a clear look, but frightening flashes of …faces. Horrified faces. Some standing along the tracks, waving as if all were just fine. People went insane. Insane, I tell you. And the violence began. Acts of rage I can't describe, but I've witnessed. Some of them formed gangs. Tribes, onto themselves. The train became segmented. Doors were barred any way possible. I secured the mail room because I had the appropriate means to do so. That didn't stop people from… climbing over the roof. Seeking entry through the windows. It was a dark time. A terrible time, that went on and on forever."

"How did you survive?" Jimmy asked. "Without food or water?"

"The train had stores, you understand," Festus explained in a weary voice. "Ample stores to feed everyone on board. Those provisions became vital as you might expect. And after they were gone… in only a week, mind you, the odd thing was… no one was hungry or thirsty after that. You asked me earlier… what I clean myself with. I haven't had to move my bowels since I stopped feeding, as impossible as that sounds."

That was met with disbelieving stares.

"Not that it mattered. Dying of thirst or starvation is a horrible end for anyone, but we were deprived of death in those ways as we were deprived of stopping the train, you understand. People died, by each other's hand, but as for dying for lack of food or water? No. No one did. And that only shattered more minds."

"We met some of those passengers," Mackenzie said. "And… we dealt with them most violently."

Festus thought about that. "You shot passengers?"

"Close to a hundred, by my reckoning."

"They might not have been passengers. They might have been other things. Monsters taking on the appearance of passengers."

And they did just that, Nathan thought.

"How long have you been on this train?" Festus asked.

"Hours," Mackenzie replied.

"Days," Jimmy added, and he got agreement on that from Mackenzie.

"You *think* that," Festus said warily. "Thing is, you might very well have been on this train for weeks. Months even. Or… or even seconds. You have no way of knowing, but you will when you start aging. Look at me. I knew I was on this train for a hundred and twenty years and a bit. I probably look a hundred and twenty years old. But you said only minutes ago the train has been missing no more than ten years. My point being… here? Time means nothing. Reality is dream, and dream is reality. Ghosts walk. Monsters exist. Mortals become immortal. I should be dead, sweet Lord above, and yet…"

Festus paused. "I can't die. Not from failing health, it seems. Or from lack of food and water. Believe me when I say I've wished for death. Every time I've opened and closed one of those doors, hoping something would do me in. I leave them open at night, or whenever I sleep when there is only perpetual day. They're closed when I wake up. I was fearful of this at first but… now I don't care. That's how it was you came in here. No one else has managed to enter when the doors were locked."

Both Eli and Gilbert looked to Mackenzie at that point, their expressions alarmed.

"So, we can't get off?" Jimmy asked.

"The train won't let you off," Festus replied. "Not if it can help it. I've tried, let me tell you, I've tried. I've gone places. Explored worlds, so to speak. Drawn by a gentle pull I can't explain, but if you let it, that pull will always draw you back to the train. To another door, and whatever lies beyond. How many cars you pass through? See any of them other places? Those other worlds?"

No one answered.

"We've been places," Nathan said for them all.

"Then you know what I'm talking about. I've seen all I've wanted to see and more. Probably could have stayed in some of those places. Maybe even died, as there are things that will certainly kill a man out there. Yet, in the end, all I ever wanted was to get back on the train and get back home. To my world."

"We'll find our way back," Nathan said.

"You sure about that, youngster?"

Nathan didn't answer.

"I don't mean to scare you," Festus said. "I'm just saying what is. And you don't have to go right away. Stay awhile, if you want. Take that money. Take all of it. I got no use for it. No more than a house fly got use for it. But… when you're ready to leave, if that is your intention, then maybe you'll grant me a last request."

Mackenzie was already nodding. "We'll take you with us."

That caught Festus off-guard. "No, no, not that. I… don't want to go beyond the mail car. Not one step. Weren't you listening to me? You *can't* get off. The train won't let you get off. We're… trapped here. For all eternity. Or until something kills us outright. I'm too old to explore anymore. No, when you go, I want you to shoot me. Every bullet you can spare. Here."

Festus tapped his chest.

"And here."

He tapped his forehead. Three times. "Especially here. To make sure I don't come back, ever."

Nathan shifted from one foot to the other. Gilbert was shaking his head, while the others didn't quite know what to make of Festus.

"We'll find the caboose," Mackenzie said. "And get off this train."

"No one gets off this train."

"We will."

Festus studied them all in turn. "How many cars have you walked through already to get here?"

"Hundreds," Mackenzie said.

"There's *thousands* out there. *Hundreds* of thousands. I know. I stopped looking because I got too old. Best thing for us all is to sit around in a circle. You boys got the bullets. Just decide on the one who gets to shoot himself, after he's done the others. That's the only way off this train."

"What do you know about a Chinaman?" Nathan asked, remembering that scene of a solitary figure wearing robes, with his hair tied back in a long ponytail, disappearing in a tunnel mouth.

The question visibly perplexed Festus.

"Going into a tunnel. All by himself. The night before the tunnel was opened?"

"I don't know. Why do you ask?"

Nathan didn't reply as he wasn't sure why he asked. He just remembered the scene as it played out in his mind, but it felt right.

"Never mind," he finished. He looked over at the others. "I don't see any point in staying any longer."

The men eyed each other.

"You can't stay?" Festus asked.

"No," Mackenzie said. "We're going to try to get off this thing."

"You'll grow old trying. Or worse."

"Suppose so."

Festus nodded. "Well, it was nice talking to you, boys. Been a while since I could talk to someone who knew what I was talking about. I'd say good luck, but chances are… you'll walk out that door," he pointed to the one ahead, "only to come back in through that one." He indicated the door they'd come in through. "I've seen it happen. Folks who were on the train, I thought long dead. They just march through here. Don't even see me. They're aged as well. Staring, just looking ahead, seeing what's in the next car over. Happened a dozen times over my lifetime here. You'll see."

"We'll see," Nathan sighed, not liking the sound of that and not wanting to hear any more. He looked at Gilbert. "You got all the cash?"

As an answer, Gilbert bent and hoisted a mail bag. There were others on the floor.

"Tie them together. Hang them off your neck." Nathan said.

"Not three hundred thousand, but it's better than nothing," Jimmy said.

"What's beyond that door?" Nathan asked Festus, pointing at the one ahead.

"I don't know. Could be anything."

"Well, when the train was nothing more than a train, before it went into the tunnel. What was behind that door?"

Festus had to think. "Livestock car."

"And after that?"

"Prison."

"You had a prison car hitched?" Eli blurted in disbelief.

Festus half-shrugged. "Passengers didn't know. Only us. It was in the back along with a handful of North West. Six constables. One corporal."

"Anything else?" Nathan asked.

"One storage car. Then the rear."

"All right, then."

"All right nothing." Festus shook his head and didn't bother hiding his doubt. "You'll see. I listed three cars, but it could be ten thousand between here and the caboose. If the caboose is still there."

"Thanks all the same, Festus," Nathan said, and tipped his hat.

"One last thing," the old clerk said. "You probably already know this. But it's worth repeating. Always close the doors behind you. Always. Lest… something follows you… into this reality. Or the next."

Nathan's spine tingled at the words of warning. He tipped his hat at the old man once again.

The men made quick work of tying off the money bags and hanging a pair around their necks. Festus watched them all through his dirty eyeglasses.

"What about them bags you took from those one-eyed passengers?" Nathan asked Gilbert.

They looked to where the bags were dropped on the floor.

"Give me a second," Gilbert muttered and dropped everything before landing on his knees. He opened one and pawed through the contents. A frown quickly soured his face.

"The hell is this?" he said, upending the bag and dumping everything on the floor. There were combs, brushes, and soft crumples of paper, as well as small items no bigger than one's finger, and other various things that the men couldn't identify.

"The hell is all that?" Eli said, equally disgusted. He extended a boot toe and went through the mess, while Gilbert upended five more bags. Each contained different contents, although some were similar.

"That a wallet?" Jimmy asked, pointing the shotgun.

"Where? Oh." Gilbert opened it up and a smile cracked his greasy face—only to sour again when he pulled the bills out. "The hell is this? This ain't money."

He held it out.

Mackenzie took it and couldn't make sense of it at all. He passed it on to Nathan.

The bills—a considerable multi-colored wad—were covered in those odd characters. There were no numbers, and the pictures in the background were scenes of places Nathan had no idea existed, which didn't really surprise him.

"Ain't anything we can use," Nathan said and tossed the bills onto the floor.

"The hell is this?" Gilbert said, holding up a poker deck of thin, especially durable cards. One side had pictures of those odd characters, while the other showed only more characters, but with an odd black strip through the middle. "The hell is *this?*" he repeated.

The cards were passed around and puzzled over.

"Strange," Jimmy said, running a finger over one inflexible edge.

Eli was sniffing at one of the smaller containers, which he'd opened, and discovered a bright red stick of rouge inside.

Gilbert held up one of several sets of what appeared to be reading glasses, except the lenses were for one eye, and the glass was black, or red, or even blue. The frames were weird as well, going from a glossy black to white and every other color and shape in between. Gilbert eventually left them alone and went through some of the wallets. He only found more of the same.

"Nothing," he finally said. "Not one damn thing."

"We best be moving," Jimmy said to them all.

Nods all around.

"Sorry about the mess," Nathan said to Festus, indicating the strange contents spilled on the floor.

"Don't worry about it."

Nathan studied the little old clerk.

"You be careful out there," Festus said.

That summoned a little smile to Nathan's face. "We're the careful types."

Festus smiled back. "Don't forget my last request, now."

"You sure about this?"

"Oh, I am. I am. I hope… I hope to God, you'll never know… what I know."

Nathan supposed so.

"Go on then," Festus said. "I hope you find what you're looking for. And I hope, where I failed, where others failed… I hope you get off this train."

Without another word, Nathan tipped his hat to the old mail clerk. He then eyed each of the men with him and settled on Eli.

Who stared back with a barely noticed nod of understanding.

Nathan looked back at Festus, released a weary sigh, and then walked to the door. One after the other, his gang followed him.

Except Eli.

Eli stared down at the little man, who stared back while clutching the varnished arms of his chair.

Eli worked the lever of his Winchester and pointed it at Festus's head. "You ready, then?" he asked.

"I am, sir. And… thank you. I couldn't have done this without you."

Eli thought about that for about two seconds before blowing out the back of Festus's head. When the old clerk hit the floor, Eli worked the Winchester again.

Festus asked for every bullet they could spare.

Eli spared him five.

42

"The hell you doing all the shooting for?" Mackenzie asked.

Eli turned away from the corpse crumpled upon the floor with his legs dead and dangly on the chair. "Last request," he said, walking towards the gang. His bulk obscured the dead mail clerk, and for that, Nathan was relieved. He didn't need to see Festus again.

"You all ready?" Nathan asked when everyone had gathered.

"You want to carry one of these?" Mackenzie asked of his mail bags stuffed with cash.

"Hell, no," Nathan said while holding a gun, cocking the hammer as he did so. "You're doing fine."

The joke wasn't funny, not with Festus lying just twenty feet behind, dead and finally gone.

Or so I hope, Nathan thought.

And hauled open the door to the next car.

Passenger car.

"Looks familiar," Mackenzie said, studying the place.

"Thousands of cars," Nathan said, lowering his gun. "Feels like we've gone through that now."

"Move on, then," Eli said. "Festus is already starting to stink."

That's what got them moving in the end. The smell of one dead old man. Night shone through the windows, without rhyme or reason. Two oil lamps provided pale light, one at either end.

Eli was in the rear and allowed the door to close. As the others walked along the aisle, he stopped, considered the door, and opened it.

Mail car. Still.

He closed it, holding his rifle, thinking as the train moved along. He held onto the latch, wondering if he should open it again. In the end, he left it, adjusted the mail bags of cash hung about his neck, and walked after the others.

They ambled up the aisle, strung out like a night patrol on alert. The weight of the train's riches hung about their necks, and offered little comfort, but it was nice that they had something to show for their misery. Winter coats swished at their heels, while their boots clumped softly. Well-crafted berths remained unchanged, but the dark seemed to swallow them whole, in the middle of the car.

"Well," Nathan declared. "Least we got the cash."

"Now all we gotta do is get back so we can enjoy it," Mackenzie said.

No one said anything to that.

"At least now we know what happened to the train," Nathan said.

"We don't," Mackenzie pointed out. "We know what happened to the *passengers*, and how everything went all dark and such, but we don't know *why* this is all happening. Why it got dark and stayed that way. Why we're still… walking through car after car after car."

"We may never know," Jimmy Norquay said. "We might be on this thing forever. Just like Festus back there. Until, maybe, we stop in a car and give up. Until some other gunmen come walking through, and we beg them to kill us."

"Christ, Jimmy," Gilbert muttered, glancing left and right.

Mackenzie stopped just past the midway point, inspected a berth, and stepped inside it. Once at the window, he stooped and glanced outside at the bright field of stars.

"What's wrong?" Nathan asked.

Mackenzie didn't reply right away, and that silence bothered Nathan. And where he was, checking on what was outside the train, shook loose a memory.

"Mackenzie?"

"Yeah?"

"What the hell got your attention back in that car with all them one-eyed things?" Nathan asked out of the blue.

"You really want to know?"

"C'mon, Mack. Out with it. Nothing's gonna bother us now. Not after what we've seen and heard."

Mackenzie turned away from the window, half of him cloaked in shadow.

"I saw something back there," he said. "Something that bothered me."

"All right, what's that then?' Eli asked and stopped in the rear. The others were all ears.

"The sun," Mackenzie explained. "Through the mountains there was a sun. The train was going around the mountains, maybe a little off course, but it looked like it was going towards the sun. Remember a while back, on the flatcar? That… green sun on ahead of the train? What I saw was… bigger. Much bigger than that and… I don't say this lightly, Nate. I think… I think it was bigger, because it was closer."

That silenced the lot of them.

"You didn't see it right," Eli said.

"Oh, I saw it right. Until Nate started yelling at me. Now, I'm not saying this to worry you. But I am saying… we might have another problem here. That sun looked bigger. We might be getting closer to it. I don't know what that all means, but part of me, part of me is thinking… we won't be on this train for a hundred years like old Festus. Something is going to happen long before that. Something is going to happen soon."

No one said anything for moments, taking in that grim bit of news.

"So what do we do?" Gilbert asked.

"Like we're doing now," Mackenzie said and scratched at the side of his head. "Try and find the end of this thing, before she bends herself straight up in the air like she did, shaking us out the end like the last few candies from a box."

"It did feel like that, didn't it?" Gilbert smiled.

"What if we can't get to the end? Nathan asked, dreading the question.

"I don't know, Nate. I just don't know. Ain't no sun out there now, so maybe it's all good. I'll—we'll know next time we see it. How much bigger it is. How much closer it's become."

That was as good as could be expected, Nathan supposed. He took hold of the latch and pulled it open.

Blackness. Metal creaked and groaned within, and fresh air hit his face, but otherwise it resembled a tunnel leading to a castle's dungeon. There wasn't much light, and the light there didn't last long when the other men shuffled behind him. What Nathan could see didn't look like any vestibule they'd passed through earlier, and he remembered the last tunnel he'd walked through.

"I hate this part," he muttered, before straightening his father's hat on his head and cautiously stepping forward, venturing deeper into the dark. It didn't feel like metal underfoot, but rather dried rock. He held his Colt before him as he walked, his fingers grazing the wall, which felt like the leather stretched across the ribs of a pliable frame. The floor shifted just a little underfoot, as if he were moving from plate to plate.

Mackenzie's outline was two steps behind him. The other men were shadows, shuffling forward, treating the floor as if it were a sheet of thin ice.

Mackenzie placed a hand on his shoulder. "Just me," he said. "Everyone link up."

Mackenzie's hand flexed, and Nathan pulled him along, following the wall. He swung his gun hand to the right and cracked it off metal. "Narrow tunnel," he said.

"Narrow enough," Mackenzie agreed.

They kept walking, in total blackness that Nathan liked less with every step. There was no difference between closing his eyes and keeping them open. A dozen more steps and Nathan halted, his hand against the wall.

"What's wrong?" Mackenzie whispered.

"Everyone still here?" Nathan asked.

"Hell yes we're still here," Eli said.

"I'm still here," Gilbert said.

"I'm here, too," Jimmy sounded off.

"Anything behind you, Eli?" Nathan asked.

A pause then. "Not a goddamn thing. Just the dark."

"Can't see the doorway?"

"Not a goddamn thing, I said. I closed it, on account of what Festus said about closing the doors."

Always close the doors behind you. Always. Lest… something follows you… into this reality. Or the next.

"What's that?" Mackenzie said. "On ahead."

Light. A pinprick of light, way off in the distance.

Nathan got walking. At one step, the rock became dirt, and the air became sweet to breathe.

Not twenty minutes later, the tunnel ended.

"My sweet Lord," Mackenzie said at his shoulder.

The passageway opened to a flat plain, where wild grass grew to one's knee, and gently swayed to the barest of breezes. A gold sky shimmered overhead, coloring the evening. Not another thing could be seen on that vast stretch of land, and the sight of all that emptiness stopped Nathan two steps back from the tunnel's end.

"What?" Mackenzie asked.

"Just wait," Nathan said. "Remember the crabs?"

That stopped them all.

"That was desert," Mackenzie said, gripping his shoulder. "All I see is good old Saskatchewan prairie."

Nathan wasn't sure of that.

Sensing that unease, Mackenzie pushed by him and carefully stuck his head outside of the tunnel.

His shoulders slumped when he studied the area around the tunnel mouth.

"What's wrong?" Nathan asked.

"You best see for yourself," Mackenzie said and backed away from the opening, his face gone slack with disbelief.

The rest of the gang pushed forward and exited the tunnel. Nathan saw it first.

The door was a black rectangle in an impossible reality. Nothing framed the opening. Nothing kept it up, but it was there, a magical, sorcerous doorway of non-light where men were cautiously emerging. Once they saw that amazing breach in the very air, their mouths hung open.

Jimmy Norquay stepped around the door, and flinched as if a bull had goosed him with both horns.

Nathan went back there and saw. Drawn by the moment, the others did the same.

There was no depth to the door. The opening was merely height and width, suspended upon the land by laws no one could understand. One couldn't see the doorway from behind, as it was nothing but air, but if one merely leaned forward, that void-like blackness crept into view.

"This is some unreal shit right here, boys," Eli said from the other side, sizing up the door as he leaned one way and then the other.

"There's no thickness there," Gilbert said.

"Just a flat plane on one side," Mackenzie added and tensed. "Hold on."

The door was shrinking, its dimensions steadily decreasing, and gaining speed. If any of them thought about diving back into the tunnel, the few seconds it took to realize the doorway was shrinking made it too late to do so.

In a span of three breaths, the doorway was gone.

The gang stood around the place where the portal existed. Gilbert even extended his rifle and swished it through the empty space.

"Gone," Jimmy said.

Mackenzie let his breath out in a sigh. "Unbelievable. Amazing. Shocking and far-fetched. I can't think of any other words to describe what we just saw."

"How about bullshit?" Eli asked.

Mackenzie frowned at the man. "We're walking through *worlds*, here. Worlds."

Eli and Gilbert glanced around, not impressed with what they saw.

"All right, so where the hell are we?" Nathan asked.

"No idea," Mackenzie replied. "But I bet if we just stand here… and relax…."

He trailed off, even closed his eyes.

Nathan didn't need to close his eyes. He felt the pull already.

"So gentle," Mackenzie said, a smile spreading across his face.

"As gentle as a whore's tug on your weasel," Eli said. "That's *your* weasel, Mackenzie. I prefer a firm grip and a yank on mine."

"This is important," Mackenzie declared. "To finding our way back. The pull, the tug we're feeling. It's important. It's a clue, somehow."

Without a glance at any of them, Mackenzie took his bearings on where the door had been, sighted a sun to the west of the disappeared portal, and faced north.

"Least the sun looks normal," Mackenzie muttered.

And it did.

"This way," Mackenzie said and starting walking through the knee-high grass.

Jimmy Norquay reached down and grabbed a handful of the prairie grass. He inspected it, even took a sniff.

"Well?" Nathan asked.

"Grass," Jimmy reported, rubbing a few strands through his fingers.

"But where?"

Jimmy shrugged and looked to Mackenzie's back.

Eli and Gilbert walked by the two men, following the new trail. "Have a sniff for me while you're at it," Eli said with a smile.

"Me too," Gilbert smirked.

The two gun runners marched in Mackenzie's tracks.

"This isn't Saskatchewan," Jimmy said to Nathan.

"No?"

"For one, it's winter."

Nathan knew that. "Or at least it was winter."

The two men regarded each other, remembering how time twisted and bent inside the train.

Without a word, Jimmy got walking after the others.

Squinting at the western sun, Nathan followed.

43

Once again they marched.

Strung out in single file, wading through prairie grass that reached their mid-thigh. Flies buzzed around them, close enough to be shooed away or grabbed for, but never caught. The insects didn't seem interested in the men's blood, however, and that was a good thing. The land was flat in an ungodly way, and the horizon seemed to roll away from them in all directions. There wasn't even a range of noticeable hills or mountains, and if it wasn't for the sun falling in the western sky, or the subtle pull they were all feeling, Nathan figured they would be lost.

As it was, far as he was concerned, they *were* lost. And in another desert.

"Sure as hell hope the crab things that got Leland and Shorty ain't around here," Gilbert remarked, reminding Nathan of the lost men.

"Ain't none of that foolishness around here," Eli said.

"How would you know?"

"Remember the desert? The way the ground was all chewed up?"

"Oh yeah."

"Not saying there might be something *like* the crabs around. Or worse."

"Jesus, Eli. You think so?"

"Just saying is all."

Nathan frowned, smelling a lie.

"Aren't any crabs around here," Mackenzie said, still leading the way, his rifle over his shoulder. "But there might very well be something different. Just keep your eyes and ears open."

"Like what?" Gilbert asked.

"I don't know. Anything."

Gilbert shook his head and sized up the horizon.

Jimmy Norquay was a watch tower, scowling at the landscape to the right, while holding Shorty's shotgun in both hands. At times, he slowed down and cupped a weed, nipping the stalk between his fingers before releasing it. He'd walk a distance before another ordinary weed took his attention. Every so often he would glance back at Nathan, as if to check he was still back there.

Nathan tipped his hat at him once and got ignored.

"Bet we see some buffalo around here," Gilbert said. "Geez, that would be some good eating. One big old buffalo. Skin the thing right here and start up a fire. Have ourselves a cook-up."

"What are you gonna burn?" Eli asked.

"There'll be trees around here."

Eli scanned the horizon. "Ain't nothing around here, Gilbert. Not one goddamn thing. Least with the desert there was something to look at. There's nothing here except dirt and grass. And whatever the hell Jimmy roots up."

"What is it you're rooting up, there Jimmy?" Gilbert asked.

"Plants. Flowers. Weeds."

"Why's that?"

"Trying to figure out where we are."

"Any idea?"

Jimmy shook his head. "No."

"Keep working on that then, Jimmy," Gilbert said, in as chipper a mood as any Nathan ever saw him in, despite everything that had happened.

"Wait until night," Nathan told them all. "When the stars come out. If we're anywhere near where we want to be, I'll know."

"And if not?" Eli asked.

Nathan didn't answer him.

They continued to walk, sweat rolling down their faces, until they took off their coats one by one. Even then they were sweating, considering they were still dressed for winter in the mountains. Nathan dearly wanted a bath and a drink, and hoped that the air would carry that smell of nearby fresh water, but it did not. Every so often, he'd check on the sun, watching it sink toward the horizon. He saw no looming sun that Mackenzie had warned them about. The trail they left in the grass had disappeared some fifty paces out, leaving an unblemished sea of grass.

The men didn't talk much, not even when Mackenzie stopped them for a rest. The mail bags full of money were starting to become a burden, and the men were now resenting the added weight around their necks.

No one approached them.

Nothing was seen.

It truly was an empty landscape.

Too tired to comment on it, the men kept walking, guided by that little pull that was strongest when they stopped for a breath. The barest force that nudged them to their feet and continued to steer them north.

The sun descended, and the sky went from gold to orange, with a few purple swaths of cloud for extra color. The flies didn't thicken with the evening, which was fine by Nathan, but once again he was damn unsettled by the lack of anything around them. No landmarks, no animals, and no people. The lack of any other bugs even bothered him.

They stopped an hour before nightfall. Mackenzie simply halted and dropped his belongings into the grass. With his hands on his hips, he turned and rubbed his head with his scarf. The others got in close and did the same, and a campsite as good as any other was made, such as it was.

"Jesus Christ," Eli declared. "My two feet are about to drop off."

"My two feet are wearing through my boot soles," Gilbert added. "I ain't never walked so damn much in all my days."

Looking up at the darkening sky, Nathan had to agree.

"Nothing for a fire," Mackenzie said.

"Nothing to eat or drink," Eli had to point out.

"I'm too tired to eat or drink anyway," Gilbert said as he spread his coat out onto the grass, flattening it. He then dumped a mailbag full of cash onto the makeshift bed, and that was his pillow. Figuring that wasn't a bad idea, the others did the same, forming a small circle where each man's feet pointed inwards.

"Don't suppose we should post a sentry?" Mackenzie asked.

"What for?" Eli asked back. "Ain't nothing here."

"Just in case."

"There ain't nothin' *here*, Mack," the gun runner stressed.

"Not a goddamn thing," Gilbert threw in for spice.

"Not a goddamn thing," Eli picked up. "The only thing I might be worried about is getting a deer tick interested in my dirty bits, and I ain't worried about that."

"The wildlife could come out at night," Mackenzie said.

"From where?" Nathan asked, joining the conversation. "There's nowhere to hide during the day."

"Yeah, stop with the worrying, Mack. You're scaring the beans 'n bacon outta Jimmy over there."

To his credit, Jimmy lay on his back, legs crossed, shotgun nearby, and stared at the deepening night.

"Well, just sleep light then," Mackenzie said.

"Sleep light," Eli scoffed. "Yes, all right, I'll sleep light. Hear that, boys? Mack wants us to sleep light."

Gilbert answered with a snore.

"I second that," Eli said and settled down for the night.

No one spoke, but Gilbert continued to snore, until Eli reached over and swatted the man across the chest. Still mostly asleep, Gilbert flailed back before rolling onto his side. His snoring ceased.

The stars were being shy, but they were up there.

"Warm night," Mackenzie said in a weary voice.

"Quiet, too," Nathan said, hearing mostly the buzzing absence of noise.

"Hey Jimmy," Mackenzie asked. "This must be familiar to you, seeing as you're from Tail Creek."

Jimmy didn't answer.

"Notice anything at all?"

Silence. Then, "No."

"Nothing?"

"Not a thing."

Mackenzie pressed on. "I suppose you were just a lad, anyway, when you were around Tail Creek. Before it all burned down."

Burned down. That extracted a memory that Nathan didn't like. Jimmy looked to be in his mid-thirties, but he could have easily been the same age as Leland. Tail Creek had been a Metis town in Manitoba, and a sizeable one at that, before a prairie fire scorched it from the map. The subsequent destruction to the buffalo herds ensured the town was never rebuilt.

Then he remembered Leland saying something about meeting Jimmy in a residential school.

"I recall that Tail Creek was close to a thousand Metis at one time or other," Mackenzie continued on.

"Mack?" Nathan asked.

"Yes?"

"Go to sleep."

Mackenzie was quiet for a while, then, as if realizing what he was bringing up might be bad memories for Jimmy, said, "Yes. Good idea, Nate. In the morning then. Ah… sorry, Jimmy. If I dredged up… well. Sorry."

"I'm fine," Jimmy said a touch stoically. "I don't remember anything from then. I was too young."

"How young was that?"

"Mack," Nathan stressed.

"Right. Sorry. Sorry, Jimmy."

Mackenzie settled back then with a sigh and an energetic rustling that suggested he wasn't pleased with himself, but he left it at that. Nathan decided to not say anything more on the matter. They all had their ghosts. Nathan had his own. And even though the men sleeping about him were his partners, there was no way on God's earth he was going to talk about his parents with any of them. Not during this business.

He figured Jimmy was pretty much the same.

Quiet. So damn quiet on the plain. Wherever they were.

The night sky slowly came into existence, a calming shift from deep blue to black that slowed the heart and the mind. The stars were once again being shy, however, and Nathan doubted he would be able to stay awake. By the sounds of things, he was already the last to fall asleep. There were one or two stars shining up there, but the full glory of the known constellations was nowhere in sight. He doubted he'd remember them, anyway.

Each blink became heavier, longer, than the one before.

And before he finally did succumb to sleep, Nathan listened. Heard the men breathing about him.

And just under the press of his coat into his ear, he heard the train.

44

Nathan woke first in the morning and cursed himself for falling asleep—although he had to admit, he'd slept pretty damn good. He sat up, looked around, and saw nothing more than that awesome emptiness surrounding them. The sky was a light blue with a few streamers of cloud stretched across it, but nothing else.

Nathan stood with a groan and saw that nothing had changed during the course of the night. No wind blew across the prairie, and the air tasted dry but good.

"See anything?" Jimmy asked, his dark head resting against a mail bag and bundled scarf.

"Nope."

"Another day of walking?"

"Looks that way."

Jimmy sat up and looked around.

"You okay, Jimmy?" Nathan asked.

He flashed a squinty eye at Nathan, held his gaze, and then got to his feet. "I'm fine," he said, but Nathan didn't quite believe him.

Eli and Gilbert struggled to stand, and Eli in particular placed both hands to the small of his back. He took in that vast land and shook his head.

"Another day," Mackenzie said and rose, looking to the north. "Maybe we'll reach another one of those shelters that saved us from the crabs."

"Maybe we'll meet something worse than the crabs," Eli said.

"Well, let's eat and find out."

"Fuck you, Mackenzie."

With no breakfast to be had, the men gathered up their belongings, got a bearing on where the pull was taking them, and started walking in that direction.

The morning was warm, and the sweat of the previous day clung to the men. Their clothing stank with dried perspiration. Only Nathan still had his hat, and that provided some shade from the sun, but by noon, the men were once again stripping down to their pants alone. Their armloads were heavier, and their breaks more frequent. With nothing to drink and no water in sight, their energy quickly sapped, and their progress slowed. They didn't talk much, saving their breath for the seemingly endless march across the great plains. Whenever they stopped for a rest, it became that much more difficult to rise. Nathan checked his boots every now and again, fully expecting to see holes in the bottom. The others were gasping and staring at their path ahead, where nothing but endless grass awaited.

Mackenzie was no longer ahead of the gang but walking alongside Jimmy. Both men were brown from the neck up, had their bare torsos burned red right down to the waist band. Eli and Gilbert dragged their feet behind them, also with their shirts off, and just as roasted.

Nathan's boots crunched dry grass as he stared ahead, panting, and wondering just how far it was to the next doorway. He looked left and right and almost stumbled in his own feet, which prompted him to keep his attention on what he was doing. *Cold.* He wished for the cold. Wanted that as well as a cold drink more than anything. He'd give his share of the train money just for a taste of snow scraped off the side of the Rockies' back. Every time he closed his eyes, it took just a little bit longer to open them. The left side of him sizzled under the sun, and he realized the desert they'd crossed wasn't so bad after all.

The sun was scalding. Searing. He continued to wear his hat, which eventually felt like a roasting pot. The cloth band inside pressed against his temples and head like a strip of hot leather. Nathan lowered his head and walked on, struggling to keep pace with the others. He perspired, his sweat damn near sizzling on his bare skin, like lard stuck to a frying pan.

Around late afternoon, Mackenzie and Jimmy stopped and swayed.

"Rest," Mackenzie croaked and dropped to his rump in the grass. He rolled over, pressed his face into those coarse strands, and stayed there. Jimmy actually staggered, and Nathan knew what he was thinking. If he sat down, he might not have the strength to rise.

"Yuh," Eli whispered, his hard-case demeanor burned away by the sun. Gilbert dropped his belongings and nearly fell over until Eli reached out and stopped the fall. The pair sat down like men in their eighties. Once on the ground, they lowered themselves onto the grass as if the very earth was a sun-bleached coffin. Their rib cages, hairy and sunburned, fluttered weakly.

Nathan stopped and met Jimmy's gaze.

"I know… what you're thinking…" Nathan whispered, feeling parts of his mouth popping free of whatever foul resin had sealed them. He couldn't generate any spit at all in his mouth or throat, both of which felt like the topside of scorched canvass.

Jimmy only stared.

"You're thinking…" Nathan said, "if I sit down… can I get back up?"

Jimmy managed a feeble smile. "Doesn't matter," he rasped. "Don't think… I could… take another step."

Nathan heard that.

They dumped their loads and lowered themselves, and Nathan discovered even the grass was hot, but not unpleasantly so.

"Can anyone… weave us … some blankets?" he asked.

No one answered.

"Just wondering," he finished and stretched out on the ground.

No one spoke. For a very long time. And the peace of that unending prairie remained constant.

Nathan's eyes cracked apart, and he licked his lips. The sun was lower in the sky, but that didn't matter. He wasn't going anywhere. The others didn't stir, didn't even moan, and they'd either fallen asleep or were just as done as Nathan. He thought to pull his winter duster up and over his frame, but discovered he'd perched his ass on it, and he didn't have the strength to yank the thing free.

"Contrary bastard," he whispered at the thing.

So he lay there, on his back, staring straight into the depths of the sky, and wondering if he could fall into it. Perhaps the sky was a secret ocean, and he could just plunge into its cloudless depths.

He opened his eyes again, realizing that he'd drifted off. Eli or Gilbert was snoring.

Mackenzie was groaning.

"Mack?" Nathan whispered. "That you?"

"Yuh."

Nathan gathered his strength. "How you doin'?"

"Not good, Nate."

"Yeah. Same here."

"Festus… was wrong… about the starving," Mackenzie got out. "And dying. Of thirst."

"Maybe." Nathan whispered.

"Listen. I'm gonna… fire my rifle."

That widened Nathan's eyes. "What?"

"You heard me. Don't make me… repeat myself." A clicking of metal then, followed by a long moment of silence. "God. Damn."

"What?"

Mackenzie sighed and released a dusty chuckle. "Can't lift the damn thing."

"Just shoot it then," Eli said in a voice that couldn't have belonged to him.

"Jimmy's in the way."

"Goddammit, Jimmy."

"Wait," Nathan croaked.

He was on his back, pointed away from the others. His hand found the grip of a Colt, and he pulled the thing free, but not far. *Damnation*, he thought blackly, it was a wonder to think he was freezing his ass off in Alberta not two or three days ago, and now he was almost cooked on an endless patch of grass.

He rested the pistol on his thigh. Took a moment to cock the hammer, which he almost didn't do.

"We might… call attention… to something we don't want," Nathan said to his partners.

"We're dead, anyway," Gilbert whispered in an old man's voice.

"Do it," Eli said.

"Yuh," from Mackenzie.

"Jimmy?" Nathan asked.

No reply, and just when Nathan thought the man might have already slipped away, he croaked. "Do it."

With no spit or strength to reply. Nathan gripped the gun two-handed and lifted it just above his belly. He aimed for the sky and squeezed the trigger. The gun bucked in his grip, and he almost dropped it, but managed to hold on.

"One," Nathan said in a shaky voice.

He drew back the hammer and took a firmer hold of the weapon. With a breath, he squeezed the trigger again. The shot rang out, the gun kicking in his hands. He dropped the piece, the bare barrel flailing him across the belly, hot enough to make him flinch.

Nathan eased back and didn't move anymore. Didn't care, really.

Strung out on their backs as they were, unintentionally in the shape of a star… they waited.

Nathan closed his eyes, the dark made red by the sun. He hauled his father's hat over his forehead. That was better, not by much, but a little. His temples throbbed in the shade. And at some point, just before he drifted off, the throbbing once again sounded like the dreamy locomotion of a struggling train.

45

Hands grabbed his ankles, and Nathan's eyes fluttered at the hard contact.

He heard various grunts from shadowed faces overhead, felt fingers lifting him off the hot ground. He swayed, distantly aware of being carried, until his drooping backside hit a hard edge and painfully lit up his mind. He was dragged over that edge, his sunburned skin screaming all the way, until he landed on hard wood.

Nathan realized two things then.

He was in the back of an open wagon, and there were people with him. Who they were, he didn't know, but he heard them all the same.

Just before he passed out.

He woke again, spat hay, wondered why that was so. With a lurch, he rolled himself over and felt the bristly ends of yet more hay stab him all along his back. Nathan adjusted himself, realized he was on a blanket, and settled back in time to see fine lines of light seeping through thick timbers overhead. *A barn*, he realized. He was on his back in a barn.

"What the hell?" he muttered and tried to get up. His world spun, giving his senses a savage spin, and forced him back down.

"Take it easy, Nate," Mackenzie advised. "Just relax until you're strong enough. Water bucket's to your right."

Nathan turned his head. Sure enough, a bucket sloshing water was right where Mackenzie said it was.

"Get him a drink, goddammit," Eli swore in a low voice. "Christ Almighty, Mack. Telling the man there's water right there and knowing goddamn well he ain't got the strength to pinch piss out of his weasel. That's goddamn torture."

"Goddamn torture," Gilbert repeated.

"And you call us the hard ones. God *damn*."

"God *damn*," Gilbert tacked on.

No reply from Mackenzie, but Nathan heard him move around until a hand touched his shoulder.

"Can you lift your head, Nate?" Mackenzie asked.

Nathan struggled to his elbows, seeing the men scattered around the interior of a spacious barn. The doors were to his left and wide open, the dirt sprinkled with strands of hay.

Looking like he'd been seared by hellfire himself, Mackenzie crouched nearby and had a wet cup of water in his hands. He helped Nathan to a sip, and let him take it down before giving him another.

"Take that slow," Mackenzie advised. "Very slow. Don't drain it down in a few gulps. Eli did that and spewed it up all over himself."

Nathan did so, feeling the life creep back with every swallow. "Damnation," he sputtered between sips. "If that. Don't taste. Good."

"Yeah," Mackenzie said with a little smile.

"Where are we, Mack?"

"In a barn. On a farm. In the middle of nowhere. Got here last night, just as it got dark. Barely remember it all, really. We were in such a poor state. Slept most of the night, until a little while ago. That's all I know. That and the people who brought us here."

"People brought us?"

"They heard us. A mile away, they said. Friendly folks. Real friendly. They were in a wagon heading home. Heard the shots and investigated. Found us on the prairie, and thought we were all gone. Weren't, though. So they came and loaded us into the wagon."

"I wasn't loaded," Gilbert said. "I climbed on."

Mackenzie smirked. "That's right. Gilbert climbed on. Jimmy almost did it, but he sorta just half-loaded himself into the back before he ran outta steam."

"You get their names?" Nathan asked.

Mackenzie shook his head. "Nah. I wasn't much for talking. None of us were."

Suppose so, Nathan thought, not remembering anything of the rescue. "So we're in Saskatchewan?" he asked.

"Yeah. I think. We might be just inside the Manitoba border as well. Jimmy thinks the same, too, except... well. Except for it being summertime."

Nathan stared at the man. They'd boarded the 311 in the Rockies, in the dead of winter.

"Yeah," Mackenzie said. "I know. We all know. We'll get the straight of it sooner or later. For now, just lie back and settle in. Drink your water and get your strength back."

Nathan relaxed, letting the last swallow work its magic. He looked to the open barn door, and noticed Jimmy sitting on the dirt just inside the shadows. The man had a face full of thought going on, staring outside while tugging on his beard.

"You okay over there, Jimmy?" Nathan asked.

The Metis man turned his head at the question and, in the warm shade of the barn, smiled ever so faintly.

Some time later, chickens clucked and swore at someone shooing them out from underfoot. People approached the barn, and Nathan, now sitting and just taking it easy, watched as two folks wandered into sight. There was a man, holding a pot, while a woman carried a stick with clay mugs hanging from its length. They were an older couple, perhaps in their fifties, with silver creeping into their otherwise dark heads of hair. Nathan saw they were Metis, their skin sun-browned and healthy, and had the look of hardworking plainsfolk.

"You men feel like a late lunch?" the man asked in an oddly calming voice. *A late lunch.*

"Yes, Ma'am," Eli and Gilbert replied as one.

The couple went about handing out mugs, and the spoons to go with them. The broth was chicken, with pepper and salted to flavour, and filled with soft chunks of carrots and potatoes.

Considering the state they were in, it was the best meal Nathan figured he'd had in a very long time. Not since dining at his own table, with his mother and father.

"Begging your pardon, Ma'am," Mackenzie started after finishing his soup in short time. "But we were wondering where we were."

The couple appeared bemused at the question.

"You're here," the man said after a bit, revealing a smile with only half its teeth.

"Where's here?"

"On the prairie."

"Saskatchewan?"

That got another smile.

"Manitoba?"

The smile widened.

"Not Alberta?" Mackenzie stressed.

"Not Alberta," the woman said as Gilbert finished off his meal with a belch and a quick wipe of his face with the back of his hand. He gestured for more with a hopeful smile and the lady obliged.

"We like to keep this place secret," the man said, his dark eyes sweeping over them all.

Nathan noticed that the man lingered on Jimmy just a while longer.

"We like to keep it secret since… we noticed the mail bags you were carrying there."

"Ah," Mackenzie took up. "Have no fear of that. Or us. I mean that. You saved us from… a most terrible death out there. Sun-scorched and left to dry out like leather. On behalf of my boys, I, we, thank you both. For your help and compassion, and nursing us back to health."

A round of thank you's then, from the gang, including Nathan.

"My name's Mackenzie," Mackenzie said and then went around the barn, introducing the others. Jimmy included, who Nathan thought had an odd expression on his face.

"Bichem," the older man introduced himself. "Henry Bichem. And this is my missus. Marie."

Nathan hadn't taken his eyes off Jimmy, so he caught the subtle stiffening of the man's back upon hearing the words.

"A pleasure, Mister and Missus Bichem," Mackenzie carried on. "Again, thank you so much for your kindness and hospitality. We owe you a grand debt. If you're not adverse to the idea, we'll gladly pay for our lodgings here. And your trouble."

Henry Bichem placed the pot on the ground and straightened. "No need for that. But if you feel partial to leaving a gift, that's entirely your choice. As for our trouble? No trouble at all, but we do hope you… ah… respect our property while you're here. Until such time as you're able to move on."

"We most certainly will," Mackenzie said.

"You men finish that off," Henry Bichem pointed at the pot. "Marie will have something a little more solid for your supper."

"You're too kind, Mister and Missus Bichem."

The couple smiled at the train robbers, ignored their weaponry, and made their way out of sight.

Jimmy watched them go.

"Pleasant enough folks," Mackenzie said after a time.

"The hell you offering them our money for?" Eli grumped.

"Because it's the right thing to do," Mackenzie said.

"It is fair," Gilbert said.

"I just would've appreciated a little more notice before you offered, that's all," Eli said.

"Didn't think it would be a problem."

And the argument began, on what the Bichems had done for them, and what would be fair compensation as well as a little extra to show their appreciation for being saved.

Nathan didn't hear any of it. Any amount of money to the Bichems was a fair price, in his mind. What really interested him, however, was those little looks between the old couple and Jimmy Norquay.

Who looked like he'd just seen the white, sheet-covered ass of a ghost.

Henry Bichem wandered into the open barn door later that day. He stopped in the shade and inspected them all, as if wondering what to do with them. Three chickens kept close to his heels, picking at the pebbles and casting curious looks at the barn's inhabitants.

"I'll get you another bucket of water," Henry Bichem said.

"You got a farm here, Mr. Bichem?" Mackenzie asked.

"We do. Small one. Does us fine."

"Livestock?"

"Yep."

With that, Henry Bichem walked out of the doorway, the chickens strutting behind him. He returned a few minutes later, carrying a single bucket, wet and sloshing, which he placed at the feet of Mackenzie. The chickens waited upon the threshold, as if not trusting the gang.

"There you go," Henry said in that calm voice of his that reminded Nathan of Leland Baxter in a way he couldn't identify.

"Thank you again, Mr. Bichem," Mackenzie said. "We greatly appreciate it."

"You're welcome. Me and Marie have been talking about you. You stay here as long as you need. Until you're fit to walk."

"That's very generous."

Henry regarded them each in turn, lingering just a second longer on Jimmy.

"When supper's done, we'll bring it out to you. Our table's small. Kitchen's small, really. Everyone couldn't fit in it."

"Out here is fine for us."

Henry nodded and looked about. "It's warm. Dry. Only the chickens will bother you, and they don't make any noise after sundown. No rain is coming. You'll be comfortable out here. It's peaceful. Safe."

And it was. From the sound of Henry Bichem's voice to the barn, it was all very comfortable. Nathan thought of his parents' home and their farm, growing up there, and his father's face when he told him he wanted to be a lawman. And then a farmer. Nathan rolled a strand of straw between his fingers, remembering his mother then and her favorite bedtime stories.

"We do have room at our kitchen table for one," Henry Bichem said, directing his brown-eyes at Jimmy. "If you wish. You'd be welcome."

The request caught Jimmy off-guard. He was still for a second or two, then lifted his chin. "That would be fine. Real fine."

"Come on, then," Henry said. "Leave your friends here. Marie and I would like to talk."

Again, Jimmy hesitated. "I'd like that, too."

With a glance at the others, Jimmy got up off his winter duster, brushed off his shirt, and stroked his beard flat.

"You ain't getting any prettier, Jimmy," Eli told him.

Jimmy shot him a warning look, but without any fire behind it. Henry Bichem studied him, however, amused by his dust-off and hasty grooming.

"No lady folk here," Henry told him. "Except my missus, and she's been with me for nearly thirty years. Just saying, you understand."

Jimmy's beard usually hid his smile, but not the one that appeared on his face just then.

Without another word, Henry led him away.

Boots scuffed dirt as the two men walked away, the sound oddly pleasant to the ears. There was a far-off creak of a door opening, then its closure.

"Guess we weren't fine enough for supper," Eli muttered.

"You heard the man," Nathan said. "The kitchen's small. That's reason enough."

Eli ignored him and looked at Mackenzie. "You sure do know how to grease talk someone, Mack. That's a gift."

Mackenzie lay upon a hill of hay and didn't budge. "If minding your manners is grease talk to you, it's no damn wonder you are what you are."

"All those please and thank you's didn't get you invited to the supper table."

"Wasn't my intention."

They stopped talking then. Gilbert was lying back, resting, and soon cut loose with a single snore.

That didn't seem like a bad idea to Nathan, who looked outside, taking in an old fence maybe a storm away from collapsing, and the open prairie beyond that.

Perhaps two hours later, Henry and Marie Bichem returned, with Jimmy behind them. They carried a basket of fresh baked bread, a huge pot of baked beans, yet another water bucket, and plates and spoons.

"Damnation," Eli muttered as he took a plate handed to him. "I might never want to leave here, Ma'am. If you keep feeding us this good."

That placed a smile on the older lady, and she handed him a clean handkerchief.

"When you're done, just place everything on the ground," Henry told them. "We'll get it all in the morning."

Nathan realized Jimmy wasn't sitting down. In fact, the man had what looked to be a clean change of clothes on, as well as a pair of shoes, replacing the man's boots.

"You not sticking around, Jimmy?" Nathan asked.

"No," the man replied quietly. "The Bichems have a spare room in there. They offered it to me for the night."

"We're quite fond of Jimmy," Marie said, lowering her head as she said the words.

At which Jimmy, clearly pleased at the words, shrugged and said, "I'm quite fond of you, too, Ma'am."

"You men will be fine enough in here," Henry declared. "Come on then, Mother. Jimmy. Cards are waiting."

They wandered out of sight, leaving the men to their supper.

Halfway through their meals, Eli said, "They've taken a shine to old Jimmy. Makes me wish I was Metis."

"They're probably glad you aren't," Nathan said through a full mouth.

Eli let that one go.

The sky turned red, a deep, troubling color that forecasted foul weather, and yet, the darkening evening was calm and tranquil. Nathan and the others sat back and watched it in silence. At times, Nathan thought he could hear laughter from the house, just around the barn's corner. Then all grew quiet again, until the crickets started their singing.

That was the nail in Nathan's coffin.

He didn't think there was a sweeter, nor more relaxing sound on the prairie.

46

"Mother?" Nathan asked.

"Yes?"

"If you… had a chance…" a deep yawn broke his thought. "Would you… want to go…"

"To a place like this?" she asked with a smile, and held up the book. She sighed, long and dreamy, the sound nudging Nathan just a little more to sleep.

"I don't know," she said. "A story is one thing, and I daresay I wouldn't be as brave as Alice. But you know something…"

Nathan didn't answer.

"I do think…" she began.

By that time, Nathan had fallen asleep.

But somewhere just before dawn, his mother's voice ended the thought that she'd started so long ago, that he'd actually heard, but just forgotten… in sleep.

"I do think that there are other worlds out there… just waiting for us to find them…"

*

Nathan awoke to the sound of Gilbert farting in his sleep.

Not five seconds later, a rooster got to crowing, keeping him awake. Not impressed, he rolled off his duster, stood, and made his way out the barn door. It was perhaps an hour after dawn, and the Bichems' old farmstead was quiet. Nathan stood outside the barn, spotted the outhouse they'd been using, and made his way there, scuffing up dirt as he went. He did his business and returned, taking in the layout of the farm. There were two barns, a pair of uncovered wagons, and fences. He didn't see any livestock this morning, but that didn't bother him. A single road led away from the farm, going east, and cut straight into the prairie, where it disappeared after a good distance.

Nathan, however, felt a tug to the north.

It had been there all while he'd been in the barn, but easily ignored. This morning however, it felt a little more insistent. Which was fine with Nathan. Looking over the farm put some peace in his heart, but he wanted to get going. It was time to leave. It wasn't his home, wasn't his time, and that especially bothered him.

It was winter, somewhere. It was *rightfully* winter.

When he returned to the barn, the others were awake.

Nathan stood in the doorway. "Rise and shine, boys. I don't know about you, but I think it's time we got moving."

"Yeah," Mackenzie agreed, pulling himself up from his bed. "I do too. I'm feeling the pull."

"I'm feeling two pulls," Eli said. "One of them is for the nearest shithouse."

Nathan gestured for him to get moving then.

A little later, once the men had decided upon leaving, Henry and Jimmy came out of the house. Breakfast was another meal of warmed beans, along with more bread. The food was simple but filling, and even Eli remembered to thank the old man for his hospitality.

"You're more than welcome," Henry said and turned to leave. "I'll be back for those plates a little later."

"We'll be leaving this morning," Mackenzie informed him, stopping the man in his tracks.

"Oh?"

"Yes," Mackenzie faltered, not knowing exactly how to go about explaining what had happened to them. "We have to move on. We're… expected elsewhere."

"You're more than welcome to stay."

"I know. We know. And thank you kindly for that. But we really must be moving on."

Henry eventually nodded, smiled faintly, and walked on back to his house. Jimmy watched him go.

Eli and Gilbert got to picking up and organizing their gear.

"So what did you talk about last night, Jimmy?" Mackenzie asked him with a smile.

"Everything," Jimmy replied, watching the ongoing preparations. "They're… good people."

"No argument there," Nathan said. "But best we leave them now. We'll get moving after we pack our belongings together."

"Already got a hundred dollars from us all," Mackenzie said. "For their troubles."

"I didn't agree to a hundred," Eli said, straightening.

"Didn't ask you about it," Nathan said in a tone not to be contested, and Eli went back to packing.

Mackenzie stepped in close to Jimmy and whispered, "Actually, two hundred, but Eli doesn't have to know about that."

"I'm not going, boys," Jimmy announced.

That stopped them all.

"What?" Mackenzie asked, slack-jawed.

"I'm not going."

"What do you mean you're not going?" Eli asked.

"No need to go. I've decided to stay right here. Like I said, they're good people."

Nathan couldn't believe his ears, and by the others' expressions, neither could they.

"Them beans weren't that good," Eli said.

"They were damn fine to me," Jimmy said. "Anyway, I'm not going and that's that. You can take my share of the money, too, for that matter. I'm done. I'm giving up the life."

The men exchanged looks.

"You'll take and keep your share," Nathan said in a voice that no one challenged. "That's yours."

"It is yours, Jimmy," Gilbert said in a somber voice, none too pleased about the man's decision. "Fair's fair."

"Yeah," Eli said. "I agree. Another matter entirely if you were dead, but you ain't. So take your money and shove it, Jimmy."

That put a smile on the man's face.

"You're really going to stay?" Mackenzie asked.

"I really am. Already talked it over with Henry and Marie. When you're ready, we'll fix you up some saddlebags with food and such. Nothing fancy. Some buffalo pemmican in there. That's good stuff. Tried it myself this morning."

But something didn't seem right to Nathan, and when he met Jimmy's gaze, the man looked away from him. Nathan wasn't overly smart, but he smelled something sour.

"Which way you headed?" Jimmy asked Mackenzie.

"North. That's the pull."

Jimmy became silent for a moment. "You still feel that?"

"Yeah, why?"

"I don't."

That quieted the men.

"You don't feel that, Jimmy?" Mackenzie asked.

"No. Not since I got here. All last night, in fact, while I was sitting and talking, and especially once I bedded down for the night. Didn't feel a thing. It's like… like I'm where I'm supposed to be."

"That why you staying?" Eli asked.

Jimmy nodded.

But as God was his witness, Nathan sensed there was more. Jimmy might not be feeling the same pull the rest of them were feeling, but there was something else going on.

In any case, the four men gathered up their belongings and prepared to leave. Jimmy kept his guns, but handed over three sticks of dynamite to Mackenzie, as well as a fresh box of matches, which Henry had passed along. Marie came outside and handed off a few water skins for them each, along with two satchels full of provisions. Nathan handed over the two hundred dollars, which produced smiles all around.

"Well, that's that, then," Mackenzie said and nodded at the Bichems. "Thank you again for saving us. And your hospitality. Not many would do that."

"You're welcome," Marie said, her hands clasped before a white apron. She and her husband stood on their front porch, watching the men about to leave. Henry raised his hand, while Jimmy backed away from the train robbers until he stood almost at the halfway point between the two groups.

"See you around, Jimmy," Eli said and started walking. Eli wasn't one for good-byes.

Jimmy waved.

"Take care, Jimmy," Gilbert said, backing up a few steps. "I was happy to have you as a partner."

"I was happy with you, too, Gilbert."

Pleased with that, Gilbert nodded and started after Eli.

Mackenzie smiled and nodded. "You take care, Jimmy. If you change your mind, just come running."

"If I change my mind, but I won't."

"No, I suppose not," Mackenzie said and, on impulse, walked up to the man and gripped his hand, then his shoulders in a hug.

Then he walked away, and didn't look back.

Nathan regarded his gang on the march, then he looked at Henry and Marie Bichem. Then at Jimmy.

He strode over to Jimmy and stopped not two feet away.

"What's going on here, Jimmy?" he demanded in a whisper. "You might've fooled the rest of the boys but I smell something here. What's going on? Them folks got something on you?"

Jimmy stared back and slowly shook his head. He was about to say something, caught himself, and then, with an embarrassed look, he leaned forward so that only Nathan could hear.

"Keep this to yourself," he said. "At least until you find the next passenger car. If you find it."

Nathan nodded that he would.

"You know I met Leland in a residential school, right?"

"I know."

"I… never knew my parents. I only got memories. Faces. Rooms. That sorta thing. Then they were gone. I can't remember anything much. Leland used to say… it might have been the shock of the fire. The one that burned down Tail Creek. Same fire probably killed my folks. See, thing was… I had *grandparents*. On my mother's side. I remember them in my dreams. On those nights when I needed company, they'd visit me. Just to let me know they were watching."

"All right," Nathan said. "So?"

Jimmy's brown eyes became moist then, and he clenched his jaw shut to damn the flood of emotion that unexpectedly took hold. Nathan lost his own power of speech at the sight, but Jimmy pulled it in, smiled, and nodded back at the old couple waiting on their front porch.

"Those two people are my *grandparents*, Nate," Jimmy whispered, holding his gaze. "I never knew their names, but… on their fireplace mantel, they had photographs. Old, wrinkly photographs of my mother and my father and… their baby son. My parents, Nate. Those people over there are my grandparents. My mother's mother and father."

Nathan still couldn't speak. He glanced over at the Bichems.

"And you know what?" Jimmy asked.

Nathan shook his head.

"They said…" and Jimmy clamped down on another surge of emotion. He held it, until the moment passed, then, "They said that my mother and father… would be home in another day or two. That they'd gone southeast, into town. And that they would very much like to meet me."

The fright rushing through Nathan was real. "Christ Almighty, Jimmy."

"I know," Jimmy whispered back. "I know, but I have to stay, Nate. I *have* to. I have to see if they're *real*. You can understand that, can't you?"

"Yeah. Yeah, I can."

"So… you go on. Don't worry about me. I'm not worried about me. I'm more worried about you fellows getting home. You see… I'm already home, Nate. I don't feel that pull anymore because I'm home. And I hope… you find yours."

With that, red-eyed and smiling tightly, Jimmy Norquay reached out and gripped Nathan's shoulder. He gave it a fond squeeze and a shake, and left it at that. Then he nodded that Nathan best get going.

"All the best to you, Jimmy," Nathan said quietly. "You're a good partner. A good friend, in the short time I knew you."

Suddenly having nothing else to say, Nathan sighed and waved to Henry and Marie Bichem. They waved back.

Nathan nodded at Jimmy one last time and walked away.

The little gang of four stopped once to look back and saw the little farmstead in the distance. There was very little activity, and no one could be seen. Jimmy and his grandparents had perhaps gone inside and were settling in around their kitchen table.

Nathan felt just a little bit envious.

The gang continued walking to the north, guided by that mysterious pull, and when they stopped to look back at the farm for a second time, the prairie had swallowed it up.

47

They found the outhouse just as the sky faded to evening pink.

Built from slabs of old wood, the forlorn shithouse shack had a sickle moon cut into a door that looked ready to fall off. A length of rope hung in the place of a proper doorknob. A second length of blue fabric hung from one corner of the roof, and probably flew quite well in a good breeze. There was no good breeze to be had, however, so it hung to one side like a county fair ribbon.

"Funny place to have a goddamn shitter," Eli Gallant said.

"Damn funny place," Gilbert echoed.

"Shitter or not," Nathan said. "Best to check it out. Just to be sure."

"Why don't you open it, then?" Eli put to him.

"Goddammit, Eli. Just when I was starting to like you.…"

Eli smirked and scowled at the deepening hues overhead. "You best stay to your own bedroll, Rhodes. I ain't the loveable type."

"He ain't," Gilbert said with a slow shake of his head.

Nathan cracked a smile but was stopped by the growing ache in his shoulders from the weight he carried. He dropped his gear, took out a single Colt, and aimed it at the door.

"That's it," Eli said. "Show us how tough you are."

"Just cover me is all."

As an answer, Mackenzie dumped his armload and readied his rifle. He took up position to the right of the door, and aimed. Eli and Gilbert tossed their gear aside and readied their firearms. They parted and stood at angles, aiming at whatever might be lurking within.

Nathan was only half aware of what they were doing. He focused on the door. A bug of some sort buzzed by his ear, but he ignored it. The wild grass surrounding the decrepit outhouse swayed ever so slightly, as if aware of the approaching gunman.

Nathan drew back on the Colt's hammer, the click sounding like the sinewy snap of bones.

He reached out for the rope of the front door and saw a short piece of wood jammed at the base, to keep the portal closed. Nathan kicked that away and pulled the door open.

His stomach lurched.

"Jesus H. Christ," Eli Gallant said behind him.

"And all his disciples," Mackenzie added.

Before them, clear as the sky overhead and simply too unreal for the mind to grasp, even though they had seen plenty beforehand… was a dark tunnel, some ten feet long perhaps, leading to the interior of a passenger car. An empty passenger car, with light spilling in from grimy windows. The spatial dimensions were not even right, as the width of the car was greater than that of the outhouse, and yet, by some unknown folding of space and time, there it was.

Contained within the dilapidated shithouse walls, was the next reality.

The tunnel wavered, as if the gateway would not last for long.

Nathan stared at that trembling portal and shook his head in disbelieving wonder. The door cracked on leather hinges held together by rusty nails, and the sound broke his paralysis.

Gun still in hand, he quickly gathered up his clothing and gear, as did the others.

Not ten seconds later, he ventured into that unstable tunnel, with Mackenzie and the others at his back. The walls, roof, and floor were an oily black that shivered, but after a few steps, the familiar vestibule walls came into view. Nathan stopped at the tunnel's end and peered inside the moving train car.

"Well?" Mackenzie asked from behind.

"Looks safe enough," Nathan said.

"Go on then," Eli urged. "Before something closes on this end."

Nathan stepped into the empty passenger car, checking the first few berths and eyeing the unlit light fixtures that swayed overhead. Nothing hid between the seats, and nothing made a noise over the locomotive clatter of the train. Movement outside the car's windows caught his eye. The glass was filthy and obscured the shapes somewhat, but… Golden sky, shimmering, shining, bouncing pure light off concentric rings of varying degrees of purple.

The sight transfixed Nathan, until the things that distracted him in the first place dropped below the upper window frame, soaring into sight.

Birds.

Gigantic birds flapping wings that blazed gold. The colors were eye-popping. The creatures were long-necked, with saw-tooth beaks. Claws drawn up to the underbelly, which didn't appear feathered at all, but rather the color of singed copper.

Then he realized what they really were.

"Oh my," Mackenzie said from behind him, staring at the birds keeping pace with the train. Mini-suns flashed by the windows, causing the men to shield their eyes, but the birds stayed with the train.

"Birds?" he asked.

"Not birds," Nathan corrected, remembering other stories his mother once read to him. "Dragons."

Dragons.

Those were indeed dragons flying alongside the train. The knowledge stopped the four men in their tracks. They leaned forward and stared, grateful for the solid woodwork of the berths, utterly spellbound by what they were witnessing. The great beasts soared, unconcerned with the speeding locomotive. Leather wings snapped, generating enormous lift, but otherwise they coasted, riding air currents like waves. So focused they were on flying, the dragons left the train alone.

Mackenzie leaned into a window, rubbed a section clear with a shirt sleeve, and peered outside. He watched the flying creatures for a long moment before attempting to see what lay ahead. There he stayed, transfixed.

"Anything, Mack?"

Mackenzie glanced back, his face full of concern. "It's closer."

The others approached the windows and pressed their cheeks to the glass.

Sure enough, that troubling sun was closer. Bigger. And the train was making its way for its fiery center.

"We gotta get off this thing," Gilbert said over the rattling and sized up the interior.

Nathan was already pulling on his winter coat and scarf and adjusting his gear for quick access. Once he had the coat on, he checked the inner pocket for the three sticks of dynamite Jimmy had given him.

Jimmy Norquay.

Though he'd only known the man for a short time, Nathan wished he could have known him a little longer. Frowning, he checked on the box of matches, as well as his Colts. Once prepared, he stepped out from the berth and marched towards the end of the car. Dragons flew on the other side of the train, some close enough that their massive forms darkened the interior. Gilbert took aim at one of the windows, fearful of the soaring beasts.

Nathan reached the next door and waited for the others. Mackenzie was next, with Gilbert behind him and Eli hurrying along in last place, keeping his rifle above the seats.

"Ready?" Nathan asked when they'd all gathered.

Eli took cover within one berth and aimed at the portal. Mackenzie and Gilbert did the same.

"Open that bastard," Eli said.

Nathan yanked the door across.

Snow whipped into his face, driven by a freezing wind. Nathan flinched at the drop in temperature and shied behind the nearest wall. He pulled his scarf up and over his face. With a look at the others, he peered through the doorway.

The scene was maddening.

In the passenger car they currently stood, there were dragons flying alongside them.

The next car, however, was a wintry flatbed coated in perhaps two feet of snow.

Where dirty sunlight lit the interior they stood in, the flatbed was obscured by blowing snow. Two different weather patterns separated by only a finger of metal. Two different worlds separated by the thinnest partition. The sight was unreal. Jaw-dropping. Ball-clenching.

"I'm going insane here, Mack," Nathan said over the rising wind.

"I'm already crazier than a two-dick coyote," Eli declared softly. "But this…" and there he trailed off, unable to finish.

"Certainly an eyeful," Mackenzie replied, pulling up his own scarf to protect his face.

"Eyeful my ass," Gilbert said. "This is crazy. *Crazy*."

For moments they stared down the snowstorm and didn't say a word. It could be their world, but the lack of landmarks didn't allow them to be certain.

"It's a flatbed, Mack," Nathan finally pointed out.

"Close the door. Maybe it'll change."

Nathan tried closing the door. The door would not close. He scowled and tried all his might to move the latch, but it didn't budge. In the end, he stood back and kicked at the thing, stomping hard heels into the metal.

The door remained open.

"You contrary piece of shit," Nathan swore and thought about Jimmy's dynamite. He quickly discarded the idea, knowing he would probably do more damage than good.

"Hell with it," Eli said, pulling his own scarf up and over his face. "We're already dressed for weather. What's thirty feet?"

Gilbert covered his own face.

"Let's go," Nathan decided. He carefully stepped onto the snow-covered flatbed. There was no gap, however, no visible couplings, as the doorway opened directly onto the white and narrow plane. The cutting winds had sculpted sizeable drifts in the center of the flatbed, and wild flurries pelted the peaks. The snow surrounding the drifts first reached mid-shin, but quickly reached Nathan's knees. It was a wet snow, a late winter snow, clingy and as thick as cement. Even as he stood there, the snow sticking fast and whitening his form, he knew that the longer he waded around in this shit, the whiter, wetter, and more miserable he would become. The platform hidden underneath wasn't slippery at all, but to his dismay, the flatbed's distinct edges were not five feet from where he stood.

Beyond that, nothing except a whirling, shrieking wall of white. There was no land to be seen, and as far as he knew, they might be racing across two narrow rails without any ground below it. Ahead, he couldn't see the next car. Perhaps it was from the speed of the train, or maybe they were passing through a blizzard.

Nathan swung around to the others, who set their feet and leaned into the gale, sizing up the task ahead. He waited for their thoughts.

"Go on," Mackenzie waved, holding his rifle with the other. "Quicker we get across the better."

Gilbert and Eli stood at his back, twin wraiths hunched over with rifles at the ready.

"Come on then," Nathan said, making himself heard over the wind. "And watch the roofs for passengers."

With that, he started stomping through the fat drifts.

<h1 style="text-align:center">48</h1>

Snow lashed into the four men making their way across the flatbed. Nathan put a hand to his father's felt hat and angled his head into the crosswind. The front of his duster was already blasted white. A large drift as high as his hips lay to his right, and past that, perhaps a five-foot-wide walkway to the opposite edge. There was nothing ahead, no lamplight, no sign of a train car waiting. All there was, was that gnashing wind, the stinging snow, and the white ribbons gusting off the edges of the flatbed. There were no mountains surrounding them, no forest, no nothing that resembled western Alberta.

Nathan placed one boot into the snow after the other, the cold penetrating his gloves and the exposed bits of his face, but little else. He walked slowly, mindful of the edge of the flatbed, and the milky nothingness that flashed by beyond that.

Thirty feet by his guess, into a void of white. The crosswind intensified, blasting him, crumpling his father's hat and seeking to rip both it and him from the exposed walkway. His frame was now thick with snow, the ice pelting him with huge suffocating clumps. Eli Gallant was cursing, but the wind stole the man's choice words for the storm.

Forty feet, and still no sign of the next car. Nathan squinted into that harsh squall which seemingly became stronger, furious at the men for challenging it. He tried shuffling through the snow until it reached his knees, which required him to lift his boot entirely free before stomping back down.

Nathan forged on.

Fifty feet, and all that he could see was that dismal drop to the left, just a leap away, and the growing wall on their right. The way ahead remained nothing more than a savage curtain hiding everything past ten feet. Underneath their footing, however, the flatbed's wood and iron was the bedrock shoring up Nathan's sanity.

"See anything, Nate?" Mackenzie hollered from behind.

Nathan made sure both his feet were down before glancing over his shoulder, surprised to see Mackenzie not two paces on his tail. Gilbert and Eli were at his back, their hair blowing madly in the wind. They all resembled sick snowmen, white, but with a cancerous black just underneath.

"Nothing," Nathan yelled back.

That prompted Mackenzie to crane his neck to look ahead.

Nathan resumed his stomp and stagger of a walk, weathering the wind and moving forward only when it seemed to diminish. His coat blew about his legs despite being buttoned to the knee—any more and he risked toppling over.

Sixty feet, and the storm only got worse.

A blast of wind ripped past Nathan and the entire world disappeared. He staggered, still stubbornly holding onto his hat, caught in a tempest. White streamers surfed the crest of the nearby snowdrift. Snow cut across his eyes. On reflex alone, Nathan dropped to his knees, and placed his shoulder to the slope of the nearby drift. The stormy air raked over his bowed back, and almost tore his hat from his head.

Nathan wouldn't have it.

He made a fist about the battered brim and held his hat fast to his head. If it left his skull, then the boys at his back would be on their own, because he would leap off the flatbed to reclaim it. Shuffling along on his knees became an energy-draining slog. He swept away snow with his free hand, and even collapsed at times and getting icy mouthfuls.

Seventy feet.

No passenger car.

But an otherworldly growl perked Nathan's ears, and he stopped to listen.

Nothing, only the raging wind. Grimacing, the cold seeping past his outer and inner layers, he resumed his painful crawl.

Only to hear that disturbing sound again. A deep but rising buzz, like a dozen men hauling a rope through an eyelet as if their lives depended on it, but more *mechanical.* The buzz spiked, pitched, and dropped partially because of the raging wind boxing his ears, but he sensed there was more to it. Much more. And it was getting closer.

Of that he was certain, just as certain as he was of its danger.

He crawled faster, pushing through heavy snow and wishing he had one of those dentist-invented plows. His shoulders ached from his efforts, but he kept on clearing the way, knowing it was easier for the others. The cold finally breached his gloves, icing his hands, chilling his fingers. His hands drove through the snow, swept the top layers away, so that he could move up to his knees, then repeat, in a locomotion mirroring the hellish train they were trapped upon. Jimmy Norquay was no fool. Grandparents or not, the peaceful, warm tranquility of that farm was a distant dream and one that—

Nathan's hand punched through a crust of snow, all the way to the bottom, and then nothing—but air. His forward movement sucked him down just as an entire mantle of snow fell away, clefted cleanly in the middle by a frosty set of iron couplings. Nathan crashed his elbow off the flatbed's edge, and his entire arm sang out as if dipped in fire. That paralyzing grip forced Nathan to lash out with his other hand—the one holding onto his father's hat. He hit the flatbed edge straight across the chest, with enough force to stun him for a second, just enough time to gaze down into what seemed to be a rushing avalanche right below him.

Framed between two black lengths of railway.

Then he was hauled back by the ankles, while Mackenzie and Gilbert screamed.

Nathan turned his head just before the flatbed edge cracked off his chin. His flailing arm got hooked and yanked free, sending another shot of agony up its length and crisping his brain.

"You okay, Nate?" Mackenzie was shouting. "You okay?"

Nathan realized the man had placed himself between the drop-off and himself. Nathan nodded.

"Goddamn flatbed ended right there," Gilbert shouted over him. "We're gonna haveta jump it."

Jump it? Nathan thought, the pain slowly receding. Jump to the next *flatbed?*

Nathan got himself to his knees and nodded to Mackenzie that he was fine. The men huddled together as the roaring drew closer—an intense repeating sputter that echoed in the storm.

Not echoing, Nathan realized in a moment of clarity. There was more than one coming closer.

"We gotta go," he croaked as he rose to his knees. He studied the gap.

Five feet. No more. One leap, without a run, but it would be close. Snow covered the next flatbed over, and icicles drooped like magical fangs from the exposed edge.

He still had his hat, though, and Nathan drew strength from that.

He stood, shakily, the winds buffeting his upper frame. He kicked at the snow covering his side of the flatbed, until a small clearing revealed the iron and wood edge. All the while, that wildcat purring whipped his attention to the other side of the train. Whatever was making the noise was on both sides now, and drawing closer, still.

"The hell you—"

Waiting for, Eli Gallant finished as Nathan jumped.

The wind buffeted him, and he felt himself veering to the left as his boots clattered onto the flatbed. He lunged forward, falling flat, while his left arm dangled off into infinity. That sensation of swinging in the frigid wind was all Nathan needed to regain his wits. He hauled his arm back to safety.

Just as Mackenzie landed in a heap beside him, in an explosion of snow. Nathan shied away from that and crawled back from the flatbed's cliff. He heard the others shout, but he didn't bother replying. Nathan didn't want to be caught crawling another eighty feet to the next flat car when whatever was making that ungodly buzzing noise finally closed in upon them.

A quick glance over his shoulder, however, informed him that the others had made it across. They were on their hands and knees again, but behind him.

So they crawled, scuffling through the deepening snow while that bobcat growling only got louder. At the forty-foot mark or so, a glow briefly penetrated the blizzard depths, ahead and to the left. Then it was gone. Its appearance stopped Nathan for a few heartbeats.

But an inhuman yowling got him moving again.

"The hell is making that noise?" Gilbert yelled out, but no one answered him.

The wind seemed to diminish. The curtains of snow slackened and grew thinner. As the weather weakened, Nathan's fright swelled, urging him to crawl faster, but stay low, for fear of being discovered. He was coated in white now and not easily seen. Or so he hoped.

The buzzing grew in volume. Multiple suns streaked by, some closer than others, running parallel to the flatbed. Outlines could be seen, but the details were blurred by blowing snow. And that hideous caterwauling continued and got louder, as if a band of those alien pirates that had harpooned the Great Serpent and Archie Whasisface had finally tracked the train robbers down.

A sun charged the flatbed from the left as one angry buzzing spiked above all the others. A second later, an inhuman banshee yodeling cut the air and frightened Nathan bad enough that he dropped into the snow.

Not before glimpsing that sun—no bigger than, say, a small wash basin—

fly over his head in a roar of smoke and heat and fury. There was a mass behind that fiery comet blazing over him, and he thought he saw shining metal, just before he went flat and breathed in a face-full of smoke.

Nathan started coughing.

A second later, he felt his shoulders grow hot and saw that they were on fire.

Nathan rolled onto his back, extinguishing the flames, while other suns blazed through the wintry gauze surrounding the flatbed. Mackenzie pushed past in a rabid flight reflex, shoving him aside to escape.

A boot heel crunched against his shoulder before pushing off.

Then Gilbert and Eli were moving past him. Gilbert tracked the moving suns with his Winchester while Eli stopped and helped Nathan to his feet.

"Get up, Rhodes," Eli barked into his face. "The pirates are back."

Pirates? Nathan's expression asked.

"Yes, *pirates!* Goddammit! Now *get moving!*"

Eli whirled him around and shoved him towards… a door. Underneath a rack of fearsome icicles was the ice-glazed door of the next passenger car. Mackenzie was already there, hauling the thing open, while just to his left, and oddly out of place, was a burning oil lamp.

Mackenzie disappeared inside the car and Gilbert was right behind him.

There was a roar that drove Nathan's head into his shoulders, and the flatbed shuddered under a heavy weight. Eli was already turning at the noise, his face slackening at what he saw. Nathan looked as well and wished he hadn't.

An immense thing had landed atop the flatbed, angled up alongside the amassed snowdrift. It spewed smoke and flame out the ass and underneath, where overturned pots flared fire. Even as Nathan watched, the snow underneath the chrome chassis melted in alarming rivulets, creating a raging fog. The metal glistening in that magician's cloud and the forward section of the vehicle snapped to one side, shining an impossibly bright light towards the men. Handlebars were spread over an elaborate working of metal pipes, pistons, and drums, the manner and purpose alien to Nathan.

But then it came to him.

As the rider detached himself from its steed.

A chrome visage much like the dragons they'd just seen was mounted above the sunlamp, and the thing's jaws worked as if demanding fresh meat.

But that only held Nathan's attention for an instant, for the man-thing riding the metallic dragon horse was dismounting.

They weren't pirates. At least, not the pirates that had killed Archie and the Great Serpent. This was something else, every bit as alien, however, and smiling a yellow-toothed smile while extracting a curved cutlass that buzzed with red light. The owner was perhaps a head taller than the men, at least as wide across the shoulders, and dressed in what looked like expensive leather. A pot helmet adorned with spikes covered its head, but the face was open, and its features shocking. Reptilian, yet similar to a man's face, its eyes covered in black spectacles of a style that Nathan had never seen before.

The thing threw its arms wide and cut loose with a scream that caused Nathan's very balls to seek higher ground.

Eli whipped up his Winchester and fired.

The first shot hit the monster's leather chest and shut him up.

The second shot twisted him to one side.

The third shot actually smashed out one side of the thing's sunglasses and cracked its head back with a wire of black oil.

That last shot, however, killed the creature, which toppled onto the flatbed without a sound. The glowing sword skidded sideways, buzzing, melting snow until it reached the flatbed's edge and flipped over in a wink. The dragon's head roared. The thing it was attached to flared to life, the fiery parts smoldering heat and smoke, just a second before the unit blasted off the flatbed, leaving its dead rider behind.

Two more suns charged into view, running up the side of the train and angling towards the two men.

Nathan didn't care, he was already running.

He blasted through the open doorway, and Eli was a heartbeat behind him. Gilbert slammed the door shut and took aim upon it, while Mackenzie was standing back in the aisle, crouched and peering out the windows. The snowstorm had weakened to half its strength, and visibility was that much improved.

What the men saw, however, didn't lift their spirits.

"The hell are they?" Nathan yelled out.

Mackenzie was already taking aim with his rifle. "No idea. Thought they were pirates."

One of the riders streaked past the passenger car, screaming all the way, and fired a weapon. Broad bands of green light blew through the train's windows in explosive sprays of glass. The tops of cushioned seats erupted into flames. The overhead compartments splintered as if smashed from above and fell to the floor. Flames burning the cushions and woodwork waved madly until blown out by the winds surrounding the speeding train.

"*Jesus Christ!*" Eli Gallant roared through the smoke and chaos. He went to a berth and sent a shot through the glass. Growling all the way, he hunkered down, cleared the window frame of shards, and poked his rifle's barrel through the opening.

He fired three shots off at the things speeding alongside the train.

"They ain't pirates!" Eli roared in between shots. "*They're robbin' the train! Just like us!*"

Crouched in the aisle, Nathan exchanged shocked looks with Mackenzie.

A second before a second barrage of destructive green light smashed through the *other* side of the train, and sliced a narrow path of destruction from right to left, as the rider blazed past on its screaming metal dragon. Glass sprayed across the interior. More seats were shredded and set aflame.

And within that very same second, one of those bursts of killer light blew Mackenzie's head completely apart.

49

In the split instant it took for the green light to blow apart everything it came into contact with, it took Mackenzie's life as well. The sight of the cattle rustler's face exploding whilst utterly astonished would haunt Nathan for a very long time. Bone and face matter flew across the interior, most of it thankfully missing Nathan, and when he looked back, Mackenzie's headless corpse was splayed out in the aisle.

"Mack's dead," Nathan yelled out, and pulled his guns "Mack's dead!"

Gilbert and Eli lifted their heads.

"Those sorry sonsabitches," Gilbert huffed with a poisoned glare.

An equally pissed-off Eli thumbed fresh shells into his Winchester, tossing aside a bandolier as he emptied it. "Bastards killed the only educated peckerwood I liked," he said, with a murderous scowl. "Watch my back, Gilbert."

"Watchin' it, Eli."

Eli Gallant went to work.

Leather riders shot past the train on their metal dragons, the very air spewing smoke in their wake and becoming easy targets to anyone adept with a hunting rifle. Thing was, Eli didn't have just any hunting rifle. He had a Winchester. Furthermore, he wasn't just a decent shot, Eli Gallant was a goddamn *marksman*. And he knew a cooler head resulted in a much higher kill count.

Which he went about demonstrating.

One of the dragon riders flashed by the broadside of the train, much too far out to track, but there were plenty of others. In fact, some of them appeared to be rising above the train only to come down on the other side.

Eli shot one, punching its helmet to one side and twisting the rider. The metal dragon it rode veered off and crashed into something with a frightening mine-blast of snow. Eli shifted, then held his fire until he got the shot he wanted. Another dragon pitched forward, the front of the metal beast tipping violently facedown and ass-up, flinging its rider free with a yodel that morphed from pure battle rage to surprised squeal.

The door to the car slid open, surprising the three men. A rider stepped forward with a hand cannon raised.

Gilbert Butler, true to his word, watched their backs and put a bullet through the unprotected throat of the rider. A torrent of green gushed from the killing wound, polluting the front of the creature's leather coat. The thing did a spastic jig for all of a split second before it dropped dead. A second rider was behind it. The creature fired, sending a green spread of killer light through the rear walls of the train car.

Through the haze, Gilbert blew out one of the thing's knees. The creature dropped, losing its weapon. Gilbert fired three more shots into the rider, each bullet connecting, each bullet shoving the thing outside and away.

Before it disappeared.

Thunder knells rattled the train's walls and roof, causing Nathan to look up.

Those devastating light weapons shredded the ceiling. Carpet jumped off the floors and sizzled down to the bare iron underneath. One berth erupted into flame while another exploded in a mesmerizing flash of feathers. Nathan lunged from one berth to another, watching the ceiling and keeping low to avoid the same fate as Mackenzie. Light beams punched through the flimsy metal and wooden compartments like a super-powered Gatling gun, but with a much higher rate of fire. More beams razored through the ceiling at an angle, marking the flight of a rider passing overhead, while two more lines ripped through the walls in a lethal crossfire.

Nathan threw himself to the floor to escape that destructive scissoring.

Above him, a tremendous weight hit the roof.

A glowing sword stabbed through the varnished ceiling in a burst of splinters. A powerful force dragged the blade left, down, then right, before completing a square. More fancy wooden compartments fell from the ceiling. Smoke blew through destroyed windows while the upholstery burned. A black boot resembling an iron block stomped through the ceiling, forcing open a well-cut lid. Shapes steadied themselves before unleashing rapid fire blasts at the train's floor. Light beams slammed into the once decadent furnishings of the Majestic 311. Fancy glass fixtures exploded. Berths jumped as if stomped on by giants. Fires ignited and smoke whorled in savage crosswinds.

Then the boarders ceased firing.

They're going to drop in, Nathan realized.

He already had the stick of dynamite out and its fuse lit. He ran past Mackenzie's headless corpse and chucked the stick through the breach. He was rewarded with several peals of surprise—and glimpsed a hand actually reaching out and catching the dynamite.

A second before the explosion engulfed the boarders and flung them away.

Gilbert continued firing through the open doorway, which was blocked by the very rider he'd killed. Eli worked his Winchester, connecting with most shots and even blasting some of his targets out of the saddle entirely, dumping them in a snowy wasteland.

"Hey, Eli!" Gilbert shouted, crouching, with his back against a smoldering wall. "There's a bunch of them on the flatbed. I think they're gonna charge us."

"Well, then, don't let *'em*, Gilbert!"

"I'm reloading here."

Nathan heard that, and he turned and raced through the smoking aisle, stomping over debris or kicking it aside. He fired through the burning doorway, sending whatever his Colts had screaming at the alien train robbers. He reached the second last berth, which still was untouched in the firefight, and ducked within.

"Thanks Nate," Gilbert called out, rapidly thumbing shells into his Winchester. "I'm ready here."

With that, he shucked off a bandolier, worked the rifle's lever, and eyed the open doorway.

Nathan shook the spent casings from his Colts and reloaded, dropping one shell in his haste and not bothering to pick the damn thing up. There was no time. A fiery explosion erupted outside the train, and Eli cut loose with a peal of murderous delight.

"These cocksuckers ain't that tough!" he roared.

Nathan wasn't so sure.

Gilbert stood, turned, and fired off three rounds before quickly returning to cover and dropped into a crouch.

The wall to the left and right of his head blew inwards in jets of fiery green, driving the gun runner to the floor. More beams sliced through the passenger car's end, destroying those fine berths and forcing Nathan and Eli to the carpet.

"*Christ*," Eli growled. "These weasels are turning my guts!"

"I heard that," Gilbert agreed.

"Get ready to run," Nathan said as he lit the fuse of another stick of dynamite, producing that familiar sidewinder hiss.

That shut up both gun runners.

Nathan rose to his knees and tomahawk-chucked the dynamite out onto the flatbed, where it disappeared from sight.

For a second.

The initial blast was immediately joined by a much larger, very much expected second, third, and fourth explosion, which shook the train right down to its steel wheels. The wall Gilbert once had his back to blew in and upwards, removing a huge section of the roof there. Snow gusted in, dousing the flew flames born from the blast.

For a moment, Nathan stared.

From underneath a pile of debris, Gilbert lifted his head, his face whitened and staring.

"The hell was that?" a bewildered Eli asked.

Nathan didn't know, but what he said was, "We better run."

He got to his feet. Eli helped a staggering Gilbert, who scanned the floor for his rifle.

"Leave it," Eli shouted, and so Gilbert did.

The smoke allowed them a little cover, but Nathan guessed the unexpected explosions—which he still didn't know about—gave them a few seconds to get clear of the passenger car, which, to this point, had the living shit kicked out of it. He pounded up the aisle, his duster flailing in his wake. Things continued to burn around him, and those metal dragon riders circled the moving train. Nathan tracked each vehicle's front light fixtures, which looked like small suns. Only thing was, the riders weren't even firing at them. At least not at the moment.

Ahead, the next passenger car door waited, materializing out of the smoke and offering escape.

Nathan reached the door and turned, his gun at the ready.

Eli and Gilbert were only paces behind him and closing, but so were the riders.

As one, the otherworldly riders saw them sprint for the car's end. They altered their flight paths and converged. They commenced firing, splitting the air with those fearsome beams. And, right in the open, were the two fleeing gun runners.

They're dead, Nathan thought, just as he gathered enough of the frigid air to scream.

Yet not one light beam came close to hitting either one of those lucky bastards.

The train still powered ahead with a single-minded determination, and the riders couldn't bring their weapons to bear upon their moving targets. Their flying dragon machines shrieked overhead and across the passenger car. They blew apart the last few windows, shattered the last few light fixtures, and made a smoking cheese out of the other half of the train car, but they were all hurried shots, wide shots, fired at moving objects *from* moving objects.

Nathan opened the door and ushered the two men inside. He followed them and slammed the portal shut. Darkness engulfed them. The familiar dark of a vestibule, and at the other end, another door, with a single grimy window set into the wood at the top.

Eli was already there, opening the door, allowing a winter wind to buffet their faces.

When they all stopped and stared at what lay ahead.

"Christ Almighty," Eli whispered.

The three train robbers stood just within that dark threshold, where wind and snow pelted their staring frames. The attacking riders had been busy—not only were they firing upon the passenger car Nathan and the others had occupied, they were also aiming at the one the men sought. The opening of the door did not offer an alternate reality as they'd hoped; rather, they piled right into another passenger car that had sustained terrible damage to its interior. In fact, half of the car's roof had collapsed, forming a ramp that greeted the three men, while the berths underneath flashed and burned.

Eli slammed the door closed, waited a second, and opened it.

Same car, same destruction.

Eli slammed and opened the door again. No change.

He tried a third time, and scowled at the same result.

"No time," Nathan said and felt it to be true. He pulled his second Colt and faced the door they'd just come through.

"We can go up and over," Gilbert said, pointing with his own pistol.

That got the others thinking. Eli regarded Nathan, who shrugged.

That was enough for Eli Gallant. He looked at the first step and saw there were no pitfalls. With that, he started ahead, and Gilbert followed. Once in the car, however, they faltered, searching for the best way up.

Nathan holstered his weapons and, knowing the bikers would be following, took out his last stick of dynamite. He lit the fuse from a flurry of flames consuming a berth. He jammed the stick into the slot at the door's base, where it rolled loosely, but stayed.

Didn't matter, it wasn't going to roll towards them.

Taking a breath, Nathan raced between the two gun runners. *"Go!"* he shouted as he took two steps and launched himself at the fallen roof. He slammed down, chest first, his teeth rattling. He managed to get a foot into a crack underneath, which he used to push forward while searching for a handhold. The wind blew his hat off his head, but the chin string kept it to the back of his neck. Nathan grunted, took the time to find his grip, and pulled himself up.

Into a windstorm.

The dynamite went off behind him, but Nathan didn't even feel the blast. The train was traveling at an impossible speed, and the roof was both slick and gritty with ice and snow. He wore gloves, but it would be a chore to crawl along the roof.

"You back there?' he shouted and half-turned his head towards his shoulder.

That was when he glimpsed it.

The sun.

Closer than ever. In fact, the train—and the hundreds of cars between the engine and Nathan's precarious position—were heading right for that ball of fire, straight down the middle of it. A perfect circle of yellow burning through the falling snow, glaring like the indifferent eye of some mythical beast. The attacking riders buzzed around the last train car and the ones after that, assaulting a section of the great machine like angry mosquitoes. Smoke rose from the last car, from damage done to both sides, but the rest of the locomotive appeared unaffected. Nathan then realized there were no mountains to be seen. Nothing below, in fact, except the infinity of open, empty space.

Eli grabbed Nathan's foot, jarring him back to the present.

"Climb!" the gun runner roared, his rifle slung across his back. Gilbert was beside him.

Nathan hauled himself onto the remaining roof and spread himself flat. The wind assaulted him from behind, wanting to hurry him along. He resisted as his coattails blew up over his legs and ass, waving madly about his chest. Nathan scowled and peered ahead.

Fifty feet at least to the next car.

He started crawling, keeping his mass spread out over the snow coated roof. Snow blew about his face, but he didn't dare adjust his scarf. Hand over hand, elbows and knees, he slunk forward a few feet and checked over his shoulder.

Eli was right there behind him. Gilbert was in the rear. The men's hair flailed in the downwind. In the distance, the riders continued attacking the train. That was fine with Nathan. He turned back, a crust of icy snow slashing his chin, hard enough to wake him. Spread out as he was, however, it was far safer than being on two feet.

Thirty feet, and he looked over his shoulder.

The riders were still attacking the train. A couple of fireballs erupted some five cars back, spouting huge black clouds that rolled and billowed against the ever-expanding face of the sun. The blast caused Eli and Gilbert to stop and look back, and the sight of that monstrous cloud paralyzed them. Several of the riders blasted through those dismal thunderheads and disappeared.

The clouds raced towards Nathan and the gun runners.

"We got smoke coming!" he shouted.

Gilbert pulled his scarf up, as did Eli. Nathan struggled to get his over his mouth just before the train charged through those rolling black curls. Nathan pressed his head against the freezing roof and dug his fingers into the icy crust, feeling his whole person tremble with the train's passage.

Five seconds, then he opened his eyes.

They were behind the main cloud, but more smoke streamed from the forward cars, dimming the sky. Nathan looked back, assessing the damage, when the glowing sun lamps of those monstrous metal dragons veered off to the left and right of the train. He squinted, discerning the graceful arc of their turns, their lamps slowly brightening until they fixed back upon the remainder of the speeding locomotive.

A handful of riders raced towards the train robbers.

Nathan felt his stomach freeze when he realized they were coming straight towards them.

"They're coming back," he roared.

Eli and Gilbert glanced over their shoulders.

"Crawl!" Nathan roared and doubled his efforts. Behind him, the men did the same, chuffing, clawing, kicking free ice and snow as they shimmied forward.

Twenty feet, and Nathan glanced back.

The sun, the almighty sun, impossibly huge in the sky, and the train a thread stretching out towards it.

Five smaller suns twinkled and burned as they got closer.

Nathan picked up the pace, risking a safe crossing, but he didn't have a choice. On the roof, they couldn't fire their guns. They needed both hands and legs to keep from falling into that endless abyss the train raced over.

Ten feet, and Nathan checked again.

Five riders, less than a quarter of a mile and gaining fast, their heads bent low over their metal handlebars.

"They're on us!" Gilbert shouted.

"Keep crawling," Eli roared back.

"Keep crawling," Nathan roared as well.

Five feet.

Above the dire locomotion of the train, the angry growl of the dragon riders filled Nathan's ears. He glanced back in reflex, knowing he shouldn't when he was so close, but he was unable to help himself.

Just before the gunfire started up again.

50

Green beams of light blazed from the oncoming riders, splitting the smoky streamers marring the increasingly orange sky. Some of those flashing dashes missed the edges of the train entirely. Most, however, bit deep into the very roof of the train. Every impact blasted a hole through the metal in a burst of ice and snow, and every shot came closer to the three men crawling to safety.

Or what they hoped was safety.

Not taking kindly to being shot at any time, Gilbert—scraggly bearded, high-strung, mole-faced Gilbert—couldn't keep his gun in his holster.

"*Goddamn sonsabitches!*" he roared and pulled pig iron. Legs spread wide, and clutching at an unseen handhold with his other glove, Gilbert fired his Colt at the riders tearing through the orange sky towards them.

"Quit it, Gilbert!" Eli shouted at the man.

Two feet from the rear edge of the car. No more. Nathan clawed for it.

"Gilbert!" Eli screamed.

Gilbert continued firing.

Nathan clutched at the edge, feeling its firmness and relieved to be able to hold on. He immediately glanced back. The train was charging forward, and the riders were coming in far too fast. Three of them blurred past, overshooting the stretched-out gang. One actually dove out of sight *under* the train, while the fifth…

The fifth had slowed, anticipating the rushing locomotive.

And fired the dreaded hand cannon their kind seemed to favor.

The beam lanced through space and time and took the Colt out of Gilbert's hand—no, that wasn't right. The blast took Gilbert's hand *off* at the wrist, sending the weapon and the hand still holding it tumbling over the edge of the train.

Gilbert was screaming. He drew his arm in tight to his chest, grabbing at a charred stump with his good hand.

And sliding sideways because of it.

Until Eli grabbed his coat by the shoulder, and held on.

Which was right about when the train inexplicably doubled its speed. The jolt caught them all off-guard, with Gilbert skidding towards the edge of the roof and an endless fall. The dragon rider whipped by Nathan, who reached out and clamped a hand onto Eli's other hand—who was entirely occupied by Gilbert's swinging weight.

Gilbert kept on screaming.

Eli's head snapped back with the strain of his outstretched limbs.

And Nathan felt himself sliding forward, his chin scraping ice as he slid towards the corner and the empty space beyond. He skittered at an angle, twisting, when his boot dropped and hooked into something solid, halting him. Nathan dug in and pulled back, and that jerked Eli's head up.

"*Hold on*," Nathan got out through clenched teeth.

Eli's squinty eyes blinked back at him.

Before the train, the goddamn train, increased its speed once more.

The lurch in power again sucked Gilbert to the edge, skittering him along until he was practically stretched out alongside the other men. There he stopped with a pained scream. Feeling the tension from his hooked fingers all the way up to his shoulders and neck, Eli held on, flat on his back, and released what Nathan thought was a pure grunt of despair.

But the gun runner held on.

He held on with every goddamn thing he had.

Gilbert's legs went over the edge.

Then his waist, where he buckled, bent over that curl of metal, where the balance of weight and awkwardness of the hold tipped the other way. He slid along the edge, until he came to one final stop, practically side-by-side with Eli. One more lurch in speed, and the luckless Gilbert would be dragged past the men, towards the rear. That very action would twist his companions off the roof, and take them both with him.

Perched there like he was, with the wind raging in his beard and hair, Gilbert gazed up at his companion and friend for God only knew how long.

Eli still didn't let go.

Even when a look of peace swept over the other gun runner's scraggly, mole-dotted face. And a little smile split the man's features.

A second later, the force of the speeding train ripped Gilbert Butler from

Eli Gallant's grasp like a hangman's noose bouncing a corpse, and he was gone from sight.

Still on his back, his fingers hooked into a claw, Eli Gallant didn't move an inch. His frame trembled on the train's roof, the ends of his coat furious in the wind. Nathan thought he would scream, but he did no such thing. He stayed that way for only a second, maybe two, before digging his heels in and pushing himself away from the edge, while pulling on Nathan's arm.

Eli turned himself over, grabbing Nathan with his now free arm. When the gun runner turned his head, the man's stone-cold expression was a terrifying thing.

The train sped up another notch, reaching speeds Nathan thought impossible.

But this was the 311.

The *Majestic* 311.

For her, nothing was impossible.

51

The solid object Nathan's boot had caught hold of was a short outcropping—a roof—to shield the platform below from the elements. It took strength and effort, but Eli used Nathan as a meaty ladder, climbing over him to reach safety. Once Eli was in better position, they both descended from the roof and swung themselves onto the platform below. There was ample railing, frost-covered yet solid, which they clung to for their very lives. There they stayed, absorbing the fact that only they remained of the original gang. They both stared at the thing just a few feet away.

Directly across from them, across a gulf with a set of iced-over couplings, was a door the color of hoary brass.

The wind rustling their frames, Nathan and Eli exchanged looks.

"We can't stay here," Nathan said.

Eli unslung his rifle from his back. "I don't want to stay here," he said grimly. "I'm sick of this fucking train."

Nathan understood that. Taking a moment to study the gap below, he readied himself and jumped across. Seconds later, Eli joined him on the other platform. The glass in the window was grimy, smeared with filth, but light glowed from within.

Nathan pulled out one of his Colts and cocked the hammer. Eli placed his shoulder against the other side of the door.

"Ready?" Nathan asked, taking hold of the latch.

"Ready."

Nathan slid open the door and rushed inside, gun first. Eli was a step behind him.

They stopped just inside the threshold, framed in light, snow, and wind blowing past them.

It wasn't a passenger car. Nor was it a livestock car or a storage car. They stood inside a long chamber, a sizeable chamber, in fact, lit by flickering candles deeper inside. Hundreds of candles, of which the closest winked out from the sudden blast of air. The biggest of these candles was set within a curved piece of brass, held up by what appeared to be snakes. Light flowed from the overturned pot of that fixture, granting the men just enough to see what lay inside the chamber.

Sitting on either side of the wide chamber, wider than any passenger car, was a series of statues. Feeble candlelight glinted against bulbous bellies the color of brass. Metal faces, their eyes closed over benign smiles, sat in meditative poses. The figures were large, twice the size of Nathan, yet radiated both warmth and peace.

The door slammed shut behind the two men, spinning them around.

"You do that?" Nathan asked.

"Hell, no," Eli blurted. He immediately checked the dark around the ends of the car. The interior was much more spacious that the exterior had them believe, but by this time, it didn't surprise the men. Aboard the Majestic, physical dimensions meant very little.

Searching and finding nothing, Nathan and Eli stood shoulder to shoulder and faced whatever waited for them. There, in the dark end of the car, an odd but pleasant smell reached out to them.

"The hell's that smell?" Nathan asked.

"Hell if I know," Eli remarked. "Smells like the powdered ass crack of a fancy city whore."

"No city whore I ever met."

"Like you would know."

Nathan scowled and didn't think much of the man's comparison. He started walking, his footfalls echoing in the vast room. Eli followed, his rifle up and seeking targets. It was warm, the pleasing heat one wanted when coming in from a bone-chilling cold, and while comfortable now, it would be unbearable soon. As they neared the candles, the light grew stronger and the statues more distinct. They were indeed made of brass, their metal skin polished and gleaming, all the way up to their smiling faces. Their bare bellies, fat and oversized to the point of caricature, drew the eye. Black paint topped off their fleshy heads, or what Nathan figured was paint. Some of the statues sat cross-legged, with their hands in their laps, while others had their fat arms folded or lifted in a stiff hello. Despite their strange appearance, they weren't offensive to gaze upon. In fact, they were oddly calming with their little smiles.

The two men passed five statues on either side. It was a good ten more to the glowing brazier ahead, and the light beyond revealed at least an equal number.

"Place is big," Nathan whispered, conscious of an echo.

Eli didn't reply, as if already aware of those very things.

Underfoot, the train gently rocked, lulling the two men to sit and relax and forget about what had just happened outside.

The brazier was the size of a wagon wheel, set upon with three thick legs of brass that had an almost fibrous quality, like that of tree roots, etched about upon their surface. Coals burned within, and Nathan swept his free hand over the heat, making a fist at the end. The candles burned stronger here, and that exotic scent was becoming more and more pleasing to Nathan with every passing second.

"Ain't nothing in here," Eli said, his rifle held at his hips.

Nathan didn't reply. He pointed with his gun.

There, at the very edge of the light, seated upon the floor like the statutes, was a figure. A *man* figure, sitting back-on to them, dressed in fine robes of red and dimmed gold.

A long tail of hair hung from the nape of his neck.

The sight of him stopped Nathan. He recognized the man.

It was the same figure who, so long ago, under the light of a full moon, had entered a dark tunnel at the base of a mountain, and was never seen again.

Until now.

*

The five metal dragons—single-engine cybernetic flight cycles—circled back.

The train's unexpected burst of speed had thrown the riders off, but that was a minor thing. They increased their own speed, racing along the cars, until they reached their target. The damage to the car was notable, but it was the three lifeforms, now two, that interested them the most. They were of a race very much valued.

Carefully matching the speed of the train, the riders settled down and magnetically coupled with the damaged locomotive. Two landed below while the others landed on the roof itself. They dismounted, their own boots magnetic to secure their footing. The wind whipped about their frames, but their stylish coats of black leather and personalized pieces of armor didn't budge. Weapons were unsheathed, a collection of heavy hand blasters and energy blades, and smiles erupted from underneath black sunglasses and spiked helmets. Their pointed teeth and scaled features marked them as one of the Reptiloid order, a largely omnivorous race that would, quite frankly, devour anything they couldn't breed with.

They exchanged a few words and turned towards the end of the train car.

Weapons in hand, they started forward.

*

Eli raised his Winchester and took aim at the seated figure. Nathan did the same without hesitation.

"That the one who went into the tunnel?" Eli asked.

"Looks like him."

"Little bastard," Eli said with venom.

"Hey, you," Nathan directed at the man. "Get up and turn around."

The man in the fancy robes did nothing of the sort.

"I'm warning you," Nathan stressed in a dangerous voice.

Eli moved to flank the seated man, casting an equally dangerous and very much impatient glance in Nathan's direction.

Nathan's anger swelled inside him at being ignored and he marched forward. "Get the hell—"

Up, he was going to say, but a hand—a three-fingered hand—reached out from the shadows and clamped down on Nathan's gun wrist.

And twisted.

Nathan flew over his heels and landed flat on his back, all the wind in his lungs escaping him. He rolled over, gasping, stunned, desperately trying to claw air back into his chest and failing miserably.

Eli whipped the Winchester around until it was pointed at the masked man's head—the same masked man with the same weird pajamas they'd met in the saloon.

Eli fired, the shot flaring in the dark.

The man in black ducked, swept aside the rifle, and punched Eli twice to the body—two blazingly fast strikes that crumpled the gun runner. Eli dropped to his knees, his rifle falling with a clatter, and slowly bent over as if in worship.

Nathan still had a hold of his Colt, and he lifted the weapon.

The man in black whirled so very fast, kicking the gun out of his hand. It skittered along the floor before disappearing in the dark.

The three-fingered hand grabbed Nathan by the coat collar and dragged him into the light. He dumped the train robber on the floor and then fetched

Eli, dragging him forward by the boot. The man in black released the gun runner when he was next to Nathan.

Nathan got in a good lungful of air and that settled him down, but he still felt physically rattled, no matter how much he wanted to fight. The interior felt warmer now, and sweat started to ooze from him.

The man in black stood between the two robbers, those odd fists clenched and ready to inflict punishment if needed.

Nathan got down a second and third lungful, the shock leaving him. He painfully regarded his guard and squinted in confusion. He thought for an instant that the attacker was the same individual from the saloon. The same one who had given him the silver locket. The eye slit in this man's mask, however, changed that.

The eyes were black, but the flesh surrounding them looked to be gold.

A subtle stirring turned Nathan's head, and he realized the man in the fine robes of red and gold was facing them, though he remained seated, his face draped in shadow.

Just then, a booming crash came from the door at the far end of the car, the same one Nathan and Eli had entered. A pair of glowing swords punched through the metal—one cut down along the seam, the other cut up. Smoke wafted from those blades as a harsh sawing threatened to make Nathan's ears bleed. When the weapons reached the ends, they withdrew.

And the door flew inwards.

Five figures charged into the car, and Nathan knew they were the same riders pursuing them. The five didn't give any commands, they simply raised their weapons and fired.

Green light beams spat through the chamber—and stopped upon a shimmering wall of orange that only appeared when the beams struck it. The five riders continued to shoot. Two of their number drew secondary hand cannons and fired those as well, and a veritable light show that reminded Nathan of the Northern Lights pummeled the orange wall, absorbing the shots upon contact. A tracery of light as fine as spider silk extended back from that mystical protective barrier, and ended…

Nathan's eyes widened.

The man in black had retreated to one side.

The man in the fine robes had lifted a hand, where that intricate weave of light ended in his outstretched palm. And, as Nathan watched, it leaned forward, revealing the features of an older man with very orange eyes.

It lifted its other hand and spoke, syllables given sound upon a voice choked with gravel.

Nathan didn't understand one word, but the five riders stopped firing their weapons. In fact, they dropped their guns just before great glowing bands of orange seized them all. The riders screamed, one at first, then the others joined in, grunting, high-pitched squeals that bespoke terrible pain. There was a shimmering, a crackling of energy, and the bikers were lifted from the floor like unwilling fence posts.

The magician—no, the *sorcerer*, as Nathan now thought of him—watched the five levitating attackers. Those glowing orange eyes peered out from underneath a lowered brow, only partially revealing an expression of loathing. The riders continued to squeal, almost unbearably so, and perhaps those sounds annoyed the sorcerer.

Whose outstretched hands clenched into fists.

The five riders crumpled inwards upon themselves in a frightening crackle of bones and a splatter of liquids. Nathan couldn't see the exact damage done, but he certainly heard.

The orange bands suddenly disappeared, and five dead rags of meat splashed to the floor.

The silence after those messy deaths was an ominous thing. Nathan could only gawk at the very much dead creatures at the other end of the train car. A force grabbed Nathan then, and his head whipped back to the glowing eyes of the Sorcerer.

Just before a mighty invisible force lifted Nathan and slammed him against the belly of a statue.

<h1 style="text-align:center">52</h1>

Nathan's arms and legs were splayed across the statue's belly, his spine bent uncomfortably. He looked down his nose and sighted Eli across the way, similarly spread over another statue. Eli grimaced and attempted to worm himself free, but he was held fast. The once benign smile upon the statue's face appeared sinister as it stretched Eli's struggling form across its bloated belly.

"The hell is this?" Eli grunted, all teeth and vinegar, and dearly wanting to put an end to the man in black and the seated Sorcerer.

"Let me handle this," Nathan grated, glad that he could at least speak.

"The hell you gonna do?"

"Talk to him."

"You sayin' I can't talk to people?"

Nathan rolled his eyes. "Shut up, Eli. For once. We both know you're shit when it comes to talking to people."

Fuming, Eli shut up, but he was none too pleased about it. Eli wasn't the best at speaking when speaking was important, and now that the riders were dead and gone, it was best to parley with the Sorcerer…or at least try. Nathan still had one of his Colts, as well as a knife. And to his knowledge, Eli still had both his Colts and a boot knife.

Not that either one of them could use the weapons in their current state.

His attention turned to the glowing eyes of the Sorcerer.

"Hey there. Yeah. Thanks for… killing those bastards." Nathan dipped his chin towards the dead biker creatures. "Appreciated. They got… they killed… two of my friends. We're not enemies here. We had our guns out because, well, we didn't know your intentions. But if you killed those things… I think we're on the same side. I think."

The Sorcerer didn't move, didn't flinch, content to study the trapped train robbers.

"How'd you do that anyway?" Nathan asked.

"Christ Almighty," Eli growled. "Why don't you ask him where the shitter is?"

"Will you shut up and let me talk?"

"Then *talk*, goddammit. Don't be making fucking small talk about his magic tricks. Talk about something important instead of the goddamn weather. You wanted to parley, so parley, ass kisser."

That stung Nathan, and he glared at the trapped gun runner. After a moment of resetting himself, he turned his attention back to the Sorcerer, who hadn't killed them yet. That was a good sign, he realized, despite the stern expression upon the man's face.

Or at least, Nathan assumed it was a man.

The man in black slipped between them, hands by his side.

"We…" Nathan started and thought about what he could say, what he could offer these creatures, locked away in what felt like a church of some kind, except… what manner of thing could kill others by crushing them with bands of orange light? He had to admit, it had been a sight to behold, and then he scolded himself for his drifting thoughts.

"We're trying to get off this train," he started again, figuring the best approach was with the truth. "We… wanted to rob her."

"Holy shit," Eli moaned from the other side.

"What now?" Nathan fired back, pissed at being interrupted.

"Why don't you tell him we shot and killed innocent people as well? Except they were all monsters when we killed them?"

"You gonna let me talk or not? 'Cause right now, you're a needle in my pee-hole. You understand that?"

"Ain't no needle small enough to prick *your* pee-hole, Rhodes."

"Fuck you, Gallant."

The Sorcerer's eyes glowed, and he muttered an alien syllable, which tightened the invisible shackles around both men, pulling their limbs tighter from their bodies, plying their backs even more over the statues' bellies, to the point of breaking.

The grunts from the two men filled the chamber.

"Wait," Nathan groaned, his eyes becoming slits from the pressure. "Wait. We… we only want to get off the train. We made a mistake. This wasn't the train we wanted to rob. We were in the Rockies. Waiting for another train. This one came through the tunnel. This one. We boarded her, and life's been a fucked-up misery ever since. There were seven of us. Now just us, and we only… *Christ*, my back is *breaking* here. We only want to get off! Figure we could… get to the caboose… and undo the couplings! Roll to a stop! *That's all! That's all!*"

As his discomfort bled into pain, Nathan's speech grew more desperate. Louder. Faster.

"We didn't kill anyone that didn't pull on us first!"

The invisible force increased upon his joints and sockets and spine, stretching him past his breaking point. His teeth ground to the point of cracking, and water misted his vision. Nathan knew he was seconds away from hearing—and experiencing—a very agonizing death.

"We met him in a saloon. And he gave us a silver locket! With a woman's face in it!"

He almost shrieked the words, not knowing why he said them at all in the first place, but he did, anyway.

And the pressure being exerted upon him remained in place for a long second.

Then stopped.

Not all at once. It took a few seconds, of which Nathan and Eli could only growl and sputter in pain, wondering if their limbs would be ripped free before their spines snapped in half. When it stopped, the statues' invisible vices actually relaxed a bit, back to when they were merely uncomfortable.

The man in black stood before Nathan.

The appearance of the thing surprised him. The creature's eyes studied him intently.

"That's right," he panted. "We met you before. Not you, exactly, but someone like you. Same… outfit and everything. He gave us a locket. In my coat. Right side, inside breast pocket."

The man in black reached out and opened Nathan's coat. He pawed around inside the winter duster, three fingers exploring until the pocket was discovered. The thing's eyes narrowed, and Nathan didn't know if that was a good or bad thing.

The man in black extracted the silver locket, letting the chain dangle from its fingers. The silver gleamed in the firelight.

"That's it," Nathan said in relief. "That's it."

The man in black ignored him. He brought the jewelry piece to the Sorcerer, who actually studied it. The man in black opened the locket, showing the picture of the woman within. In moments, the Sorcerer's expression faltered and became a reflective thing. He took the locket from the man in black and draped its length across his palm, where he traced the shape with a finger.

All the while staring at that lovely face.

Nathan wasn't the brightest of folks. He'd be the first to admit it, but he possessed enough sense to understand that there was obviously a connection between the woman in the locket and the Sorcerer. He knew the Sorcerer was the man responsible for the disappearance of the 311. He didn't know how, but seeing as the man could kill with bands of light and seize men with invisible shackles, making a train disappear didn't seem that big of a magic feat. The question remained *why*, and that, Nathan supposed, was easy enough to figure out as well, once you got a fire going in the old thinking stack. A lot of men had died in the construction of the railway. A lot of lives of honest working folk, a good number of them from China or someplace else, looking for an honest existence and facing hardships and injustices no one deserved. How many countrymen were subjected to cruelty and ridicule and treated like shit, only to be sent to their deaths with no more regard than one disposing of a piece of paper just used to wipe one's ass.

Nathan's thoughts whirled, but he figured he was on the right path of it. He only recognized the Chinamen in that dreamy replay he and the other gang members once watched aboard the train, but who knew what other nationalities might've been sacrificed in the making of the railway, in the construction of that damn tunnel.

And if he had the knowledge, the power, to get revenge on the heartless bloodsabitches responsible for making the lives of so many a living hell— well, he'd sure as hell make them pay. Damn straight, he would.

"You did this," Nathan said to the Sorcerer. "With the train. You did all of this."

The man in black didn't move. The Sorcerer's shoulders sagged just a little, but then firmed up.

"I did this," the Sorcerer spoke, from a mouth and throat that sounded like it hadn't tasted water in years.

The words dissipated upon the air, replaced by the familiar, underlying locomotion of the train.

Chump…chump…chump…chump…

"I did not know…" the Sorcerer slowly explained, "that she would be… on board. The train. *This* train. When I… cursed it. To this. All of this."

His shoulders sagged again, and the orange light that was his eyes dimmed just a little.

Nathan wasn't a heartless man, and even Eli Gallant had to feel the sadness emanating from the Sorcerer.

The pieces fell together then.

"She was on the train when you cursed it," Nathan said. "Just before all this happened. And you found out somehow. Maybe saw her in the window as the train passed by. Maybe… you got on the train, boarded it like we did, but to look for her. You found that locket. In an empty berth."

The Sorcerer didn't respond.

"Maybe you couldn't find her. After… years of searching. So you sent someone else to search." Nathan looked at the man in black. "Or maybe you were both searching at the same time, but the other one went off on its own. That one had the locket, to recognize her. If he found her. But he didn't. He couldn't. Or… perhaps he'd had the locket long enough that he'd recognize that face anywhere. So he passed it on to me… maybe hoping I'd meet up with you. To let you know he'd hadn't found her yet."

Nothing from the Sorcerer.

"How long," Eli asked from across the way, surprising Nathan, "have you been looking for her?"

The Sorcerer didn't look up. For seconds the only sound was that of the train, but then came the whisper of, "Forever."

Nathan believed it.

He didn't ask who she was, exactly. The Sorcerer obviously loved her, and for his revenge on the railway, she had been the price to pay. Obviously, the Sorcerer hadn't been aware of her traveling on the train, but that was life, Nathan mulled, knowing how damn cruel it could be.

He wanted to say he was sorry. He wanted to ask more questions, to get greater details about the curse upon the train and the reason behind it, but he knew that wasn't going to happen. One look at the Sorcerer told him that.

"Forever," Nathan repeated, weighing the word, thinking he might know how much time forever was, but figuring he didn't have a clue. Was forever a year on board the train? A hundred and twenty years or more? As it was for old Festus, whom Eli had put out of misery upon request. Or perhaps forever was an even longer period of time for poor Archie Willmoore, who'd eventually become one with the Great Serpent, exploring vast ocean depths, heedless of time entirely.

Blessed Sacred Heart of Mary, Nathan thought, repeating the oath Mackenzie and Jimmy so often liked to say. *Blessed Sacred Heart of Mary. And the Holy Ghost.*

His brain hurt from the weight of his thoughts.

And then, without warning, the vices holding Nathan and Eli in place vanished. The men crumpled to the floor, grimacing, as the blood resumed flowing through their limbs and backs.

"Forever," the Sorcerer said, still holding the locket, but now watching the two men. "But… this train's journey… will soon end."

His face hardened. "Go."

Eli looked to Nathan for clarification.

"Go?" Nathan asked. "Go where?"

"Anywhere you wish," the Sorcerer said. "There is no escape. Only…"

And with that, the man in black lifted an arm and pointed. Behind the Sorcerer.

An oil lamp, so very much out of place in that supernatural sanctum, weakly flared to life. Beside it was another door.

Only doors. Nathan realized, finishing the Sorcerer's sentence. *Only doors*.

He exchanged looks with Eli, who looked around his feet for his rifle.

"Leave it," Nathan told him, then to the Sorcerer. "Thank you."

The man in the long robes studied him for a short time, before returning his attention to the locket. And the face inside.

The man in black made no move to stop Nathan or Eli as they walked around the seated Sorcerer. The figure still didn't move when the two men hurried to the door.

Eli reached it first, and with a glance at Nathan, drew one of his Colts.

Nathan pulled out his remaining pistol.

With one last look at the mysterious chamber of the Sorcerer, and learning perhaps something of the how's and why's of the Majestic 311's mind-twisting fate, the two men opened the door.

A second later, they went through.

53

The little platform they stood upon shifted underfoot, prompting the two men to grab hold of the nearby railing. Ahead, across an open gap and the exposed couplings, was another door. To their left was a ladder attached to the wall. And beyond that, little else except a whitening sky.

"The hell he mean by that?" Eli yelled from the other side of the door, making himself heard over the wind and the moving train.

"By what?"

"You heard him—that shit about this train's journey will end. Will *soon* end."

That *was* unsettling. Nathan certainly didn't have everything figured out, but the Sorcerer's words were indeed ominous. The train's journey would soon end. What did it mean? For not only Nathan and Eli, but for all those creatures and realities, and… dare he think it… the *worlds* they passed through to this point? Would all of that end with the train's journey? Would Jimmy and the place with his supposed grandparents (and perhaps even parents) cease to exist? Even though Jimmy said the force pulling him, pulling them all, had ceased once he reached his grandparents' farm, would all that be gone with the journey's end?

And what was the journey's end anyway?

Even with all those troubling thoughts, Nathan still felt that little tug pulling him towards the next door.

The impulse to climb the ladder grabbed him. Nathan ignored answering Eli for the time being and started climbing the rungs. When he reached the top, he stuck his head above the roof of the train—no more than eye level.

All words left him then.

This train's journey will soon end…

The sun was bigger, perhaps twice the size of what it was the last time he'd gazed upon it. And the train, the *train,* was a straight line heading right for its center, so far off that Nathan couldn't rightly place where the front of the locomotive was. The iron tapered off into a speck, and the sun's increasing glare pained Nathan to see any further.

Not that it mattered.

"What?" Eli barked from below. "What is it?"

Nathan climbed back down. "The train's headed for the sun."

Eli scrunched up his face in a mixture of confused horror.

"Straight into the center," Nathan said. "We gotta get to the caboose. And right now."

There was no argument from the gun runner.

They jumped across the coupling gap, onto the next platform. They entered the train car with guns ready, and saw only another passenger car. Nathan didn't bother with searching the berths for monsters or money, he merely thundered down the aisle, an impending feeling of dread powering him forward. The sun was going to swallow the train whole, and everything on board. Of that, Nathan had no doubt.

The two men ran through the car, then another. They were then surprised to discover a livestock car, but the cages were filled with skeletons of not only horses and cows, but people as well.

Then another passenger car. And yet another.

Then a prisoner car, with about a dozen cages housing all manner of twisted alien creatures, all of which screeched at the two men as they raced through. There was not one man or woman among them, so Nathan and Eli let them be.

All the while, Nathan wasn't sure if the sweat coming off his face in rivulets was from the winter clothing he still wore, or the ferocious heat of the nearing sun.

To his credit, Eli Gallant saved his breath for the run, not saying a goddamn word.

The pull still led Nathan along, and every door he opened.

They weren't going to make it.

They *had* to make it.

The *pull* was still there. That ever-present, maddening *pull!*

They had to—

Nathan and Eli gasped and shuddered, their strength nearly exhausted, when they opened the next door and stopped dead in their tracks.

"Well *fuck*," Eli snapped in horrified surprise, his shoulders sagging at the sight. Nathan didn't even have breath for that.

There, ahead of them, wasn't the caboose.

They stood in the rear of the engineer's cab… at the very *front* of the train.

Smoky plumes of steam whipped by the open windows, but it didn't hinder what Nathan saw before him. The familiar circular iron plate, the surface dimpled in a pattern of riveted seams. The accompanying assortment of gauges, dials, levers and hand wheels, all below a narrow collection of brass piping and blackened knobs. A ratty-looking coat hung from a peg. A shelf held a pair of dented mugs and a smudged oil can between them. A frayed seat, the cushion imprinted over the years by a sizeable ass, lay to the right. Above that, a lamp burned on a secured perch.

And right there, slowly turning about as if realizing he had company, was the enigmatic engineer. Nathan knew he'd heard the thing's name, but he couldn't remember. The engineer stood in front of the open portal to the fire box, where coal and wood fed the locomotive's terrible hunger. The engineer's smiling face was still devoid of flesh, and the nearby lamp colored his skeletal features a harsh orange.

Eli turned back to the door, to return through it, in an attempt to change the reality once again. Except the door was no longer there. Just the huge bin carrying the Majestic's supply of wood and coal.

And ahead of the Majestic 311, the sun *loomed*. A great ravenous ball of fire that hurt the eyes to gaze upon. So enormous, in fact, that Nathan might've been standing in front of a mountain face and looking straight up to marvel at the sheer size of it. The heat was cringing, but as close as they were, they remained untouched by that death-dealing surface. The thunderous energy of the steam engine boomed within the cab, as if it were threatening to explode at any second.

The engineer watched them with black eye cavities, empty except for the little flickers of light deep within. Its smile was unrelenting. It made no move towards the two men, however. No threatening gestures. Instead, it merely stood to one side, its back partially blocking a window.

To the sides, mountains flashed by. And fresh air cut across their faces.

Cold *mountain* air.

"Nathan!" Eli Gallant cried out, saying Nathan's full name for the first time ever. "*Look*! Those are *mountains*!"

They were indeed mountains, snow-capped and wintry, very much resembling the Rockies… but they were speeding by at a dangerous pace. To jump off the train would surely break one's legs or snap one's neck. Or worse.

"*We gotta jump*," Eli shouted.

"*We can't jump!*" Nathan shouted back, his eyes flicking to the sun, then to the watchful engineer, and finally to Eli, who was already at the edge of the cab, his free hand upon the metal wall.

"*Sure as hell can!*" Eli shouted. "*Come on, before it's too late.*"

Too late? Nathan realized. It was *already* too late, and yet that damn *pull* was holding him fast, stronger than ever before, rooting him in place.

"*There's nowhere to jump!*" Nathan roared.

"*I'm going,*" Eli roared back.

And Nathan knew he was.

The two men regarded each other for a fleeting second then, but on the Majestic 311, a second seemed to be as good as a year. And in that look, the thoughts, memories, and sentiments of a shared journey passed between the two train robbers, two men who might've once been enemies, but in the end had arrived at a mutual respect for each other.

Perhaps even a little bit of friendship.

Not one to dawdle, Eli broke the moment with a sorry frown and then turned away.

He leaped off the train and was gone from sight.

54

Eli landed on his back in a plume of white and stars and then darkness. The passing of the Majestic 311 briefly thundered in his ears before quickly receding. He opened his eyes, saw the night sky overhead, and felt the frigid embrace of a snow bank slowly penetrating his duster.

Eli sat up, sputtering, and looked around.

Clear night sky, the stars brilliant and blazing. Below them, the frost-tipped peaks of the Rockies, distant and yet radiant under the glow of a full moon. An *ordinary* moon.

"Holy shit," Eli released, breathless, and rose to his feet. Cold air filled his lungs, and snow chilled his face as his scarf had long gone slack about his neck. He looked behind him and saw the black lines of the railway, going left and right.

But to his left was the disappearing rear end of the Majestic 311.

The caboose.

A lit lamp swung from its rear, and for a moment, a full second, something moved beside it as well. Then the 311 was gone from sight, bending around a curve and hidden by frosted hills. A ghostly hoot of its horn then, and all became quiet and cold.

The cold enveloped Eli then, and he shivered.

He was pretty sure that the figure was… of all things… that skeletal face of the bony sonavabitch running the train. But that couldn't be right. Not at all.

Eli stood there, glanced over his shoulder, and saw the tunnel mouth some hundred feet back, where the whole gang had boarded the locomotive. Where all this twisted maddening foolishness had begun.

"I'm back," he whispered, elated at the thought. "Jesus Christ Our Savior, I'm back."

His hands went to his neck then, and he nearly squealed the happiness that spiked through him. The mail bags full of cash were still hanging about his neck. It wasn't the full amount he'd wanted, but it was more than enough for him and…

Gilbert, he thought, and his happiness wilted just a little. Gilbert was gone, but Eli sure as hell intended to have a drink in his partner's memory. Probably a bottle, at a right nice saloon where the people were people and the women were two-breasted.

There was a snapping of a whip, then, and a harsh force clutched him around the throat.

"Gurk!" was all Eli Gallant got out before an irresistible force hauled him back, pulling him off-balance. He tried turning as he stumbled and slogged through the deep snow, trying to see who was attacking him. Both hands grabbed onto the whip, but he couldn't dig in to pull back. He tripped and fell flat on his chest. The whip ran from his neck, impossibly long, a good twenty feet or more back, to where a winter-clad rider reared his horse back on two legs.

A thunderbolt of horror struck Eli Gallant then, and he tried to whimper, but the whip about his throat yanked him to silence.

The horse was huge, black, and a creature born of night. Moonlight fluttered over the form, but the eyes were red and flaming, and the rider, decked out in a familiar winter duster, cackled a most evil laughter. That sound chilled Eli's blood and bone marrow faster than any winter night in the freezing vastness of the Rockies.

Milton? Eli mentally asked when he couldn't get the name out.

Milton Floss, Mackenzie's mouthy cattle buddy and the eighth and final partner of the ill-fated gang, left on the side of the tracks so long ago to watch over the horses. To guard their retreat when the time came.

It wasn't Milton, however.

Not even close.

As if sensing his victim's horrified confusion, the ghost rider reared back its horse once again. The beast's forelegs kicked, flinging snow and stone into the night. Then it landed, and the rider, still laughing, danced the creature around.

Eli barely had time to realize what was happening before he was yanked entirely off his feet, but he saw where he was *going*, and the sight filled him with horrified despair.

The laughing horseman kicked, driving hellish spurs into the creature's flanks. The monster took off, bearing the struggling weight of a man, charging back into the dark and terrible hole that was the tunnel mouth.

Dragging a kicking and twisting Eli Gallant behind it.

Until rider, horse, and gun runner entered that cursed tunnel and disappeared from sight.

The maddening laughter lingered, however, becoming weaker by the second, until only snow and rock and iron remained.

55

After Eli had jumped from the train, Nathan spared the gun runner only a second before looking back to the engineer and his spectral smile.

Nathan realized he still had his gun pointed at the creature. Knowing the weapon was useless against the apparition, he opened his duster and put the gun away.

The engineer watched him all the while.

Through a forward window, over the pipes and the gauges and other instruments Nathan had no understanding of, the sun had flooded the entire sky. A gigantic wall of shifting waves, bubbling curds, moving ripples and exploding stone drops. The heat blasted by his head, and squinted his eyes, but he didn't burst into flames as he thought he would.

This train's journey will soon end.

Seemingly pleased with the train robber's decision, the engineer showed his back, checked his gauges, and placed a bony elbow upon the nearby windowsill. The ghost stuck his head out the window. There, the engineer's haunting smile blazed, and it nodded eagerly at the immense light that was the sun.

Blinding.

Mesmerizing.

And the pull was stronger than ever, yet it no longer pulled Nathan forward. It kept him right in place and held his head fast. It kept his eyes open and wide, so that he could see... *everything* that would... *become.*

This train's journey will soon end.

The words fluttered through his mind, but as the last word faded, Nathan wondered about Jimmy Norquay.

Jimmy's pull had ended on that farm.

As the Majestic 311 charged into the face of the sun, where everything seemed to crystallize and shimmer as if running through a blizzard of stars, Nathan looked up, transfixed by the window that shuddered and shook as raw sunlight dissolved the very metal. More light pierced the cab of the Majestic, finding holes as small as pores and punching through, transforming the interior into a blinding web.

The engineer, with his maniacal grin still in place and his head still outside the window, reached up for a lever and cranked it.

The train's steam whistle blasted overhead, jolting Nathan where he stood.

The sun…

This train's journey will soon end.

And as those words petered out like before, as the light engulfed and dissolved the cab, the ghostly engineer, and even Nathan himself…

Nathan screamed.

And the world screamed with him.

56

"What's wrong little fella?" a woman asked.

"Straps are too tight on him," said a man.

A hand reached out and tugged on the harnesses keeping Nathan in place.

"Nope, seem fine to me," the woman said, her expression dark with puzzlement—and all the more lovely because of it.

"Goddamn car seats," the man said. "I'll get a new one."

"I don't think it's the car seat."

"Sounds like it."

"Is it the car seat, sweetie?" the woman asked, her face leaning out from around a mountain, except it wasn't a mountain, but another car seat. A second face darted into sight from the other side, young and concerned, and meeting Nathan's gaze for a fleeting instant.

The man smiled at him before turning away, disappearing behind a slab of upholstery.

The woman reached for Nathan and caressed his fat cheek. That simple contact alone summoned a smile.

"He's smiling now," the woman said.

"I smile too when you touch me like that," the man said.

That drew a warning from her. "Watch yourself."

"What? He can't understand me. Be something if he could, being only five months old and all."

The woman turned back to Nathan, traced the curve of his cheek down his chin and up the other side. She reached up then, pleased, and adjusted the hat on his head that kept him warm.

"You relax now, cutie," she said to him and smiled. "You relax, my little man. We got about an hour to go before we get to grandma and grandpa's house. Bet they'll be so happy to see you. They can't wait. Can't wait."

With that, she smiled again, touched his nose, and leaned back into her seat.

Allowing Nathan a wide look at the windshield, and the sun passing overhead, warm and glowing and high in the sky. He didn't really know what the sun was, or the glass for that matter, or the intricate controls and displays of the SUV's dashboard.

He didn't care, either.

All he knew were the two faces of the people before him, just out of sight. And that, somehow, for reasons unknown, they loved him, and he loved them back.

That was enough for him to kick his little bare legs.

"Watch this," his father said. He reached for the ceiling, where his fingers tickled the top.

The sunroof opened slowly, revealing more of a beautiful sky.

"*Ohhh*," his mother said, glancing back at her baby boy, to make sure he was seeing what they were seeing.

He was.

His broad toothless smile conveyed exactly that.

And as the SUV snaked its way through the Rockies of Alberta, a little giggle passed through the mountainous expanse, and lasted a very, very long time.

About the Author

Keith C. Blackmore is the author of the Mountain Man, 131 Days, and Breeds series, among other horror, heroic fantasy, and crime novels. He lives on the island of Newfoundland in Canada. Visit his website at www.keithcblackmore.com.